William Bedford has had i̶ ̶ ̶ ̶ ̶ ̶ ̶ ̶ ̶ ̶ ̶ ̶the
Independent, *Punch* and *Harpers & Queen*. His short
stories have appeared in the *Daily Telegraph*, *Encounter*,
London Magazine and the *London Review of Books*, and
several have been broadcast on Radio 4. He is the author
of three previous novels: *Happiland*, which was short-
listed for the 1990 *Guardian* Fiction Prize, *All Shook
Up* and *Catwalking*, as well as collections of poetry
and two novels for children: *The Golden Gallopers* and
Nightworld. He has just completed his next novel, *The
Freedom Tree*.

WILLIAM BEDFORD

The Lost Mariner

An *Abacus* Book

First published in Great Britain
by Little, Brown and Company in 1995
This edition published by Abacus in 1996

Copyright © William Bedford 1995

The moral right of the author has been asserted.

A CIP catalogue record for this book
is available from the British Library.

ISBN 0 349 10805 6

Typeset by M Rules
Printed and bound in Great Britain by Clays Ltd, St Ives plc

Abacus
A Division of
Little, Brown and Company (UK)
Brettenham House
Lancaster Place
London WC2E 7EN

For Fiona

With thanks to the Society of Authors
and Yorkshire and Humberside Arts
for their generous financial assistance.

O Wedding-Guest! this soul hath been
Alone on a wide wide sea:
So lonely 'twas, that God himself
Scarce seemed there to be.

SAMUEL TAYLOR COLERIDGE,
'The Rime of the Ancient Mariner'

Contents

Rechabite

One

You do strange things in the blackness of grief. If I had ever seen *Rechabite* I would never have signed up for her summer voyage to Iceland. But I had been grieving for my old friend and skipper Joseph Proctor for over a year, and missing my girl Miriam for months on end, and I was in no state of mind to be making sound judgements. I had the letter from Satan's Hole telling me where I might learn something of Miriam, and I went searching for *Rechabite*'s skipper without any of my natural fisherman's caution.

I found him in one of the barking yards near the bottom of Kitty Witches Row. He was standing in the gateway to the yard, his hands clenched behind his stiff back, his eyes squinting into the sun. He was a tall, stern-looking man, strong and angular, his broadcloth coat and velvet waist-coat coal black, his grey hair scraped back on his naked head. Most of the skippers I knew wore the hard hats that were fashionable in those years. When he looked at me, his eyes were like muddy ice.

'Skipper Everitt?' I asked him direct. 'Of the *Rechabite*?'

He nodded briefly, taking his time to answer. 'That's right.'

'I heard you were looking for a fifth hand, skipper?'

'Did you?'

'For the summer voyage.'

Everitt's eyes never left off studying my face. He had grey, calculating eyes, bloodshot with tiredness and flecked with broken veins, but still alert, watchful. His manner was frigid and cold, tense with some clenched passion. At some time, his nose had been badly broken, the skin beneath his left eye stretched and pitted with scars that looked like the cuts of a breaking winch rope. His cheeks were tanned hard by the salt and sea winds. He looked the sort of skipper who would never leave the tiller to his second hand.

'Where did you hear that?' he asked indifferently.

'In the Guillemot, skipper. Some of the men were talking.'

He smiled then, as if he had put money on my answer. 'What's your name, fisherman?' he said in the same flat tone.

'Samuel Vempley.'

'Do you know what Rechabite means, Mr Vempley?'

I nodded, puzzled by his calm smile. 'Total abstainer.'

'That's right, Mr Vempley. Total abstainer. No alcohol. God put water on this earth, Mr Vempley, not alcohol. Alcohol is Satan's work.'

I shrugged. So, he was a God-ranter. I had known worse. And if he was short-handed in the middle of summer he wouldn't worry too much about what God thought. It was already late for the voyage to Iceland.

'You get information in the Guillemot, skipper,' I told him cheerfully. 'Who's sailing. Who's short of a hand. How the fishing goes. You can't get information anywhere else.'

Everitt recognised my tone of voice. He watched me for a second, making up his mind. 'Is that so?' He smiled in his unfriendly manner.

'In my experience, skipper.'

There was a shout from one of the men at the copper tubs. They were boiling a mixture of oak bark, tallow, red ochre and Stockholm tar for the sails. I recognised the smells. Most skippers bark their sails every year to protect them from mildew, and the crew have the pleasure of the job. But at sea, you see sails of every colour, from golden amber to black and deepest brown, depending on the mixture the skipper prefers. A fleet of smacks is like a floating rainbow, all according to the barking.

'Those are our spare sails,' Everitt told me. 'Ready for when we get back. Shall we have a look?'

He walked towards the coppers and I followed him.

The man who had shouted stood ready at the first tub, a long sweeping brush in his hands. The mainsail and mizzen were spread out on the ground ready for the barking. Harwich smacks only tanned their jibs, and used cutch instead of bark. It was the Grimsby skippers who introduced tanning for all a smack's canvas. Everitt must have got the idea from them. The man by the tubs nodded cheerfully as we walked up to him.

'This is Jack Walmsley, *Rechabite*'s third hand,' Everitt said.

Walmsley nodded cheerfully, holding his hand out to me. 'How d'you do, matey,' he said. 'Looking for a berth?'

'That's right.'

'You'll be well suited on *Rechabite*.'

The skipper coughed and stared at his third hand.

'How are we doing, Mr Walmsley?' he asked impatiently.

Walmsley never blinked. He nodded promptly towards the boiling liquid as if nothing else had ever entered his mind. 'That hot enough for you, skipper?' he asked. 'I can never judge myself,' he added with a wink in my direction.

Everitt peered into the copper, ignoring the man's cringing smile. I could hear the bark bubbling. Steam rose in the hot air. As the men watched their skipper, a gull landed on the wall that surrounded the yard and screeched noisily at the bright sun.

'What do you think, Mr Vempley?' Everitt asked.

'Sounds all right to me,' I said.

'You can tell by the sound?'

'It's been heating a good few hours,' I said. 'Judging by the sweat on your men's faces.'

The skipper smiled his thin-lipped smile.

'All right then, Mr Walmsley.'

Walmsley swung the sweeping brush over his shoulder and nodded to a couple of lads who were standing by. 'Let's get it done,' he shouted. The lads leapt forward and started to haul buckets of bark out of the copper. They had to mind their hands as the liquid slopped into the metal buckets. Walmsley stood ready by the mainsail and the first of the buckets was tipped on to it. As the liquid hit the huge sail, he started working madly to spread the bark around. His arms were thick as warp ropes, and the muscles stood out like iron. He had tattoos of green mermaids all over his arms. Sweat poured down his face. As he worked frantically with the long sweeping brush, the lads fetched more buckets and tipped them on to the massive mainsail. The red ochre soaked into it. Men stood around in the yard, watching and laughing.

'You admire my red ochre, Mr Vempley?' the skipper asked me quietly.

'It's a fine mixture, skipper.'

'The colour, you mean?'

'I like red ochre.' I nodded.

He seemed to delight in hearing what he expected to hear. His lips were a tight line of sarcasm.

'As long as it does what's wanted,' he said ironically.

We watched for a moment longer and then Everitt glanced impatiently at his pocket watch.

'Why are you out of a berth, Mr Vempley?'

'My skipper died,' I told him.

'I'm sorry to hear that.'

'Joseph Proctor, *Wings of Morning*.'

'A well-smack?'

'Yes, skipper. Out of Yarmouth.'

'When were you indentured?'

'Eighteen sixty-nine. Aged fourteen. From Peterborough workhouse.'

'To Proctor?'

'Yes.'

'No parents?'

'They died.'

He watched me for a moment, still holding his silver pocket watch. 'You seem to have had your share of misfortunes, Mr Vempley.'

'Most people do, skipper.'

He nodded, thoughtful. The men went on working and shouting at the mainsail. It was nearly finished. They would move on to the mizzen once the mainsail was well covered, then do another coat. It would dry quickly, ready for collecting when *Rechabite* got back from her first few days' fishing in local waters. The smacks always worked the local grounds for live fish before setting out on the fourteen-day journey to Iceland.

'How long were you with Proctor?' Everitt asked me after a pause.

'Seven years, skipper. He died January last year.'

'So I heard.'

He glanced at me, his eyes searching my face suspiciously. Eighteen months was a long time to be away from the fishing.

'I've been on the whelkers,' I explained. 'I couldn't face another liner, not immediately after *Wings of Morning*. She was a fine vessel. And I had things to do.'

'What sort of things?'

'The funeral. The house. His wife died two years ago. They had no family. The smack was sold at auction.'

Everitt nodded.

He seemed to make a sudden decision.

'I heard about the auction,' he said brusquely. 'It was a sad business.' I thought he had probably gone along to bid for some of the fine equipment. I hadn't had the courage to go myself, to see *Wings of Morning* auctioned off. And he obviously knew all about Joseph Proctor. Most fishermen along the east coast had known Joseph. 'I need a good man for hand-lining,' he went on quickly, wanting to get things agreed now that he had settled his mind. 'We need a successful trip this summer. You've been to Iceland?'

'Yes,' I said. '*Wings of Morning* went every year I was with her.'

'We sail tomorrow afternoon,' he said. 'Late tide. I have to buy a spare set of long-lines. You can find our bait for us?'

'Skipper?'

'You said you worked on the whelkers? I need twenty-five wash of whelks for long-lining on Smith's Knoll. Just for a few days, until the sails are dried. We might get down to Gabbard & Galloper. Depends how they're biting. Live fish for the well. Price is high at the moment. You find me twenty-five wash of good whelks at a decent price, Mr Vempley, and I might think you're worth hiring.'

I smiled. 'I can manage that, skipper,' I told him.

'Right then.'

I made to leave the yard, and then turned as if I had remembered something. I didn't think a little arrogance would hurt.

'You don't have anybody else in mind, skipper?' I said.

He looked surprised, wary. 'In mind?'

'I mean, I could look for another berth if you weren't able to take me on *Rechabite*. Only I need this summer voyage.'

He almost laughed at my sarcasm. There were not many experienced fishermen waiting around Yarmouth in the middle of the hand-lining season, and if they were in Yarmouth in July they probably weren't worth hiring.

The skipper knew that as well as any man.

'No, I don't have anybody else in mind, Mr Vempley,' he said with his tight smile. 'You will suit me very well indeed.'

'That's all right then,' I told him.

At least he wouldn't imagine I was desperate.

I walked back to my lodgings in the Rows, the sun high above the Yarmouth sandbanks, the breeze fresh off the sea, and for the first time in months, my heart felt a little less heavy.

Two

I had to celebrate that night. Not that I felt like drinking. I have never been a drinking man, whether you think it Satan's brew or the Lord's. But you can't leave the shore without raising a glass to all you leave behind. I had my suit of navy-blue pilot cloth with the velvet collar, and my blue bell-bottomed trousers. The leather boots I had bought for an evening out with Miriam, and they were still stiff and squeaky from lack of wear. What reason had I for wearing such smart gear? A gansey jersey and fearnoughts suit me most of the year. But I put my best clothes on and combed my hair. I found my favourite corner seat in the Guillemot, and wished myself well in best Yarmouth corn brandy.

It is a town carved out of the sea.

The day I arrived I was overwhelmed by the smells and the riotous noise of the quays. I was fourteen, and in all my years had never seen such excitement, even at the travelling fairs. The village where I grew up was isolated and quiet, and I had spent the past two years locked in a dingy workhouse with only my blind grandmother for comfort, and they only let me see her when she was dying and too ill to recognise my voice. I thought the Yarmouth Rows might be a taste of hell, or heaven. I was frightened as well as excited, thrilled and terrified in the same breath. But I trusted Proctor: I liked him from the start, the minute he and his kindly wife Alice came to collect me from the workhouse. When I thought my life was over, they took me from the cold wards and cruelty of the workhouse, and offered me a new life.

But Yarmouth was still a rare town to a village boy. There was a stench of fish and oakum everywhere, pitch and black tar on the salty air; geraniums seemed to be growing in all the window boxes and most of the houses boiled shrimps in their tiny front rooms; along the crowded quays, the acrid smoke and tang of kippers rose from the dozens of curing houses. I had never been so overwhelmed by noise. The skipper took me round the crowded lanes, the rope-walks and boat-builders, the shipwrights and smithies and caulkers' yards, the narrow alleys where women sat in the sun and gossiped, mending fishing nets and smoking clay pipes. He wanted me to see everything. At least the smithies' forges reminded me of the village where I grew up, but I had never heard the language coming from the riggers' lofts and the decks of the fishing vessels. In the chaos, I nearly got run over by the two-wheeled troll carts which rushed the fish through the narrow lanes. You got out of the way, or they ran you under.

'You'll soon get used to our ways,' Joseph Proctor told me, laughing at my confusion. I knew the laughter was kind. After two years in a workhouse, you learned to recognise kindness.

'I hope so,' I told him in my excitement.

He ruffled my hair and bought me my first bag of cockles, fresh from the sea. I don't think I had ever tasted anything so wonderful. From the beginning, I knew this was the life for me.

It was nothing like the village where I was born.

Hepstone was in Northamptonshire, with treeless fens to the south and wooded scarp country to the north. My father used to say it was blealy, meaning it was bleak and damp, but I never found it bleak. The fens were golden with wild reedbeds, alive with weird and colourful insects, singing with coots and bitterns. There were sedge birds mocking the songs of their neighbours in the fields, wildfowl swarming in the rivers. The sun made the flat countryside blaze, the woodlands dance and dazzle with whispering light.

I suppose my father taught me how to use my eyes. I know I loved him. He was a quiet, easy-going sort of man, good-natured and full of fun. We used to go looking for snails' shells and birds' nests together. He called snails' shells pooties, and he had rare names for all the flowers. Red campion he called cuckoo flowers, and purple loosestrife were long purples. In the streams, the sticklebacks were struttles. I learnt most of what I knew from my father. We even had a *Universal Spelling Book*, and an old copy of *Old Moore's Almanack* on a shelf in the downstairs room, though I don't suppose I learned much from them.

My mother grew up in Stamford. They met at the summer fair in 1850, and always told me they fell in love at first sight. She was Susan Taylor then. They got married more or less straight away, and I was born two years later. I had a sister in 1854, but she died after a few days. She was named Beatrice. I used to put spring flowers on her grave because my mother liked flowers. She was with us a few days, my mother used to say, but in our hearts forever. My mother was a simple, rather muddled woman, loyal to her family but not very intelligent. She adored my father.

And there was my grandmother, blind Elizabeth Vempley. She came from Ringmer, in West Sussex, and travelled to our part of the world when her husband was hanged for rioting in 1831. She went blind when I was nine years old. She used to sit for hours going on about a world where the workers had a little land, kept pigs and a donkey and a few cows, wild bees for honey and wood for the fire from the heath all round. It all came out of her dreams, I used to think. We never knew any of that in our village.

Hepstone was what they called closed, which meant that everything belonged to the landowner. He was worse than some fishing gaffers. He had a rule that all his workers had to attend church every Sunday. If anybody in the family didn't go, he interviewed the father. You can imagine how that would be, all cold arrogance and not a lot of understanding. Boots had to be polished too, and I can remember my father sitting at the table Saturday nights doing the family's. If one of the village girls had a baby before getting married, she had to leave the village, and the parents had no say at all. The farm-workers had to wear corduroys at church, and if they wore anything else he said they were getting above their station. He could inspect any of the cottages between six in the morning and six in the evening. Not that they were worth inspecting. We had two rooms upstairs, and two down, with a ladder to get to bed. But we had an apple tree, and I loved that, and fresh vegetables in the garden. My father dug the garden morning and night before going about his day's work.

There were rules about the garden. The land had to be dug and not ploughed, with one half planted with wheat and the other half with peas, beans, potatoes or some other vegetables. The food had to be consumed by the family, or by the pigs, but we couldn't sell it. All the rows of vegetables had to be planted pointing inwards from the road so that the landowner could see they were straight and properly weeded.

My father was always scathing about that landowner. 'You can't sneeze without his damn permission,' he used to say when he was annoyed. 'You can't breathe.' I never heard him swearing otherwise. Hipt, my mother called it, when my father lost his temper.

I suppose we had good times. It was a lovely village, with yellowstone thatched cottages and sparrows and swallows nesting in the thatch, gardens full of woodbines, spindling sedge and traveller's boy. We had ghosts and poachers, and a ranter who sang hymns; a witch lived in one of the cottages by the woods: they all walked in the main street of our village, and nobody told much difference. There were elm trees round the small green and will-o'-the-wisps the village girls called Jenny-burnt-arses. I went crow-scaring in the big fields, rambling among the bullrushes and reeds in the fens. I ran free until my father was killed.

He had a serious accident with a threshing machine. The landowner said it was his own mistake. I was twelve. My mother simply gave up. She couldn't live without my father. She used to sit by the fire, rocking backwards and forwards, staring into the empty grate. Within three months, she was dead. They moved me and my grandmother into the workhouse. The landowner said he needed the cottage.

I don't suppose the Peterborough workhouse was any worse than the rest of them. It was hard, being separated from my grandmother, but I soon learned the rules. They didn't care much about relatives. Husbands and wives were separated. Nobody was going to worry overmuch about a boy not seeing his grandmother. I found a way of surviving. I did what I was told. When my grandmother was dying, they let me see her for a few minutes, but she didn't know who I was. She talked about characters in *Pilgrim's Progress* and people she had known in the village. She had a thing about Presbyterians: couldn't stand them. She mentioned Thomas Paine and William Cobbett, but I wasn't sure I heard right. She couldn't see me.

They buried her in the workhouse graveyard.

I was lost after she died.

In the Yarmouth Rows, I began to find my life again.

I began to grow.

The Proctors had a tall, rambling house at the bottom of Sailmakers Row. There were miles of narrow lanes in the Rows, some of them hardly wide enough for a man to squeeze through, with upper floors overhanging the lanes so closely that neighbours could reach out of their windows and shake hands across the street. In the narrowest lanes the houses joined overhead, like a tunnel of darkness, with tiny dark courtyards where washing and starching were done, and nasturtiums and scarlet runners growing in boxes to bring a bit of colour.

I don't know where the Rows got their name. Some fishermen reckon the lanes are based on fishing-net patterns, but others say the building was entirely random. There are miles of houses, and every Row has a poetic name, like Kitty Witches Row, or Money Office Row and Adam the Barber's. Sailmakers Row had originally been called Budds, but somebody changed the name for easier remembering. Whatever they were called, they were always busy. Even in the middle of the night you could hear fishermen going off to their vessels and the watchman crying the wind, 'East is the wind, east- north-east, past two on a cloudy morning.' I dreamed that cry at night when I was at sea. I heard it in my darkest moments.

There was poverty in the Rows, but Alice Proctor kept her house like a new pin. She had flowerpots in the windows, and fresh flowers in all the rooms. Joseph used to whitewash the front of the house every time he came home. There was always the smell of fish, and Alice boiled shrimps in her kitchen like the rest of the wives, but the house smelled as clean and fresh as a country garden, the kitchen hanging with herbs, the furniture waxed and polished. It was a house polished to a glow, I always thought, like a cube of sunlight. When we were at sea, I dreamed of the Rows, just as some lads at home are always dreaming of the sea.

It was a wonderful life for seven years, sailing with Joseph Proctor, learning the life of a fisherman. Joseph taught me everything a man needed to know to earn a living as a fisherman, and a lot more about being happy.

And then in the autumn of 1875, I met Miriam Geddes.

She was a herring girl, working on the farlins. She had grown up in Yarmouth, but followed the fleets as far north as Wick for three or four years, which is why I never saw her when we were younger. We were both just twenty when we met. She made me forget how my father died, and how my mother mourned him to the grave. She was dark-haired and warm-voiced. When she spoke, I felt my stomach turn, like a lad with butterflies. She had tiny white scars on her fingers from gutting the herring, and her ears were pierced for gold earrings. Her lips were thin and soft. She made me forget my blind grandmother. She made my life turn over.

I cannot think about her now.

The pain is too raw.

'She was here, in Satan's Hole,' the letter from Grimsby told me. 'For a few days. Then she left. But I think I know what happened to her. I can't write it down here. But I can tell you.'

In January 1876, Joseph Proctor died. He was sixty, and suffered a heart attack while we were long-lining on Botney Gut. He would have been pleased with what we caught. We threw the catch back because he was no longer with us. He died at sea, his wife's name on his mouth, his friends all around him, which was a blessing. I think he couldn't wait to follow his wife. I was holding his hand when we closed his eyes.

In the spring of the same year, Miriam disappeared. She left no message. None of her friends had any idea where she had gone. I searched like a drunken man for weeks. I began to live in the beerhouses. There was no sign of her. She might never have lain in my arms. I threw dried seaweed into the waters off Yarmouth for a chance of good luck and then I found work on the whelkers. Slowly, I went into my grieving, like a drowning man sinking beneath the waves. I had been grieving ever since. The work on the whelkers numbed my pain, though I did not forget. I was beginning to drink regularly at the Guillemot, until the morning the letter arrived. The letter from Satan's Hole. I could not imagine what she was doing there. No fisherman in his right mind would go to Satan's Hole. No man of any decency. There could be no place on earth worse to hear from.

I read the letter a final time, and raised my glass to the yellowing ceiling of the back room of the Guillemot. You can't leave without saying goodbye to the things you leave behind. Even if they are all dead. Or memories. Ironically, I thanked Charles Oliver Everitt for offering me a chance to journey. It had to be somebody. It might as well be *Rechabite*.

In the morning, I would begin a new voyage.

Three

I was down on the quays by six the following morning, glad to be back in comfortable fall-front trousers and gansey. I have a gansey jersey knitted with rings and rainbows, the patterns all telling a fine fortune I heard from a gypsy on the Lerwick quays. Pale sunlight lifted out of the sea. I breathed the salt air and shook the alcohol out of my mind. It was a clear, warm morning, the light dazzling off the sea, herring gulls racketing over the wide quays and bustling fish merchants. Dozens of schooners and cutters rode bare masts in the roadsteads and a breeze tossed white water off the banks. I had my gear in my shoulder-bag, ready for going aboard *Rechabite*. But first I had to find our bait.

A set of long-lines on a smack such as *Rechabite* would consist of sixteen dozen lines each thirty fathoms long, two such lines making what we called a piece. Attached to each line were the snoods, lengths of line approximately thirty inches long, and these in turn carried the hooks. The snoods were fixed every eight or twelve feet depending on how many hooks you were using to a piece. A string of lines might be as much as twelve miles long, with six thousand hooks baited with whelks. You can imagine the business in that. I had spent the past year learning all about it, sailing with Leonard Beatniff on the whelker *Primrose*.

I walked along the quays until I found the *Primrose*. She

was a fine vessel, a single-masted cutter rigged fore and aft
like a sloop but with running bowsprit. Beatniff had fixed a
well amidship for the whelks, and she worked the Wash and
coastal waters as gaily as any smack I had ever known. I had
seen some rough seas on the *Primrose*, but she never took
much green water over her bows. I hailed the skipper and
then waited. I knew he would still be sleeping down below.
I had sailed with the *Primrose* for nearly a year, whelking in
Lynn Deeps and along the Kentish shore. I knew Leonard
Beatniff thought nothing of welcoming the sun. He came up
the companion after a few minutes, rubbing the sleep out of
his eyes.

'That you, Samuel?'

'Nobody else.'

He grinned at me blearily, and clambered on to the deck,
stumbling against the boom. He was a big, friendly man,
clumsy until the *Primrose* was riding a sea and then agile as
any young fisherboy.

'What the devil time is it?' he grumbled, blinking and
shielding his eyes from the morning sunlight, the dazzle off
the leaves of the trees along the quay. He groaned when I
told him.

'What you after, Samuel?' he asked grumpily, settling
against the mainmast and lighting his pipe, the sleep still in
his eyes. A cloud of black smoke drifted out to sea, and he
grinned at me happily.

'I'm signed on, for the summer voyage.'

'You leaving us?'

'I need to visit Grimsby.'

He shook his head, puzzled, letting his pipe go out.

'Never heard of anybody needing to visit there,' he said
glumly. 'Who you signed with?'

'*Rechabite*,' I told him.

'Charlie Everitt?'

'That's right.'

'What you need to see in Grimsby, Samuel, that makes
you go mad?'

'He seemed all right.'

'If you like your religion passionate.'

I laughed.

'And I reckon he sent you for a good price on bait,' the skipper suddenly grinned, seeing the reason for my early-morning call. 'He pinches my crew, and then wants cheap whelks. Trust a man of religion to go for a bargain. I only got expensive whelks for Charlie Everitt.'

'Come on, Leonard!'

'No, I don't reckon I got any cheap whelks for *Rechabite*.'

'You know I have to go!'

'Go why for the Lord's sake?'

'The letter.'

I had told Leonard all about the letter from Satan's Hole.

'You still bent on Satan's Hole!' he exclaimed.

'Yes.'

'You must be losing your anchor.'

'I have to find out about Miriam.'

The skipper sniffed and held his tongue.

He made a fuss of filling his pipe again with black tobacco.

'You know I never liked that girl,' he said after a few moments.

'I liked her.'

He sighed, glancing up from the deck. The *Primrose* was lifting up and down with the tide. A huge herring gull perched on the bowsprit and screamed at the flapping stay-sail. Leonard never reefed his sails down at night. He was usually too drunk.

'What do you need?' he asked finally. 'For *Rechabite*?'

'Twenty-five wash,' I told him.

A wash is the old Winchester measure, three shillings for twenty quarts and a pint of water. We would take forty wash to Iceland, but for the local fishing twenty-five would see us fine.

Leonard sighed again and shrugged, knocking the old tobacco out of his pipe and stretching reluctantly. He rubbed his eyes vigorously with the back of a hand and pushed his pipe into his jacket pocket. It took him a while to get going in a morning.

'I suppose I could manage that all right,' he said.

'Thanks, skipper.'

'Money in the hand.'

'Naturally.'

'You wait here while I fetch George and Andrew.'

He clambered over the bulwarks and up on to the quay. He was still yawning as he walked away. I could hear him grumbling aloud. George Salmon and Andrew Howie would be sleeping off their drink in one of the beerhouses. The second hand, James Allward, would be down when he was ready. He had a married woman in the Rows he visited whenever her husband was away, and he liked to take his time.

Lighting my own pipe, I thought about the year I had spent with the *Primrose*. It might be a way of life if you hadn't tasted deep waters. I could never settle to sleeping in my own bed at night. But the whelking was a lively business.

Huge quantities of whelks come from Harwich and along the Kentish shore, especially in the long-lining season on the Dogger Bank or coastal waters. There were forty cutters working from Grimsby alone. At Lynn the whelks were caught in round withy baskets with a hole at the top and baited with refuse fish in about thirty fathom of water. Leonard preferred long-lines which he called trots, the snoods baited with small live crabs. The whelks seized the crabs and held on so firmly you could easily haul them to the surface. Whelkers such as *Primrose* were fitted with a well so that the whelks could be kept alive for the smacks. It was profitable business for the whelkers, and Leonard had been doing the trade for years. He had a crew of four, and they all slept at home every night.

He got back with George and Andrew within an hour, which was less than it might have been, and after a strong brew of tea and some fresh fried haddock, they started measuring the whelks into nets.

'You going to see the midnight sun, Samuel?' George Salmon asked me solemnly as he ladled out the live whelks from *Primrose*'s well. The whelks would be stowed in nets and then rowed round to *Rechabite*, trailing from the long-boat's stern. 'You going to cast the hand-line?'

George always talked in this poetic fashion.

'Must be losing your anchor,' Andrew Howie grinned, and I knew Leonard had told them I was heading for Satan's Hole.

'Just measure the wash,' the skipper growled at them now, smoking his pipe complacently while they worked.

'Only making conversation,' Andrew complained.

I saw him winking at George Salmon.

When the twenty-five wash were measured and into nets, Leonard gave them a scribbled invoice and told them not to let the whelks go until they had the money in their hands. And to bring it back smart. They rowed away, laughing and talking, and I sat on the tiller while the skipper made another pot of tea.

'You think you doing right, Samuel?' he asked me when he brought the mugs of steaming tea up from the galley.

'I have to go, Leonard.'

'But to that Godforsaken hole! Nobody in their right mind visits Satan's Hole.'

'I know.'

'It's a dark address for a girl to be writing from,' he said.

'She didn't write.'

'She has friends there though. They wrote.'

I drank the tea and shrugged.

'It's my business, Leonard.'

'I know that. You expect me to keep quiet?'

'It might help me forget Joseph,' I added.

'You don't want to forget him.'

'Stop grieving then.'

Leonard nodded, then shook his head.

'He was a good man, but you don't have to go on grieving. He wouldn't want that from you. It ent natural. But
mebbe you're right. Iceland takes a lot of things out of a
man's mind. You forget things in Iceland.'

We were silent for a moment, drinking our tea, and then
I asked him about Everitt.

'He's a good fisherman,' Leonard admitted.

'I heard that.'

'Ought to be.'

'Why?'

'Fishing family. Long way back. He was born in Harwich,
they say, not long after the French wars. Not much fishing
done in those years. Harwich was the greatest fishing port on
the east coast when I was a lad. It was the Orlibars introduced the first well-smacks in Harwich, back in the last
century, and they developed long-lining on the Dogger.
Clever buggers. You listen to some fishermen you'd think the
Orlibars invented fish along with the fishing.

'It was Everitt's grandfather who owned smacks in
Harwich. When the fishing fell off, he refused to leave, and
for years Everitt's father went on struggling to earn a living.
He failed, despite all his efforts. In the end, he was forced to
move to Barking. I think they went there in the early 1830s,
though I don't know other than I've been told. Samuel
Hewitt had the Short Blue Fleet in Barking then, and it was
Hewitt introduced ice to keep the fish fresh, which meant
the fleets could stay away from port for as long as there was
good fishing. Nobody thought about the men. Everitt's
grandfather always called Samuel Hewitt the Devil's
Prophet.

'By the time Charlie Everitt took over *Rechabite*, they had
bad pollution problems in Barking. You couldn't keep the
fish there. He went back to Harwich for a time, and then to
Gorleston for a couple of years. By then, Hewitt had moved
the Short Blue Fleet here to Yarmouth, and most of the
trawling fleets came with him. The liners just followed.'

'And the whelkers,' I grinned.

'Got to follow the fishing, Samuel.'

'I know.'

Leonard sighed and finished his tea.

'They do say the Lord was a fisherman, Samuel,' he said. 'Always remember that. We should cast our nets the same side as the Lord, and then we won't go far wrong.'

'Don't you think Everitt believes that too?'

'He might,' he said warily, avoiding my eyes.

I leaned forward, punching his knee. 'Leonard?'

'I'm not saying anything, Samuel. The man has a right to his own reputation. He's done me no harm.'

'But you've heard things?'

'*Rechabite* lost a couple of lads. Nobody made any accusations. These things happen. I just don't reckon Joseph Proctor would have lost 'em so easy, or lived so easy with it on his conscience. But I don't know what I'm saying. I go to bed most nights sodden on corn brandy, and it's not my place to be talking about other men's deeds.'

I stood up then and stretched in the warm sun. The heat was rising out of the sea. I felt tired, restless. I didn't want to listen to Leonard's stories. I was going to Satan's Hole with *Rechabite*, and then on to the frozen wastes of Iceland. I wanted to see the sun kiss the sea. I wanted to find out what had happened to Miriam Geddes, why she had left so suddenly. In my heart, I might hear more than I wanted to hear somebody say, but I couldn't change my mind now.

I said goodbye to Leonard, and went off to find some lunch. I had the afternoon to kill, and then it would be time for *Rechabite*.

Four

I found *Rechabite* moored down the quays. She was an
eighty-foot ketch with the mizzen for'ard of the tiller to leave
room for dropping the lines from the stern. On the dandy-
rigged ketches the mizzen was aft of the tiller and caused
confusion with the lines. *Rechabite* looked as if she had been
built for working the rough seas of the Dogger, and I liked
the red ochre of her sails, the graceful curve of her bows and
transom stern. They were loading ice into the holds ready
for the trip. The prime fish would go live into the well, the
poorer specimens be gutted and iced for the local market. I
stood and watched for a moment, seeing the way she rode
the moorings, listening to the men laughing. Then I noticed
Jack Walmsley waving to me from the tiller.

He was fooling about, saying something to the group of
men round the mainmast: two or three grown fishermen,
some young apprentice boys. Walmsley danced up and down
the deck, hurling lumps of ice at one of the boys, and the
men all roared with laughter as the lad skidded and dived to
avoid the showers of ice. Walmsley seemed to want me to
watch. I walked to the edge of the quay and leaned against
one of the bollards.

'Mr Vempley,' the clowning third hand smiled, making a
mock bow.

'That's right.'

'You hear, boys, that's right!'

They all laughed nervously. The boy dodging the ice stood still but kept his eyes on Walmsley. A thin, sallow-faced man stepped forward and reached out for my shoulder-bag. He had grey straggly hair hanging down the back of his neck and a boil on the side of his face.

'Henry Purvis,' he said, taking my bag. 'Second hand.'

I jumped down over the bulwarks and slipped on the ice. The men from the ice barque were already leaving. Walmsley nodded at one of the lads and he ran to fetch a long-handled brush to clear the deck of ice. The other two boys stood by the mainmast, one of them watching Walmsley nervously, the other leaning nonchalantly against the mast.

'Samuel Vempley,' I told them, nodding briefly.

The younger lad blushed, glancing at Walmsley. He looked no older than twelve or thirteen. 'That's Robert Allison,' Purvis told me. 'Francis Campbell is the lad clearing the deck. The other's John Pinney.' He nodded towards the second boy at the mainmast who stepped forward and shook my hand cheerfully. He looked slightly older, fifteen or sixteen, good-humoured and lively. He had a wide grin and firm handshake. 'Welcome aboard, Mr Vempley,' he said as Walmsley snorted.

Purvis seemed to be on edge. He flinched, ducking his shoulders, when there was a crash from the hold where the men were shovelling the ice into the shelves ready for the trip. 'You been on *Wings of Morning*, Samuel?' he said without much interest, staring at the young apprentice busily clearing the ice off the deck.

'That's right.'

'And *Primrose*,' Walmsley shouted. 'Don't forget the whelker. We got our bait through Mr Vempley, Henry. Got to have good bait to make a trip.'

'They loaded it all right?' I asked Purvis, ignoring the third hand.

'Yes,' Purvis said indifferently. 'That's right.'

'They good whelks?'

'Skipper thinks so,' Walmsley answered for him.

In the bows, I could see another lad loosening the tyers on the jib and staysail. The bowsprit was already free to be run out.

Walmsley lurched towards me with his rolling gait. He was grinning, enjoying himself. I could smell the drink on his breath. 'You ent Poll Brock, by any chance?' he asked, coming close and leering into my face. 'Come aboard in disguise?'

I flinched away from his stale breath.

'Is the skipper not aboard?' I asked Purvis.

Walmsley went on as if I hadn't spoken. 'Only I don't like Poll Brock,' he whispered. 'She has a cast in her eye and she brings bad luck. We don't need bad luck on *Rechabite*. We can make our own.'

Henry Purvis laughed nervously and then had a coughing fit.

Walmsley turned on him. 'You laughing at me, Henry Purvis?'

'Get on with your work, Jack.'

'Yes, sir.' Walmsley nodded. 'Right away, sir.' He turned back to me, deliberately ignoring Purvis. 'Poll Brock could easily disguise herself as a fisherman,' he said with his mocking sneer. 'Pretend she knew what she was about. Handy with the lines. Indentured fisherman. You ent that kind of article? You ent come among us to raise havoc?'

I bent down and picked my gear up.

I hadn't met a fisherman yet who wasn't superstitious.

'I knew a skipper once reckoned his Aunt Katie was a witch,' I said levelly.

'Is that so?' Walmsley grinned.

'It is. Once, when he was having a bad trip, he got a red-hot poker and went right round the boat shouting, "Come out you old bugger!" He wouldn't sail if she came anywhere near his smack.'

'A wise man.' Walmsley nodded sagely.

'A stupid man.' I smiled. 'He could never find the fish. He was too busy dreaming witches. I don't reckon intelligent fishermen believe in things like that.'

Walmsley straightened. He was grinning, but his eyes were small and lifeless, like black seas. He had a broken nose, same as his skipper, but it was flattened to his face as if it had been punched with a hammer. He was enjoying himself, but he would stick a knife in your throat and watch the blood bubbling out with the same grin on his pock-marked face.

I glanced at the other men without taking my eyes off Walmsley. I could see Purvis and the two apprentices watching me. The third lad was leaning on his sweeping brush. Purvis picked at the side of his face. An older, white-haired man had climbed on deck from the companion and was leaning in the hatchway, beaming happily as if we were putting on a show. I thought it might as well be now as later.

Then suddenly everybody swung into action.

'Skipper coming,' Henry Purvis shouted, and Walmsley grabbed my gear and made for the companion, shouting at me to follow him and see my new quarters. I was halfway down the companion when Everitt climbed down over the bulwark and Purvis rushed up to him, telling him the smack was provisioned and ready, shouting orders to the waiting apprentices.

At the bottom of the companion, Walmsley dropped my gear and turned into the galley. 'New hand, Benjamin,' he yelled. I peered into the galley and saw the galley-boy jump, knocking a pan off the side and then another as he tried to retrieve it. He had a round pink face and terrified eyes, and his skin was delicate as a girl's, flushing with panic. He couldn't have been much older than twelve. He was scrubbing pots with a scouring brush and went on with his work when I handed him the pans. Walmsley leered at him and winked at me. 'Got bad nerves,' he said. 'Easily upset, ent you, Benjamin?' The boy blushed again, ignoring me as he tried to work. Walmsley laughed crudely and pushed past me into the cabin, crushing me against the door. He had shoulders like an ox and barely fitted in the entrance to the aft cabin opposite the galley. 'This is our little home,' he sneered. 'Skipper has second aft cabin. Not that he ever leaves the tiller.'

'Thanks,' I said.

'Make it your home.'

'I will.'

'Skipper doesn't like to see new hands until we leave port,' Walmsley explained. 'Get in the way. You know how it is. Welcome aboard.'

He shook my hand, and I felt my bones crushed by his thick fingers. The fingers were gnarled and filthy, covered in white scars. He chewed his nails. He grinned straight into my eyes and then turned to go.

As he passed the galley, I heard him hiss nastily at the young boy in the galley. 'I eat eyes,' he whispered jeeringly. 'I like eyes. I suck 'em out and swallow 'em.' I stepped out of the cabin and saw him clambering up the ladders. When I glanced at the boy, he looked terrified, pink-faced and near to tears. I waited until Walmsley had clambered back up the companion ladders and told the boy not to worry.

'He means it.' The boy began to blubber.

'No, he doesn't.'

'He treats us real cruel,' he went on. 'He says he's going to kill us.'

I touched his arm and smiled at him. 'Benjamin!'

'Yes.'

'You listening to me?'

'Yes.'

'Good. He can't treat you cruel when I'm around,' I said. 'I'm the new hand, let him try and make a meal of my eyes. Right?'

'Yes.' The boy nodded unhappily.

I laughed at him, punching him on the arm.

I left him scouring pans, and went back into the aft cabin. The cabin was filthy. There was no ventilation because the hatch had to be kept shut to keep the water out and the skylight was fastened down to prevent the glass being smashed by the seas. On either side of the cabin were two tiers of narrow bunks, like shelves with sliding doors. The narrow space stank of sulphur fumes and plug tobacco. There were globules of tobacco juice all over the floor, and the hinges and brass fittings were green with verdigris. The smell was foul.

'Fifth hand!'

The shout nearly had me off the bunk. I pushed out of the cabin and clambered up the companion. The skipper was standing by the tiller. He was dressed in his working gear now. I stumbled, getting over the companion, and went to the tiller. The lads were hauling the mainsail halyards, and I could hear Walmsley shouting orders from the bows. Everitt stared at me contemptuously.

'You don't think it polite to report to your skipper, Mr Vempley?'

I knew then Walmsley had walked me into this one, but I wouldn't say anything. I nodded and apologised. Everitt watched his men working for a moment and then suddenly pointed to a white card pinned to the mizzen.

'Read that please, Mr Vempley.'

I went and studied the card.

'In the sweat of thy face shall you eat bread,' the words told me.

'You understand?' Everitt asked me.

I nodded.

'You're sure?'

There was something savage, remorseless in his smile: he kept hammering at me with his eyes.

'I'm sure,' I said plainly.

The skipper smiled, satisfied. 'Cast your line the same side as the Lord, Mr Vempley, then God will provide.'

I nodded again.

'The Lord was a fisherman,' I said.

He studied my face as if I might be uttering blasphemy,

and then smiled his unpleasant smile. I could see his fists clenched together at his sides, and his teeth were like polished ivory. I hadn't noticed his teeth in the barking yard.

'We will be long-lining from the boat on Smith's Knoll,' Everitt told me conversationally, suddenly seeming to relax.

'Yes, skipper.'

'You can take the first trip with Edwin Wallis, our fourth hand. Do you have a favourite hymn, Mr Vempley?'

I shook my head: no.

'Mine is appropriate for fishermen, I think,' Everitt smiled. 'You might know it. Sing along with me if you recognise the words.'

To my amazement, he suddenly started singing. He had a loud, tuneless voice, and it carried the length of the smack from the stern to the thirty-foot bowsprit. As he sang, the other men joined in while they worked, Jack Walmsley raising his voice as loud as he could, drowning the sweating boys at the halyards. Weakly, I recognised the hymn, and joined in as well as I could. I hated hymn-singing almost as much as sermons, which was what they mostly were: sermons set to music.

When we were finished, Everitt smiled directly at me. The singing seemed to make him feel better. He repeated some of the words. '"Will your anchor hold in the storms of life/When the clouds unfold their wings of strife/When the strong tides lift, and the cables strain/Will your anchor drift, or firm remain?"' He took a breath and sighed. 'Fine words, Mr Vempley.'

'Yes, skipper.'

'Will your anchor hold, Mr Vempley?'

'I don't rightly know, skipper.'

'Perhaps we shall find out?'

I shrugged. 'I do my work,' I said, watching Walmsley toiling with the lads at the main halyards, hauling them up and trying to keep the gaff square to the mast, sweating and heaving in the evening sun. He shouted all the time at the lads as if they couldn't work without his bawling voice in their ears. When the halyards were belayed the peak was swigged up until the sail began to girt at the throat. *Rechabite* was obviously going to go out under her mainsail only. There was too much breeze to risk a full rig inside the harbour. 'I do my duty,' I added vaguely. There was something dispiriting about this ritual: humiliating while everybody else worked.

Everitt smiled at me complacently. He was watching every move on the smack. 'We have nothing to do but save souls, Mr Vempley,' he told me with his self-satisfied smile. 'That is the Lord's work. Welcome aboard *Rechabite*. You may get about your business.'

Seeing that I was dismissed, I made my way for'ard and watched as the apprentices heaved the bowsprit out. Another lad was busy loosening the tyers on the jib. When they were ready, Purvis said something to the skipper, and he went and took the tiller. The massive tiller post was carved with religious figures, and the oak tiller swung in Everitt's hands as if it was light as a feather. 'Cast off for'ard,' Everitt shouted. The lads on the quays loosened the ropes. 'Cast off stern,' the skipper called. 'Get the drogue ready.' The drogue was a heavy old sail that was kept in the stern and could be dropped overboard if we needed to slow down suddenly. One of the apprentices was busy getting her clear.

Jack Walmsley seemed to be everywhere, giving orders, lifting and shoving. The skipper went on shouting his commands. *Rechabite* left the quays like a feather caught on the wind. The huge mainsail stiffened and suddenly we were heading for the harbour entrance. With a shout, Walmsley told the lads to get the jib and staysail secured to the bowsprit and the mizzen ready for hauling. The topsail was already being hoisted. We were going to be under full sail as soon as we left the harbour. Strictly speaking, the bowsprit shouldn't have been out until we were abreast of the pier heads, but we had right of way departing the harbour, and Everitt was obviously in a hurry.

'How does that seem, Mr Vempley?' the lad John Pinney asked me, pausing for a breath as *Rechabite* slipped through the lockpit.

'We're in a hurry,' I laughed.

'Fish won't wait for us.' The lad grinned.

'Mizzen halyards,' Walmsley roared from the stern.

'That's me,' the lad whispered, and fled before I could say anything else.

I saw Walmsley knock him across the head with his fist and then point to a flapping sheet. I felt the sea lift *Rechabite* out into the clear water, and saw the red ochre of the main-sail gleaming in the evening sun. The roadsteads were crowded with vessels, schooners and yawls, cutters and little mizzener dandies. There were a dozen fishing ketches like our own. A sloop was heading in for the quays.

But we were heading out to sea.

I felt the surge of the old excitement, the freedom of deep water.

After a quick glance round, I climbed back down the companion and said hello again to Benjamin. The boy was crying. When he moved his hands from his face, I saw a cut down his left cheek, streaming with blood. The cut looked like it had been made with a gutting knife.

'Who did it?' I asked him in surprise. He shook his head. 'Nobody came below,' I said half to myself, staring at the fresh blood. 'Nobody left the deck.' Was I certain? He refused to answer my questions. I went into the filthy cabin and stowed my gear in the locker beside my bunk.

Five

We took a course NE for Smith's Knoll and settled into the wind under full sail. Swarms of seagulls followed us out to sea. To the west the sky was turning a delicate pink as the sun climbed down below the horizon. Ahead of us, darkness already twinkled with summer stars. Benjamin Bulpit had dinner ready by the time we were an hour out, roast beef and suet pudding with dumplings and treacle duff, and brought it on deck in tin plates so that we could eat while we were working. There was plenty of scalding-hot tea to wash it down. The tea was sweet and black as tar. The galley-boy always boiled the tea in an enormous copper, adding sugar and creamed milk as we went along. The skipper took his food at the tiller.

We were heading for night fishing, and my first job would be to help Edwin Wallis and some of the apprentices bait the lines. In long-lining the hooks were bought already on the snoods, with the snoods tanned and the long-lines tarred. Everitt had a complete set of lines ready baited in the eighteen-foot longboat, and the lines we were baiting were the spare set, ready for the second haul.

Edwin Wallis was the white-haired older man, stocky and short like a lot of fishermen, his face tanned mahogany brown. He wore gold-rimmed spectacles perched on the end of his nose.

'It took me years to get this colour,' he joked about his tanned arms as we hauled the bags of whelks out of the well and carried them to the coils of lines heaped amidships by the fish hatches. 'I'd have managed it a lot quicker if I'd been a kipper.'

'And hotter,' I laughed.

'That's true,' he beamed. 'But I've always been short.'

'Most fishermen are,' I responded, knowing the joke that was coming.

Wallis nodded cheerfully. 'They do reckon the taller variety died out,' he said solemnly. 'On account of falling overboard. You think that's so, Samuel?'

'So I heard.' I laughed again, though I was tall enough myself and had trouble not knocking my head when I was down below.

'I've been fourth hand on the *Rechabite* for eleven years,' Edwin told me as we lifted the last of the bags of whelks out of the well. 'I never got any further on account of my lack of powerful ambition.'

He seemed pretty pleased with himself by his own account.

When we had collected enough whelks for the lines, we settled down cross-legged amidships and began cracking the shells with iron mallets. You can use other fish for bait, mussels or herrings, and even lugworms. Lugworms will attract the cod away from any other bait, but they're expensive and fiddly to get on the hooks. The great thing about the whelks is their firm, muscular flesh. No trouble fixing a hook in that. We took two lines to bait each, which would normally take an experienced man about an hour. John Pinney and Richard Buss joined us, and Nathan Chapman, the oldest lad among the apprentices. This was the crew who would take the first set of lines out in the longboat when we reached Smith's Knoll.

'Looks like we'll be laying by the stars.' I grinned at Edwin Wallis as we settled into the work.

He shook his gnarled head solemnly, concentrating on a

large whelk and munching a mouthful of shag tobacco. The smell of the stuff made me want to give up smoking. I only smoked the weakest stuff myself. 'Cod are allus hungry,' Edwin said, as if I had never been to sea in my life. 'Cod are allus eating.'

'Like you, Edwin,' John Pinney laughed.

'That may be so, young Pinney, but the Lord made me what I am.'

'He must have had a rough day then,' Pinney teased him.

I finished my tea and went on with the baiting. The skipper was at the tiller, watching the burgee, keeping an eye on the full sails. Like most of the skippers I'd known, he hardly seemed to use the smack's compass but guessed the grounds by the changing colours of the water. I stuck a hook into my thumb and cursed.

'Take your time,' Edwin said calmly.

'We're in a hurry,' I reminded him jokingly but in a lower voice.

None of the lads spoke. I saw John Pinney glance at the skipper and then change his mind. We were obviously making for a quick trip, and I guessed the *Rechabite* needed the market. Everitt must be short of funds, or hauling close to the wind.

'Not much gained by hurrying,' I said quietly. 'In my experience.'

I saw Nathan Chapman watching me. He was a hard-faced lad, eighteen and strongly built, with unfriendly, crafty eyes. I guessed he kept his peace by being silent. He gave me a surly look.

'You got your skipper's ticket, Mr Vempley?' he asked unpleasantly.

'No.'

'I intend getting mine.'

'Is that right?'

'I finish indentures end of this season.'

'I hope so.'

'I got a good character.'

I didn't know why Chapman was saying all this. Edwin and the other two lads went on baiting all the time he talked. You would think the skipper was deaf. He seemed not to be listening.

'Is it that unusual then?' I said casually.

'How do you mean?'

I sniffed and concentrated on my line, pretending not to mean anything.

'Is what unusual?' Chapman said again aggressively.

I looked up with a surprised expression.

'For somebody on *Rechabite* to finish their indentures?'

I thought Chapman was going to have a go. He turned white. He glared at me and then glanced at the skipper. Nobody else spoke. We went on with the baiting.

At the mainmast, Henry Purvis was playing an accordion. 'Daisy, Daisy' drifted over the empty sea. The sky was full of evening stars. I could see Robert Allison, settled beside him on the deck, carving a smack out of a length of soft white wood. Fishermen did all sorts of things at sea to pass the time. I had carved a few white-wood models myself.

On *Wings of Morning* they liked mat-making. The skipper would buy cloth clippings and a few yards of sacking before every trip. The men cut the cloth into strips about half an inch wide and two inches long and threaded them into sacking. The result was a lovely mat for taking home at the end of the voyage. Making music was the other favourite pastime. Sometimes during the summer months there could be days and nights on end during which there was not enough wind to fill the sails and the sea was as calm as a puddle. When that happened you could see other smacks becalmed, and hear men playing their accordions. Without wind, there was nothing to stop the sound carrying over the sea for miles.

Some of my happiest hours had been spent listening to the night music when the smacks were becalmed.

'I see you loaded a good supply of candles,' I said conversationally, regretting the way I'd antagonised Nathan.

There was always plenty of time for trouble when you were at sea. I should have kept my mouth closed the way Joseph Proctor taught me. 'You save them for Iceland?' I asked with a brief smile in Edwin's direction.

'That's right,' Edwin nodded.

Joseph Proctor had always taken a hundredweight of tallow candle to Iceland. When they're hungry, cod will snatch at anything white just because it gleams in the water, and you could catch two score of cod with a short length of candle cut off and fixed below the hooks on the hand-lines. Some fishermen also used a cast lead fish on the shank of the hand-line hook. They could be bought ready-made on the hook, or the apprentices would make moulds from wood or a piece of potato and cast and fit their own. Joseph was willing to try anything on *Wings of Morning*.

There was a shout from the bows and Richard Buss got up to go and look. I could see Walmsley, struggling with one of the jib sheets. We went on working. From the galley, Benjamin came to collect the plates, and watched us for several minutes baiting the lines. His face was still swollen from the cut, but the skipper had given him some ointment. According to Benjamin, he had cut himself with one of the fish knives, holding it up to get it sharpened. When he went back down the companion, I lit my pipe and stood up for a moment, feeling the cooler night air on my face.

'You're a religious man then, Edwin?' I went on cheerfully, trying to make amends for whatever had upset the atmosphere.

'That's right.' Wallis nodded.

'Methodist?'

'Primitive Methodist, Samuel.'

I nodded. 'The religion of the poor.' I smiled.

'How do you mean?' John Pinney asked, sounding interested.

'Wesleyanism is a religion for the poor, Primitive Methodism is a religion of the poor,' I explained. 'That's what my old skipper used to say.'

'Sounds a bit clever to me,' Nathan Chapman muttered. 'True though.'

'Truth is in the Bible,' Edwin said seriously. 'Nowhere else.'

'I wouldn't know about that,' I laughed.

'I seen all kinds,' Edwin went on relentlessly. 'All varieties.'

'How's that, Edwin?' John Pinney insisted.

'I seen Independent Methodists, Magic Methodists, Methodist Unitarians, New Connection, Quaker Methodists, Primitive Methodists. I seen every variety. I even seen Tent Methodists and Welsh Jumpers in my time. I never seen anybody find truth outside of the Bible.'

Richard Buss came back from the bows and settled down to his lines.

Edwin Wallis was still in full fervour.

'Man is a poor blind fallen wretched miserable helpless sinner without grace, Samuel,' he told me in a garbled rush of words, 'and grace can only be found in the Bible.'

I finished the line I was baiting and leaned back against the low bulwarks. The bulwarks were less than three feet high and you could go over in a second if you weren't careful where you were putting your feet. I lit my pipe and grinned at the stars. Edwin noticed the grin and shook his head sadly.

'You're not a religious man then, Samuel?' he said.

'Does it matter?'

'Not to me,' he said with a frown, as if he couldn't believe a grown man could be so foolish. 'But it might matter to you.'

'I'll let you know when it does.'

I saw Benjamin clambering back up the companion, a shoulder of beef slung over his back. He paused for breath at the top of the ladder, and then lurched across the deck towards us. The skipper glanced at him quickly, and then went back to the stars. Benjamin dropped the beef at our feet and knelt down to force a hook and line through the middle of the meat. When it was ready, he carried it to the stern and heaved it overboard, securing the rope to a fastening. A swarm of hungry mollies swooped screaming after the meat, but it was gone beneath the waves before they could reach it. The beef would be towed for a few days to get rid of the taste of salt. Benjamin was sweating and panting for breath.

'In the sweat of thy face, Benjamin,' I told him with a grin.

He looked at me blankly and then smiled back.

At the tiller, the skipper suddenly looked up and spoke.

'We don't take the Lord's word in vain, Mr Vempley,' he said in a voice so quiet I hardly heard him. 'Not on my vessel, if you don't mind.'

I spat over the side and took another line for baiting.

Spitting was supposed to bring misfortune, but I didn't care.

'Bibles and witches,' I said under my breath. 'You'd think grown men would know better.'

But none of the men found my words amusing.

And I should have known better. You couldn't deride the beliefs of fishermen, even if they were nothing more than magic and fortune-telling. You couldn't make fun of a man's beliefs: they might be all he had between the decks and the deep green waters. Even superstitions had to be respected on board a fishing smack. I smiled to myself, thinking about Joseph Proctor and his ridiculous sayings.

Proctor wasn't religious, but he was as superstitious as the next man. He would never sail on Fridays, or go on board *Wings of Morning* if he'd seen a parson or a black cat. You couldn't mention pigs or pork on *Wings of Morning*. His wife Alice was just as bad. She refused to do the washing if Joseph was sailing in case she washed him away with the dirt, so heaven help us if we sailed on a Monday morning.

Joseph believed everything nonsensical except religion, and true religion he would simply mock. Some skippers read aloud from the Bible when they were laying their lines.

Joseph read from *Robinson Crusoe*. On one of our trips, I saw
him throw an entire night's catch over the side because they
were such poor quality, and then stand at the tiller and wave
his fist at the skies. 'There you are, you old bugger,' he
shouted, 'hev that for your breakfast and see how you like it.'
But he could alarm himself with his blasphemy. On a trip to
Tea Kettle Hole, when we had been becalmed for three
days, he climbed up the mainmast rigging with a gutting
knife in his hand and threatened to behead the Lord if he
didn't send us some wind to shift the sails. He was shaken to
a stunned silence when a breeze lifted off the sea half an
hour later.

Joseph was as daft as any man if it came to superstition.

This voyage was obviously going to be full of such
pleasures.

Six

We reached Smith's Knoll by summer darkness and the skipper ordered the lowering of the longboat. While Walmsley and two of the lads prepared to do that, the skipper shouted me to his side. I went and stood with him at the tiller.

'You know what to do, Mr Vempley?'

'Get the smack hove-to, skipper,' I told him.

'Show us your skills then, Mr Vempley.'

'Yes, skipper.'

I took the tiller and put the helm down to bring the smack's head to the wind. The *Rechabite* responded to my hand like a girl dancing on the ice. I glanced at the skipper and then started shouting the orders.

'Drop the jib, Mr Purvis,' I shouted, and saw Purvis leaping about with one of the boys in the bows. 'Back the staysail when you're ready,' I called. I saw them hauling the staysail sheet a'weather to prevent the smack coming round, and then Purvis easing the main sheet until *Rechabite* steadied to the wind. She rode hove-to like a gull riding the rough water. She was a lovely vessel, nearly as delicate to handle as *Wings of Morning*. I glanced at the skipper, but he stared ahead at the darkening seas, allowing me to have my hand. When the rocking motion of the smack told me we were ready, I stepped back and offered the tiller to the skipper.

'Bring me some prime cod, Mr Vempley,' Everitt said with a tight smile. 'Not too much rough.'

'Right you are, skipper.'

I went to the port bulwarks and started to climb over the side for the longboat. Edwin Wallis and the three lads were already aboard. I saw Walmsley lounging towards me, offering to help me over the side. When he had my arm, he gripped it as if he was going to break it. I flinched and struggled to pull free but his hand was like a vice.

'You be careful now, Mr Vempley,' he said quietly. 'Men have been lost drawing the lines.'

'I'll be careful,' I told him, 'you needn't worry.'

He let me go and wished me good fishing in a louder voice so that Everitt could hear. I clambered down into the boat and took the bow seat. Edwin was in the stern. The lads were doing the rowing. We pushed off from *Rechabite* a few yards and then dropped a line anchor. I could hear Everitt shouting the men to get ready to tack. We had a coal brazier in the stern of the longboat to warn any passing smacks that we were fishing and to give a bit of warmth in the long night.

Rechabite now sailed off under easy canvas, laying lines across the tide from the transom stern. The lines were always lain across the tide so that the snoods would set clear of the main line. The baited lines were coiled down in trays in the smack's stern, and I could see Henry Purvis and Jack Walmsley paying them out. Light anchors were used along the length of the line to keep it in place, and *Rechabite* might sail seven or eight miles before the whole set was out. In the darkness, we soon couldn't see her barked sails. We had nothing but water and stars and the immense silence for company.

'That's it then,' Edwin Wallis said as *Rechabite* disappeared into the darkness. 'Time for a smoke, I reckon.'

I felt the boys in the boat relaxing, saw Wallis lighting his pipe. The fourth hand dropped more wood on to the fire. In the centre of the longboat was a miniature well for keeping the fish alive. I got my own pipe and lit it.

'You ever been lost in fog, Samuel?' Edwin asked me cheerfully.

'Once or twice.'

'I got picked up by a schooner one night,' Edwin went on. 'Took me to Holland. Six weeks I was, getting back.'

'I bet Everitt was pleased.'

'This was before *Rechabite*. I sailed with my dad a good few years. He was lost off Cape Farewell. We worked out of Harwich. I only been with *Rechabite* since my dad drowned.'

Nathan Chapman took a flask from his pocket and took a long drink, lifting the flask high and swallowing greedily. I could smell the corn brandy. He offered the flask to John Pinney and Richard Buss. Edwin shook his head gravely.

'Drink is the ruination of good men,' he muttered.

'I ent a good man.' Nathan grinned.

'I reckon we worked that out already,' Edwin told him.

But Nathan wasn't listening.

'You know my dream?' he said. 'My dream of getting lost on the fog banks?'

'You going to tell us?' Pinney laughed.

'I dream I'm lost on the fog banks, and a koper picks me up.'

Pinney and Buss both laughed. The kopers were the Dutch trading ships which brought aniseed whisky and tobacco to the trawlers working in the fleets. The whisky sent the men mad and the tobacco poisoned them. The kopers also sold pictures of women produced in Holland and France. The pictures soon sent the men mad if the drink didn't.

'I get hauled aboard a koper,' Nathan sighed, 'and spend the rest of my years drinking whisky and sleeping with wicked women.'

'They don't have women on the kopers,' Buss told him.

'I heard they did,' Nathan insisted.

Edwin threw more wood on to the brazier and stared up at the skies. There always seemed to be more stars when you were out in deep water. In Iceland, the sky seems to be nothing but stars, millions of them going on for eternity. There was no moon, but the sea was brilliant with light. To the north-east, I could see a fire burning, and guessed it was another smack's boat, working the tides. There were men all over the sea, lonely in small boats, lifting up and down with the wash of the sea.

'Where you from, Samuel?' John Pinney asked me.

'I was indentured in Yarmouth,' I told him.

'You don't sound like Yarmouth.'

'I grew up in a village not far from Stamford. I ended up in a workhouse. My father worked on a farm. He got killed. I was indentured out of the workhouse.'

'Like me,' Nathan Chapman grunted.

'All the best fishermen come from workhouses,' I grinned. 'Where were you then, Nathan?'

'Hackney.'

'Hackney!'

'Everitt did the rounds. Got a lot of lads from Hackney. He reckoned they had nothing to lose.'

I knew half the trawling fleets were manned by lads from workhouses and orphanages, the worst of them from reformatories. Even on the liners, skippers were having to turn to the workhouses for labour. Every year, hundreds of lads absconded or ended up in prison on the treadmill. You had to be lucky to enjoy a life fishing.

'I could go back to Hackney,' Nathan said dreamily, as if he was talking to himself. 'I might one day. Show the bastards. When I got money and a silk waistcoat. See the women laugh at me then.'

He sounded resentful, his voice slurred with corn brandy. I guessed he'd been drinking on board *Rechabite* and wondered how come Everitt didn't smell the alcohol on his stinking breath.

'My family have always been in fishing,' John Pinney said cheerfully.

'From Yarmouth?'

'That's right. Four generations. My great-grandad did the Iceland trip. We go back further than the Everitts. They're comers-in to us Pinneys.'

'You better not let him hear you say that,' Edwin laughed.

'I don't mind Everitt. He knows the fishing.'

'Fucking religious bastard,' Nathan muttered in front of me.

'He does,' Pinney insisted. 'He knows the grounds, and the smacks.'

'Fucking maniac,' Nathan said more loudly.

I felt the side of the longboat sway and water sloshed over my feet.

'I don't like that language,' Edwin shouted from the stern.

'You know what you can do about it,' Nathan shouted back.

'Yes, inform the skipper, and see what he thinks then about your indentures.'

There was a tense silence. I could hear Nathan breathing heavily from all the corn brandy he'd swallowed. The air stank with the stuff. I went on calmly smoking my pipe, trailing my hand in the cold water, watching the rocking motion of the stars. It would be wonderful to have a knife-fight in the middle of the sea, a dozen miles from your berth.

Richard Buss suddenly started speaking.

'I grew up on a farm,' he said. 'I worked the harvest. I didn't know about the fishing. This man came to the school one day and said there was good money and a fine suit of clothes for any boy who wanted to be a fisherman. I didn't ask my father. We never had enough to eat anyway, despite living on a farm. I signed the papers and they took me away that evening. I haven't seen my family in two years.'

Nathan Chapman grunted, snoring in the bottom of the boat.

I could hear the tears in Buss's voice. He looked no more than fifteen, tanned and healthy but miserable in his new life. He had probably signed indentures for ten years, and there was no law to help him break them.

'What about Benjamin?' I asked, trying to distract the boy's unhappiness. 'He doesn't look like much of a fisherman.'

Pinney and Wallis laughed.

'Poor sod,' Pinney said.

'I reckon he has a hard time with Walmsley,' Edwin agreed.

'I don't like Walmsley,' I admitted.

Edwin turned serious. 'He's a dangerous man, Jack Walmsley,' he said. 'You watch your back, and your reputation. Nothing worse than a gossip on a small vessel. We are a kingdom to ourselves. We are alone on the deep waters. Jack Walmsley would sell his soul for a bottle of corn brandy. I believe he already has.'

'Does he pick on Bulpit?'

'He picks on anybody who will stand and take it,' Pinney said in a quiet voice.

I could tell there had been trouble between them in the past.

I imagined John Pinney had held his own. 'What about Benjamin?' I said again.

Edwin Wallis sighed. 'He shouldn't be with us at all,' he said. 'He ran away from school. He's not twelve years old yet, and if he is, he doesn't behave it. He's a child. He ran away and signed indentures and his poor mother has been trying to get him back ever since. She wrote to Everitt three times. I saw the letters. Everitt never replied. I don't condemn him for staying with the law, the boy signed indentures and there's no denying that, but I do blame him for not replying to a distressed mother.'

There was a silence.

'Did nobody let her know?' I asked.

I saw Edwin glance at Nathan Chapman, and Pinney

leaned forward and squeezed his shoulder. When they were sure Chapman was asleep, Edwin nodded in the darkness.

'I wrote and told her,' he said.

'Somebody had to,' John Pinney agreed.

'Quite right,' Richard Buss said quietly.

We lay almost motionless on the deep sea, and I felt the stars moving above us, the moon rising from a remote land of ghosts. You could easily believe in ghosts when you were anchored in a longboat in the endless wastes of the sea. Men have gone mad and jumped overboard waiting for the smacks to come back to the fires of the longboat. Men have driven themselves wild with aniseed whisky and murdered each other before the smacks could return for the lines. I thought suddenly of Joseph Proctor, reading to me from *Pilgrim's Progress* while we were out in *Wings of Morning*'s longboat, reciting the wonderful list of names. I heard his voice, and the tears suddenly came to my eyes. I would never forget those wonderful names: Mr Money-Love and Mr Hold-the-World; Old Man Pope and Mr Save-All; Great-Heart and Lord Carnal Delight. I knew them all by heart from the days when my blind grandmother chanted them aloud by the fire in our cottage: Lord Luxurious and Sir Having Greedy; The Valley of Humiliation. I knew them from my grandmother, and then again from Joseph Proctor, along with Cobbett and Tom Paine. Joseph Proctor knew them all. He was a fine man. He would not have tricked a boy to sea and denied the wishes of a grieving mother. He would not have done that even to save his own life. He would not have hurt anybody.

'Samuel?'

I looked up and saw John Pinney watching me with concern. Edwin Wallis was peering at me through the darkness. I rubbed my eyes and grinned at them.

'You all right?' they both asked.

'I'm fine,' I told them.

We smoked our pipes, and sat on in the silence, and while we waited for the agreed time, slept to the lulling of the waves. I hadn't slept for nearly twenty hours, and even the longboat seemed comfortable on a warm night. The sea rocked us to sleep like a cradle.

I woke with a start, and heard Edwin giving orders to start hauling.

Nathan was awake by now, and he and Richard Buss did the rowing, taking the stern oars. John Pinney and I sat in the bows and leaned for'ard, hauling up the line and passing it back along the side to Edwin who took the fish off the hooks before coiling the line down in the stern. The fish he dropped into the well amidships. We had several miles of line to haul, and unless *Rechabite* tacked back along the line to meet us, we would have to deal with the entire catch.

I could feel the sweat pouring down my face within minutes.

'What a life,' I joked to John Pinney. He grinned at me, wiping his own sweat out of his eyes.

'Just pray the sea doesn't make up,' he said.

'I do.'

'Don't you worry about the sea,' Edwin said cheerfully. 'I can deal with that.'

'Oh yes.' I laughed at him over my shoulder.

'Don't you know, Mr Vempley,' John said mock-seriously. 'All Mr Wallis has to do is tap the sea with the blade of the weather oar and he tames it as calm as a pond.'

We all laughed, Richard Buss nearly losing his fourteen-foot oar as he slipped in the stern seat, Nathan choking drunkenly as he struggled with the lines. I laughed with the rest of them at Edwin's solemn warnings.

'You think that's very funny,' he said, shouting over our din, 'but you know what my father used to say?'

'What's that, Edwin?' John managed to ask.

'You are all right so long as you fly towards the sea and never fly from it, for if a little water tumbles over the bow you can bail it out, but if a sea gets under your billage it may turn you over.'

For some daft reason, we all roared with laughter.

In Edwin's mouth, the most sensible advice about the sea sounded like a parson's sermon.

Then with a shout, Nathan Chapman saw the *Rechabite* tacking steadily towards us, and we all sobered up quickly.

Seven

Back on board *Rechabite* we got the prime cod into the well and then gutted and iced the rough. While we were doing this, Walmsley and Purvis took the longboat and Francis Campbell and Robert Allison and laid the lines for another catch. It seemed daft, sending the two youngest lads in a short-handed boat, but Walmsley said they didn't need help with his fine muscles. The work would go on like this for days.

I was tired, but worked by the fish pounds with the other lads. Edwin Wallis dealt with the live cod. Live fish had to be pricked before going into the well, a needle being pushed into the swim bladder to let out the air: if you didn't do that the fish would rot. Being the best of the catch, you handled them with great care. They were lifted carefully out of the longboat with a net and never dropped on the deck, and once they were pricked slipped into the well tail first to avoid breaking their necks. The coaming to the well funnel was amidships, and the hatches down to the fishrooms for'ard and aft of the funnel. Fish could live in the well for months without being fed. I once took *Wings of Morning* into Yarmouth for her yearly refitting, and found an eight-pounder swimming around in the well.

An experienced fisherman like Edwin Wallis could prick the live fish in a force ten gale, but the gutting was more complicated: you were using razor-sharp knives, and you had to watch what you were doing.

'You take the heading, Samuel,' Nathan suggested.

I had my own heading knife, and sliced at the fish with a will. Nathan and Richard did the splitting and gutting and then threw the fish down the hatch to the fishrooms. John Pinney was looking after the catch, stacking it in ice on wooden shelves. There were fishrooms to the port and starboard sides of the well funnel, giving access to the aft and for'ard quarter. It wasn't my favourite job, working with the ice, even on a hot night in July: the ice took the skin off your hands, and the slime from the fish left a stench on your clothes for weeks. The cod livers we threw into large wooden tubs where they would be collected throughout the trip: there was good money to be got for cod-liver oil.

It took us an hour to deal with the catch, and then I stumbled to the aft cabin. The older men always slept in the aft cabin, the lads for'ard where the bows take green water. I'd spent many years of sleepless nights trying to cling to my bunk in the lurching, heaving for'ard quarters.

But tonight I didn't think there'd be trouble sleeping. I took a mug of tea from Benjamin in the galley, and then settled down on the edge of my bunk. The cabin still stank, but I was too tired to be much bothered. I glanced down at my seaboots to kick them off, and then noticed the door on my locker was unfastened. Nobody worried about keys. I knelt down and looked inside. The gear had been moved. I searched through the locker, but nothing had been stolen. I was going to shut the door when I found the letter pushed to the back of the clothes; the letter from Satan's Hole, telling me there might be news about Miriam. It had been unfolded and then put back creased. Somebody had read it.

I put everything back where it was and lay down.

I closed my eyes, and went to sleep.

When I woke, the cabin was dense with tobacco smoke. Henry Purvis was sitting on the bunk opposite mine, smoking a clay pipe. Walmsley sat on the floor with his back

against the coke stove. He had the sleeve of his gansey jersey
rolled up beyond the elbow, and I could see his wrist and
arm covered with inflamed ulcers and angry sea boils. The
blood and fish guts stick to your arms when you are gutting,
and if you don't wash properly the skin soon becomes
inflamed. The boils on Walmsley's arms seemed to be suppurating. He winked when he saw me leaning up on my
elbow.

'Enjoyed your sleep, mate?'

I remembered the disturbed locker, the unfolded letter.

'You want to try washing.' I nodded at his wounded arm.

Before he could speak, the door into the cabin opened
and Benjamin came in. He was carrying a bucket of boiling
water in one hand and a bowl in the other. I smelt the paraffin straight off, and recognised the mixture of paraffin and
treacle fishermen sometimes use to ease suppurating boils.
Benjamin had a wire scrubbing brush clenched underneath
his arm.

'Set em down, lad,' Walmsley grunted.

I saw Benjamin go white when he glanced at the inflamed
ulcers. He put the bucket down and turned to go but
Walmsley grabbed his arm.

'You ent leaving?'

'I got the duffs boiling, Mr Walmsley.'

'Won't taste no better with you watching 'em.' Walmsley
grinned.

I sat up on the edge of my bunk and stretched my arms.
Rechabite was tacking under light sail so we must be laying a
fresh set of lines. I wondered why the skipper hadn't called
me on deck.

'You know what to do?' Walmsley was saying to the lad.

'No, sir,' Benjamin blushed.

'To get rid of 'em?'

'No, sir.'

'Got to scrub 'em. Take 'em off.'

'I can't do that.'

'Somebody has to.'

'That's wire.'

'You won't hurt me.' Walmsley grinned again. Benjamin was beginning to panic.

'You want to leave the boy alone,' I told Walmsley.

He gave an exaggerated jump, pretending to notice me for the first time.

'I thought you was asleep,' he said.

'Did you.'

'All the snoring.'

'Let me use the brush,' I suggested bleakly, holding his look.

'The boy's supposed to make himself useful,' Walmsley protested innocently. 'That's only right, ent it, Henry?'

'That's right.' Henry Purvis nodded glumly.

'The boy's got to feel likely,' Walmsley went on with a sneer.

'Leave him alone.'

Walmsley continued as if I hadn't spoken.

'He makes tea like cat's piss,' he said, appealing to Henry Purvis. 'I never tasted owt like it: mushy vegetables and burnt fish, puddings half water and beef black as charcoal. He must have learned to cook off his mother. You learn to cook off your mother, Bulpit? She teach you to feed the pigs?'

Benjamin's eyes filled with tears and I could see his lips trembling. His face was white with fear.

'Give it a rest, Walmsley,' I snapped, suddenly angry. I detested him. I detested all the bullying rant and cruelty. I let my fury show.

Walmsley loved it. He began to smile. He would delight in a fight. He would protest like a whining girl and then produce a blade from his back pocket and gut you before you could turn round. I thought he was mad.

'You got a friend, Benjamin!' Walmsley said with a leering smile.

'You heard me.'

'You got somebody to look after you.'

'Get out,' I told Benjamin quietly.

'You want to think yourself particular lucky today, boy.'

Benjamin darted out of the cabin and back to the galley.

I got down off the bunk and stood over Walmsley. It had to be now. I turned my back on him, knelt down and opened the locker. I felt inside as if I was looking for something, and then stood up with my gutting knife in my hand. I waved the knife slowly in front of Walmsley's face.

'You leave him alone, Walmsley,' I said quietly. 'You hear me?'

Nobody said anything.

Walmsley kept smiling but his eyes were lifeless. Very slowly, he leaned forward and took the wire scrubbing brush. Without looking at me, he began to scrub at the ulcers and boils. White pus ran down his wrist. He dipped the brush into the bucket of boiling water and went on scrubbing. His eye never flinched at the scalding water. There was blood and pus all over his fall-front trousers.

As I left the cabin, he was smearing paraffin and treacle ointment on to the wounds, then rolling up his sleeve to do the other arm. Henry Purvis never moved. They were both laughing as I closed the door. When I got out of the cabin I breathed the fresh air like a drowning man, then I went and found Benjamin and asked him to show me round the smack.

I kept close to him in the days following.

I talked to him about the fishing, and got to know *Rechabite* nearly as well as I'd known *Wings of Morning*: at least I could find my way around, there was no hidden darkness where I might get a knife between the shoulders or a club across the back of the neck. I took my turns working the lines from the longboat with Edwin and John Pinney, and hardly saw Jack Walmsley and Henry Purvis. The fishing and gutting went on relentlessly day and night. The fishrooms were filling with iced fish, the well was beginning to get some fine specimens for the live market. I hardly exchanged a word with the skipper.

I thought *Rechabite* was a fine smack.

As I said before, she was an eighty-foot ketch with her mizzen for'ard of the tiller and staysail and jib rigged to the bowsprit. I reckon her beam was twenty feet, and her depth maybe twelve. There wasn't much room below if you lifted your head. Edwin Wallis said she was registered at seventy-seven tons. There were cabins for'ard for the lads and galley and cabins aft for the men. You reached the aft cabins down the companion, and could go for'ard to the bows through the fishrooms which were either side of the well-funnel. A coaming covered the well-funnel amidships, and there were hatches down to the fishrooms for'ard and aft of the coaming. The funnel was four foot square, but opened out beneath the fishrooms into a huge well for the live fish.

Like all the well-smacks, *Rechabite* had been specially built for bringing back choice cod alive, and the well was part of the vessel itself. Two caulked bulkheads were built amidships across the hull from keelson to deck, enclosing a large watertight compartment. This was the well. A constant supply of sea water flowed through the large auger holes bored in the bottom of the vessel below the waterline. You had to be careful with those holes: in a bad storm a smack might heel wildly, and if any of the holes came out of the water, air might get into the well and a considerable quantity of water blow up through the funnel, killing most of the fish. There was no cracking-on or driving into hard seas in a smack with a well full of live fish. You could kill the lot in a hard blow.

You also had to be careful with the fish. Every morning, one of the lads had to climb down into the well to make sure none of the fish had died. Round fish such as cod and haddock move freely about the well, but halibut or plaice tend to lie on the bottom or sides, choking the holes and preventing the free flow of water. Dead fish have to be removed as soon as possible. It was the one job I loathed. Climbing down into the dark and slimy pit of the well was like swimming through a solid mass of giant maggots. I had nightmares about the well for years. Access to the well was through a hatch on deck covered with an iron coaming. The four-foot square tunnel down into the well meant there was plenty of space for the fishrooms on port and starboard, allowing passage along each side of the vessel below the main deck.

It was in the fishroom that Walmsley caught me, on our last day of fishing. I was going through the fishroom from the galley to see if John Pinney was in the apprentices' cabin for'ard. The aft door slammed behind me, and when I turned round, Nathan Chapman was leaning against the door. Then Walmsley stepped through the narrow for'ard door from the passage, and closed it behind him. Both men were holding gutting knives loosely at their sides.

'You checking the catch, Mr Vempley?' Walmsley said with a smile.

'What do you want, Walmsley?'

'You don't think John Pinney knows how to stack a shelf?'

I kept my eyes on Walmsley, listening for any sound from Nathan. *Rechabite* was working under full sail, and I might not have heard it if he moved. I turned slightly and leaned back against the shelves of iced fish. If he had a good throwing hand, Nathan could have lodged his knife in my back before I even saw it. I felt for my own knife, but it was with my gear in the cabin. Walmsley saw the movement, and grinned with pleasure. 'You won't need your knife.'

'Not against you,' I sneered.

He laughed. 'You hear that, Nathan!'

Chapman said nothing. He looked nervous. If I was going to make a move for either door, it would be the aft door where he was standing. I didn't reckon he had the nerve for knifing anybody, not judging by the sweat running down his face.

Walmsley was swinging the knife in his hand.

'I don't like you, Vempley.'

'Is that right?'

'I don't like you interfering.'

'I'm terrified.'

'I don't like your smell.'

There was silence. I could hear the skipper shouting something to Henry Purvis and the second hand's hoarse reply. I guessed Purvis would know what was going on down below. I felt the smack ride green water, and wondered how long it would be before Edwin Wallis missed me.

'I don't want you on this vessel,' Walmsley said finally.

I shrugged. 'Isn't that down to the skipper?'

'Not when he hears what I got to tell him.'

'In the middle of the summer voyage?'

'Plenty of fishermen looking for a good berth.'

'Not for hand-lining off Iceland.'

Walmsley sniggered. 'You're that good then, are you?'

'I can manage a line.'

'It'll take more than that, Vempley. It'll take more than good fishing. Skipper's a religious man. He doesn't like drinking. He doesn't like women. Not certain kinds of women.'

I knew he was referring to the letter. I stood away from the shelf and turned my back on Nathan. I'd had time to think, and I knew what I had to do. I stared at Walmsley, clenching my fists ready so that he would know I was going to do something.

He grinned at me in anticipation.

'Not women who work in Satan's Hole, Vempley,' he said with his cold sneer.

I let out a shout of rage and made as if to attack Walmsley. He flinched and then crouched down, snarling and holding the gutting knife in front of him.

'Come on then,' he roared.

But I was already turning away. Before he could see what I was about, I spun round and hurled myself at Nathan Chapman's legs. I went forward faster than Nathan could move. I crashed into the deck at his feet and then had him by the legs before he could react. I lifted him straight off the deck. He wasn't expecting that. His head hit a maindeck beam with a sickening crack. He let out a cry. I could hear

Walmsley thumping down the fishroom towards my back. Nathan cried again. With a huge effort, I flung him round as Walmsley reached us and pushed him towards the knife. If the knife had been firmly held, it would have gone straight into his back. As it was, the blade clattered to the floor and Nathan fell heavily against the wooden shelves, his face hitting the well-deck as he went down, blood running from his forehead. Walmsley stumbled clumsily over him and then scrabbled to his feet, desperately trying to find his knife.

I was out of breath. I bent down and picked the knife up. I waved it casually in front of Walmsley's face and then hurled it the length of the fishroom so that it thudded into the far door. It quivered for several seconds.

'I'll kill you next time,' I said quietly.

Walmsley was red-faced and his breath came in great gasps. He seemed too surprised to speak.

I turned and let myself out of the fishroom.

In the bright sunlight, I went up on deck and leant against the bowsprit. Green water flew in my face. I could hear herring gulls, following our wake. I got my breath and stopped my hands trembling.

In the fishroom, I'd learned something.

On that first day, Jack Walmsley could easily have got down through the hatch into the fishroom and from there into the galley to cut Benjamin Bulpit's face. And if he could do it, I was pretty sure he had.

I didn't know what else he could do.

Eight

We fetched an incoming tide and reached Yarmouth a week after departing. Everitt saw *Rechabite* berthed. She was a heavy smack with fine lines, and because of the tide took a lot of stopping. The sail was reduced steadily, and even as we approached the roadsteads Everitt had the drogue unfurled and ready in the stern. The bowsprit was run in for safety.

When we were safely berthed, Everitt started shouting his orders for the catch. The bobbers were already waiting for us on the quays, clowning and skylarking in the dawn sunlight, irritating everybody with their buffoonery. It was their job to unload the iced fish from the fishroom into big wicker baskets and carry it off for the morning market. Jack Walmsley and Henry Purvis kept a count of the iced fish as it left *Rechabite*, and Everitt was everywhere, seeing to the unloading, checking that all was well. It took the lumpers an hour to clear the fishrooms of iced fish.

Then the fun started.

The merchants had already swarmed aboard to check the live fish in the well. They argued a price with Everitt and decided the quantities they wanted, and then we had to begin unloading. The cod for the merchants was swept out of the well with a laddenette and lifted on to the deck. Everitt had ready orders for seventy score, the fish to be crimped on deck.

'You handle the crimping?' Edwin asked me as we began the unloading.

I got my knife and waited by the well. John Pinney and Richard Buss had the laddenettes. When we were ready, Edwin pushed the coaming off the well and Everitt stood and watched us.

'You know what you're doing?' he asked when he saw I had my own crimping knife.

'I've done plenty.'

Everitt frowned. 'These are mine,' he said with a scowl. 'You make sure you do them right.'

He watched carefully as Pinney climbed down into the well. He came up with a huge squirming cod in the laddenette. A prime cod might be four feet long and weigh fifty pounds, and threshing about in the laddenette could easily knock a man off his feet if he didn't watch what he was doing. John swung the laddenette round to the deck where Edwin grabbed the cod by its tail while I lunged after the head. I held the fish firmly with my left hand and struck it on the nose with the cod knocker. It immediately went limp, stunned from the wooden bludgeon. The stunning makes the fish shut their mouths and gills and prevents toughening when rigor mortis sets in. As Edwin let go of the big cod, I knelt down on the deck and slashed a pattern of lines and stars into the fish's flesh with my crimping knife. The crimping proved to the merchants that the fish was freshly killed from the well, not taken iced from the fishroom. In London, they paid a good price for crimped fish.

By the time I had crimped the first cod, the two lads had lifted another couple of fine specimens from the well and Edwin was already making his grab for the tail. Again, I went for the hold behind the head, and brought my bludgeon down on the fish's skull. It was alive one second and stunned lifeless the next, ready for my crimping blade. I felt the muscles in my arms tighten. The deck was awash with water and slime, and I could hear herring gulls screaming over the masts, scavenging for offal. It never failed to surprise me, this sudden shock of death, with life squirming in your hands one second, violence the next. As I worked, I soon forgot Everitt's watchful eyes. My wrists were aching. There were seventy score of live cod to be crimped, and my eyes were already smarting with salt sweat. Edwin was reaching for a new fish before I had hardly begun my work. I felt hot and my head was aching, my hands slippery with silver scales and slime.

'That's it, Samuel.' Edwin laughed with pleasure. 'That's fine. You're a codbanger no mistaking.'

He seemed to be filled with delight. The delight of killing.

Codbangers was what people called the fishermen.

I went on with the bloody work.

It took us two hours to crimp the live fish for the merchants.

Everitt watched the whole operation, then saw the order carried off *Rechabite* before coming back and standing by the coaming. I was washing my hands, drinking a mug of tea Benjamin had brought from the galley. Edwin Wallis was pouring cold water over his gnarled head. John Pinney and Richard Buss were resting.

'You did a fine job, Mr Vempley,' Everitt said.

'I told you I do my work.'

'So you did.'

'But not for pleasure.'

He raised his eyebrows, questioning. I swallowed my drink and massaged my arms.

'I don't like crimping,' I said.

'It proves the fish were alive.'

'Alive when we crimp them.'

Everitt shook his head. 'God gave man dominion, Mr Vempley.'

'As long as he can afford the price.'

Everitt smiled then.

'The rich pay for their pleasures, Mr Vempley. We profit from their indulgence.'

'Right.'

'Right?' he asked quietly, recognising the scepticism in my tone.

I shrugged. 'Not my business, skipper. I'm a fisherman. I just don't like crimping.'

Everitt nodded, pleased.

'As long as you do it right,' he said, and walked away down the deck to where Jack Walmsley was finishing business with the bobbers.

I drank my tea, and after a rest, we had to finish emptying the well.

Live cod that hadn't been sold were stored in codchests in the harbour. The wooden codchests were made of battens a few inches apart to allow free circulation of water. They were kept floating near the quays. The top was planked over except for an oblong opening which was closed by a padlocked cover when the chest was in the water. Each chest could hold forty large or a hundred small fish, and the fresh movement of water would keep them alive long enough for the next market. If *Rechabite* sailed before the fish were sold, one of the merchants would handle the deals for the skipper and show him the figures when he returned.

I didn't have to help with this job.

I sat by the mainmast, drinking my tea and watching, relaxing in the warm sunlight. Everitt wanted me to get another load of bait from *Primrose*, but I could do that when I was rested. When the tea was finished, I smoked a pipe of tobacco, and enjoyed the fun with the codchests.

Everitt had got Henry Purvis and Nathan Chapman working on the codchests. They hoisted the first of them out of the water with lifting ropes, brought it alongside, and then stood in the longboat while John Pinney and Richard Buss again fetched the live fish from the well with their laddenettes, this time swinging them over the side and down to the waiting longboat. With a lot of shouting and splashing, Purvis and Nathan got the leaping fish into the codchest, and when it was full, fastened the cover with the padlock. Once the first of the codchests was safely anchored, they fetched another. The work went on for most of the morning, and I was glad I hadn't got Chapman's aching head in that heat. His head was still bandaged from the blow on the deckbeam.

'I fell out of my bunk,' he told the skipper sourly the morning after our fight.

'Fell out of your bunk?'

'I was half-asleep, skipper.'

Everitt eyed him sharply. 'Does that mean drunk, Mr Chapman?'

'No, skipper. I never touch strong drink. You know that.'

Everitt stared at him icily. He obviously didn't believe him, and was weighing up whether it was worth asking anything more. He decided not to bother.

'I doubt that very much, Mr Chapman,' he said as he dismissed the lad. 'Just don't let your head be an excuse for not pulling your weight.'

He kept Chapman on watch for hours after that, to teach him some sort of lesson. Emptying the codchests in the swaying longboat was probably his idea of a joke. Or a punishment.

Once the catch had been unloaded, we were free for a day's rest.

I took an advance on my money and walked down the quays to the Guillemot. Leonard Beatniff was in his usual corner, emptying glasses of beer with George Salmon. He seemed pleased to see me.

'You need more bait?' he grinned, raising his glass to the yellow ceiling of the Guillemot.

'Another twenty-five wash,' I told him, fetching my own beer and joining them in their corner. 'Skipper wants it tomorrow. They're loading ice now. We're heading for Leman & Ower and maybe Botney Gut if we can't fill the well.'

'For Yarmouth?' Leonard asked, interested in *Rechabite*'s sailing plans. He was always interested in new customers.

'Grimsby,' I told him.

Everitt had heard the market was higher in Grimsby.

Fishermen always followed the markets, after they'd followed the fish. It was a life of always following something. I drained my glass and smacked my lips.

'I haven't touched a glass all week,' I sighed, my eyes closed with pleasure. 'Skipper doesn't approve of drink.'

George Salmon went to get refills and I sat up and looked round the bar. Everything always looks different when you get back, even if you've only been at sea a few days. I grinned at Leonard.

'You were right about Everitt, he's a steady fisherman.'

'Like his father.'

'But he cracked on.'

'In a hurry,' Leonard laughed.

George got back with our glasses.

'Why's that?' I asked Leonard curiously.

'He needs the money?' Leonard suggested craftily.

'We all need money.'

'I'll drink to that.' George Salmon grinned.

'Some more than others,' Leonard persisted.

'Why?'

'I hear he's been hauling empty lines for some time.'

'I didn't see much evidence of that,' I told him sceptically.

'Tides change.'

'And catches,' I nodded, 'but we caught plenty of fish this week.'

Leonard grinned at me under his thick eyebrows.

'You always brought *Wings of Morning* good luck, Samuel. Joseph Proctor told me that himself. You brought the fish swimming to the surface, they were that eager to bite your hooks.'

We all laughed, and I gave up asking questions. I wasn't going to get much sense out of Leonard, or at least any more than I'd already heard. If Everitt was running short of cash, this trip might have made the difference, depending on the market. It didn't matter to me anyway. He drove his *Rechabite* hard, but he didn't take any risks that I could see.

'If he wants to catch a lot of prime fish, that's fine by me,'

I told my old friends. 'We all get a share of the profits.'

Jack Walmsley must have come into the bar through the back door. He probably heard my voice. He sidled up to our corner and was sitting down before I could tell him where to go. He made sure I saw him, so that I wouldn't go for a knife or broken bottle. The minute he sat down, he held out his hand to Leonard and George, introducing himself as *Rechabite*'s third hand. His breath already stank of ale, so he must have started drinking the minute his boots touched the quays.

'Jack Walmsley,' he said cheerfully, beaming and nodding at everybody round the table, making himself at home. 'Friend of Samuel's here. That bait you caught us was prime stuff. I never seen such whelks. I shall recommend the *Primrose* to every man what asks me.'

'I thank you, Mr Walmsley,' Leonard said cautiously.

Walmsley beamed with generosity and didn't stop for breath, nodding his head towards me. 'You got a good ship-mate here,' he said. 'I seen a lot of fine fishermen, but not as handy as Samuel. He crimps faster than any man, and them's Charlie Everitt's own words. He learnt his trade properly, our Samuel.'

'He had a good skipper,' Leonard said warily.

Walmsley nodded, his mood changing immediately. He looked solemn enough to be inside a church.

'We all respected Joseph Proctor,' he agreed with a deep sigh and shake of his head. 'A tremendous man. A real gentleman.'

'I didn't realise you knew him,' I said, surprised, caught off my guard by Walmsley's naturalness and spontaneity. He was the easiest liar I had ever met. 'He never mentioned knowing you.'

'Everybody knew Joseph.' Walmsley grinned at the other two, ignoring me. 'Famous, he was, with his *Wings of Morning*. Everitt bought a load of gear at the auction. Not one to miss a bargain, Charles Oliver Everitt. A real enthusiast for a bargain. Now there's a famous man.'

He roared with laughter at his own good humour and went and fetched us all fresh drinks. He'd noticed the glasses without even asking. We all got another pint of what we had been drinking.

Sitting down, he seemed to be finding something amusing, and then addressed his words straight to Leonard Beatniff.

'He fights as well,' he said, glancing at me as if for confirmation. 'He crowned one of our lads harder than some bare-knuckle boxers I've seen. That Nathan Chapman, he's a lad, isn't he, Samuel? A vicious sod, but he picked the wrong man this time. I went along with him because he said he wanted to set something right, but I didn't know he was going to draw a knife. I had mine with me, you know, Samuel. I couldn't stand and see you knifed. Not for a clown like Nathan. But the lad knows better now. He's got a head like a swarm of bees. Says he can't hear nothing but buzzing.'

I stared in amazement at Walmsley. He winked back as if we had berthed together a dozen years. I almost laughed out loud at his nerve. He lifted his glass and grinned cheerfully.

'I reckon you'll end up in prison, Jack Walmsley,' I told him.

'I hope not, lad.'

'It wouldn't be for doing nothing.'

He went on grinning. 'That's not friendly, Samuel.'

'Why should I be friendly?'

'You don't know me. I don't hold no grudges.'

'Maybe I do.'

He roared with laughter at that. 'Maybe you do,' he repeated, shaking his dirty-haired head.

'Or Benjamin Bulpit,' I suggested.

He looked genuinely surprised. 'Why should he hold grudges?' he asked innocently.

'The way you torture him?'

'I never laid a hand on the lad.'

'Not for want of trying.'

'Samuel!'

'But I'm looking out for the lad,' I warned him. 'I'm interested in his welfare.'

'Welfare.' Walmsley snorted with derision.

'That's right,' I said coldly. 'He signed indentures. He's going to finish them. I'll see to that.'

Walmsley seemed to bridle at my words. He drained his glass and gave me a look I wouldn't have wanted to see in a mirror. He stood up then and dropped some coins on the table.

'Buy yourself another drink, Samuel. It's the last I'll stand. A gift for what you did to Nathan. You'll not get another chance.'

He turned and walked away without waiting for my answer.

With a grunt, I swept the coins on to the floor.

'Bastard,' I said under my breath.

Leonard and George said nothing.

After a minute, Leonard got down underneath the table and started searching through the sawdust.

'What the hell are you doing, Leonard?' I asked him, shifting my feet out of his way.

He came up with the coins in his hands.

'Can't waste good money.' He grinned at us.

We drank to Jack Walmsley's damnation, and then I found my way back to *Rechabite*.

'Twenty-five wash of whelks in the morning,' I told Leonard as I left.

'Twenty-five wash of whelks it is, Samuel,' he cried.

'And mind your back,' George Salmon added.

I knew that was advice I was going to need.

Nine

The fish were biting on Leman & Ower: cod and haddock, halibut and plaice, some spawning whiting and a score of saithe. We had pink dawns and cloudless skies, and the green water was flat as a windless pond. I had seen rougher water on the Wash, where *Primrose* caught most of her whelks and the sea seemed to merge into the land. Laying her lines, *Rechabite* needed a full set of sails, and working the oars of the longboat bruised your arms. Even the tides were sluggish and lifeless, rocking us on muddy water, and the immense skies were like open mouths, dragging us towards the horizon.

The more we caught for the well, the more Everitt relaxed. He had codchests rented in Grimsby, and another skipper in Yarmouth had confirmed the rumours that the market was high. The best fish are always caught in the winter season, when cod has ice in its mouth, but we were catching some fine specimens for the well, and packing the rough stuff in ice. John Pinney warned the skipper that we would soon run out of ice. Francis Campbell and Robert Allison, the two youngest apprentices, spent every hour of the day baiting the spare lines. Even Benjamin came up from the galley to help with the baiting when he had time.

'Good fishing, skipper?' I said one night when the gutting

was finished and Walmsley had taken another set of lines in the longboat.

Everitt agreed pleasantly. 'The Lord is with us, Mr Vempley.'

'And the fish.'

He didn't bother to respond. Glancing up at the sail, he breathed in the night air and was content. I had never known a skipper take so much of the responsibility for the tiller. A smack's great sail power makes her far from light on the helm, and most men have to shout for help in anything of a breeze. Everitt never asked for help. His arms must have been like iron, tensing the huge tiller. He never even looked tired.

'You don't want a relief on the tiller, skipper?' I asked him.

'No thank you.'

'Most men would.'

'I have strong arms, Mr Vempley, but that's nothing to boast of. A gift from God. Like the fish,' he added wryly.

I could see Edwin Wallis in the bows, smoking his pipe and watching the white water. John Pinney was at his side, relaxing after the fishroom. In the stern, Francis and Robert were lazily cracking whelks, while Benjamin leaned against the bulwarks, his eyes closed.

'So many stars,' I said quietly. 'You wouldn't imagine.'

Everitt nodded. 'There always seem more out at sea,' he said.

'Yes.'

'You don't miss the land?'

'I wouldn't want to be anywhere else on earth,' I told him.

'Or having a family?'

I wondered briefly if he knew about Miriam. The opened locker slipped into my mind. Walmsley might well have told him about the letter, my reason for wanting to visit Satan's Hole.

'I might have married,' I said, deciding to be direct.

'Oh?'

'There was a girl, on the herring. She went north a few months ago. I haven't heard from her.'

Everitt seemed satisfied. 'A man should be married,' he said after a pause. 'Settles him down. Gives him something to work for.'

I was hardly listening to him.

For a moment, I felt a terrible loneliness, seeing Miriam's face in my mind. Then it passed. The familiar ache returned.

At the tiller, Everitt didn't seem to notice. He kept his eye on the mainsail, waiting for the tide to turn. The staysail was backed and the jib dropped. The tide was almost motionless, but in an hour it would turn and the snoods on the line would no longer be streaming in the right direction. If our good fortune held, the hooks would already be full of fine cod.

'Did you never think of going on the trawlers, Mr Vempley?' he asked after a long pause.

I shook my head. 'That's not for me.'

'The fleeting?'

'I wouldn't want that,' I admitted. 'The life sounds rough.'

'Godless,' Everitt said emphatically.

There was a lot of drinking on the fleets, and brutal violence. The kopers saw that they were well supplied with aniseed whisky and tobacco. The long, empty hours in overcrowded smacks saw to the rest.

'I like real fishing,' I told the skipper.

'There's a skill to trawling.'

'Not the same.'

'No,' he mused. 'I agree. But I've seen some rare skills on trawlers.'

'You went on the fleets?'

'Briefly.' He nodded. 'When my father died. Before *Rechabite* was rightly mine. I sailed with Coffee Smith's, out of Gorleston. Hubert Caldicott, on *Plough Boy*. I've seen that man take a trawl warp in his mouth and sense the nature of the bottom from the vibrations in the line. A trawler skipper has to know his grounds, Mr Vempley, or he'll lose a trawl on the rocks faster than he can haul nets. Another night, I watched him take a lead-weight and cover it with tallow so that he could judge the depth and contours of the ground by the colour of the sand we picked up. "We're like blind men groping round with sticks," Hubert Caldicott used to say, but he knew every trick there was to find the gulleys where the fish might be hiding.'

I recognised the admiration in Everitt's voice.

'He sounds a fine fisherman.' I nodded.

'He was,' Everitt said quietly. 'But not a fine man. He knew how to catch fish, but he spent his money as fast as he found it. Women and alcohol, they catch as many fishermen as fishermen catch fish, Mr Vempley.'

I thought for a moment about Leonard Beatniff and the crew of *Primrose*. They managed to catch whelks without bothering too much about women. I wasn't so sure about alcohol. It seemed all right to me, though I wasn't about to say that on the *Rechabite*. At least Joseph Proctor would have agreed with Everitt about that. He never allowed alcohol aboard *Wings of Morning*, although he would have been just as strict about Bibles.

'We don't want religion on *Wings of Morning*,' Joseph used to say. 'Causes too many arguments. We catch fish, and leave souls to parsons.'

'Did you know Joseph Proctor?' I asked absent-mindedly, not thinking about anything in particular.

Everitt's eyes never left the mainsail, but I noticed his hands tighten on the tiller. His mind worked faster than a feeding seabird, but I was getting to know him gradually.

'Did Joseph Proctor approve of alcohol?' he asked casually.

'No,' I replied. 'He never let a drop on board *Wings of Morning*.'

I was glad I could answer frankly.

Everitt smiled. He was too sharp for me. 'That's not what I asked,' he said, 'but let it pass. A man does what he likes with his own vessel.'

'He thought the kopers should be outlawed,' I said.

'I never met a sensible skipper who didn't.'

'No. They do a lot of damage.'

'They do harm, Mr Vempley,' Everitt corrected me. 'They ruin men's souls.'

'And minds.'

'I don't know much about men's minds,' he said flatly.

'Or care?'

I felt the silence. He never looked at me, but I didn't care if he knew my thoughts. I wasn't going to be kept quiet, just because I didn't hold with his religion. I'd found my own kind of religion in the books Joseph Proctor lent me, his essays of William Cobbett, Tom Paine's *Rights of Man*. Tom Paine was enough religion for me. Tom Paine, and *Pilgrim's Progress*. I had my own mind.

In the bows, I saw John Pinney stretching and yawning, shouting goodnight as he went below to rest. Edwin Wallis went on smoking, happy with the stars and his pipe. He hardly seemed to sleep, Edwin, but worked as willingly as any other man on the smack. He said the salt air kept him awake, and he only slept nights when on shore.

'Did you know Proctor?' I repeated my question.

Everitt nodded. 'I'd heard of him. And *Wings of Morning*.'

It would have been difficult not to have heard of *Wings of Morning*, living and working from Yarmouth. She was a fine smack, and skippers are always interested in other vessels. She also returned to port with some record catches, which was even more interesting for competing skippers. They listened to rumours the way women listen to gossip. Joseph Proctor had even tried some new grounds, especially west of Faroes, and his skills were known throughout Yarmouth. Even with four or five hundred smacks working from the port, it would still have been difficult not to have heard of his adventures on the fishing.

'She was a fine smack,' I said quietly.

'Still is, Mr Vempley.'

'I find it hard to think of her without Joseph.'

He nodded. He seemed willing to talk this way. For most of the trip, he had been frigid and isolated, concentrating on the fishing, cold and unfriendly at the tiller. I never saw him smoke a pipe. He drank mugs of scalding-hot tea, and ate his meals on deck. He was not the kind of man you would share your memories with. But tonight, he appeared less stern. He kept his watch, but didn't freeze me out.

'He was a good skipper?'

'He was.'

'You said you were with him straight from the workhouse.'

'That's right. Fourteen.'

'It's a rare berth, seven years.'

'Yes,' was all I could manage to say.

Everitt stared ahead into the bright darkness. He seemed pensive, thoughtful.

'I believe an indentured boy should be taught his trade,' he said.

'They're not all so lucky.'

'That is true. There are wicked skippers as there are wicked men.'

'Yes.'

'But you would not expect to find it otherwise.'

'Maybe not.'

'You have to deal with the wicked, and hope for the true.'

'I was fortunate then.'

'Indeed.'

We seemed to be agreed, but I sensed something in the skipper's voice, an uneasiness, or a deliberation.

He went on after a moment's silence.

'He wasn't a religious man?' he said seriously.

I shook my head. It didn't seem to matter.

'He was a good man,' I said.

Everitt smiled.

'That's not the same thing, Samuel, is it?'

It was the first time he had called me by my given name.

'Isn't it?' I asked.

'You can be good by nature. Just as you can be wicked by nature. Doing God's will is something different.'

I had no answer. I didn't really want to answer. This was not my kind of argument. I rarely knew what such talking was about. I lit my pipe and told the skipper I was tired. He didn't seem to mind. He went on staring ahead into the darkness, and I excused myself and went down the companion to the galley. I needed my rest.

Benjamin was in the galley, brewing tea.

'You want a mug, Mr Vempley?' he asked.

He seemed happy, red-faced from the steam of the galley, free and easy when Walmsley was not hounding him. He had a fine time talking and joking with Francis and Robert, watching them bait the lines.

I hoped he was beginning to enjoy the fishing.

I let him pour me a mug of tea and leaned in the doorway of the galley. He polished the brass fittings at the sink and lowered the wick in the lamp.

'Why did you come to sea, Benjamin?' I asked him.

He blushed, his eyes very blue in the dim light of the galley. There was a yellow glow from the lamp, and silence in the aft cabin.

'My father died,' he said after a moment, seeming confused by my question.

'Yes.'

'I thought he would want me to be earning.'

'You could have earned money on the curing. Or the fish market.'

He nodded unhappily, then shook his head as quickly, biting back the tears with a determined frown.

'I thought I could earn more at sea. To help my mother. She can't manage too well on her own. I was told there was good money to be earned at sea, so I signed on. I didn't want to go on the trawlers. They say bad things about the trawlers. But I thought it would be all right on *Rechabite*.

They all said Mr Everitt was a religious man. I wanted to earn money for my mother.'

The words all came out in an eager rush, as if he was trying to explain himself. I could see the tears in his eyes, and hear the tremble in his reedy voice. He was a child. He should never have been at sea. I couldn't imagine why Everitt wouldn't let him go, except that decent lads willing to sign indentures were getting harder to find, and a lot of experienced fishermen had gone with the trawlers to the fleets. The liners were left with family members or boys from the institutions. A lot of them weren't worth signing.

I ruffled Benjamin's hair and told him to get to his bunk.

I desperately needed my own sleep. In an hour or so, *Rechabite* would be tacking back along the line, ready to collect the fish from Walmsley's haul. The gutting and icing of the catch would begin again. It would be my own turn for another trip in the longboat. I lay down and went to sleep almost immediately, Joseph Proctor's warm voice ringing in my ear, the strong rhythms of *Pilgrim's Progress* lulling my tired mind. In the warm darkness, I had no memory of Miriam to disturb my heart. I began dreaming about her the minute I fell asleep.

Ten

Joseph never liked Miriam Geddes.

'She has come-to-bed eyes,' he said.

'She's all right.'

'And she can give you a few years.'

'She's my age!' I protested.

'So she tells you.'

I think he was suspicious because I found her dancing on the quays. I told him she was a dancing mermaid, and he said I must be out of my mind. It was September, and we were just returned from one of our best trips to Iceland. In the morning, we would have to begin unloading the catch.

There were fires burning along the quays where the herring girls lived for the season. They were housed in wooden huts, six girls to a hut, with a coke stove for cooking and warmth, and a bunk and a locker for each girl. The herring fleet visited the port every September, nearing the end of its journey from Lerwick to Lowestoft, and the girls were obviously throwing a party on the last night before the fleet departed. I could hear singing and the haunting notes of a violin, and there was a smell of freshly cooked food drifting deliciously across the water.

'I shan't be long,' I told Proctor.

'You'd better not be,' he warned. 'I don't tolerate late-nighters on *Wings of Morning*.'

I shouted goodnight to Proctor and climbed over the bulwark on to the pontoon. Most of the crew had already gone to their lodgings. The skipper and second hand were staying on board to look out for the catch. I felt like seeing the dancing.

A large crowd had already gathered, chattering and warming themselves round the fire, enjoying the hot food. Three men were playing pipes and a violin, the music animated and rousing in the crisp night air, several young couples already dancing by the light of the leaping flames. One of the fishermen in the crowd offered me a flask of corn brandy, and I took a long swallow. We had been weeks in Iceland without anything to drink. I thanked the man and asked where I could buy my own. The brandy made my eyes smart. When I had a bottle of my own, I went on watching the dancing.

The music was getting wilder. The man on the violin responded to the clamour of the crowd, bowing and scraping at his instrument, waltzing in a kind of trance as the notes rose higher and higher and the haunting melody drove the crowd wild, several of the herring girls dancing in a kind of delirium. I felt the excitement, the blood beating in my head. I glanced across the pontoon to where *Wings of Morning* lay in the darkness. The light from the fires reflected in the water. In the roadsteads, dozens of small fires burned in the sterns of the herring drifters, bobbing up and down with the tide. The sound of an accordion drifted restlessly on the chill air.

Then I noticed the girl.

She was dancing alone, moving slowly and sensuously to the music, indifferent to the commotion all around her. She seemed to be living in her own world, dreaming the sound of the music. The two men on pipes had lowered their instruments, and the man with the violin was following the girl, keeping his eyes on her all the time and weaving

rhythmically backwards and forwards in front of her, swaying from side to side as he played, his chin resting on the
polished wood of his instrument.

The girl danced round the fire. She lifted her arms and
held them high above her head. She spun round and round
and then slowly lowered herself to the ground. Some of the
men shouted her name, but I couldn't hear what they were
calling. Women in the audience started clapping. The girl
lifted her face to the flames, and flew rapidly round the
circle, flinging her hands out to men in the crowd, shaking
her head and letting her hair fall over her shoulders. She was
wearing a grey woollen dress with a neat white collar, and
her hair shone in the sparkling light of the fire. Her eyes were
closed and her lips slightly open.

She came steadily closer to the man romancing her with
his music. He was caressing her, making love to her with
his violin. He knelt on the ground and she danced seduc-
tively in front of him, touching his shoulders with her
hands, stroking his face with the tips of her fingers. Then
she was off again, almost running to the far side of the fire,
leaping into the darkness and kicking at the embers of
wood, floating through the showers of sparks. The crowd
went wild, chanting and clapping their hands, and the men
with flutes joined their companion on the violin, their
music rising to an anguished frenzy, an aching, passionate
melody drifting out into the dark night, mesmerising in
the autumn cold.

And suddenly, she was standing in front of me. I could
hear her quick hard breathing, see the perspiration shining
on her forehead. She stopped, with her hands on her waist,
her breasts heaving, her mouth slightly open. She had
wide, high cheekbones, and her eyes were bright with
laughter, wild with her own exertions, the shouts of the
men, the thrill of the music. She had thick dark hair hanging loosely over her strong shoulders. When she smiled, I
felt my stomach lurch, and she seemed to know what I
was feeling, laughing at me quickly, taunting. She reached

out her hand and touched me very lightly on the side of the face.

Without thinking, I stepped forward and put my hands round her narrow waist. I saw the surprise and then panic in her eyes. A woman in the crowd gasped and some of the men shouted angrily. Before anybody could move, I lifted the girl off the ground and held her tightly above me, her legs kicking in the air, her hands fluttering for my arms. She stared down at me helplessly, and I felt a drop of her sweat on my forehead. I held her for a long moment, and then lowered her slowly to the ground, and she was gone, darting into the firelight, leaving me surrounded by the cheering men, my eyes searching for her in the crowd, trying to follow her quick movements, make her out among the heat and shadows.

That was Miriam.

We walked out together every time *Wings of Morning* berthed in Yarmouth. I didn't care what anybody thought. I refused to listen to Joseph Proctor. My mind was full of music. My dreams lived with Miriam in a kind of paradise.

It was a cold winter that year.

Cold enough even for young lovers.

About a week after we met, she took me skating.

'I'm going on the ice,' she announced when I called at her lodgings early in the morning. She lived in a house in the Rows. I had come straight from unloading *Wings of Morning*. 'I'm going skating,' she said, pulling on her coat and grabbing hold of my arm.

'Skating?'

'That's right.'

'I've never been skating.'

'Then I'll show you.'

There was a big field on the outskirts of Yarmouth which flooded almost every winter, and if the days were cold enough, froze to a sheet of ice. In the early years of the fishing, skippers bought their ice from the farmer, and some smack owners still preferred to buy field ice, delivering it to the smack by horse and cart. When the field froze, people went there skating. There was midnight skating, and roasted chestnuts. Lovers wandered off into the darkness of the surrounding fields. The religious folk talked of disgrace and scandal.

I told Miriam I had no boots, but she borrowed a pair from her neighbour and laughed when I said I was tired. She wouldn't listen to arguments. She refused to hear me say no.

I think I fell in love that winter morning.

When we arrived, dozens of couples were already skating across the field, crowds of children racing in dazzling circles through the pools of red sunlight. It was a hard frosty morning, and the sun hung over the field like a ripe blood orange. A woman from the market was selling roasted chestnuts, and the sounds of laughter and hiss of steel skidding across ice carried over the frozen countryside.

'You go on,' I shouted at Miriam from the edge of the ice as she skated away towards the centre of the field. 'I shall come.'

I felt awkward and out of place. I fumbled with the straps on my skates. I felt lost away from the quays and green water.

I could hear her calling me.

'I'm coming,' I mouthed, my breath white frost in the blue morning, my face hot with embarrassment.

I could see her skating across the field.

'You're scared,' she laughed, spinning and waving as she flew past.

An elderly couple stumbled and fell with loud shouts of amusement, the woman shrieking and kicking her legs in the air as she struggled to keep her balance, the man laughing at his own clumsiness. Several children whirled around Miriam, calling her name, laughing and chanting, and she chased after them with great pushes on the ice, catching them and spilling them over, then dancing away before they could reach her.

I got on to the ice and she skated to where I was standing

and took my hand. 'You won't fall,' she said, smiling at me. 'I won't let you.'

We stepped out on to the ice and I felt my balance go, the ground moving underneath my feet. It was worse than being at sea in a force nine gale.

She held my arm.

'Steady,' she said with a confident laugh. Her voice was deep, her eyes blue with the ice. 'You must slide,' she said gaily. 'Let me show you.'

We slid out across the ice and I felt the cold on my cheeks, the field and hawthorn hedges gliding around the horizon. I felt dizzy, out of control, and barked a nervous laugh.

'This is fun,' Miriam said wildly.

'Yes.'

'This is lovely.'

We were out in the centre of the field. The sky was spinning round and I could see the sun turning in a strange circle towards the horizon. I opened my mouth wide to catch my breath and let out a shout of pleasure. Vaguely, I saw the other skaters whirling past. I could feel Miriam's hand on my arm, firm and steady, gentle and guiding. As she kicked gaily forward, I noticed that the leather straps of her skates were a brilliant deep red like the sun.

The cold was making it difficult to breathe. A rime of frost half an inch thick had formed on the ice overnight, and the steel blades of the skaters drew wide circling patterns in the sunlight, gleaming as the light changed and the sun climbed up into the cloudless sky. Beyond the field the horizon seemed empty and endless, and gulls wheeled in the startling blue, screaming out of the sea.

I clung to Miriam's hand, laughing and gasping for breath.

We seemed to be dancing through sunlight.

'This is wonderful,' I cried to the racing sky.

Miriam was laughing helplessly. 'I can't hold you much longer,' she kept shouting, but went on clinging to my arm, her skates hissing through the ice. Then as we turned and zigzagged around the field, she suddenly broke free, and despite my cries for help, was gone, racing away in front of me so that her skates threw hissing blue sparks around her feet and I couldn't hear the words she was shouting.

'I love you,' I called into the freezing air, and the words hung like frost in the rainbowing silence.

'I can't hear you,' she mouthed back, a shimmering ghostly figure at the edge of the field. 'I can't hear you.'

I slowed down and reached the edge of the ice, falling down clumsily on the frozen grass. 'I love you,' I said under my breath, trying to control my breathing. I looked up and saw Miriam floating eerily towards me across the ice.

She held my hand, and knelt down beside me.

'I love you,' I said, looking at her with surprise.

'Yes.' She nodded. 'Yes.'

Her eyes were very blue. She had a thin mouth, her lips touched with pale, delicate pink. She was wearing a neat green hat to go with her coat, and her cheeks shone with excitement and the cold. She was breathing rapidly.

'I could just eat some hot chestnuts,' she said when she gathered her breath, pretending nothing had happened, nothing had been said.

A crowd had gathered at the brazier, buying chestnuts from the market woman, warming their hands at the blaze. We stood up and went and bought some. They burned our mouths, and we swallowed handfuls of frost from the grass to cool them down.

For the first time, I kissed her.

I walked her back to her lodgings. She had lived in the same lodgings for years, keeping her room even when she worked away from Yarmouth with the herring fleets.

'What happened to your parents?' I asked her.

'My father drowned, off a Faroes fishing smack. When I was eleven.'

'I'm sorry,' I said.

'He drank,' she said with a shrug. 'He was probably drinking.'

We were silent for a moment. A lot of fishermen went overboard when they were drinking, tumbling into the darkness without a sound, slipping into the sea with a shout nobody heard or a surprised gasp of welcome: the death that had always been waiting for them.

'And your mother?' I asked her gently.

'She moved to Aberdeen with another fisherman when I was fifteen. I was working the curing houses by then. I started on the farlins as soon as I could handle a gutting knife. I always work the farlins during the herring season.'

It was good money, gutting the herring.

When she had gone, I stood outside the tiny house for a long time, thinking about what she had told me, and then returned to *Wings of Morning*. When I told Joseph Proctor of my day, he roared with laughter.

'Skating!'

'So!'

'At your age!'

Miriam and I became lovers not long afterwards.

Wings of Morning was on the quays for refitting, and Miriam's landlady had gone to Cornwall to visit her daughter, so she was in the house alone. We went for a drink in the Guillemot, then walked back to the empty house. I felt lightheaded, foolish, and my hands were trembling. We went up to her room and sat on the narrow bed. Winter sunlight filtered through the attic window. Far away, I could hear herring gulls screaming over the market. Miriam breathed awkwardly at my side.

'I missed you,' I told her. 'I kept thinking about you.'

'I know.'

'Do you?'

'What did you imagine?'

'I don't know.'

'It's the same for me. I will miss you always. I will never stop thinking about you when you are away at sea.'

I closed my eyes and felt my heart ache with longing.

'Samuel,' she whispered as I leaned forward, clenching my hands together to stop them shaking, trying to control my breathing.

I looked up at her.

'Yes?'

'Don't be shy.'

We slept together that night. In the morning, we got up and dressed and went down to the foreshore. The sea was grey and cold, washing icily from the frozen sky, thundering up the deserted shores. As the sun lifted out of the horizon, we could see the sails of dozens of vessels bobbing with the tide beyond the harbour. I had my gutting knife with me and caught a fish in the shallow water beyond the creeks. Miriam lit a fire. She collected wood and wrack while I fanned the flames. We roasted the fish in the flames and then ate the hot sweet flesh with bread Miriam had wrapped in greaseproof paper. I had never tasted such delicious food.

'Isn't it fine?' I said, wiping my mouth with my hand.

'Yes,' she laughed, cleaning her hands in the sand and watching the lights of the smacks out beyond the harbour. She warmed her hands at the fire and watched the flames dancing in the early-morning light. We could hear plovers and oystercatchers crying in the dunes, and there was seaweed dancing backwards and forwards in the tumbling surf.

'I could live like this,' I told her.

'In the open?'

'Travelling around, eating my own food, living on the land.'

'Be a bit cold,' she said with a grin.

We sat quietly, enjoying the flames of the fire, adding more wood from the pile Miriam had collected.

Beyond the roadsteads, a thin fog was drifting from the sea, and the bell on the buoy began ringing, the sound drifting mournfully across the cold, flat water.

'I could go with you,' Miriam said simply.

She shivered as she said the words, and then turned and warmed herself in my arms, burying her face against my shoulder. For the first time since I was twelve, I no longer felt lonely.

Eleven

I woke up to the sound of men yelling, the skipper's voice roaring into the hot night. 'Dogfish on the line, dogfish on the line.' I was out of my bunk before I was awake. I grabbed for my boots and scrambled up the companion ladder. The deck was mayhem. Edwin Wallis was already toiling at the stern, hauling at the last of the long-line. An enormous nursehound dogfish threshed and flailed across the deck at my bare feet, John Pinney and Richard Buss stabbing at it frantically with heading knives. By the well coaming, Nathan Chapman was struggling with another nursehound, the creature's jaws clamped on a large cod, gnawing at the flesh as Chapman hammered at it with a gutting knife. I could hear Nathan sobbing. Blood and fish guts slithered around the deck, making it impossible to stand. I sat for a moment, stunned, then jumped up and grabbed my knife. I didn't bother with my boots.

I slipped across the deck to where Edwin was still struggling. He was leaning far out over the transom stern, hauling at something on the line. Out to the starboard, I could see Walmsley standing in the longboat, cursing and fighting another of the nursehounds, hacking at it with his heading knife. The fire in the stern of the longboat sent sparks flying into the darkness and there was a hissing sound as water splashed into the flames. The longboat was lurching sickeningly in the waves being created by *Rechabite*. I could hear the skipper raging at the tiller, trying to hold *Rechabite* steady and see what was happening to his lines. His voice was hoarse from shouting. He kicked wildly at a dogfish slipping across the deck, and howled with rage as it slithered away through the scuppers.

I had never seen such carnage.

The lines were dancing with skeletons.

Nursehound and spotted dogfish lay dead all over the deck.

'God help us,' I heard John Pinney gasping, sitting on the deck surrounded by white skeletons.

In the longboat, Francis Campbell was crying.

The nursehounds must have got at the lines before Walmsley had a chance to begin hauling. They had wreaked havoc. Every cod we brought up was stripped to the bone. The few live cod that came struggling to the surface were being torn to pieces by the sea rats, their jaws clamped to the fish even as we hacked them to bits. The cod were being eaten alive. Severed heads stared at us with huge, bewildered eyes.

Then suddenly it was over.

The anchor at the end of the line was hauled over the side. Edwin Wallis sat numbly in the stern, coiling the anchor into the tray. The lads on the deck sat with their heads in their hands, surrounded by half-eaten fish. Dead nursehounds littered the deck round their feet. The skipper was standing motionless at the tiller.

We must have sat like that for half an hour.

When Everitt finally began issuing orders, his voice was like sandpaper, hoarse and rasping.

'Clear the decks, and start baiting the lines,' he said blankly.

I struggled to my feet and went and found my boots. Nathan Chapman was still crouched on the deck, his head forward on his knees, sleeping in nervous prostration. I got my boots on and fetched a long brush from the for'ard

stores, and began sweeping the decks clear. The dogfish
made a splash as their heavy bodies slithered through the
scuppers and hit the water. The skeletons disappeared
beneath the waves without a sound. I worked steadily with
John Pinney and Richard Buss, and saw Edwin already
beginning to bait the lines. It was another half-hour before
Jack Walmsley climbed aboard and slumped down on the
well coaming. The skipper didn't bother to ask him what
had happened. Dogfish hunt by night and there is not much
you can do when a swarm of them attack the lines: they've
done their work before you can haul the first snood.
Walmsley sat on the coaming, staring over the port bows. He
seemed stunned, motionless. As the light dawned on the
horizon, his face looked carved out of the dark. His eyes
were wide and empty.

I heard him start talking.

'It's that boy,' he said in a croaking whisper.

The skipper glanced at him and then away.

'I told you he would bring bad fortune.'

Henry Purvis was helping Edwin bait the damaged lines.

I waited for the skipper to give orders. The lines that were
already baited would need to go over the side. A fresh crew
would have to take the longboat and begin laying again.
There were fish to be caught if we were going to fill the
well. I felt nervous, listening to Walmsley.

But the skipper didn't stop him.

'I did warn you,' Walmsley went on viciously. 'I said no
boy that colouring ever made a fisherman. He's too pretty,
too delicate. He's not our kind. He ought to be wearing
dresses.'

The skipper spoke then.

His voice cracked across the early light, making several of
the men jump, startling Walmsley out of his monologue.

'There are lines to be laid, Mr Walmsley,' the skipper said
icily.

'Skipper.'

'There are things to be done, Mr Walmsley.'

Walmsley got to his feet and leaned briefly against the mainmast, supporting himself and breathing steadily. He had his head lowered, his shoulders hunched against the dark. He stood straight and turned and faced the skipper.

'I told you he would bring misfortune.'

'And I refused to listen to you,' the skipper said bleakly, glaring straight into Walmsley's exhausted eyes. 'I refused to listen to you, and now I'm telling you to prepare the lines.'

I knew then I would have to leave *Rechabite* and go with Edwin in the longboat. My stomach lurched. I went on sweeping the deck as if the skipper might not notice me. I thought of Benjamin down below in the galley, brewing the first mugs of tea for the dawn sunlight. He had stayed below all the time we were trying to hack the dogfish from the lines. I knew that sooner or later the skipper would remember he hadn't come when all hands were called on deck. I cursed myself for not fetching him.

'Longboat hands,' Walmsley suddenly bellowed.

He was sweating. In the early-morning light, I could see the sweat shining on his face, fish scales glimmering silver on his neck and arms. He was covered with fish slime. As he shouted his orders, I could hear the cold fury in his shaking voice. He looked demented.

I got my gear when the longboat was ready and climbed over the side.

I have never felt such dread.

I was trembling.

But I had to go with Edwin. It was our turn in the longboat and the tide would be turning any moment. I sat in the stern of the lurching boat, and closed my eyes as Nathan and John Pinney took the oars. Edwin sat wearily in the bows. Richard Buss was asleep before we were a hundred yards away from *Rechabite*. I could still hear Everitt shouting his orders, the smack sailing across the tide to get a good lay for the lines. On deck, I could see Henry Purvis working at the damaged lines, cracking the whelks and getting them on to the hooks. The fishing went on regardless. I heard

Walmsley's voice for several minutes, giving orders for top-sail and jib. When I couldn't hear it, I closed my eyes.

We were out six hours, and when we finally returned, there was a deathly silence on the smack. Everitt was at the tiller. Francis Campbell and Robert Allison were hauling the lines from the stern. There was no sight of Walmsley and Purvis. I clambered over the side, and stood shakily by the transom while Edwin and Nathan followed. We had never had so little help getting the lines back on deck. I stared at Everitt. He hardly noticed the fish, the fine cod we had hauled. I thought the smack might turn head into the wind if he wasn't watchful. John Pinney scrambled on to the deck beside me and then I heard the laughter.

I was down the companion before the skipper could say a word.

The galley was empty. From the cabin, I heard voices. A body seemed to be jammed against the door. I hurled myself at it and heard Henry Purvis curse. The door slammed into his back, and he lurched sideways into the iron stove. I stood in the doorway. I could feel the blood pounding through my head. I had my gutting knife in my hand.

Benjamin was lying on his back on the deck.

Henry Purvis must have been holding his arms, twisting them behind Benjamin's head. The cabin door had knocked him sideways. Walmsley was still crouched over the boy, kneeling on his chest, glaring at me like a wild animal. He was stuffing cod livers into the boy's mouth. Every time Benjamin tried to close his mouth, Walmsley punched him in the stomach. He gagged and vomited. There was blood on his face where the delicate skin had scraped against the metal bolts in the floor. He was crying like a child, sobbing and choking.

Walmsley was demented. I kicked him in the side of the head. He clung on to the boy and I had to kick him again, stunning him with the force of the blow. I was still wearing my steel-capped seaboots. The thud of the boots sounded hollow in the hot cabin, and as Walmsley fell sideways off the boy I went at him again, kicking him savagely in the ribs. I heard Walmsley grunt with pain. I kicked again. Purvis was shrieking and there were shouts from the companion. Then Walmsley was struggling to his feet, his eyes wild with fury. I aimed a kick straight at his back and he went sprawling across the floor beside the stove. I went forward, gripping the gutting knife.

If Edwin Wallis and John Pinney hadn't grabbed my arms I would have killed him. I wanted to kill him. Benjamin was choking on the floor and Henry Purvis was whining and complaining about his head, but I just wanted to get my knife into Jack Walmsley. He flailed backwards into the bunks and stared at me as if he couldn't believe what was happening. There was blood running down the side of his face where he had caught his head against the side of the bunks, and he clenched his arms round his ribs as if they might be broken. I kept shouting, struggling to get free. I think for a few moments I must have gone mad.

But Edwin and John pulled me away. They watched Walmsley, threatening him with their own gutting knives while Benjamin scrambled into the galley and vomited into the bucket. Henry Purvis started to cry.

The skipper climbed down the companion.

He ordered us on deck and then went back below to deal with the cut to Walmsley's head. He had a medicine box in his own cabin. He was down below for half an hour, and while he worked, we started gutting the fish and pricking the live cod for the well. Nobody spoke about what had happened. Benjamin refused to leave my side. My hands were trembling as I used the heading knife.

John Pinney worked with me. He was ashen, his own hands trembling, fumbling with the fish. 'We saw what he was doing,' he said in a hushed voice. 'You aren't on your own.'

'No man can do that.' Edwin Wallis nodded. He was wearing his gold spectacles. He looked suddenly old, his eyes watering when I thanked him.

'Stay close,' I told Benjamin.

The boy was too frightened to cry. I have never seen anybody so terrified. He knelt beside me. He kept glancing towards the companion, touching my arm. Edwin Wallis watched him, and I thought he was going to break down with pity.

'No man can do that,' he kept whispering.

When the skipper came back on deck, Henry Purvis was close behind him. He had a bruise on his forehead. The skipper nodded towards the tiller and Purvis took over from Nathan Chapman. Chapman came and joined us working at the catch. The skipper came for'ard and stood beside the well coaming.

'You saw what happened, Mr Wallis?' he asked mildly.

Wallis nodded. He couldn't speak.

'Mr Pinney?'

'I did,' John said, his voice firmer, his look direct. He kept the skipper's eye. 'I saw it all. And would confirm it.'

'Aye,' Edwin managed to mutter.

Everitt nodded curtly. His lips were white. He understood the threat.

'There will be no need for that,' he said icily.

'No?' Wallis said, suddenly very calm and angry.

'No.' The skipper tried to smile. He shrugged. 'The boy was not hurt. Things got out of hand, that's all. A bit of rough and tumble.'

'He could have choked,' I said.

It was the first time I had spoken.

'He could have died.'

Everitt's face was haggard as death. He looked lost, frozen in some unspoken fury. He would not stand being crossed. When he did begin to speak, his voice was shaking. Where he clenched his hands together, there were white marks from the broken nails.

'He did not die, Mr Vempley. He lives. I take it that is not a ghost at your side.'

I felt a flicker of anger at his sarcasm.

I met his eyes, and held them.

'He may even return to his duties,' the skipper said with a forced smile. 'He will be quite safe now from Mr Walmsley's resentment.'

'Resentment!' I laughed. 'You call it resentment!'

Everitt stared at me from within some hidden nightmare of hell. His eyes seemed to freeze my mind, destroy my will.

'Have you ever seen the lines after dogfish have been at them, Mr Vempley?' he asked moodily.

I flinched.

I was suddenly sweating.

Everitt watched me, waiting for my answer. A blank depression seemed to have sunk over his mind. His skin was yellow. His eyes looked dead.

'No,' I said. 'Not till last night.'

Everitt nodded. 'Then you will understand the men's feelings.'

'I'm one of the men,' I pointed out.

'But it has not happened to you before. You are a fortunate man.'

'That might be true . . .'

'Pray it doesn't ever happen again.'

'And the boy?'

I don't know how Everitt controlled himself. He could see the mood of the men. He might have shouted John Pinney to a silence but he wouldn't risk Edwin Wallis. He seemed surprised by Edwin's manner, caught off his guard. The fury with me burned clearly enough in his eyes.

'The boy should go below and make tea,' he said coldly.

Benjamin tried to stand.

'He should go to his duties,' the skipper went on in the same pitiless voice.

He never once looked at Benjamin.

Benjamin went below, and we stood face to face on the swaying deck. The crew were watching. Nobody was doing any work.

Everitt talked so quietly I could scarcely hear him.

'Do you know John Wesley, Mr Vempley?'

'I can't say I do.'

'He wrote very wisely about children.'

'Is that so.'

'He understood their nature. He understood all our natures. Is that not true, Mr Wallis?'

Edwin sat on the edge of the coaming, staring unhappily at the deck. He nodded his head reluctantly.

Everitt went on talking, his voice remorseless in the tense silence.

'"Break their wills," he said in one of his sermons. "Break their wills betimes. Begin this work before they can run alone, before they can speak plain, perhaps before they can speak at all."'

'What was happening in that cabin was nothing to do with John Wesley,' I said angrily. 'The boy wasn't being punished. He hadn't done anything wrong. He was being choked alive.'

The skipper ignored me. He was not talking for my benefit.

'"Whatever pain it costs,"' he went on relentlessly, '"break the will if you would not damn the child."'

'Amen,' Henry Purvis said at the tiller.

'Amen,' Edwin Wallis muttered, raising his eyes.

Everitt didn't take a breath. '"Let a child from a year old be taught to fear the rod and to cry softly,"' he said in a strange, intense voice, as if he was remembering something he had heard, seeing some awful cruelty in his mind. '"From that age make him do as he is bid,"' he went on, '"if you whip him ten times running to effect it. Break his will now, and his soul shall live and he will probably bless you to all eternity. I will kill or cure. Amen."'

'Amen,' Edwin said yet again, this time more loudly.

'Amen,' Henry Purvis chanted at the tiller.

I caught John Pinney's eye. In his embarrassment, he looked away. He was frightened. Then he looked back, and we held each other's eyes.

For the first time I felt the real terror of the skipper's icy fury.

He came very close and whispered into my face.

'You do not know what happened while you were laying the lines,' he said quietly. 'You do not know what offence may have been given.'

I would not be cowered.

'Not much,' I said back, 'if I know Benjamin.'

The skipper smiled.

'But you do not *know*.'

There was nothing I could say.

In that smile, I saw the bleak fires of hell, where the righteous wreak such havoc.

Twelve

The afternoon Benjamin Bulpit died, the sea was like yellow mud and the skies a darkening sultry bruise. There was no breeze, and the tremendous heat drenched us in sweat. The air was like hot dust in our mouths. We had filled the well and secured everything in the fishrooms. The younger lads had started scouring the decks with a mixture of cod-liver oil and ash from the galley stove. Nathan Chapman and Richard Buss were polishing the brass fittings. In the dog hours, John Pinney made a half-hearted attempt to get the lads singing, but nobody joined in. Everybody seemed to be waiting for something to happen. There was a strange silence over *Rechabite*, as though the attack of the nursehounds and the tension between Jack Walmsley and myself had unsettled the whole crew. Even Edwin was affected. In a kind of daydream, he was riding the bowsprit, watching the sluggish leaden-coloured sea wash against the bows of *Rechabite*.

Jack Walmsley was on the tiller. He acted as if the fight had never happened. He was even friendly with Benjamin, showing him how to fry meat without burning it, giving him a hand with the last of the vegetables. We had a feast of roast beef and fried potatoes one night, and treacle duff that was sweet enough to turn a village scold into an angel. The attack on the lines had lost us a whole tide: we had taken another three days to fill the well, and Walmsley seemed determined to give them some pleasure.

'You give us a break when I've had enough, Samuel?' he asked cheerfully. 'You know the course. Skipper won't mind.'

'Maybe,' I said sourly.

Walmsley had a way of making you seem ungracious, putting you in the wrong.

I didn't believe a word of his lying performance.

'You know what he told me,' he went on relentlessly. 'He told me you were the best man at heaving-to he had ever seen on a smack, short of a skipper, if you understand my meaning.'

'I understand your meaning,' I said sarcastically.

He ignored me.

'I bet he puts it in the log,' he said with a loud laugh. 'I bet he writes Samuel Vempley down as a fine helmsman. I reckon you can count on that.'

I wandered over to the stern and watched the seabirds screeching after us. Benjamin had just dumped a bucket of offal over the side, and the gulls were having a fine time, diving for the rich food. I could hear Benjamin singing in the galley. He seemed to have recovered from his fright, feel better now that Walmsley was being friendly. The skipper was in his cabin, writing the logbook and the records of the catch. Like all skippers, he kept a careful record of his catches. He always liked to know where *Rechabite* had found the best fish biting.

I must have dozed off to sleep.

The scream woke me.

With a jerk, I banged my head against the mizzen boom. I could see Walmsley at the tiller, and for a moment thought I must be dreaming. He turned and stared aft, his face gone ashen, his hands leaving the tiller for a brief moment before he recovered. As the tiller swung to port, the smack heeled and drove to the wind. The mainsail went slack. I saw Edwin Wallis leap from the bowsprit and Henry Purvis run to the mainsail halyards.

'Down below,' Walmsley shouted, but I was already running for the companion. Another scream stretched the airless heat. 'The galley,' Walmsley yelled again, and then seized the tiller and began shouting orders to the lads. Richard Buss and John Pinney were already helping Edwin with the halyards. Henry Purvis was at the mizzen. The huge mainsail found the wind once more and lost the slack. The jib and staysail tightened.

The next scream was the last. It rose to a high-pitched shriek, like a kettle steaming with boiling water. My skin froze. I would never forget that scream for the rest of my life.

I slipped on the iron ladder and crashed to the deck below.

As I struggled to find my feet, I saw Everitt coming out of his cabin. He had a pen in his hand. There couldn't have been more than a few seconds between the first scream and my scrambling fall down the companion. As I straightened, Everitt reached the galley. He stopped abruptly in the doorway.

Benjamin nearly knocked him over.

He ran out of the galley and pushed me back against the wall. I fell again, I was so surprised. Benjamin started to climb. As he climbed, his feet slipped on the metal rungs but he clung on with his hands. He climbed frantically, as if *Rechabite* was on fire. I couldn't take my eyes off his hands. The skin of the right hand was red raw. It looked as if it was boiling. I could smell hot fat and burnt flesh. In the kitchen, there was a hiss of burning fat. Then as if my eyes had suddenly opened, I saw the smoke pouring out of the galley and the flames licking upwards to the deck, and Everitt rushing into the galley to try and douse the flames. I lifted myself on to the bottom rungs of the ladder and started to climb.

I reached the deck as Benjamin went over the side.

Walmsley was still at the tiller.

Edwin Wallis had just finished securing the mainsail halyards.

John Pinney was charging across the deck, colliding with

Richard Buss, pushing him savagely out of the way. As he ran, he shouted Benjamin's name.

But Benjamin was already in the water.

By the time we reached the bulwarks, he was sinking beneath the waves. His heavy seaboots carried him down before we could throw a rope. He was under before we even had one unfastened.

To follow after him would have been death.

Rechabite had gone thirty yards before we saw him disappear into the sea. She would be half a mile away before we could launch the longboat to try and find him.

'Benjamin!'

I started to climb over the bulwarks and would have leapt into the seas after him if John Pinney and Richard Buss had not grabbed hold of my arms. I was yelling as I fought to be free.

'Benjamin!'

I don't suppose I knew what I was doing.

There was an ache in my shoulder, a dull pain at the side of my head. A huge bruise was already forming on my forehead. I sat at the bulwarks for an hour, staring at the white heat of the sky. The sun seemed determined to burn a hole in my head. I heard the screams of seabirds, and they were the cries of the dying boy. I drank some water when it was brought to me, and watched the skipper take the tiller. He looked shaken. His face was white and his mouth was a tight line of shock. The scars and mauled skin on the side of his face were livid in the brilliant sunlight.

'The pan was full of boiling fat,' John Pinney told me when he came to sit beside me later that night. 'He was getting ready to fry potatoes.'

I nodded, swallowing hard. There was a painful lump in my throat.

'He must have knocked the pan over, tried to rescue it with his hand. The fat was all over the floor. Everitt scalded his foot trying to quench the fire. There's a bucket of peeled potatoes, waiting to be fried.'

I don't think I wanted to listen to any more.

I was exhausted.

'You should get some rest,' John said apprehensively, touching my arm.

'I'll be fine.'

'Still.'

'Yes.'

I managed to stand up, and lowered myself down the companion. I felt feverish, shaking. I needed some ice to put down my neck.

It was in the port fishroom that I found Robert Allison.

He was crouched against the far door, sitting on the floor against the shelves of iced fish, trembling with terror. When he saw me, he started to flinch and cover his head with his arms. I closed the door behind me and knelt down at the opposite end of the fishroom.

'I'm not coming towards you,' I whispered in the icy room. 'You can open the other door and leave.'

He peered at me through his clenched fingers. He seemed to be pushing himself into the wall, trying to climb into the racks with the iced fish. I got right down on the floor so that he could see I couldn't move in a hurry. My shoulder was hurting like hell, and I had to talk through gritted teeth, my head was so bad. I managed to smile at the lad.

'Why are you here, Robert?' I asked him.

'Nothing,' he said through his teeth.

His teeth were chattering with the cold.

'Nothing?'

'Nothing.'

'There must be something.'

'No,' he whispered through the frosted air.

I let him rest. I took a lump of ice off the racks and held it against my forehead. I closed my eyes. The pain began to ease.

'Did you see something?' I asked quietly.

'No.'

'Were you in here when you heard Benjamin cry?'

'No.'

'When you heard him screaming?'

'No.'

'That was Benjamin screaming. You were right to be frightened it was that.'

'No.'

I paused and listened to the boom and creak of the smack. She was making fast water. We would be in the Humber Estuary in a few hours. I heard the low voices of shocked men talking, the slap of a loose sheet and the skipper calling his tight orders. The skipper was still taking the tiller. He was in agony with his scalded foot.

'What did you see, Robert?' I asked the boy.

He was thirteen. He was from the Norwich workhouse and had signed indentures in Yarmouth. He had untidy curly hair and black teeth. We could never get him to clean his teeth properly, though there wasn't much fun in that with only a bucket of saltwater for washing. He hardly ever opened his mouth, and did as he was told as if he was permanently terrified. He was a child, and still a year older than Benjamin.

'I see nothing,' he said suddenly, making me look up.

He was watching me now. His eyes were round, completely white. He was trying to get up. 'I see nothing,' he said again.

'All right.'

'I ent going to tell.'

'It's all right, Robert.'

'I ent going to speak.'

I managed to stand myself.

'You don't have to,' I tried to say, but he wasn't listening.

'I gone blind,' he said in a sudden rush, and then opened the fishroom door and was gone, slamming the door behind him. 'I gone blind,' I heard him say in the darkness.

I stood in the silence for a long time, listening to the movements of the smack, then went through to the cabin and fell straight into a restless feverish sleep.

Satan's Hole

Thirteen

The cry for all hands on deck woke me, and I grabbed my clothes and scrambled up the companion, rubbing the sleep from my eyes. *Rechabite* was already approaching the lockpit, and the great tower over the fishdocks loomed to starboard over the low, sprawling town and muddy waters of the estuary. I stood by the mizzen and listened as Everitt shouted orders, and all the time I was peering ahead to the pontoons and the busy harbour. This was where Miriam had gone. I searched the quays as if she might be waiting for me. In the clamour and bustle of the arrival, I hardly heard the skipper's commands or the shouts and calls of the men as we bumped into the turbulent waters between the high walls of the lockpit. I was sure in some insane way that Miriam would be waiting for me on the quays. She would be there, and the dream would be over.

And then suddenly Robert Allison left the sheet he was hauling at the mainmast and ran to the bulwarks. We were just entering the lockpit, and with a shout, he clambered over the bulwarks and leapt from the smack, scrambling up the iron ladders at the sides of the lockpit and disappearing among the crowds on the pontoon before any of us could make a move. Crowds always gathered on the pontoon when smacks were returning from the fishing grounds: families and friends, owners waiting to check the catch. They yelled with delight at the spectacle of an absconding apprentice, but nobody offered to lend a hand. Robert had made his escape within seconds.

'Get the drogue!' Everitt shouted as *Rechabite* lurched into the churning waters of the lockpit. 'Don't let him get away.'

John Pinney and Richard Buss were working feverishly with the drogue, hoisting it over the stern and unfastening the tyers. Henry Purvis and Nathan Chapman were pulling the mainsail sheets down. I could hear Purvis cursing under his breath, sweating as he heaved at the sheets. Francis Campbell was waiting by the skipper for orders.

Everitt seemed wild with fury.

'The drogue,' he kept thundering at Edwin Wallis who was in the bows, struggling to secure the bowsprit. The bowsprit had already been run in: you always make sure of that when entering a lockpit: outgoing smacks have the right of way, and you can do a lot of damage with a thirty-foot bowsprit charging into the pontoons. Edwin wouldn't leave the job until the bowsprit was secure. I wondered if he sympathised with the boy.

'Give a hand,' Everitt snapped at Francis Campbell.

Francis ran as if he'd been scalded.

At the for'ard bulwarks, I could see Walmsley balancing dangerously on the rail, waiting for the smack to draw level with the second set of iron ladders that ran down the sides of the lockpit for maintenance work.

'Don't let him get away,' Everitt was shouting again, and as we reached the end of the lockpit and the second set of ladders, I saw Walmsley make a grab for the side and start climbing. *Rechabite* was slowing through the dark waters now, held down by the heavy drogue. I had no time to think about things. My mind was full of Miriam and Benjamin Bulpit and Robert. And I knew why Robert Allison had fled the smack. I made my decision without listening to Everitt.

'I'll find him,' I told the skipper, clambering up on to the bulwarks after Jack Walmsley.

'Vempley!'

'I know the town.'

I was gone before he could order me otherwise. I reached for the iron rungs of the ladder and hoisted myself off the bulwarks. The mainboom swung dangerously close as *Rechabite* swept past. I could see Everitt glaring at me and then struggling to keep the smack away from the walls as she left the lockpit. The bowsprit was already safely secured. Edwin Wallis waved from the bows and then *Rechabite* was through, tacking to starboard and away towards the pontoon moorings.

I clambered up the lockpit ladders. A wash of spray following *Rechabite* slapped against my boots. I could hear men laughing at the top of the lockpit, and several hands reached out to help me over the wall.

'He's long gone, matey.' One of the men grinned at me.

'You want to try Satan's Hole,' another man suggested to the amusement of the crowd. 'They like a bit of fun, these lads.'

I thanked them and pushed my way through the crowd. Hundreds of people were on the pontoons. There was music coming from the west quay, and the gas lamps were beginning to burn. I walked past the main market, looking for Walmsley. The narrow lanes and alleys behind the pontoons were dark and empty. I could smell the sea. A seagull screamed eerily down one of the alleys. It was early evening, and the sky over the estuary was dark with banks of cloud. It would soon be too dark to find anybody in the warren of brothels and drinking houses in Satan's Hole.

I found Walmsley at the top end of the market, lighting his pipe.

'Skipper send you?' he asked, grinning at me through a cloud of black tobacco smoke.

'I know Satan's Hole.'

'I bet you do, Samuel.'

He pushed his tobacco tin back into his pocket.

'You don't seem in much of a hurry,' I said, puzzled.

'I know where he'll be.'

'Is that right?'

'Done this before, has our Robert.'

'He was frightened of something,' I said without thinking.

Walmsley glanced at me quickly, and then covered the sharp look with an attack of coughing. When he finished, he grinned at me and started walking.

'Allus goes to the same place,' he said.

I followed him quickly.

'Is that right?' I wasn't much interested.

'Has a friend, does Robert.'

I recognised the sneer in Walmsley's voice.

'He's thirteen,' I said.

'Old enough, Samuel.'

We reached the main square outside the docks. Walmsley took his time, but he obviously knew where he was going. There was better lighting in the square, and the pavements were made up. Crowds jostled outside the shops. Gas flares burned brilliantly in the early summer evening. Shop windows were flooded with light. There was music again, coming from the beerhouses and music halls.

We saw a crowd at the top of an alley, and two women flailing and punching at each other with bare knuckles. 'Look at that then,' Walmsley grinned at me.

'Let's get on, Walmsley.'

'No hurry, Samuel.'

We watched the women. They were clenching coins in their hands so that they couldn't tear at each other's hair or eyes without dropping the coins. The first to drop the coins would lose the fight. One of the women already had a nasty yellowing bruise down the side of her face and she was grunting and breathing heavily. Gangs of men in the street and at the top end of the alley yelled and jeered their approval, making bets and urging the women on, roaring with drunken laughter. There were screams from some of the women in the crowd, and dozens of prostitutes lounged outside the music halls, their faces garish with rouge, their eyes sullen with lack of sleep and alcohol.

'We're going,' I told Walmsley as one of the women aimed a punch straight into the face of the other and the crowd roared with delight. I pushed my way back to the main street. Walmsley followed, scowling.

'You ent got a happy heart, Samuel.'

'I want to find that lad.'

'Do you now.'

'You said you knew where he'd be.'

'I wonder why.'

'He's a boy, Walmsley. He's frightened. How would you feel in this hellhole?'

'I grew up here.' Walmsley grinned at me cheerfully.

'What!'

'That's right, matey. I grew up in Satan's Hole. On account of being abandoned here by my mother. Lovely kind of bringing up, if you know what I mean!'

With a loud laugh, he nodded across the main road and set off. A horse and cart nearly ran us down as we crossed the rutted road.

'Where are we going?' I shouted, catching him up.

'To find young Allison. Just through the market it is. His sister brought him up. Before they moved to Yarmouth. She came back here when he signed for the smacks. She rents a room in Atkinson's Cut. When she has some money. Depends how many customers she's had.'

You could see the market from streets away. The red and yellow fumes from the gas flares hung in the air like a shroud. Some of the traders had candles in hollowed-out turnips, tarred flares burning outside butchers' shops. The warm air was rich with the smell of food and drink: hot chestnuts and Yarmouth bloaters, cheese and roast meats, gin and illicit beer, aniseed whisky and corn brandy. Hundreds of housewives crowded among the stalls, thick shawls wrapped round their shoulders against the night air, wooden clogs ringing on the cobbles. A tingle-airey played noisily at the entrance to the market, and young girls brushed against us, grinning and touching our faces, pouting and trying to grab hold of Walmsley's arm. Just inside the market, there was a peepshow, and hordes of youngsters stood outside, waiting to see the obscene paintings.

We pushed through the crowds. A rat-catcher suddenly danced in front of us, live rats running up and down his arms, a wire cage dangling from his hands. A girl was following the rat-catcher, her eyes fixed feverishly on the pages of an open Bible, ignoring the shouts and jibes of the crowd, chanting the words aloud in a defiant, hysterical whine. Young boys and girls from the penny gaffs fought over bottles of cheap whisky. I could see Walmsley drinking from a flask he kept hidden in his pocket. He was beginning to lurch as he walked. He put his arm round the shoulder of one of the girls, and I had to pull him free.

At the far end of the market, Walmsley let out a shout of pleasure. He saw Praying Billy before I did. Billy worked all the ports. He carried a bottle of spirits in which a lump of swollen flesh bobbed up and down. According to Billy, this was his tongue, cut out by savage tribes in South America for telling the Lord's truth. You could read the story of the tongue on the slate he kept hanging round his neck. If you gave him money, he wouldn't curse you. If you tried to push past him without paying, he opened his mouth and showed you the raw red flesh where his living tongue had once been.

'You seen one of our lads, Billy?' Walmsley was already asking when I caught him up.

Praying Billy had insane, unfocused eyes. He peered at Walmsley as if he was the devil escaped from hell. Walmsley tapped the slate hanging round Billy's neck and offered him a drink from his flask. With a furious shake of his head, the speechless man began to move backwards, staring at the bottle in horror. Walmsley grabbed hold of his arm.

'Robert Allison?' he asked again.

Billy shook his head and suddenly held out his hand.

'Give him something, Samuel,' Walmsley laughed, and walked away.

I handed a coin over. The red eyes never left my face. As I tried to get away, he grabbed my wrist and came closer. His face was inches from mine. I could smell the whisky. With a grin, he opened his mouth wide and kept tight hold of my wrist. I had to force his fingers back to get free.

By the time we got to Atkinson's Cut it was dark. The door was down a cut between tall buildings. There was no light. The stench of the cesspool under the entry made me feel sick. Families lived five or six to a room in Satan's Hole, breeding grounds for cholera and typhoid, smallpox and dysentery. The children starved or worked in the brothels. The last time I was in the port there had been enteric fever in the public wells, yellow maggots in the drinking water.

A young woman opened the door and glared at Walmsley. She was holding a candle, and in the light from the pathetic candle flame we could see the fever burning in her eyes, the angry red mottling round her neck. The stench from the cesspool made me gag.

'Ruth not here?' Walmsley asked.

The woman opened the door wider and we stepped into the hall. The narrow passage smelled of damp and rotting cabbage and brown wallpaper hung in strips off the walls. There were no back doors to these houses, and no staircases. You used ladders to get to the upper floors.

'Ruth Allison?' Walmsley shouted, bringing his face close to the woman's.

'You want to be friendly?' The woman smiled vaguely at him.

'Sure,' Walmsley grunted. 'Not with you though, pet.'

The woman screeched with laughter, waving the candle around in the darkness, watching us craftily all the time she laughed. She had no teeth.

'Let's have a look,' I muttered to Walmsley.

We climbed the ladders to the first floor. They were tied to the walls. I gave the woman a silver coin and she held on to my leg as I scrambled up. The rooms were dark. Straw and blankets were scattered on the floor, waiting for the men and women to come back from the music halls and brothels. Only children slept in the darkness.

'Well, he's not here,' I said when we had searched each of the rooms.

Walmsley seemed edgy, nervous. He kept glancing round the rooms and listening.

'I can see that,' he muttered.

'You think the girl's left?'

'Dead more like,' Walmsley said, glancing at me as if I was simple.

'Then he's on the run.'

'He won't get far.'

I thought about the boy, terrified out of his mind, searching desperately through Satan's Hole for his sister. He was still wearing his fishing gear. It would be impossible for him to get out of town without somebody stopping him. Lads on the run were easy to see if they were still wearing fishing gear. In the countryside, the villagers would turn him in sooner than spit: they didn't want absconding fisherboys in their workhouses. If he didn't get caught, he would end up living in Satan's Hole.

'Best get back,' I said as our candle began to burn out and splutter.

'Yes,' Walmsley agreed.

I thought he was probably scared of the skipper.

As we climbed back down the ladders to the stinking entrance, a baby was crying in one of the rooms, and a child's voice sang a lullaby.

Fourteen

Everitt had calmed down by the time we got back to *Rechabite*. The smack was secured, moored at the bottom end of the market ready for unloading first thing in the morning. Everitt was standing at the tiller, staring at the clouds that raced across the hazy moon.

'He got away, skipper,' Walmsley told him.

Everitt hardly seemed interested.

'Is that right?' he said indifferently.

'Sister isn't there any more.'

'You asked?'

'Looked everywhere, skipper.'

Everitt shrugged.

'Our fortune,' he said quietly. 'We seem to be having bad fortune this trip, Mr Vempley.'

'Yes, skipper.'

'Maybe you brought it with you.'

'I wouldn't know.'

'No, you wouldn't.'

He was still preoccupied, forcing himself to listen to us, lost in his own thoughts. He stood rigidly at the tiller and watched the bows lift with the slight tide inside the harbour. We had a fire burning in the brazier in the stern. The rest of the crew were down below, getting a sleep before the morning's work. A watchman walked slowly up and down the pontoons, calling the hours. The gas lamps burned yellow in the dark.

'We can try again in the morning, skipper,' Walmsley suggested helpfully, but Everitt shook his head firmly, suddenly gathering himself again and glaring at Walmsley.

'He's long gone, Mr Walmsley,' he said. 'And if you did find him he won't be worth the trouble.'

'No, skipper.'

'You can set yourselves to find me two new lads.'

'Yes, skipper,' Walmsley said quickly, ready to please, rubbing his hands.

'What about Benjamin?' I asked.

The skipper stared at me, and for a second I thought he had forgotten who Benjamin was, then he nodded curtly, turning away. There was no legal requirement to notify a death at sea on a fishing vessel unless the smack was damaged in the same incident. If the drowned boy had no family, there was nothing to report. I felt sick at the thought of Benjamin, floating at the bottom of the sea, his body white and bloodless, seaweed dancing round his fingers. We had to tell his mother.

'Well?' I asked the skipper.

'He had no family here,' Everitt pointed out coldly.

'We should tell somebody,' I insisted. 'Get a message to his mother in Yarmouth.'

Again, I thought Everitt had forgotten. He stared at me for a moment, and then nodded again. He was probably thinking about the letters the poor woman had written to him about her son.

'I shall do that,' he said with an effort. 'First thing in the morning. Once we have the catch unloaded, you will help Mr Walmsley find me two new lads. *Rechabite* can't sail two hands short.'

'Why me?'

'You know this port?'

'Yes, skipper.'

'Where to look?'

'The usual places, skipper,' Walmsley interrupted with a laugh, but Everitt wasn't listening.

He was watching me now.

I guessed he knew about Miriam.

'Why me?' I asked again levelly, tired and suddenly angry, worried about Robert Allison and what he had seen in the galley, disturbed by Everitt's cold, sneering smile.

He let out a laugh: a sudden abrupt cough like a bark.

'Being as how you have business in Satan's Hole, Mr Vempley,' he said flatly, smiling at me without humour and rubbing his hands together. 'Being as how you are familiar with the district. And now, goodnight to you, Mr Vempley. You can take the first watch, as you seem somewhat restless.'

He turned, and was gone before I could speak.

With a grin, Walmsley followed him down the companion.

I got myself a mug of tea from the galley and then roasted a potato on the fire in the brazier. The wood glowed hot red and sparks flew out over the transom stern as I poked the potato. It smelled good in the night air. I couldn't hear a sound, apart from the creak and rattle of the gear, the slow wash of the tide in the lockpit. The water was racing now as the tide turned, and I sat against the mainmast, drinking the tea and eating the hot potato, the skin thick and crunchy, the white potato inside scalding my mouth. I took a swallow of water from the bucket we kept hanging by the mainmast, and stared up into the endless skies, the racing cloud, the moon glimmering and shining above the estuary.

It was gone two in the morning when Edwin Wallis joined me.

'First watch, Samuel?'

'Hello, Edwin.'

'Everything calm?'

'Calm enough.'

He sat down beside me on the well coaming and started

to light his pipe. His gold spectacles shone when the moon touched them. He took his time lighting the pipe.

'You lost Robert then?'

''Fraid so.'

'Got away.'

'You wouldn't find him in Satan's Hole.'

'He didn't go to his sister?'

'You know about her?' I asked.

'She brought him up. He usually goes there. Done it before. She fought for that lad. He went to the fishing to help her out.'

I shook my head. My mind was filled with thoughts of Benjamin and whatever had scared Robert down in the galley. He had seen something. He knew what had happened to Benjamin Bulpit. Now he was gone, before talking could do him any harm. I filled my own pipe and listened to the knock of the ropes against the moorings, the warbling of curlews along the distant foreshore.

'You going with Jack Walmsley in the morning?' Edwin asked.

'That's what the skipper wants.'

Edwin nodded. He was thoughtful, fretting about something. He knocked his pipe out on the coaming and leaned forward, talking in a low voice so that nobody listening from the companion would be able to hear.

'You make sure you get a lad who wants to come,' he said.

'What?'

'Wants the life.'

I shrugged. 'They all want the life.'

'Until they got it.' Edwin nodded ironically.

'How would I know?'

'Find a lad who's done a trip. Knows the fishing. Walmsley's none too particular. He won't care, as long as you sign somebody.'

I watched Edwin carefully. He kept his voice low. He must suspect somebody might be listening. *Rechabite* pulled at her ropes and Edwin reached into his pocket. He pulled out a sheaf of newspaper cuttings.

'Walmsley's none too particular,' he said again, handing me the cuttings. They were yellowed with age and badly creased from being inside Edwin's wallet. I unfolded them and glanced questioningly at Edwin. He shrugged as if they could explain themselves.

'This is a rough port,' he said.

'I know that.'

'Have a read.'

I glanced through the cuttings. They were familiar enough. Most fishermen who could read had seen them over the years. They were from the *Leicester Mercury* and the *Lincolnshire Chronicle*. I had even seen a faded copy of the French *Le Figaro* that Joseph Proctor kept in his locker in his cabin. The stories in *Le Figaro* were all to do with scandals. The French journalist said there was a system of slavery operating in Grimsby as infamous as any in the world.

'I remember *Le Figaro*,' I told Edwin. 'All the fuss.'

'And then nothing done about it.' Edwin nodded gloomily. 'Nobody bothered enough to put it right.'

'What do you expect, Edwin? When men are making money?'

Edwin smiled at me shrewdly.

'Read the cuttings, Samuel,' he said.

'I already read them.'

'Read them again.'

I shrugged impatiently and glanced at the faded print. The first cutting was a letter printed in the *Leicester Mercury*. It was from some distressed mother who had lost her child. The story was headed Legalised Kidnapping and was about one of the biggest owners in Grimsby. 'I have four children in my family,' the letter started:

My son, being the oldest, was twelve years last November. He was going with another boy to take his father's dinner.

They were met by a strange lad, dressed very fine, and he
made himself friendly with them. He asked them if they
should like to go to sea, and showed them some money, and
said the life was a happy one. These poor boys listened, and
went with the lad to a man who treated them and told them
what a lot of money they could get, and that they would
have two shillings a day and ten shillings on engagement,
which was false, for they have had nothing, but poor lads,
they agreed to go. In about two hours after they had seen the
man they were sent to Grimsby, and the poor parents were
left in trouble. This man took them. We never knew where
our boy was for two or three days. Then we were told he had
gone for a fisherman. It put us about very much. We were
told to write to Mr Gothard. We did so, though I am no
hand at writing. I wrote several letters, and got no answer
from them. I sent paper and stamps, and still no answer
came. Was not this cruel? I thought I would lose my senses.
Then we heard he was drowned. He ran away and tried to
come home, but he was hunted and took back to Grimsby,
and was sent to Lincoln prison for twenty-eight days hard
labour. And then was forced back on the fishing. And was
drowned. Lost forever.

The second cutting was from the *Lincolnshire Chronicle*. It
was about the articles that had been published in *Le Figaro*,
which had been widely reported in the English press. 'The
City of Lincoln rings with indignation at the treatment these
lads receive at the hands of the authorities,' the article began.
'They are brought from Grimsby by train, and heavily
chained together are marched through the busiest part of
town for more than a mile to the prison.' The article went on
to claim that the boys were frequently drunk by the time
they arrived at the prison because the police escorting them
sold them alcohol, taking the last of their money before
delivering them to the treadmill and the oakum-picking at
the prison.

   I tried to hand the cuttings back to Edwin.

'A lot of indignation?' I smiled.

'And nothing else.' He nodded. 'Read the rest.'

'I don't want to read them, Edwin.'

'Read!'

He seemed determined, hunched forward on the coaming, staring furiously into my eyes.

'There's no call to be so outraged.'

'Read!' he said again in an angry, low voice.

I shrugged wearily and took the cuttings back. I unfolded them and stared at the faint print. The one on top was from the *Leicester Daily Post*, a letter from an anxious father desperate for news of his son:

> I was employed out of town for a short time last summer, and on my return I found that my son was missing. On making inquiry I learned that he was at Grimsby on a fishing smack. We received a few lines from him, but no satisfaction. I was very uneasy about him until the end of December when a friend came to tell me that he had seen my son in great trouble at Grimsby, and that he would very much like to get home. My friend advised me to fetch the boy back, but I had not the means to go and see after him. I have a parent's feeling, and am in great trouble about my son. He is the eldest of eight children. It is not likely that I shall be able to go to Grimsby, trade being so bad. Since December I have heard no news of him, and whether he is dead or alive I cannot say.

A woman from Leicester wrote:

> I am one of the mothers who are suffering through the practices of the Grimsby men. My eldest son disappeared in July last, and I did not hear a word about him until the middle of November, when I saw a youth, who told me my son had been on a fishing smack with him, but he was in Grimsby gaol for trying to get home. They had both been flogged with a rope while out at sea. Was not this very poor

*news to be the first after so long a silence. I found myself
greatly in need of some kind friend's advice, so I made my
way to the Rev. Mr Owen and told him of my trouble. Mr
Owen took great interest in my case, and proved to be a
friend in need. His first kind act was to write to Lincoln to
ask if the boy described was there. He soon received an
answer that my son was locked up there for three weeks for
trying to get home from Grimsby. A day was fixed for me to
go to Lincoln to see if anything could be done. When I got
there I was told it was the second time my boy had been in
gaol for trying to get home. When he came out of prison he
was taken back to Grimsby, and sent out to sea. He was out
both Christmas Day and New Year's Day because he had
offended his master. It thus seems that if they offend once
there is little or no forgiveness. I heard no more for several
weeks. As all was silent I was in hopes that all was well, but
in February came the fearful news that my son had started
to come home again, and had been caught, and had been
sent to gaol for a month. His master, being short of lads, sent
for him out of prison a few days before his month expired.
That makes the third time he has been shut up in Lincoln
Gaol. Is not that enough to break a parent's heart. I truly
hope I shall meet with some kind friend who will give me a
little advice in this sad affair, as I find it a great load for a
mother to bear.*

I felt a cold sense of outrage reading through the cuttings.
Edwin was watching me all the time, smoking his pipe complacently, but his eyes shining with anger. As I read, he kept
his watch on the companion, listening for the sound of anybody moving below. I held the cuttings for a moment,
staring across the harbour to the west quay where the herring girls had their huts during the season. I had heard
rumours about the kidnappings before, but there are always
stories among the fishermen. What else are men to do miles
from land in the emptiness of the sea: they tell stories to pass
the time. I had never seen such cruelty. In the liners, the

crews are nearly always experienced fishermen, and the fisherboys come from fishing families. The trawlers were different. Because of the shortage of labour, the crews were often made up of apprentices, lads of eleven and twelve from orphanages and reformatories, workhouses trying to find places for their boys. Under the law, absconding boys could be sentenced to three months' hard labour for desertion. Hundreds of lads went to prison every year, leaping ashore and running away as the smack went through the lockpit. Just like Robert Allison. Many more were drowned. Benjamin Bulpit could lie at the bottom of the sea, and nobody cared except his grieving mother. Robert Allison might end up living in a brothel, and the courts wouldn't turn a hair.

I turned to the final letter in the file. It was from a mother in London, and was again published in the *Leicester Mercury* who had been running a campaign to help stop the abuses:

> In September, my son suddenly disappeared. He was four-teen. I applied to every police office in London for two months. I could glean no tidings of him. At last my sister received a letter from him. It appears he was decoyed from home by a lad years older. They got so badly off that they took refuge in the Romford Union. During the two days they were there a Mr Gothard, a smack owner from Grimsby, saw them, and he writes me my son legally bound himself to him for seven years. I have written. I have pleaded his ignorance, his youth, his inexperience of legal documents. The boy states it was not read over to him, but Mr Gothard says unless I can pay the sum of twenty pounds he will not release my son or let me see him until the expir-ation of seven years. My boy writes me he is a thorough slave, receiving no wages, working day and night. I fear greatly I shall never see him again.

I folded the cuttings and handed them back to Edwin.

'I've read them,' I told him.

'Then you know.'

'I think I knew already, Edwin.'

'Just to remind you, Samuel, that's all.'

'Fair enough.'

'As I said, Jack Walmsley is none too particular.'

'And you think I can gainsay him?'

'You can try. None of us can do much more than that.'

Edwin pushed the cuttings back into his pocket and stood up, staring around the harbour. He had his back to me. When he spoke, his voice was tired but friendly, concerned.

'You have somebody you love in this port, Samuel?'

I glanced up. I felt a cold shiver down my back: ghosts walking on my grave in this dead hour.

'Maybe,' I muttered. 'I don't know.'

'You don't know if you are in love?'

He sounded surprised.

'I'm not sure if she's here.'

He turned and studied my face. His eyes were very blue, but beginning to fade at last, the years draining the brilliant colour. He had a fisherman's eyes, full of the sea.

'That's hard to bear,' he said. 'Not knowing.'

'People get lost,' I said, without knowing what I meant.

Edwin nodded. He thought for a long moment, watching me all the time.

'You'll know how they feel,' he said, touching the pocket where he had hidden the newspaper cuttings.

'Of course I know.'

'Good.' He smiled, then glanced up at the sky. 'It's a grand night, Samuel.'

I stared up at the stars, the faint light at the horizon. The warblings of the curlews grew louder as the sky lightened. A pink glow was already showing at the estuary.

'Is it?' I said tiredly, staring down at my hands.

'Yes,' Edwin said firmly.

He touched my shoulder, and then went down below.

I sat for a long time, thinking about Benjamin Bulpit and Robert Allison. When Nathan Chapman came on deck to take the next watch, I stumbled below and was asleep within seconds of hitting my bunk.

Fifteen

We spent the early hours of the morning unloading the frozen catch and getting the live fish into the codchests. There were four hundred codchests moored in Grimsby fishdocks, and Everitt had hired a dozen for his prime fish. Several score went straight to the merchants. By the time we finished and the lads began scouring the decks, I was impatient to be off: to search for Robert, to find the address Miriam's friend had written from. I didn't think about getting new hands for *Rechabite*.

Walmsley was cheerful as ever. He worked at the unloading all morning, took a mug of tea, and was ready. He seemed to have an animal's strength and energy.

'You ready then, Samuel?'

'Let's go.'

'Finish your tea, Samuel.'

I threw the remains of the tea over the side. I wasn't thirsty. I had slept for three hours, and that seemed more than enough with the things on my mind. In the dawn hours, I had dreamed about Edwin's letters, the chorus of voices crying the names of children in the early light. I woke up determined to take heed of Edwin's warnings.

We searched the bustling town for hours.

There was no real centre to the place. Most of the fishing families lived in Cod's Kingdom, a sprawling slum of tenements and dingy terraces built on waste ground facing the sea. Some of the houses had been built on the sands, and they said you could see the water under the wooden joists. There were no lavatories or sewers. Filth ran in the streets. There were houses built behind a tanyard which had no back doors and scrapings from the skins of animals heaped against the front windows. At Cook's Buildings, there was a cesspool under the entry and seventy people crammed into twenty rooms. Very few of the houses had a staircase, stepladders being used to get upstairs just like the tenement in Atkinson's Cut. There were riots and drunken brawls whenever the fleet returned from the fishing ground.

'He won't be here,' I told Walmsley, but he insisted on looking.

'Got to be thorough, Samuel,' he said. 'You don't know Everitt.'

We saw boys splashing round pumps, the sprinkling water making rainbows of colours as they doused their heads and bodies, chased the trickles escaping down the baked ground. In one of the yards, a girl cartwheeled through the fountains of water, and her dress caught the flashes of brilliant colour as she turned through the clouds of fine spray. We drifted around Cod's Kingdom for two hours without seeing a sign of Robert Allison, and then back to the fishdocks and the ramshackle chaos of Satan's Hole, where already the cheap-jacks and try-your-weight-stalls were busy in the streets, and the paltry shows and punching machines were opening in the market.

Everywhere we walked the roads were a disgrace: full of holes and dangerous cracks, throwing up clouds of choking dust in the summer heat. Blinding dust filled the air. There was a stink of fish in the narrow streets and tenements, and acrid smoke drifted from the curing houses into the rotting alleys and slums. Trains steamed from the fishdocks every few minutes, and the town was full of cattle and horses, farmers celebrating sales and men staggering blind drunk from the beerhouses. Walmsley stopped at several of the beerhouses, saying he had to ask around for likely lads, swallowing pints of dark brown ale.

'Got to ask questions, Samuel,' he told me blearily when I complained that we were wasting our time.

'We don't seem to be doing much good.'

Walmsley laughed and tapped the side of his flat nose.

'I'm listening,' he said in a low voice, and then winked.

In the afternoon, we visited the magistrates' court. It was in the old part of town, a dismal red-brick building with tiny barred windows and a heavy door. The court was crowded, several drunks sitting in the gallery sleeping or watching what was going on, dozens of lawyers and barristers crowding at the bar. A single policeman stood at the back of the room, ignoring the row in the gallery. He stank of alcohol.

There was only one magistrate, a man called Keetley. Keetley was well known down the east-coast fishing communities. He owned several trawlers. He had an interest in keeping the fisherboys on their smacks. A single boy was standing in front of him.

'What's the matter?' the magistrate asked without looking up from his notes.

The smack-owner bringing the charge stood up.

'Ran away, Mr Keetley,' he said. 'Picked up near Caistor. Cost me money and trouble bringing him back.'

The magistrate nodded wearily. 'What's your complaint, boy?'

The boy glanced round the court cheekily, waving to a friend in the gallery. A young girl waved back, her cheeks bright red with rouge, her eyes dancing with merriment at the proceedings.

'I got nothing to wear,' the boy said.

Keetley stared at him sarcastically.

'You're wearing clothes now. Provided by your master, no doubt.'

'I got nothing to wear when we're fishing. These is best.'

'Sold them, did you, for drink money?'

'Don't drink, sir.'

The girl in the gallery guffawed and smothered her laughter with her bonnet. Several of the drunkards in the gallery grinned at each other and started whispering to the girl.

'What's this boy's complaint, Mr Draper?' the magistrate shouted, losing his patience.

The clerk stood up and read from a sheet of paper.

'The boy states that there are only three shirts and two pairs of stockings full of holes to be worn by five apprentices when they are working the grounds. They were working off the Faroes and the boy complains of being cold.'

'I'm ashamed to walk down the street,' the boy interrupted. 'A bloke asked me whether I was wearing a shirt or a rag the other night.'

Keetley glared at him furiously. 'What's that got to do with going to sea?' he shouted. 'Plenty of people have got ragged shirts and they're grateful for it. Twenty-eight days hard labour. Any more, Mr Draper?'

The boy was shuffled out of the court and another boy wearing equally ragged clothes was brought in by a policeman.

'No luck here,' Walmsley whispered to me as we sat at the back of the court. He had been talking to the policeman. All the boys were claimed by owners, and if they weren't sent to prison would be taken straight back on board their smacks. We watched the next boy being routinely sentenced to hard labour for absconding from his vessel. He had waited until the last minute and then leapt from the smack as she was leaving the lockpit. That was the favourite trick: abscond when the smack is leaving and the skipper isn't likely to turn back to begin the search. But the police had found the lad on the outskirts of town, trying to get a lift from a carrier.

Keetley dealt with all the boys with the same brisk savage humour. None of the lads had barristers to speak for them. How would they pay. Most of the solicitors had mortgages on smacks anyway, and wouldn't be that interested in defending an absconding apprentice. The magistrates were all smack-owners.

We left the court. The sun was high in the afternoon sky. There were crowds around the corn exchange and in the cattle market and boys playing in the square in front of the church. Drunkards were already singing loudly in the White Hart, the beerhouse opposite the parish church.

'What a farce,' I muttered as we walked away from the court.

'How's that, Samuel?'

'Keetley and his friends.'

'They're respectable gentlemen, Samuel.'

I was angry, hot and tired in the afternoon sun. We seemed to be wasting our time. I wanted to go and find Miriam's friend.

'It *is* like slavery,' I said angrily, thinking about Edwin's letters.

'Slavery!'

Walmsley obviously didn't know what I was talking about.

'The only difference is that slaves get bought,' I muttered, talking more to myself than to Walmsley. 'The owners have some sort of interest in keeping them alive. These lads are signed on for nothing. Nobody cares what happens to them. It's the smacks that matter. A boy costs nothing.'

Walmsley had stopped and was staring at me, an amused grin on his broad, flat face. He had pockmarks on his cheeks, and his eyes were black with drink and ridicule.

'You from a workhouse then, Samuel?'

'That's right.'

'You got a grudge, have you?'

'I had a good skipper,' I told him flatly.

I was incensed, tightly controlled.

Walmsley crouched suddenly and then straightened. The movement was so quick I wondered if I'd imagined it. He punched me on the arm.

'You need a drink,' he said roughly.

'Do I?'

'You need a girl. I know I do.'

'What about Everitt?'

'Dancing,' Walmsley said cheerfully as if he hadn't heard.
'Dancing?'

'We go dancing, then we find a girl. Let's be cheerful,
Samuel. Iceland's a long voyage. Plenty of time for sorting
grievances.'

He went off to find a drink, and I followed him.

We spent the afternoon drinking, talking to fishermen
who might know of lads looking for a berth. There was
nobody. In the evening, we had a meat pie and roast potatoes, and then Walmsley said we should try the dancing.
There were always lads dancing, he said, grinning drunkenly
as I argued. I gave up in the end. He knew a dancing room
above a public house where you could have a good time
without the ugliness of the brothels, the fighting and violence of the penny gaffs. I thought I might ask about Miriam
when we got there. There would be girls in a dancing room.
There were girls at every corner in Satan's Hole.

The room was up a flight of narrow stairs behind the
beerhouse. There were portraits of musicians on the walls of
the stairs, but no carpet. Our boots echoed on the bare
wood. The room was long and lit by gas, and couples sat on
benches along the deep red walls. There were four musicians
on a raised dais at the far end of the room: a fiddler, a man
on a cornet, and two lads on flutes. The bare wooden floors
were thick with sawdust. When the men started playing,
drifts of sawdust lifted off the floor.

The music was wild and strange, the shrill notes of the
flutes piping behind the cornet, the fiddler working himself
into a frenzy. I closed my eyes and thought about Miriam
dancing on the quays.

'I can't dance,' she warned me the first time we spent an
evening together.

I laughed at that. 'I saw you on the quays, remember.'

'That's different. I like dancing alone.'

Walmsley fetched us beers and I tasted the strong liquid,
resting my head against the wall. I could have gone to sleep.
At the braying of the cornet, couples got up and began

dancing, whirling up and down the long room, spinning through the hot shadows, clinging together to keep pace with the music. The fiddler seemed to be playing in a trance. He bowed and swayed to his own melodies, and the dancers shouted and clapped, doing polkas and waltzes in the heat, laughing when they put a step wrong, calling for the fiddler to go on playing.

Walmsley staggered across the room and asked one of the girls to dance with him. I heard his harsh laugh bellowing in the heat. An Irish reel mourned in the hot darkness of the room. Some of the dancers had returned to their seats, their arms around each other's shoulders. A couple were kissing by the door. A girl brought glasses of beer and whisky on a tray, and I paid for more drink. The fiddler played with his eyes closed, the sweat running down his face, tears mingling with the sweat. I closed my eyes, and felt myself flowing into the music, the hypnotic sadness of the valleys, the wail of birds over the Irish Sea. My soul yearned for the music. Miriam said the soul *was* music.

When I opened my eyes, tarts with rouged cheeks were grinning down at me, drunken fishermen stared at me with vacant, stupid eyes. For a moment, I didn't know where I was.

Then I realised the girl was trying to speak to me.

'You want a dance, fisherman?'

I shook my head. 'No thanks.'

'This is my friend,' the girl mouthed above the music, nodding at the fisherman at her side. 'I don't know his name.'

Her face was flushed with drink and tiredness. She leaned forward, her eyes glazed, her lipstick smudged round her mouth. The fisherman holding her arm belched, peering at me blearily, clenching his big fists.

'You her *friend*?' he said nastily.

He leered over the word, leaning forward and poking my arm, breathing straight into my face. His breath stank of putrid fish livers. I pushed him back gently, wondering whether he had ulcers.

'Do you know Brown's Yard?' I asked on impulse, trying to avoid a fight.

The girl was stone drunk. She stank of whisky. There was a bruise on her arm, yellowing and soft in the centre. She glanced quickly at the fisherman she was with, who seemed to have slipped into a stupor, breathing heavily and leaning on her shoulder.

'This is my friend,' she said again hopelessly. 'Isn't he lovely?'

'I can see you home,' I suggested like a fool.

She laughed bitterly. 'Home! I haven't got a home.'

'Anywhere then?'

'I haven't got anywhere.'

The fisherman opened his eyes and belched again, bringing up bile and a dribble of saliva. 'We going then?' he said to the girl.

She squeezed his arm and smiled at him. 'He's lovely, ent you?'

'What?'

'I'm telling this man you're lovely.'

'Who the hell is he?' the fisherman asked, glaring drunkenly at me.

'We was just talking.' The girl giggled, and let out a shriek of laughter. 'Drunken sod. I'll have a right time with him.'

She started to leave.

'You wanted Brown's Yard?' she said, hanging on to the man's arm.

'That's right.'

'Just off Riby Square. Kelly's Kitchen and Sunshine Row. You after Charlotte Grange's then?'

'I don't know.'

'Ask for Charlotte Grange. She's all right.'

They staggered off down the room. I heard a crash as the man fell on the stairs, and the girl's raucous laughter. Walmsley left his girl and came and sat beside me.

'You doing all right then, Samuel?' he leered.

I stood up. 'I'm off,' I said.

'You going back to *Rechabite*?' he said, staring at me in astonishment, hanging on to my arm. 'You giving up already?'

'I'm not going back to *Rechabite*,' I told him, trying to pull free.

'Don't do that, Samuel,' he said with a grin. 'I got this girl.'

'I'm not for *Rechabite*,' I shouted at him.

Several people turned and glanced at us.

I smiled at Walmsley and pushed him back against the wall.

'I'm going to find somebody,' I said. 'Somebody I came to look for. You go on dancing. I'll see you later.'

I left the dancing room before he could ask any questions.

Sixteen

The night was hotter than ever, late August burning itself to a fury in the wild lurid streets. Fights broke out in the beer-houses. Music blared from music halls and dancing rooms. My mind seemed to be full of music and dancing. Down the main street, sewage ran in the gutters, and the stench filled my lungs. In the market, women crowded after me, calling sweet names, giggling their crude suggestions. Some of them were no more than children: rouged faces and croaking childish voices.

Brown's Yard was not far from the market.

A crowd of men stood at the top of the alley talking to the women in one of the brothels. It was dark. I walked warily, listening for any movement in the shadows behind me. There was a pump in the middle of the yard, and a row of bleak houses down one side. The houses were rotting with decay: rubbish piled in the gutters, weeds growing out of the damp walls. I could hear a man yelling drunkenly at the end of the row and a woman screaming from an upstairs room. A child was crying hopelessly. Gangs of boys played around the pump, throwing dice, fooling around with young girls. A woman stood in a doorway, smoking a clay pipe and watching the children. Lines of washing hung between the dismal buildings. There was a bakery opposite the houses, an old barn with rats scuttling underneath the doors.

'Hello, lovely,' a voice said at my shoulder.

It was a girl, thirteen or fourteen. She had rouged cheeks and pale lips, the corners of her mouth covered with sores. Her long skirt was torn at the waist.

'Brown's Yard?' I asked.

'That's right. Sunshine Row and Kelly's Kitchen. You wanting somewhere to sleep?'

'No thanks.'

'You can sleep with me,' she suggested, pushing herself against me.

'I said no, pet.'

I walked down the yard. The houses must be Sunshine Row. At the bottom of the yard stood a gaunt, dreary building that looked like two or three houses knocked together to form a single dwelling. It was a lodging house. There were dozens in the town. The boys at the pump asked me if I wanted a bed for the night but I ignored them. I could hear them laughing as I opened the door into Kelly's Kitchen.

A rough-looking man sat by the door on a stool. The hall was badly lit by an oil lamp and smelled of damp and rats. The man glared at me. He was drinking from a bottle. I could smell the cordial: Godfrey's Cordial, the mixture of booze and laudanum women gave to their children to keep them quiet. The hall stank of laudanum.

'Bed?' the man grunted, peering at me.

'I'm looking for somebody.'

'Fisherboy?'

I knew this was the sort of place Robert Allison was likely to be in. Absconding boys usually ended up living with the prostitutes or in the lodging houses, which were not much better than brothels.

'Not a boy,' I said.

The man cackled his harsh laughter.

'Try the brothels, brother.'

'No.'

'Please yourself.'

'I'll have a look round.'

'No you won't,' he said quickly.

I pulled the gutting knife from my pocket and showed him. He shrugged. He didn't bother to get up from the stool.

'I work here,' he said with a toothless grin.

'That's nice.'

'Kelly finds you, he won't worry about a little knife.'

'But he's not here.'

'No.'

I searched the place. There were four large rooms on the ground floor. Dozens of mattresses were arranged in rows either side of them. A rat fled from underneath one of the mattresses as I walked up and down, staring at the beds. Men and women lay in a stupor on the floor. A girl of eight or nine lay on top of the filthy sheets of one mattress, grinning at me and leaning on her elbow. There were two boys in the bed with her. A couple were making love in a corner, grunting and sweating in the rank darkness. As the woman groaned and banged against the rotting wall, I left the room and went upstairs. There were more children there, dozens of them, sleeping or drinking by candlelight. In the light of one candle, I saw the vermin crawling on the mattresses. In each room, I repeated the name of the girl who had written the letter. Sullen faces stared back at me. One girl burst out laughing hysterically, as if a name was the last thing that mattered in this verminous evil ditch of humanity. I left the last of the rooms and didn't even bother to search the attics. The shrieks of children followed me down the stairs.

In the yard, a fight had broken out round the pump. I saw knives flashing in the gaslight. A crowd had gathered to watch. I made my way round the edge of the yard. The baby in Sunshine Row was still crying piteously. As I passed, a door flew open and a man staggered out, his head streaming with blood. He slipped on the cobbles, stumbled, and then lurched away down the narrow alley. I was sick in my heart, desperate to get out of this hellhole. If Miriam had ended up here, I couldn't stand the pain the knowledge would bring.

But I didn't get out of the yard.

As I reached the alley, the back door of the house next to the bakery flew open and light flooded into the yard. The door slammed against the wall and then a man fell out of the room. I could see inside: it was a kitchen, full of women. They were all shouting. A huge, muscular woman in a bright green silk dress chased after the man, kicking at him with her boots and cursing.

'Get out, you bastard,' she yelled. Her voice was like rusty tin, scraping across the hot, fetid night. 'Don't come back.'

The man staggered to his feet. Blood was running down his face. In the light from the kitchen I saw that he was completely bald. I guessed immediately what the women were shouting about: loss of hair was one of the first signs of syphilis. The man couldn't have been much older than twenty-five. A long cut down his cheek ran with fresh blood. I stepped back quickly out of the way as he lurched to his feet and tried to make for the alley.

'Bastard,' the woman was still shrieking at him.

'You tell him, Charlotte,' one of the women in the kitchen yelled.

They were all shouting and cursing, waving their fists in the air, straining to see what was happening. In the yard, people turned and watched, laughing and calling encouragement. Some of the lads started running towards the alley.

Then the man was gone.

'Good riddance,' the big woman grunted, and turned back to the kitchen. Before she could shut the door, I stepped forward and put my foot in the doorway. The woman turned and raised her fists.

'I'm looking for Ann Babb,' I said quickly.

She paused. I didn't like the look of her fists. They were bigger than Jack Walmsley's, and she had his muscles. She stared me down, waiting for me to explain myself.

'Ann Babb,' I repeated. 'Does she live here?'

There was brief laughter inside the kitchen.

'Does she?'

'What if she does?'

'I'm looking for her.'

'Half the men in Grimsby are looking for my girls.'

I tried to smile at her.

'Look,' I said. 'I have a letter.'

'He can read,' one of the girls jeered.

They were sitting down at the kitchen table now. One of the women was brewing tea. I took the letter from my pocket and showed it to the big woman. She read it quickly and then shrugged, handing it back and standing aside. I went into the kitchen and sat down.

'Are you Charlotte Grange?' I asked.

'That's right.'

'My name's Samuel Vempley.'

'So the letter says.'

The women were putting cups out on the table, a big teapot, and I glanced round at them, trying to smile. 'I could do with a drink,' I said.

'Get him a cup,' Charlotte Grange said brusquely.

She sat down. She had a blue tattoo on her arm: a delicate tracery of patterns. A girl's name was written underneath the blue: Jenny. The woman saw me looking, and pushed the arm in my face.

'My daughter,' she said. 'Died in Stepney workhouse. Typhoid.'

'All right.' I laughed, pushing her arm away. 'I'm sorry.'

'Drink your tea.'

The women were quiet now, subdued. I could hear singing in the street and somebody hammered at a door to the front of the house, but nobody moved to answer it. They seemed to have given up for the night. They looked tired and depressed. Their faces were gaunt in the light from the oil lamp. There were three of them, apart from Charlotte Grange. She obviously owned the house.

'Mercury works,' one of the girls said suddenly. She was the youngest of the three, dark-eyed and with wild straw hair. She had a gap in her front teeth which made her look like an old hag, her smile crooked and cheeky though her eyes were dead with exhaustion. 'That's what I heard.'

The other two women agreed quickly.

I had heard women talking like this before: women in the brothels in Yarmouth. They were all terrified of disease. They would believe anything if somebody only said it worked. There was a girl in Yarmouth who kept heartsease growing in a box in her bedroom window, and several girls I had known slept with violets hidden underneath their pillows.

Charlotte Grange sighed and shook her head.

'First year I visited this port,' she said, 'one of my girls caught syphilis off a fisherman. A month after his visit, she was covered in sores. All over her chest and abdomen they were. I had a doctor then. He tried nitric acid and iodoform, but the sores spread everywhere. She was emaciated, deranged. The doctor sent her to Leeds but she died a few weeks later, screaming in agony.'

'Thanks, Charlotte.' The blonde girl laughed bitterly.

'I'm telling you so's you'll know. You use something.'

'You needn't worry,' the girl said.

One of the other women swallowed her tea and took some brandy from a small flask. She didn't offer it to the others. 'He didn't have anything,' she said. 'That bald bloke. You could tell.'

'How could you?' the blonde girl asked quickly.

'You can allus tell,' the woman with the brandy said aggressively.

'It's the eyes.' The third woman nodded. 'You can tell from the eyes.'

'What about the eyes?' the blonde girl insisted.

The woman with the brandy smiled at her blearily. 'They got natural colour,' she said, drinking from the flask. 'Men with the pox has yellow eyes.'

I knew that was rubbish. More yarns to keep them happy. You couldn't go to sea without knowing about syphilis. You might not know who you were bunking down with half the time. And syphilis lived in the dark. The first sign was usually a hard lump, then a sore throat and deep ulcers in the tonsil. Then there would be fever and aching bones. Every fisherman on the smacks had those pains most of his life: they didn't have to be syphilis. But they might be. The disease could get into your blood without you ever knowing, and if you didn't get mercury treatment before the disease spread, it could send you blind and eat half your nose away before you knew what was happening.

Charlotte Grange was talking again, staring gloomily into her tea.

'I knew the wife of one of the skippers got syphilis,' she said.

'I don't want to know,' the blonde girl muttered, but made no move to leave the table.

'She got it off her husband when she was pregnant. Doctors told her to use a wet nurse. When the baby was five weeks old it died. Wet nurse was covered with sores. The baby had syphilis. They cured her, but she didn't get compensation. She sued. They said she must have got the disease herself. She had sores all over her nipples.'

I watched the women. They seemed fascinated by what the older woman was saying, sickened and unable to stop listening. It was women gossiping over the laundry, but their gossip evil with sickness and disease.

'Stop it,' the blonde girl said pathetically. Underneath the rouge and sarcasm, I saw that she was not much more than a child: seventeen or eighteen. She had probably been in the brothel for years. Some of them started at thirteen or fourteen. There was a brothel in Satan's Hole that specialised in young girls: the owner boasting that sleeping with a virgin was a cure for syphilis. Most of his girls lasted less than a year.

The women were suddenly standing up, getting ready for bed. They joked and made a lot of noise, but I could see the fear in their faces. When they left the kitchen, Charlotte Grange sat for a long time, staring into her empty cup, thinking her own thoughts.

I couldn't move.

Was this where Miriam had ended up? And where was she now?

I held on to my cup to keep my hands steady, my knuckles white with tension, the pain in my forehead throbbing violently.

Suddenly, the older woman started talking again.

'I have to frighten them,' she said bluntly.

'Do you?'

'Make them careful. Use something.'

'Men don't always like it that way.'

'They use something with my girls.'

I nodded briefly. She looked up and there were tears in her eyes. She brushed them away angrily.

'You want Ann Babb?'

'Yes.'

'About your Miriam?'

'You saw the letter.'

'Yes.' She nodded bleakly. She stood up. 'She's not here. She went to Hull. Looking for her brother.'

'Ann Babb?'

'That's right. Her brother signed with the fleets. One of Gothard's trawlers. Ann's gone to look for him. He's thirteen.'

I felt desperate. The night seemed to be endless.

'When will she be back?'

'I don't know.'

'We sail soon.'

'On the long-liners?' she asked.

'Yes.'

'For Iceland?'

'Yes.'

She started clearing the cups and teapot.

'I'll tell her as soon as she comes back. What vessel?'

'*Rechabite.*'

'I'll tell her.'

I stood up. 'I'll come back,' I said. 'When I can.'

She opened the kitchen door and let me out into the yard.

I felt dizzy with tiredness and drink. I didn't know where I was.

What was Miriam doing in a brothel in Satan's Hole?

Who was Ann Babb?

I walked into the night, terror growing in my soul.

Seventeen

I felt as if my head was going to leave my shoulders. All night I walked the streets of Satan's Hole, trying to clear my mind of Kelly's Kitchen and Sunshine Row, trying to make sense of Miriam's journey into that hellhole. When I got back to *Rechabite*, I reeled when my feet touched the deck and Everitt glanced at me caustically, turning his back with a frown and talking to Edwin Wallis. I stumbled down the companion and lay on my bunk. I needed sleep. I needed oblivion. The clamour of the music halls filled my aching mind.

An hour later there was a hammering on the cabin door. The door flung back against the wall and I could hear Everitt shouting orders on deck. Francis Campbell stood in the doorway.

'We're sailing, Mr Vempley.'

'What?'

'Morning tide.'

'You want me?' I managed to say, coming awake, struggling out of the bunk.

'Skipper said.'

I nearly fell, crashing my shoulder against the side of the bunk. Campbell watched me warily. He was a squat, tough little boy, straight from the Hackney workhouse and determined to make his way: his eyes never missed a trick; he avoided Jack Walmsley like a plague.

'What you doing, Francis?' I asked him, irritated at being woken up, massaging my bruised shoulder.

'Brewing up.'

'Brewing up?'

'I'm in the galley,' he said. 'Until we find a new boy. You didn't have much luck.'

'No,' I said ruefully, dragging my seaboots on. I could feel the smack lurching out of the lockpit. Everitt was yelling his commands. 'No, we didn't have much luck. Now go and brew that tea, there's a good lad. I could drink a bucketful.'

I was starting up the companion when Jack Walmsley scrambled down.

'Morning, Samuel,' he boomed cheerfully. He looked as fresh as daylight, and landed on the deck with a clatter of boots, clapping his rough hands together and pumping my arm. 'You look a prize catch.'

'Give over, Walmsley.'

'Give over!'

'Being so bloody cheerful.'

'Just my nature, Samuel. I'm a glad-hearted man. Can't help that.'

'We sailing?'

'Long-lining on the Dogger.' Walmsley grinned. He turned and shouted through to the galley. 'Get that tea, Francis. Lovely as she goes. Got to catch some fish, skipper says.'

'I bet.'

Walmsley grinned with pleasure, leaning in the cabin doorway and looking me up and down. 'You had a good night,' he said with a crude laugh. 'Livening things up in Brown's Yard.'

'Sod off, Walmsley.'

I clambered up the companion and came out into brilliant sunlight. White light danced off the sea. The waves were tumbling towards the shore and already *Rechabite* was bouncing towards the estuary, following a strong easterly, under full sail. I went up to Everitt at the tiller. He hardly bothered to look at me. Edwin Wallis was standing at his side, glancing at a chart.

'Sorry about last night, skipper,' I said.

Everitt nodded briefly.

'You had no luck, Mr Walmsley tells me.'

'Nobody to be found.'

'You can try when we return. We can't make Iceland without more hands. Maybe you looked in the wrong places.'

There was something ironic in his tone, and I saw Edwin glance at him. He ignored me. I shrugged and looked at the horizon. We were heading north-west for the Great Silver Pit and Skate Hole. The fishing was good on Southermost Rough and deep into Dogger herself. I felt the pain ease in my head as the fresh air filled my lungs, and I took my pipe out of my pocket and started to fill the bowl. When I offered the tobacco to Edwin, he shrugged and turned away.

'I'll go and check the lines,' he said brusquely.

He never even looked at me.

So now I knew: Walmsley had been busy talking; telling him about my visit to Brown's Yard.

There was nothing I could do about that.

I stayed by the tiller and kept my face into the sun. The bright sunlight and fresh breeze cleared my head in minutes, and I smoked a full pipe without talking to Everitt. I needed to think, and he wasn't a man for much talking. He kept his eye on the mainsail, his hand firm on the tiller.

After a few minutes, I knocked the pipe out on the mainmast and went to the fish hatches where John Pinney and Nathan Chapman were helping Edwin check the lines. I leaned against the mainmast and watched them for a while, then knelt down and helped unravel a stretch of line. All the snoods were ready baited. The men must have been working most of yesterday afternoon while I was trudging round Satan's Hole with Jack Walmsley. Maybe it was that they resented. But John Pinney was cheerful enough, and Nathan Chapman greeted me with a cautious smile.

'We looked hard,' I told them, though my words were intended for Edwin.

John seemed surprised. 'I reckon,' he said. 'Not that easy, this time of season.'

Nathan sat back on his heels and flexed his wrists. 'Don't know why he bothers,' he said in a low voice. 'Anybody worth having has already got a berth. We managed all right last time.'

'Last time?' I asked, looking at him quickly.

It was Edwin who spoke now. 'We lost a lad before. Last season,' he explained. 'Terrible weather.'

'Terrible,' Nathan laughed.

'Blew out of nowhere. Off Tea Kettle Hole. We managed three trips short-handed.'

'Till we found Benjamin,' John Pinney said ironically. He flashed a look at me: his eyes mocking, his thin mouth tight with some hidden bitterness. 'He was a great help.'

The lines were all checked and coiled down. I sat back against the mainmast and relaxed. Again, I offered my tobacco to Edwin. He met my eyes this time. He looked uneasy, uncomfortable. As he took some of the tobacco, he glanced over his shoulder to the skipper, who was talking to Henry Purvis at the tiller. Walmsley was in the bows, chatting with Richard Buss. We could hear Francis Campbell whistling in the galley. The first meal of the trip would soon be ready: that was when a cook earned his reputation for the rest of the voyage. Already, I could smell roasted potatoes and fried fish floating from the small galley.

'We looked everywhere likely,' I said, holding Edwin's attention.

'Didn't sound likely,' he said with a frown.

'You listened to Walmsley?'

'Brown's Yard?' Edwin said, raising his eyebrows.

'That's right. Kelly's Kitchen. Sunshine Row. And other places. I had business in Brown's Yard.'

'A friend,' Edwin said with increasing scorn.

'A lost friend.'

'She'd have to be lost to be working there.'

'I didn't say she was working there.'

There was an awkward pause. Nathan stared down at the deck and smirked. John Pinney looked embarrassed.

Edwin paused, staring at me again, wanting to believe me. 'You didn't say anything,' he pointed out. 'You didn't share it.'

'Why should I?'

'Fair enough.'

He was about to get up, but I held his arm. He didn't like that.

'It is my business, Edwin, you can't gainsay that, but if you're going to listen to Jack Walmsley's evil mouthing . . .'

'I'm not. You said it was true.'

'I said she'd been seen in Brown's Yard. I don't know what she was doing there. She might have been trying to find lodgings. Kelly's Kitchen gives lodgings. She wouldn't know what kind of place it was. She wouldn't have been there if she'd known.'

I felt angry, furious at Walmsley's lies, hurt by Edwin's doubts. If I was going to survive this Iceland voyage, I had to have Edwin on my side. I had to have his trust. He was the one man on *Rechabite* the majority of the men listened to. Even Everitt wouldn't cross Edwin.

He still looked doubtful.

'A woman doesn't end up in Satan's Hole unless that's where she was intended to be.'

'You don't believe that.'

'Don't I?'

'Life's more complicated than that, Edwin, as you well know. You showed me the cuttings.'

'Yes.'

'Remember!'

'Yes!'

We were beginning to shout. I controlled my voice and

hissed at him. I could tell that Everitt and Purvis were listening, though they never looked our way. They went on talking as if they didn't know we were there.

My head was aching again.

'You think those boys *wanted* to be on the fishing?' I said furiously. 'You think they *intended* to end up like that?'

The doubts crossed his eyes again.

'Do you?' I insisted.

He shook his head, and stared blindly over the stern.

'Do you?' I hissed into his face.

'I don't know,' he said vaguely. 'I'm not sure.'

But before I could force the issue, there was a shout from the galley, and Francis Campbell clambered on deck with the food. We were all too hungry to waste time arguing. John Pinney and Nathan were on their feet before Francis was out of the companion, and by the time Edwin started to struggle up, the men were crowding round Francis to get their hot meal. I gave Edwin my hand, and he stood up slowly, stretching his tired back. He grinned at me and shrugged, but he didn't say he believed me.

As I took my own food, I saw Everitt watching me with a caustic smile. He might have been listening to every word of the conversation. I took my plate to the bows, and Everitt turned away to continue his talk with Henry Purvis. I could have cursed Edwin, but my mind was too full of Miriam and Satan's Hole. I ate my food, and wished the lot of them at the bottom of the restless sea.

After that, I spent long hours at the tiller. We made good time to the Dogger, working under full sail, green seas tumbling over the bows, white water threshing from the stern. When he wasn't busy with the sails, Everitt liked to talk about the fishing. He had worked these grounds for years, ever since his first trips as a boy. The grounds don't change. He talked endlessly about the secrets of the deep water.

The Dogger is like an enormous sea: thousands of square miles of stormy, unpredictable water. The western edge lies off the Yorkshire coast, and it extends north-east for almost

two hundred miles. The northern edge is the most dangerous, where great seas roll in from deep water and drive
against the submerged cliffs, making a deadly, confused
smother of broken water and wild spray which rages around
the smacks like a maelstrom. In winter, nobody in their right
mind goes fishing along the northern edge in case they get
caught with a northerly gale coming in and no sea-room for
manoeuvre. Fishermen call this ground the Cemetery; the
southern edge is known as the Hospital; the names tell their
own story.

Everitt knew every inch of the Dogger.

'It's all banks and flats and pits on the Dogger,' he said
gruffly, musing as if he was talking to himself. 'But at least
you can tell where you are by the stuff you bring up from the
bottom.' He always talked to me as if I had never been on a
fishing smack. I think he liked to show off his knowledge: his
secret vice. 'You get light-coloured sand with small white
shells at the east end of the Dogger,' he went on. 'A bit
nearer the Yorkshire coast it's red sand and soft mud, a fine
sign for haddock, but you get a horrible stench on the line if
you try there. Lot of big rocks. Trawlers daren't risk it. My
father used to call the sand coffee soil, it was so dark. He
claimed he could find his way about simply by dropping the
lead or looking at the colour of the water. He couldn't use a
compass anyway, or read the charts. He always preferred his
own ways.'

At times like this, Everitt almost sounded like Joseph
Proctor.

'You get sand at thirty-two fathoms on Brucey's Garden,'
Joseph told me the first night I spent on the tiller on *Wings
of Morning*. 'Mud at thirty-five fathoms on Markham's Hole,
and the same mud on Botany Gut at forty fathoms. Botany
Gut's one of the worst grounds, just an inlet in the South
Rough, near the Oysters.'

Fishermen right down the east coast would recognise this
colourful world beneath the grey North Seas. The German
Seas, Joseph called them, where hundreds of smacks had

been lost, their crews of fishermen drowned, their spars disappearing beneath the relentless waters. No wonder fishing wives said the sea was the heart's graveyard.

It took us eighteen hours to reach the southern end of the Dogger.

'We'll work Skate Hole and then westward to Hospital Ground,' Everitt told Henry Purvis when he asked for orders for the lines.

'First crew to the lines,' Purvis began shouting.

I was on the first crew. After the strong tides of coastal waters, the deep waters of the Dogger were relatively tideless, but the weather was unpredictable, so we always laid the lines from the stern of the smack. It would have been too dangerous to use the longboat. I made my way to the stern where John Pinney and Edwin were already waiting, and once we had dropped a buoy with *Rechabite*'s pennant to mark our starting point, helped them lift the first tray of lines to the bulwarks.

'You think there's fish about, Mr Wallis?' John Pinney chatted cheerfully as we uncoiled the first flakes of line.

'Can't tell.' Edwin shrugged. 'It's one of the skipper's favourite grounds. He'll know soon enough, that's for certain.'

'Get on with it, lads,' Walmsley grumbled, coming over to the stern and standing at the bulwarks. 'Let's get her fishing.' He was obviously determined to impress the skipper after our failure in Satan's Hole.

Everitt was tacking under light sail.

I wiped the sweat from my forehead and let out a shout of pleasure. 'That's the way,' I laughed as the line disappeared under the water, dark brown from the tarring which protected it from chafing on the ground. There was always something exciting about the way the coils of snoods and hooks went flying over the stern into the green water. You never knew what you might catch: a fortune or a swarm of dogfish; a dead fisherman tangled among the snoods. The lines would be left down for three hours, and when we had finished uncoiling, *Rechabite* dropped a light anchor so that we could work back along the line once enough time had been allowed for the fish to bite. We had laid almost eight miles of line.

'Gear overboard, skipper,' Walmsley shouted the minute we had the tray emptied, and with a brief nod to Purvis, Everitt got *Rechabite* hove to.

'Nice work, Mr Walmsley,' Everitt said loud enough for us to hear.

With the jib dropped and the staysail beautifully backed, *Rechabite* rode the tide as steadily as a resting seabird.

'Pray the Lord for good fortune, Edwin,' I heard Everitt saying as I climbed down the companion to fetch a mug of tea. Edwin grunted something I couldn't hear, and went off to smoke his pipe in the bows. I fetched my tea and went into the cabin. There would be an hour for rest before Francis Campbell prepared the evening meal. I lay down on my bunk and closed my eyes. The coke stove was burning, causing the cabin to stink of tobacco and wet clothing. There was nowhere to dry gear on a smack, but at least we weren't out for months at a time like the fleeting trawlers. Sitting up, I eased my long seaboots off and dropped them to the floor. My mouth tasted of salt, and I yawned, enjoying the tea and the rocking motion of the smack, listening to the sails taking the strain of the wind.

I must have slept for a couple of hours. 'Food's up, Mr Vempley,' Francis shouted through the cabin door, and I struggled up on to the edge of my bunk and started putting my seaboots back on. My sleep had been full of Miriam and Kelly's Kitchen, only Miriam was a child crying in the middle of the night, frightened of the squirming darkness, the unfamiliar sounds all around her. Other children whimpered in the cold. I got my gear on, and went through to the galley, hardly rested by the miserable sleep. After a quick meal of meat duff and suet pudding, swallowed down with half a pint of scalding-hot tea, I went back on deck to help haul the lines. I seemed to have been living this life for years, but never in such misery.

'Weather's changed,' Nathan Chapman said, climbing up the companion and rubbing the sleep out of his eyes.

We stared dismally into the sombre, choppy sea, the grey waters swelling to the horizon, banks of cloud rolling urgently out of the east. You couldn't believe the weather at sea sometimes: becalmed for hours, then devastating black squalls. We had all seen rough weather. At night it seemed worse.

To haul the lines, Everitt lowered the foresail and made short tacks back along the course of the line. It was the most difficult operation in fishing. To tack in any sea, a smack has to be sailed fairly hard because she won't come about unless she is moving smartly through the water, and then if you aren't careful you can easily damage the line. Everitt made the whole business look effortless. I watched as he gave his orders. As far as possible, he kept the wind sufficiently abeam for the smack to jog back at a safe haul, checking with the drogue if she overran the line. If *Rechabite* got too far to leeward, or the wind headed her, he would have to use the longboat or go back to the other end of the line and haul the same way as she was laid. That was a complicated and time-wasting business. Everitt made certain it didn't happen. He sailed *Rechabite* beautifully down the miles of line, and as we hauled from the stern there wasn't a hook without a huge cod. Some of the men actually cheered.

As soon as the smack's buoy had been lifted, we began the work of clearing the catch, lifting the fish off the hooks and transferring the best into the well. Most of the catch this trip was for freezing, but Everitt couldn't resist keeping the prime specimens for the well. All hands joined in this frenzied work, so that we could lay fresh lines as soon as the catch was cleared away. And as we worked, we sang.

Henry Purvis started us off. 'When I survey the wondrous Cross,' he squawked with a pious look on his pinched, sallow face. The men sang with a will, enjoying the sound of their own voices, delighted with the pleasure of a fine catch.

Young John Pinney surprised me when we finished by going straight on with 'The day thou gavest, Lord, is ended', his voice a fine, clear tenor, so that for a moment we were all silent, listening to the wind in the sails, the creak of the smack's oak timbers. Edwin Wallis broke the silence with 'Now thank we all our God', and even Everitt joined in with that, keeping his eye steadily on the sails.

'You been looking thoughtful, Samuel,' Jack Walmsley said at my side, helping with a fine green cod. 'Pensive, if you know what I mean. You all right?'

'Why shouldn't I be?'

'Thinking about that girl?' he asked with a smile.

'Maybe.'

He finished gutting the cod and reached for another. 'She in your heart, is she, Samuel?' he said as his knife sliced into the writhing fish.

I looked up into the vast sky, the cloudless night and twinkling stars. The weather had cleared. The wind was fresh on my face. There were trawlers working the banks, isolated smacks long-lining on the grounds. Where the smacks were working alone, they had fires burning in their sterns to warn approaching vessels. As *Rechabite* rode the seas, the horizon went up and down.

How could a girl I had known for less than seven months be so deeply buried in my heart?

'She's in my mind,' I said at last. 'If that's what you mean.'

He laughed ruefully. 'Amounts to the same thing.'

'Yes,' I said after a long silence.

At the tiller, Everitt started up singing again, pleased that the lines were almost cleared. 'Will your anchor hold in the storms of life,' he boomed in his tuneless monotone, glancing at me briefly as the wind took the mizzen. We went on singing until the last of the catch was safely stowed, and then brewed fresh tea before preparing the next tray of lines ready for hoisting over the stern.

In the bows, Richard Buss had the watch.

'Fleets away,' he called to the skipper, and to our starboard we saw the lights of the trawlers. A hundred vessels, sweeping through the encroaching darkness. Every man on deck turned and watched the twinkling lights, the sails lifting up and down on the sea.

Eighteen

A dozen fleets worked the Dogger, most of them out of
Gorleston. During the next few days we identified the flags
of nine fleets: Hewitt's Short Blue, Leleu's, Columbia, Great
Northern, Coffee Smith's, Gamecock, Red Cross, Durrant's
and Fenner's. They worked to and fro across the water like
a giant factory, sweeping the floor of the sea.

'I never seen the fleets,' Richard Buss told me one morning when we were waiting to haul the lines.

'They're a fair sight,' I admitted.

'Like harvesters, on the farm,' Richard said. 'Going across
the fields.'

'We never had harvesters,' I told him, remembering the
farm where my father worked. 'They got the harvest in by
hand.'

Richard nodded miserably. He always looked miserable.
'My dad lost his work because of the harvesters,' he said bitterly. 'We grew our own vegetables, but he couldn't earn
nothing. We used to collect wood but the landowners
stopped that. I used to like working on the harvest. I would
have done that if we'd had enough to eat.'

I knew he hated the fishing. He was seasick every time we
hit rough weather. At the lines, he worked with his teeth gritted, disliking the touch of the fish, jumping every time a
large cod writhed near him.

I told him about the trawlers to try and cheer him up.

'At least you're not on the fleets,' I said.

'Is this better?'

'You've no notion, Richard,' John Pinney said at his side, joining us from the companion. He had a mug of tea in his hand. 'The fleets is like floating hell.'

'Can't be that bad,' Richard muttered.

'Oh?'

'Men are quick enough to join.'

'Do anything for money, some men,' John said sagely, and I burst out laughing. 'What's wrong with that?' he asked with his innocent grin.

'You're full of wisdom, John.'

'I told you, my family lived the fishing. Generations of them. They know about the damned fleeting.'

'So why is it so bad?' Richard asked.

I told him.

Men slaved on the trawlers. They fished night and day, seven days a week, only stopping in dead calm or very rough weather.

'Like us,' Richard said ruefully.

'Yes, but we only have to shoot lines,' John Pinney pointed out. 'They have to shoot the net. You should try the difference.'

'That's right.' I nodded.

I had lifted a trawl net one summer, helping a friend of Joseph Proctor's for a few days when he was short-handed. I had never worked with the fleets. That single trip was enough for me. We shot the trawl over the side every six hours, three hauls a day without relief, and then the gutting. I was exhausted after a couple of days.

'It takes three strong men to lift the trawl over the side,' I told Richard. 'It's a hundred feet long, and the beam they use to keep the mouth of the net open is like a small tree. Even without fish it takes some lifting. When it's full, it can weigh a ton. But the most dangerous bit is getting the gear over the side: you have to be careful you don't get dragged overboard when you finally let go of the beam.'

'How do you do that?' he asked.

'Leap back as it plunges into the water.'

'Blimey.'

'The real work is getting the gear back on board,' I went on. 'All hands are called on deck, and you have to haul the net up to the port side of the vessel. Two men always begin the heaving in, and that takes at least an hour in good weather, maybe three or four hours in a storm. You can imagine what that's like, with the smack rolling and pitching all the time you're hauling. When the trawl-beam finally gets swung alongside, it takes all hands to hoist it on to deck, panting and heaving in the rough weather, sweating in their wet clothes. Once the trawl is fastened to the port rails, the second hand usually loosens the cod end and the fish deluge out of the net and on to the slippery deck. The minute that's done, the trawl has to be put back over the side, and then the crew get on with gutting the catch.'

It was the gutting that exhausted men on the fleets. The catches were so much bigger; the work went on without rest. In calm weather the job is heavy enough, but in winter the fish start to freeze and go stiff before you can pick them up. In choppy weather spray flies over the decks all the time, and sometimes heavy waves wash right over the smack, knocking the men into the mass of swirling fish and cold water. A man can be straight overboard if he doesn't watch what he's doing. And after twelve hours of hauling the nets and gutting the catch, men actually fall asleep where they're standing. That's when the accidents happen: boys hacking their fingers off, too tired to watch what they're doing; exhausted men thrown over the side by the sea. On any trawler, the work was heavier, but on the fleets, the men might be working for twelve weeks without rest or sight of land. No wonder they were tired.

'Blimey,' Richard laughed when I'd finished. 'Maybe *Rechabite*'s not so bad.'

'Maybe she isn't,' John Pinney agreed.

I saw Jack Walmsley sidling across to the rail. He had been listening all the time, leaning against the mainmast, smoking his pipe.

'You wouldn't know it from the way you lot whinge,' he said with a sneer.

'We're not whingeing, Walmsley,' I told him.

'What are you doing then?'

'Talking. You ever heard of that?'

He curled his lip and went back to his pipe at the mainmast. I saw the fear in Richard Buss's eyes, but then he smiled. I hadn't seen him so happy since the day we left Yarmouth. At least I had managed to cheer somebody up. The thought of life on the trawlers would probably keep his spirits up for several hours.

In my own silence, I went back to thinking about Miriam.

I wondered if my life would ever get back to that happiness.

We had good weather for three or four days after that, and the fishroom was soon filled with fine iced fish. The prime still went into the well, ready for a last visit to Grimsby.

But Everitt was worried about Iceland.

'We still need extra hands for the long-lining,' he said as he studied the figures for the well with Jack Walmsley. 'A few more days of fishing should do it and then we must get back. I want the well full.'

'And the iced catch, skipper?' I heard Walmsley ask him.

'To the cutter.'

'Yes, sir.'

'Tomorrow morning.'

My heart sank.

I had never worked at transferring the catch to a cutter. The trawlers in the fleets always did this, shifting each day's catch so that the cutters could get it back to the Grimsby market. But liners nearly always returned to port with their entire catch for the market. I knew Everitt was intent on getting as much fish as he could without wasting time sailing back to port. But I dreaded the idea of taking the longboat full of iced fish to the waiting cutter.

I think Everitt knew I was frightened.

'I think you might learn something,' he told me when he suggested my joining the longboat.

'Yes, skipper?'

'I heard you talking about the trawlers.'

'Yes, skipper.'

'Have you ever worked the fleets?'

'No, skipper. Just that one trip, helping a friend of Proctor's. We worked on our own. I wouldn't go on the fleets.'

'But you know a great deal about them.'

'Fishermen talk,' I said with surprise, thinking he was being sarcastic. 'They share things.'

'Quite so. I'm not criticising. Richard Buss should know his good fortune, sailing on a liner like *Rechabite*. I'm glad you told him.'

'She's a fine vessel,' I said truthfully.

'Indeed.'

'And he's a willing lad, he's trying to learn.'

'Good.' Everitt smiled in a friendly manner. 'So you will take him with you to the cutter. So that he can learn.'

I stared at the skipper in surprise. He must be mad. Why risk an entire catch with an inexperienced man and a fifteen-year-old boy.

'Isn't Henry Purvis second hand?' I said sarcastically.

Everitt laughed cruelly, enjoying my nerves.

'I'm not suggesting you should go alone. Mr Walmsley can show you the handling. He's done the job before. He worked the fleets for several years, until they wore him out. He knows all about carrying fish boxes.'

'That's right,' Walmsley agreed jovially, coming across and standing by the skipper. 'Nothing to it, Samuel. I'll look after you.'

He winked at the skipper but Everitt's expression didn't change: a look of contempt, and even triumph; a secret gloating at my fears.

'Fine,' I said quietly.

I wouldn't let them see how I felt.

I went below, and tried to sleep. In the darkness, I could feel *Rechabite* riding the seas, tacking under full sail for the fleets trawling at the horizon. In the morning, we would be right among them.

Nineteen

I slept badly that night, and in the morning, was ready at the longboat when Jack Walmsley shouted out for all hands. Richard Buss was the last to join us. He helped lift the boxes of fish out of the hatch, and Walmsley hoisted the longboat over the side. Each box had *Rechabite*'s name printed on the side so that the merchants would know where to credit the market price. It took us an hour to get the fish boxes down to the lurching longboat. Edwin Wallis and Henry Purvis stood at the rails, and Walmsley joined me in the boat: as the men at the rails hoisted the boxes out, we had to wait for a rising wave and then grab the frozen fish before it crashed down into the bottom of the longboat. I was sweating by the time we had all the boxes safely stowed.

'Release the painter,' Walmsley cried, and as Richard Buss steadied the longboat Edwin unfastened the rope at the stern of the smack. The longboat swung away, and we headed out towards the crowded seas. Dozens of trawlers were already milling around the cutter. The longboat swung and steadied against the wash from a passing smack, and then we were rowing like mad for the cutter, Jack Walmsley standing in the stern so that he could see over the top of the stacked boxes, Richard and myself pulling as hard as we could at the oars.

I could see the sweat pouring down Richard's face.

'No hurry, lad,' I told him.

He hardly seemed to hear me. The muscles on his arms were standing out, and his eyes were bulging with panic. I didn't feel much happier myself. I knew that ferrying the fish to the cutters was the most dangerous job the men in the fleets had to do. In all but the roughest weather, they had to launch the boat and row to the cutter. Even in a calm sea, with more than a hundred smacks all sending small boats to the cutter, the chance of collisions made the job a nightmare. Given a rough sea, the little boats could be capsized before they got anywhere near the waiting fish carriers, and in their heavy seaboots, men thrown from a longboat didn't stand a chance of surviving. The thought didn't cheer me up.

'Another hundred yards,' Walmsley shouted over the top of the boxes. Melting ice was already running down the sides of the boxes, but we couldn't see Walmsley behind the five-foot-high stack of frozen fish. He was clinging on, making sure he could see ahead, but all we could hear was his voice and the sound of our oars squeaking in the iron rowlocks.

'Take it easy,' Walmsley shouted now.

I turned in my seat and looked over my shoulder. The cutter was twenty yards away, rolling like a demented animal in the choppy water, longboats clustering around her lee side. In bad conditions, a longboat could be driven against the side of the carrier or underneath the transom stern before the men knew what was happening: one big swell, and the stern would crush the longboat to splinters. I clenched my teeth and cursed Everitt.

'Take our turn,' Walmsley shouted over the boxes.

'How do we know?' I yelled back.

'I'll be telling you.'

He seemed almost jovial, showing off, enjoying the excitement. A cloud of tobacco smoke drifted over the boxes, and I nodded at Richard to take a look: the fool was smoking his pipe; one slip, and he would be overboard. Even Walmsley hadn't the strength to swim in these waters.

'Steady,' he shouted as our longboat lurched to port, caught in the wash of a trawler passing too close. We could hear the men on the cutter yelling, and shouts from the men in the longboats.

At last it was our turn.

'Take it steady,' Walmsley said again, hanging on to the pile of boxes for grim life, trying to sound casual.

We rowed slowly, listening as Walmsley guided us towards the cutter. Once we got the boat alongside, he shouted at us both to ship oars and stand up. The boat lurched sickeningly as we clambered to our feet. On the deck, men were lining the rail, shouting instructions.

'Wait for a sea,' one of the men yelled down to us.

Working together, Richard and I hoisted the first box off the top of the pile and held it at waist height. We had to wait several seconds but they seemed like hours. The men kept shouting instructions: take it steady, hold on. Then in a split second the cutter's rail dipped down towards us, and we had to lift the box across the rail to the men waiting on the deck. They steadied the box, and, as the deck soared upwards and the box slid off the rail, guided it to a soft landing. There were seconds in which to do the job safely. Before the first box was off the rail, our longboat was plunging back down into the green water, lifting violently as the sea passed underneath the cutter.

We had eighteen boxes of fish to unload.

By the time we hoisted the last box aboard the cutter, a rough wind had lifted off the sea. The maindecks of the cutter were piled with boxes of fish and there were still dozens of longboats waiting to get their catch transferred. The summer squall hit the seas like a thunderstorm dropping out of the skies. The skipper on the cutter started hauling sail. The next minute, the cutter rolled so heavily that water lifted the boxes off the deck and she shipped several heavy seas over the coamings and down the main hatchway. The wind was blowing from the east, and banks of cloud rolled threateningly towards us out of the horizon.

'We're in for a squall,' Jack Walmsley shouted as we pushed away from the cutter. He was beginning to sweat now. I could see the fear shining in his eyes. 'Put your weight behind them oars,' he yelled suddenly.

As we grabbed the oars, there was a large wash of water plunging underneath us, and the longboat was suddenly boiling with spray, a huge swell throwing the boat back against the side of the cutter. There was a grinding of splintering wood, but it was only an oar cracking in half. As we pushed away again, Walmsley pulled the spare oar from the bows and took Richard's place beside me. Richard scrambled to the stern. When I looked up at the cutter, men were working desperately at the rail, trying to guide another longboat alongside.

'You wrecked the oar,' Walmsley shouted stupidly at the lad.

In the stern, Richard clung to the tiller, too frightened to shout anything back. His face was white with fear.

'Don't be a fool, Walmsley,' I yelled as green water deluged into the bottom of the longboat.

But Walmsley wasn't listening. 'Keep her up,' he yelled at Richard, and with my arms aching from the work, I pulled and laboured at the oars, keeping my eyes steadily on *Rechabite* as she rode the passing squall.

By the time we got back, the wind had dropped completely.

'You can pay for that fucking oar from your wages,' Walmsley yelled as we clambered back on deck. He was in a fury.

'Not so easy then, Walmsley?' I laughed at him.

'You what?'

'Not so simple, transferring the fish? I thought you said it wasn't dangerous.'

Walmsley was in a frenzy, white with anger and fear.

'Shut your mouth, Vempley, before I shut it.'

I saw Richard trembling, terrified of Walmsley's temper, but for the first time, Everitt interfered.

'No need for that, Mr Walmsley,' he said calmly.

Walmsley looked shaken, stopped in his tracks. 'Sir?'

'First time the lad's done the job.'

'Yes, skipper.'

'You did very well,' Everitt smiled at us. 'Both of you.'

'Didn't lose a box,' Walmsley chimed in, immediately changing his tack. 'And we had a swell. Nearly took us over.'

'You did well,' Everitt said again icily, cutting Walmsley dead. 'Not a simple job, trunking the fish. You did a good job.'

He seemed delighted. I half-wondered if he was pleased Walmsley had proved himself such a fool.

I slapped Richard on the back, and once we'd helped Edwin hoist the longboat back aboard *Rechabite*, we went down to the galley and had a mug of tea together to celebrate.

'But not again,' Richard said as he drank his tea.

'Somebody else's turn,' I agreed promptly.

For once I was right: thank God.

A week later we were becalmed.

A fine fog drifted in from the banks, and the sea became the wind's graveyard. There was nothing we could do without wind. We sat about on the decks, listless and bored, yarning or playing accordions. Edwin got out his materials for a hook rug, and Henry Purvis sat by the mainsail carving a ship. His fingers were thin and quick, and he told me he had sold several models of smacks back in Yarmouth. For a bit of fun, Walmsley and Nathan Chapman tried to catch gulls by trailing a tarred rope astern, but the birds avoided the ropes even when there were fish attached. Arguments broke out, but Everitt seemed to be everywhere when there was trouble. He wouldn't stand fights aboard *Rechabite*.

The calm lasted for four days. The fresh water became lukewarm and the colour of pea soup. The boredom was enervating. On the fourth day, Everitt took the longboat and with Edwin Wallis rowed himself to visit the skipper of one of the trawlers. He took a box of tobacco with him, and a side of salted pork. He said he would be away until night-fall. As soon as the longboat had gone, Walmsley and Henry Purvis started drinking. The bottle appeared from nowhere. Nathan Chapman seemed to have a flask hidden somewhere in his bunk. The smell of aniseed whisky drifted around *Rechabite*. They wouldn't have dared with the skipper or Edwin aboard.

It was during the afternoon that one of the Dutch kopers pulled alongside and offered to sell Walmsley some enter-tainment. The kopers were nearly all old fishing vessels that had taken to the drink trade for better money. They sold tobacco and cigars, brandy, rum and gin. The tobacco burned the skin off your mouth. The drink was all adulter-ated. Walmsley bought tobacco and aniseed whisky. I saw the money changing hands. There was also a packet of pic-ture cards. I knew just the kind of pictures they would be.

'Want a share, Samuel?' Walmsley grinned when he saw me watching.

'No thanks.'

'Have a bit of fun?'

'I said no.'

'Please yourself.'

They settled down on the deck and started playing cards. Nathan Chapman soon joined them. Richard Buss was down below, trying to sleep. John Pinney sat with me in the bows.

'Fine men,' he said sarcastically, his cheerful grin darken-ing.

'The skipper will be back by nightfall.'

'I hope that's soon enough,' John said warily.

After an hour of the heat, I went down to the cabin. I tried to sleep, but it was too hot in the airless cabin and the stink was worse than ever. I was just about to get out of the bunk when I heard Purvis's drunken voice. 'Chained light-ning,' he seemed to be shouting.

I got up and went through to the galley.

Francis Campbell was polishing the pots. On the stove, a

large pan of fat was sizzling. I stared at the fat. There was no food to be cooked for several hours. Francis saw my look and grinned.

'You all right?' I asked him.

'Why shouldn't I be?'

'I reckon they're getting drunk,' I told the boy.

'I'll be in the galley.'

'What?'

'In case Jack Walmsley wants me,' he added with a nasty laugh.

'What the hell do you mean, Francis?'

He turned to the stove and nodded at the boiling fat.

'He comes down here, he'll get that lot in his face,' he said.

'Jesus Christ, Francis.'

He didn't even seem frightened. He winked at me, and went back to his work. I left the galley and climbed the ladders to the deck. The three card players were already drunk. They were handing round pictures of women from the pack: naked women together, men and women making love. Walmsley saw me and raised his bottle.

'Never trust a sober man.' He belched.

'You look at her, Samuel,' Henry Purvis giggled, showing me one of the cards.

They were roaring with laughter.

I went back down to the cabin.

Francis was sitting on a stool, drinking tea. I paused in the doorway. 'The skipper will be back soon,' I said.

Francis shrugged. 'They reckon they set fire to one man,' he said cheerfully. 'On *Zachariah*. Poured turps over him and set him alight.'

I had heard the same story.

The men on deck were dancing, shouting. Purvis was playing his accordion. When I climbed back up the companion, Walmsley had stripped to the waist and was pouring alcohol over his head, swallowing great mouthfuls of liquor from a stone jar. Henry Purvis was dancing and jigging with his accordion, ranting up at the sky. Nathan Chapman lay collapsed on the deck, roaring with laughter, enjoying the pictures on the cards.

Later, at night, Purvis and Walmsley stumbled down the companion ladder and started shouting for Francis, but I was standing in the galley doorway. They tried to push past and then started cursing.

'I got a knife,' I said, facing them in the narrow darkness outside the aft cabin. Purvis belched, leaning against the wall. Walmsley eyed the knife.

'I'll use it,' I said quietly, moving the razor-edged blade backwards and forwards in front of Walmsley's eyes.

'That right?' Walmsley whispered drunkenly.

'Yes,' I said steadily. 'That's right.'

They let it go at that.

In the darkness, we heard Everitt's voice calling.

He put the whole crew on watch for the state of the deck. The whisky bottles were thrown over the side. Somehow, Jack Walmsley managed to hide the pornographic pictures. A few hours later, the wind lifted, and Everitt gave orders for *Rechabite* to make full sail for the Humber.

Twenty

We started our search as soon as *Rechabite* was moored. Everitt wouldn't need us for the unloading. The last of the iced fish had been transferred to the cutter by Henry Purvis and John Pinney, Nathan Chapman complaining bitterly about feeling seasick for the first time in his years at sea. Edwin Wallis could easily handle getting the live fish out of the well and on to the market.

'You've got two days,' Everitt told us. 'Find somebody, Mr Walmsley. *Rechabite*'s never sailed for Iceland short-handed, and I don't expect to begin now.'

'Right you are, skipper.'

We left *Rechabite* in darkness.

'What you got to realise, Samuel,' Walmsley chatted amiably, 'is that our skipper is a determined man. You get him wrong, and you won't enjoy the voyage. Not a day, not an hour. You won't want to go fishing ever again. I learned that first time I berthed with *Rechabite*. His dad was a right bastard 'n' all.'

We were walking down the quays. The gas lamps were already burning and crowds of women were coming down to the pontoon, chattering and shrieking with laughter, waiting for the men to come off the smacks. Some of the women were knitting, black shawls draped around their shoulders, their leather boots clattering on the slimy cobbles. In the darkness, several of them shouted out to Walmsley, but he said we were in a hurry, no time for pleasure. They jeered and called names after us, their raw voices echoing along the quays.

'You know where you're going, Walmsley?' I asked.

'Penny gaffs.'

'You're joking.'

'Better than Brown's Yard.'

'I got business in Brown's Yard.'

He burst out laughing. 'I know you have, Samuel.'

'What the hell is the point of wasting time in the penny gaffs?'

Walmsley stopped under a gas lamp and lit his pipe.

'What are we after, Samuel?'

'Hands.'

'That's right, hands. In this case, boys. Everitt would take men with time at sea, but he isn't going to get 'em. He knows that. So he needs boys. Doesn't matter what size, doesn't matter what colour. He needs boys with two legs and two arms and a longing for a bit of adventure. We give 'em money, they get adventure. A life on the wild seas. They don't have to come from anywhere particular. They just have to come. And in a town like this, which is where our skipper happens to have landed us, the only place we are going to find boys is in Satan's Hole. Beerhouses, lodging houses, Kelly's Kitchen, on the market, in the stews. And the penny gaffs is one of the most certain places. The penny gaffs is where boys loves to entertain theirselves. So that's where we're looking.'

He blew a cloud of smoke in my face, winked, and set off again towards the bright lights of Satan's Hole.

I shrugged and followed him. Maybe he was right. We had to walk through the market to reach the penny gaff Walmsley had in mind. There were beggars sleeping in the alleys and cuts off the market. The music halls and beerhouses were already packed to the doors. Crowds of men drifted in the dark streets searching for women. The whole area was infested with nests of brothels. Outside the Victoria Music Hall, dozens of prostitutes waited in the gas-lit street, chatting together or parading up and down, waiting for the finish of the first performances when the men would pour out of the halls looking for entertainment.

In the market, flower-sellers stood in desultory groups in the dark. There were stalls selling oysters, cockles and whelks, dirty pictures and pornographic stories, sheet music. A man with a baked chestnut stove was doing good business. There were tumblers and a conjurer working near the gates, a fire-eater and a magician, clowns, a Punch and Judy stall, buskers playing drums and pipes, dancing girls doing half-hearted polkas in the noisy darkness. Huddled together in the shadows, children tried to get some sleep. Despite the heat, there was a thin fog blowing off the river, trailing around the gas lamps and shop flares. Voices cried through the fog, like sirens drifting out at the estuary.

'That's it,' Walmsley said, pointing towards the entrance to a narrow alley. A dull yellow light was shining through the fog. The penny gaff was at the bottom of the alley. A crowd of hawkers stood outside, selling obscene pictures and aniseed whisky. Loud music thumped from the dingy building. 'Used to be a butcher's shop,' Walmsley told me. 'Before the butcher went bankrupt. The new owners converted it into a theatre.' Coloured lamps shone outside the entrance, and girls of eight and nine tried to grab our hands as we approached, asking us if we wanted to come down the side alley for a bit of fun. Walmsley shoved them away savagely. He paid, and we went inside.

The theatre was packed, with people dancing in the aisles, couples sitting on each other's knees in the filthy seats. Young girls in showy dresses paraded up and down the aisles, feathers in their hair, bright lipstick and rouge making their small faces garish in the flaring lights. Some of the youngest girls were doing grotesque dances, the crowds cheering obscenely, drunken men shouting coarse suggestions. In the seats, lads of eight and nine sat smoking pipes, and the stench of shag tobacco mingled with the overpowering smell of sweat and stale makeup, alcohol and vomit. I could see couples clinging together in their seats, girls hoisting their long skirts and sitting across the men. Slumped by the stage, a sickly-looking woman was breast-feeding a child, saliva running down her chin, her eyes glazed with exhaustion and whisky.

'This is mad,' I managed to shout, making Walmsley hear.

He ignored me with a quick look of contempt.

The crowd were roaring the words of a popular song. On the stage, in front of the tattered scarlet curtain, a fourteen-year-old girl was leading the singing, holding up a card with the words printed in big letters. The final word of each verse was an obscenity, and as the word approached the girl grinned foully at the drunken audience, the crowd stamping their feet and roaring in delirium, lads jumping on girls' shoulders, tiny children cheering and howling with laughter.

I stood at the back of the theatre and watched Walmsley pushing his way through the aisles. He stopped every few seats and tried to talk to one of the boys. The lads kept shoving him out of the way and he laughed good-humouredly. As he argued and struggled through the narrow rows of seats, he kept taking a flask from his pocket and having a drink. In the garish lights, I could see the liquor running down his chin.

I felt light-headed with the heat and noise.

In the aisles, Walmsley stumbled and fell, and then clambered over the backs of several seats, throwing his fists at the heads of the shouting lads. A girl clawed at his neck, and I saw him give her a thump in the stomach. She screeched as she landed in the aisle, and then leapt up again, shouting at the men around her and pointing at Walmsley. He grinned as if the whole thing was a game. When he saw me, he waved and gave a pathetic shrug, buffooning with the angry crowd.

'Have a drink,' he shouted above the din when he finally reached the back of the theatre. He waved the flask in front of my face, and I smelt the brandy and laudanum. The laudanum must have been for the boys: to confuse them, make them easier to persuade; it didn't seem to have worked. I pushed the flask away and flinched as the music suddenly became louder, bright lights glaring through the curtains, gas flares bursting into brilliant colour at the sides of the stage. As the lights came up, I could see the strippers preparing to come on and perform. Walmsley leaned back against the wall, watching the girl who was still singing on stage.

'We're not going to find any lads here,' I told him.

He nodded gloomily, draining the flask and getting another from his pocket. He looked subdued, staring sullenly at the stage, unscrewing the cap of the second flask. He offered it to me again, and shrugged when I looked away. I was too impatient to bother speaking.

On the stage, the girl was finishing her song, and suddenly there were several more girls with her, flash-dancing as the tattered red curtain was pulled aside. The girls were all young. They lifted their skirts and showed legs and knickers as the crowd roared their approval. The women in the audience seemed to be as excited as the men. The girls on stage whirled and spun through their sordid routines, their breasts bulging out of the tops of their dresses, their knickers kicked off and twirled out into the crowd. At the end of the dance, their breasts slipped out of the loosened silks and feathers, and the crowd again erupted into a roaring mob, young lads trying to climb up on to the stage, men with wooden staves appearing from behind the curtains and beating them back. As the audience rioted in their delirium, I grabbed Walmsley's arm and started to drag him out of the back of the theatre.

He vomited into the gutter outside. As he retched and groaned, I heard people laughing and jeering. One of the women under the lamppost sidled over to us and asked me if I wanted any help. I told her to clear off.

'Laudanum,' Walmsley choked through his vomit.

'You put it in the flask.'

'I ent used to it, Samuel,' he managed to splutter.

'All right for the lads?'

'Fuck off, Samuel.'

He went on being sick for several minutes, and when he managed to stand up, he looked white in the light of the lamps. He leaned back against a wall, and shook his head like a dog running out of water.

'I could drink a whisky,' he said with a rueful grin.

'That's all you need.'

'Bastard.'

He shook his head again, and ran his thick fingers through his hair, wet through from sweat. My own head was pounding like a mallet on tin roofing. I felt fed up with Walmsley's stupid tricks.

'We're never going to find a lad like this,' I told him.

'No.'

'Wasting our time.'

'Yes.'

He touched my arm lightly and pointed towards the market.

'There's a café,' he said through gritted teeth.

'I'm not hungry.'

'Cup of tea. I need a cup of tea.'

I nearly felt sorry for him. He was a wreck, stumbling in the darkness as we walked back towards the market. The fog was thicker now, gloomy in the narrow streets and alleys, while out on the river, sirens wailed and moaned. The warning bell was ringing on the buoy in the estuary.

In the warmth of the café, we had a pot of strong tea.

'Six spoonfuls,' Walmsley told the woman who ran the place.

'You fishermen?'

'That's right.'

She frowned resignedly. She had blue lovebites all over her neck and her eyes were yellow and bruised with tiredness. 'That'll be extra,' she said impatiently, glancing at the clock above the door.

'I ent in poverty row,' Walmsley told her nastily, wincing
as the pain stabbed his forehead. 'Just bring the tea, woman.'

After two cups, he began to feel better. I smoked my pipe
and asked the woman for a brandy. As I drank it, it burned
my throat and made my eyes water. Walmsley was too sorry
for himself to laugh. He finished the tea and sat slumped at
the table.

'Fucking penny gaffs,' he said miserably.

'You took us there.'

'I allus go.'

'You must be hard up for a good time.'

'I have this need.'

He stopped, staring into his empty cup. His eyes were
bleary with the laudanum and alcohol. He seemed full of
self-pity. I eased my back against the wall and watched him:
I had never seen him like this.

'I don't know what you're talking about,' I said after a
moment.

He flinched. Maybe he'd forgotten I was there. He picked
his cup up and saw that it was empty, then shouted at the
woman for more tea. She filled the pot with fresh tea leaves
and hot water.

'I had a woman, ended up in the penny gaffs,' he said
bleakly.

'A woman?'

'We wasn't married.'

'No?' I said cautiously.

'She wouldn't get married.'

'Some women won't,' I said.

'No.'

'Nothing wrong with that.'

He shrugged. 'No.'

I thought he was going to stop talking. His eyes were
closed, and he was breathing heavily: tiredness and the laudanum.

Suddenly, he started speaking again.

'She was seeing this Polish feller. Off the schooners.

Working out of Rotterdam. I never knew him. I heard about it from friends. She was seeing him when I was off fishing. I worked the fleets a few years. You know that. She was giving it to this feller when I was on the trawling.'

I could hardly watch him. There were tears in his eyes, running down his rough cheeks. He didn't notice them. His big fingers were clamped round the empty cup and he was crouched forward, staring down into some raw misery. Behind the counter, the young woman was listening without much interest. There wasn't a sound in the café apart from the ticking clock. It was two o'clock in the morning.

'I told her we was done for,' he went on. 'I couldn't stand for that. She kept crying. She couldn't stop crying. I thought she was playing up. Didn't want me to hit her. I never hit women. I couldn't bear the sight of her. If she'd touched me, I'd have broken her neck. I just left. Nothing for me there.'

He was silent again, breathing heavily.

My pipe had gone out.

'They found her in an airing cupboard,' he said abruptly, as if he had to get the words out of his mouth. He paused, surprised by the sound of his own voice. 'It was a big cupboard,' he said ridiculously. 'For hanging clothes. Airing. You know.'

'Jack!' I tried to interrupt, but he wasn't listening.

'Because the cupboard was next to a fire, she was still warm. One of the neighbours opened the door. She let out a scream. She must have thought she was still alive. They told me all about it afterwards, when I got back. There was a flush in her cheeks, and her eyes were wide open. The rope had gouged a great wound round her neck. They said her blood was bright red against the skin. She had white skin. When they lifted her down, she urinated all over them.'

The woman behind the counter stared at us sullenly, resting her head back against the wall.

'Jack,' I said again, trying to bring him round.

He just shook his head, and stared blindly into the darkness.

I had to get him a place to sleep.

Then the door in the café opened. A woman came in, glancing quickly round. She had a green shawl over her head. She nodded at the woman behind the counter and came across to our table.

'You Samuel Vempley?'

I stared at her, surprised, worried about Walmsley.

'That's right,' I said.

She smiled quickly. 'You were looking for Ann Babb?'

'What?'

'I saw you in the penny gaff. One of the girls recognised you. I told Charlotte and she said you was to come. The girls has finished working.' She smiled apologetically, as if I would understand. 'Ann's waiting for you. She just got back. Yesterday afternoon.'

I stood up, then glanced at Walmsley.

'What about him?' I asked.

The woman behind the counter folded her arms. 'I got a room behind the counter,' she said.

'A bed?'

'Two shillings for the night.'

'I'll give you a lift.'

We hauled Walmsley behind the counter and left him snoring noisily on a rough bed. I paid the woman the money in advance.

'I'll be back before he wakes up,' I said.

'No need.'

'You don't know him.'

'I've got a dog,' the woman said bleakly. 'You don't work down this dump without a dog. He tries anything, my dog will have him.'

Quickly, I followed the other girl out of the café.

In the thick fog, we made our way to Brown's Yard.

Twenty-one

It was quiet in Brown's Yard. Fog shrouded the dismal buildings, and the cobbles were wet with mist and running water. A light burned in a window in Sunshine Row, but there was no sound. In the yard, the girl tapped lightly on the door, and when the bolt shot back, pushed it open. She slipped inside, and as I followed, disappeared through the kitchen into a dark hall.

Charlotte Grange was sitting morosely at the long table, her solid arms folded in front of her, a bottle of corn brandy standing to her side. She had drunk half the bottle. When I closed the door and sat down, she glanced up at me angrily, as if I had interrupted her thoughts. A low fire was burning in the range.

'You again?'

'I'm sorry. The hour . . .'

'What?'

'It's not yet morning.'

She stared at me blankly, as if I was deranged. 'Sit down,' she said brusquely.

We were silent for some minutes. She went on drinking, not offering me a glass. The fire flared briefly and glowed in the dimly lit room.

'I been on the land,' Charlotte said abruptly.

'Oh?'

'I worked in the curing houses and the filleting sheds. I hated land gangs. Giving it away, half the women.'

'Charlotte . . .'

She glared at me passionately, her eyes wet with tears, the lines around her mouth tight with fury. She wasn't seeing me at all. Her eyes were hazy with tiredness.

'I used to be good-looking,' she said quietly, 'before I lost my daughter. You didn't know us then. She was eleven. Lovely little girl. Died in the typhoid, when we was in Stepney. You can keep London. I wouldn't go back, never. I tramped all the way up here, same as Ann Babb, only it were further. I tramped for three months, doing the land gangs, sleeping rough. I couldn't think of nothing but my little girl. She was screaming when she died. I only wanted for her to go peaceful. She was crying for me. And I was there. I was always there. She didn't know me. There's nobody left cares.'

The door from the hallway suddenly swung open.

Charlotte didn't move.

'Mr Vempley?'

The girl stood in the doorway. She was plump and had short curly hair, very dark. Her eyes were swollen with lack of sleep but she was pretty and nervous. She looked no more than eighteen.

I pushed my chair back to stand up but Charlotte grabbed my hand. Her fist was like a claw.

'You mind her,' she hissed at me across the table.

'It's all right, Charlotte,' the girl said, but the old woman shook her head vigorously, clearing the drink from her mind.

'No,' she said roughly. 'It isn't. You mind her, hear?'

'I will,' I promised.

She held my eyes for a long look, and then released my hand. Taking the bottle, she left the kitchen. The girl shrugged with a weak smile, and then went to the sink where she filled a kettle.

'I need some tea,' she said briefly.

'That would be good.'

My heart was racing. I stood up and stretched my arms, trying to control my shaking hands. I could feel the colour draining out of my face, as if I was about to faint. It was tiredness, and not knowing what I was going to learn. I walked to the door and almost walked out of the kitchen. Maybe it would be better not to know. I turned and smiled. The girl was watching me, leaning against the sink, waiting for the kettle to boil. I sat down again, at the far end of the table. When the kettle boiled, she made some tea and put the pot on the table to brew. She got cups and milk from a cupboard.

'I lived on milk once,' she said quietly, sitting down and pouring milk from the jug into the cups. 'I used to drink milk when I was tramping from Yarmouth.'

'Yarmouth?' I said vaguely. I tried not to sound startled. It seemed wrong, not to know anything about her if she had written to me about Miriam. 'I didn't know you were from Yarmouth.'

'I grew up there. I came to find my brother. I had no money.'

'No.'

'I had to walk, same as Charlotte. She was telling you.'

'How'd you get milk if you didn't have money?' I asked, trying to keep her talking.

'From the cows.'

'What?'

'Tastes all right.'

'You mean from the udders?'

'In the fields. Before milking. It's just hunger,' she said vaguely. 'I was hungry.'

She poured the tea and went to a cupboard where she found cheese and a fresh loaf. She cut a chunk of bread and chewed at the crust without butter. She left the cheese uncut. She chewed with her mouth open. She had perfect white teeth and a thin mouth. She ate as if she was alone in the kitchen.

'I had to find my brother,' she said.

'Yes.'

'He signed on the trawlers.'

'In Grimsby?'

'He was thirteen. He used to work on the market in Yarmouth but we needed money. He tramped all the way here and signed up with Gothard's trawlers. I had to find him.'

She was crying, but when I made a move to get up she reached out her hand as if she was pushing me back, blind with her tears and distress, still chewing the crusty bread. She swallowed hard, and wiped the tears from her eyes. She didn't seem embarrassed. She let the tears come, and went on eating, pouring two cups of tea and pushing one across to me. I took the cup eagerly and drank the hot tea for something to do. I had to keep control of myself. I had to let her talk in her own way.

There was a shout outside in the yard. I saw the girl jump. Her face twitched. Silence washed back across the kitchen.

'They come looking for the boys,' she said in the same abstracted voice. 'Gothard's men. Early in the morning. Thieves Row, the local fishermen call it. They often hide there, boys running away, try and buy some clothes and get out of town with a carrier. If they get caught, it's two months on the treadmill. They hardly ever get away.'

'No,' I muttered.

'My brother must have come like that,' the girl said. 'Tramping into town, and then not able to get away. Frightened and hiding. Asking strangers for help. I thought if I waited, I might eventually see him. He had to come back, if he signed on a smack from this port. Even the fleets don't stay out forever.'

I was too upset to speak. I knew what she was going to say.

After a long silence, she shrugged and smiled at me through her tears. 'You want some more tea?' she asked, and then went on immediately about her brother, telling me she had been in Hull where they had found trace of him. He had been on one of Gothard's trawlers. The trawler had got caught in fog, and the boy slipped over the side, drowning on a night watch without anybody on deck to help him. The skipper only registered the death because he knew Philip Babb had a sister working in Grimsby.

She took a deep breath.

'I'm sorry,' I managed to say.

'I had some friends in Hull,' she told me. 'They looked after me. Yesterday morning, at first light, we all walked down to the harbour. The light on the water was lovely, delicate, sort of opal flecked with pink, shining on the wide river. There were lots of gulls wheeling and crying after food, circling the silent harbour. We threw dried seaweed on to the water. The sky made the water blue, and the seaweed darkened and sank, drifting away from the quays. A herring gull swooped right down, I suppose it thought we were throwing food, lifting away with a strand of seaweed, dropping it and screaming back towards the pontoons. The tide was turning. They left me standing on the quays. I needed to be alone for a few minutes. I had to think what to tell my parents. I could hear a child crying in my mind, but it wasn't Philip. He was thirteen. I didn't hear him crying.'

I did get up now. I brewed some fresh tea and touched her lightly on the shoulder. As she cried, I knelt down beside her and put my arms round her for comfort. She leaned against my shoulder, weeping into my neck. I could feel her warm body, her breathing desperate and unhappy. I made her drink the fresh tea with a drop of brandy from the cupboard. It took her several minutes to calm down, and then she blew her nose and smiled, her eyes shining brightly, her face white with tiredness.

'You didn't want to hear this,' she said.

'Don't be daft.'

'I'm sorry.'

'Ann!'

'You got my letter,' she said seriously.

I took the letter from my pocket and showed it to her.

'I had to write,' she said.

'Yes.'

She drank another cup of tea and watched me with a concerned frown, as if she was trying to decide what to tell me.

'Miriam spoke about you,' she said, putting her cup down.

'Did she?'

'When she was here.'

'I didn't know about you,' I admitted.

She laughed. 'We worked on the farlins,' she explained. 'I knew her from a child. We both grew up in Yarmouth.'

'Yes.'

'She talked about you one night. Sitting here.'

I could hardly speak. I knew my voice would let me down.

Ann sighed and stared round the kitchen. She looked confused, miserable.

'You're a kind man,' she said abruptly.

'Kind?'

'You've been kind to me. Miriam loved you.'

'I know,' I said hoarsely.

'She only ever loved you.'

'Yes.'

'But I think she couldn't tell you.'

She watched me, waiting to see how I would react. I took a deep breath. I laid my hands on the table. The knuckles were white and my nails had dug into the flesh of my hands.

'You have to tell me, Ann.'

'Yes.'

'Please?'

'I know.'

She gathered herself and smiled.

'She needed help, Samuel. She came to me because she thought I might know somebody. It had to be out of Yarmouth, you see.'

'What kind of help?'

'She was pregnant.'

There was a long silence. I couldn't believe that.

'A baby?'

'Yes.'

'She couldn't be.'

'She was pregnant, Samuel.'

'We used something.'

'It didn't work.'

I started to tremble, and had to clench my hands together. I stood up and then sat down quickly.

'Why didn't she tell me?'

Ann shrugged briefly, shaking her head. 'She said you were upset about a friend dying. She said she didn't want to concern you.'

'A baby?'

'She loved you, Samuel.'

'But where is she? Why did she come to you?'

I was lost. I heard the sirens on the river and a voice crying in one of the tenements. An owl flew low over the crowded building, hunting the alleys and yards. There were mice and rats everywhere in Satan's Hole.

I felt cold as I stared at Ann.

'Where is she?' I asked again quietly.

'She wanted me to help her.'

'What kind of help?'

I knew what she was going to say. The words stunned me.

'She couldn't have the child.'

'No!'

I stood up, refusing to listen.

'Samuel!'

'No!'

'She couldn't face it.'

I wanted to get out of the kitchen. I wanted to get away.

'I don't believe you.'

'She wanted me to find somebody . . .'

'I don't believe you.'

I opened the kitchen door and stumbled out into the yard.

The fog was thick now, swirling in the narrow yard. The morning heat was already heavy in the airless tenements. I started to walk down the alley and then turned round and went back to the kitchen. Ann was still sitting at the table, waiting for me. She was crying again, staring down at her hands.

'Ann?' I pleaded with her.

She looked up, desperate with unhappiness, weeping as she looked away.

'Tell me.'

'Sit down.'

'Tell me.'

'Yes, sit down.'

I sat down and she dried her eyes.

'She asked me to find somebody,' she said. 'There's a woman we know in Whitby. Just outside Whitby. Boggle Hole. It's not far from Robin Hood's Bay. Charlotte uses her when it's necessary. She's a wise woman, she knows what she's doing.'

'She went to Whitby?'

'She knew somebody on a drifter. The skipper took her there.'

This all sounded incredible. Miriam had never mentioned Whitby in her life. I couldn't imagine why she would go there: I couldn't imagine a wise woman holding her in her hands. I didn't know what a wise woman was. Just the old women in dirty hovels, crowded down dismal back streets. The kind of women girls went to when they were in trouble. I couldn't think of Miriam as being in that kind of trouble. We had done things to stop it. We had known what we were about.

'But where is she now?' I demanded. 'This is mad. This isn't true. Where has she gone?'

There was another long silence.

I could hear the words inside my head.

Ann got up and fetched a letter from the cupboard. She unfolded it and handed it to me. I left it lying on the table.

The handwriting was large and scrawled across the page. It was from an address in Whitby:

We got some bad news for you, Ann. Your friend didn't do well. She saw the wise woman but the infection set in. You heard the rumours. There was a lot of folk talking, but it got calmed down. Your friend didn't get well. She died of the fever. There was nothing to be done. We are sorry for the news, Ann. She has been buried in Whitby graveyard. We hope you can tell the man.

The letter was dated the end of May 1876, a month after Miriam had left Yarmouth.

I stared at the words without moving. It didn't mean anything to me. I didn't know what they meant about infection. She must have caught something on the journey, the crowded tenements in Satan's Hole. I didn't even know how long she had been in Satan's Hole. I kept reading the words, and gradually my eyes settled on Whitby graveyard. The graveyard overlooking the sea. The sea was a cold graveyard. In Whitby, the cliffs towered into the sky and the ruined abbey stood gloomy guard above the waves. In Whitby harbour, I had eaten lobsters in a café, celebrating with Joseph Proctor a fine catch. We had drunk beer, and sang some songs.

I was too shocked to cry.

'It is true?' I asked Ann hopelessly.

She hardly bothered to answer.

'Yes,' she said quietly with a brief nod.

'It is true.'

'Yes.'

We sat for a long time. The town was waking. Cocks crowed in the yards. A church bell chimed the hours. We sat without speaking. There was nothing to say. I folded the letter and asked if I could keep it.

'Yes,' she smiled. 'Of course.'

'Thank you.'

'It's yours really. It should have been written to you.'

I had to get away. I stood up and then sat down again. My legs wouldn't hold me. I was like a boy taking his first trip to sea. The ground rolled underneath me.

Ann seemed to be lost in her own thoughts.

'He had the same hair as me,' she said very quietly, talking abstractedly to herself, warming her hands round the teapot.

'Your brother?'

'Yes,' she nodded. 'My brother. Dark curly hair, lots of it. He was a devil when he was little. Into everything. We had a back yard that hadn't got a proper gate, it was broken, and he would keep getting out there and round the lavatories. He used to crawl out of the kitchen when my mother wasn't looking and make straight for the back gate. My dad found him once, crawling round the midden, trying to reach a dandelion that was growing through the cracks. He got hold of it and he wouldn't let go. My dad said he liked the colour. He got a good hiding all the same. He was never out of trouble.'

I let myself out of the kitchen.

I stumbled into the light.

'Look where you're going, pal,' a man complained as I shouldered into him. He was leaving one of the houses in Sunshine Row. He had a sack over his shoulder and I could see blood seeping through the sacking. The sack stank of dead rabbits. He disappeared down the alley, and I followed him into the waking town.

Twenty-two

You can't think in a glass world: I was treading on glass, I was breaking glass with my nightmares. My mind was a shadow of whirls. Deeper currents than I knew swept me into dawn's delirium. I stood on street corners. I wept for the morning lamplighter. As the fog lifted, I slipped into the thickest fog of all: grief's savage hours.

When I got back to *Rechabite*, Everitt was too pleased with himself to be annoyed. He was parading up and down the deck, chatting with Edwin Wallis. 'Mr Vempley,' he called. 'Come aboard and tell us your news. How did you fare?'

'Fare, skipper?'

I had no thought for what he was talking about.

He laughed brightly, glancing at Edwin.

'The boys, Mr Vempley, the boys.'

I was too distraught to listen really. I nodded and stood by the bulwarks. The smack was lifting up and down. I felt the agonised lift of my memories, swirling in my mind like the night's fog. Out at the estuary, the warning bell on the buoy was still ringing, and the sun was obscured by a fine, thin mist. On a day like this, the heat could be awful.

'No luck then, Mr Vempley?' Everitt persisted.

'No, skipper.'

'You looked everywhere you could think of?'

'Yes.' I nodded.

'But not where I looked,' Everitt gloated. He clapped Edwin on the back and let out a laugh. 'Didn't I tell you, Edwin, Jack Walmsley would let us down.'

I remembered Walmsley sleeping at the café.

'I promised to fetch him,' I said, and then stopped, confused.

Both men watched me with amusement, waiting for me to explain. John Pinney came up on deck and leaned against the mizzen, listening to our conversation.

'I left him sleeping in a café,' I said. 'He was exhausted. He fell ill.'

'He fell drunk, you mean,' Everitt laughed.

'No . . .'

'Never mind that. I found us a lad, Mr Vempley. What do you think of that? An afternoon's searching, and I found an ideal boy. Just what we need. Six weeks at sea, just off the treadmill for mouthing his skipper. He won't mouth me. I don't allow mouthers. A fine tough lad. We could use another, but Matthew Whalley will have to do us.'

I said I was glad, not really interested. I made to go to the companion but Everitt stopped me.

'No, you can't desert the task now, Mr Vempley, when it's half finished. You must come with me to the custom house. You must witness the signing of the indentures.'

'Walmsley will be back soon.'

'I'm not concerned about Mr Walmsley. He let me down. He should be here now. I'm asking you, Mr Vempley. Seeing as how you've been such a help in our searches. You will come with me to the custom house. They are expecting us right now. The lad will be waiting.'

I went below and had a cup of strong tea, and then joined Everitt on the quays. He walked briskly on land; gone was the stiff restlessness that I was used to from seeing him on *Rechabite*. I walked at his side, and answered his questions about the places where we had looked. When I mentioned the penny gaffs, he nodded with a grimace.

'He's still obsessed with that?' he asked casually.

'Penny gaffs?'

'He told you about his woman?'

'Yes, he mentioned her.'

'Hanging herself?'

'Yes.'

'Death by one's own hand is a sure sign of damnation, Mr Vempley.'

'I wouldn't know.'

'A certain sign of God's displeasure. We do not own our own lives, Mr Vempley. Surely you recognise that?'

'I suppose.'

'They are held in trust. We are on a journey. The soul is ours to nurture. The body is a gift from God. We are not to dispose of what does not belong to us anyway. We are God's property.'

'I think Walmsley was sickening for something,' I said in his defence. God knows why I was defending him. 'I think he was ill.'

'Drunk.'

'He was sick in the street.'

'Drunk!' Everitt laughed humourlessly. 'Laudanum too, I shouldn't wonder.'

'I don't know,' I said reluctantly.

'I know my men, Mr Vempley. Jack Walmsley is a good third hand. He knows the fishing and he knows my smack, but he doesn't know himself.'

'He was sick, skipper,' I said, fed up with Everitt's sermonising.

He didn't stop. 'Give me a man who knows himself,' he said, 'and he can achieve anything. Walmsley will never get further than third hand. You, on the other hand, could be your own skipper.'

I laughed and he glanced at me angrily, not liking the derision.

'You laugh?'

'I don't think any man ever knew less about himself than I do,' I said bitterly.

He seemed interested. 'Why do you say that?'

'Things that have happened to me.'

'Ahh.' He nodded, not understanding, waiting for me to continue.

'Things that have happened to people I've known,' I said.

He dismissed my words with irritation. 'We are all responsible for our own actions.'

'You can't damage other people?'

'Not if they are free. Not if they are doing God's will.'

'I've hurt people,' I said.

I felt a panic, rushing into the words. I didn't know or trust this man, and certainly didn't want to be talking to him about Miriam: he wouldn't have begun to understand Miriam. But he seemed to have mesmerised me. I was tired, too stunned to think what I was saying.

'I didn't give them freedom,' I said.

He kept quiet for a moment after that. We had walked the length of the pontoons and gone round the main gates to the commercial docks. The dock tower and dock buildings were all gathered at the top of the commercial docks where the schooners and carriers unloaded and collected their cargoes. As we reached the steps leading to the custom house, Everitt stopped and turned to look at me. I thought I could see concern in his eyes. I must be going mad.

'I don't believe things simply *happen*, Samuel,' he said quietly. 'I believe we are responsible for our own lives. I have had to be responsible for my own life. I have had to fight the hidden demons.'

'Demons?' I laughed.

He ignored my laughter. 'We all have them,' he said. 'Women and drink for Jack Walmsley. Piousness for Edwin Wallis. Only fools go to damnation for women and drink. Being pious is the hard one to handle. Imagining you are doing God's will. Imagining you are saved by kindness. Kindness is a delusion, Samuel. You are kind. That is your demon. You will be blighted by kindness. You will refuse to judge. You cannot forgive the world's cruelty. But forgiving is God's business. You imagine doing good is the answer.'

'You seem to me to be talking nonsense,' I said steadily.

'Naturally. It is much easier, being kind. It makes you feel good. You see immediate rewards. Men like you, admire you. The boys turn to you for help. It must all be comforting in a dark world.'

'So?'

'It isn't always for their own good. My father taught me that.'

'I see.'

'He made me sleep naked on the deck.'

'For Christ's sake.'

'Yes indeed, though you meant it profanely: for Christ's sake. He punished me when I couldn't control my desires. He taught me to know God. He taught me to know myself. I have demons, Samuel. I have desires. The temptation to pity weakness. It does no good in the end. It leads to disaster. At sea you can witness that truth daily. Letting a boy learn to become slack can lead to the loss of the vessel, then a dozen men die instead of one. Giving sin a berth among your crew can send the lot of them straight to damnation. It is a practical and sound teaching.'

'It is cruel.'

'Life is cruel, Samuel. My father flogged me in front of the rest of the crew just to show them there would be no favouritism. We were all expected to do our best. That is God's way. He punishes the wicked. A skipper on a smack can take no better master. I know you suspect my motives. I know you show kindness to the boys on *Rechabite*. Don't mistake your own kindness for truth, Samuel. I am taking *Rechabite* to Iceland. In those waters, kindness can end up among the ice floes, trapped for a winter of starvation. My boys won't thank you if they have to eat each other's flesh to survive.'

He turned and led the way down the steps to the custom house.

If I had not been weak with exhaustion and misery, I

would have left him and never rejoined *Rechabite*. I would have broken my agreement. A fisherman did not do that lightly. Word soon travelled around and skippers were reluctant to give berth to a man known as a deserter. I followed Everitt to the custom house because I was too tired to argue. It would have been madness to have done otherwise.

We went inside the custom house and down a dismal corridor. Our boots echoed between the green arsenic walls. At the end of the corridor, Everitt opened a door into a dingy office. The clerk behind the desk glanced up irritably. He had long, greasy hair hanging over his coat collar and squinted at us through cheap spectacles.

'Skipper Everitt,' he beamed when he recognised Everitt.

They shook hands briefly. A boy was sitting on a chair opposite the desk, his back to the wall. I glanced at him briefly. He was a wiry, dark-haired lad, with a white scar round his neck. He looked straight back at me, chewing a lump of tobacco. When the skipper frowned at him, he spat the tobacco on to the floor and then kicked it under his chair.

'You have the papers?' Everitt asked.

'All prepared, skipper.'

The clerk pushed the indentures forward and Everitt signed quickly. The lad got out of his chair without asking and lounged to the table. The clerk was supposed to read the indentures out to the lad, but he didn't bother.

'Last indentures cancelled?' Everitt asked casually.

'That's right, skipper.'

'Can't behave?' he asked the lad directly.

The boy smirked. 'So they reckon.'

'You'll learn. Are you going to sign?'

The boy put his cross on the paper. Very few of them could write. He pushed the pen in his pocket and laughed when the clerk held out his hand. He slouched back to his chair.

When the papers were signed, the skipper gave the clerk two shillings, and they shook hands. The clerk was a pensioner from the customs, well known in the town. He spent his life preparing indentures. The collector of customs had no control over him, and let him use the office as a favour. He was in truth employed by the owners, and paid a fixed fee for every lad he handled. It was easy to see how the grand, imposing building would affect some boys. They must have been terrified.

Everitt turned and looked at the boy.

'This is Matthew Whalley, Samuel,' he said in a quiet, hard voice.

I nodded briefly at the lad.

'I see you have a scar?' Everitt said conversationally.

'You got good eyes, skipper.'

Everitt ignored the sarcasm. 'From a rope?' he asked ironically.

'I ent been hung yet, skipper.' The boy grinned.

'You will be, I have no doubt.' Everitt smiled icily.

'You ent a hanging skipper, are you?' the boy asked promptly, refusing to be cowed. I had no fears for Matthew Whalley. He was a vicious, tough twelve-year-old. He must have grown up in Satan's Hole: survive that and they could survive most things. I couldn't imagine even Jack Walmsley getting the better of this lad.

We made our way back to *Rechabite* and Walmsley was already on the deck, making a great fuss of getting the decks cleaned down. He was full of himself. When he saw us he leapt into action, greeting the new boy and congratulating the skipper on his success. Everitt ignored him. He was in too good a mood to take it out on Walmsley for last night. He gave a few brisk orders, and then went down to his cabin. We needed another forty wash of whelks before sailing, two hundred gallons of prime bait for the trip to Iceland.

'You all right?' I asked Walmsley when the skipper had gone.

'Why shouldn't I be?'

'You seemed pretty sick last night.'

'Can't stand alcohol,' Walmsley said solemnly. 'Shouldn't touch the stuff. Never learn.'

'I thought it was the laudanum,' I said sarcastically.

'Laudanum! What you talking about? You'll ruin my reputation, talking like that.'

'You obviously slept all right.'

He burst out in crude laughter. 'I slept with that girl,' he said. 'You know, behind the counter. She had a bed all right. Miserable fucking cow. They'll sleep with anybody, some women.'

I went below before he could start giving details.

In the galley, Francis Campbell was busy showing the new lad where things were kept. I brewed a pot of tea and then lay down on my bunk. In the stench of the quarters, I read through the two letters: the one from Ann Babb that had brought me to Satan's Hole; the one from her friend in Whitby telling me that Miriam had died.

I must have slept from simple grief.

When I woke, *Rechabite* was already in motion.

Twenty-three

For a moment, I wasn't sure where I was. The roll of the smack took me back to *Wings of Morning*, and I imagined I heard Joseph Proctor shouting for more wind in the sails, tossing coins over the side for a catch. Then I recognised John Pinney's voice in the galley, and climbed reluctantly out of the bunk, dragging my seaboots on to my feet. Henry Purvis was sleeping in the other bunk, and Jack Walmsley's voice rang out on deck. I went through to the galley and got myself a cup of tea. Matthew Whalley was already busy scrubbing potatoes.

On deck, I went straight up to Everitt.

'Can I talk, skipper?'

He glanced at me in surprise, concentrating on the burgee on the mainmast, making sure *Rechabite* didn't head the wind. The wind was rough, north-easterly, and we were cracking on under full sail. The estuary was already out of sight.

'What is it, Mr Vempley?'

'I need to visit Whitby.'

He burst out laughing. 'What?'

'I have business in Whitby.'

'Do you indeed?'

'A friend died,' I blurted out. 'I need to sort things out.'

I thought Everitt was going to order me below. He took

his hand off the tiller and touched his forehead, then glanced back impatiently at the burgee: it was fluttering loosely, and he made a grunting noise deep at the back of his throat. *Rechabite* lurched to port but he seized the tiller and put her right. We cracked on, the wind booming in the heavy canvas.

'You signed for a trip to Iceland, Mr Vempley,' Everitt said angrily.

'I know that.'

'Whitby wasn't included on the trip. We're looking for another catch for the well and then we shall call at Wick. That is our last stop before Orkney, Mr Vempley, as you know very well.'

I held my breath.

I knew I was being ridiculous. *Rechabite* couldn't afford to call at Whitby with an empty hold and nothing in the well. Only a man dying would bring a skipper to that decision. Even Joseph Proctor would have laughed at the suggestion. I nodded numbly. I felt my head aching with pain.

'I'm sorry about your friend,' Everitt said suddenly.

He did not look at me directly.

'It doesn't matter.'

'There will be time to mourn your dead, Samuel,' he said quietly. 'Now get to your duties. This is a fishing smack, not a pleasure voyage.'

I worked numbly for the next couple of days. Men talked to me and I didn't hear. Edwin Wallis asked me what was my bad news, and when I shook my head, he looked puzzled and put his hand lightly on my shoulder, then went away. I spent a lot of time sleeping. John Pinney kept bringing me cups of tea, and I worked at baiting the lines with Edwin Wallis and Richard Buss. We had a fresh load of whelks in the well, enough for the long trip, and everybody seemed excited at the prospect. In the great heat, *Rechabite* ploughed through the heavy seas.

When we reached the grounds, Everitt ordered the laying of the lines. Working from the stern, I helped uncoil the snoods. There was hardly any wind. I had never seen such strange weather. There was a sort of dullness in the sea, and in the sky, with a lot of big swells. The clouds were erratic purple against the dullness of the sky, drifting slowly towards the coast. There was a terrific amount of green water, rolling on towards the edge of the grounds. We were on the northern edge of the Dogger.

'This is peculiar,' Edwin muttered as we uncoiled the lines. 'I never witnessed anything like it.'

'Just heavy seas,' John Pinney suggested.

Edwin Wallis scoffed, but looked worried. 'That's what you dread, John,' he said quietly. 'Rough ground with a lot of water, it makes the surf dreadful.'

'But there isn't any wind,' John pointed out, surprised.

'That's what's so strange,' I said. They glanced at me. It was the first time I had spoken for hours. 'No wind and heavy swells,' I added. 'That's what you don't look for.'

Everitt was pacing up and down the deck. *Rechabite* wouldn't respond even to a full rig of sail. We had the lines down but they were trailing loosely behind us. We were hardly moving, drifting sluggishly with the tide. I could see the worried frown on Everitt's face. He kept rubbing his nose with the back of his hand and glancing up at the sky.

It was like that for four days. We had dawns of unnatural, bloody red, nights weirdly silent. The wind dropped steadily. The sky was like a bruise gone bad, livid and copper-coloured. The water was muddied, yellow. The life seemed to drain out of the air, and we were exhausted by the sullen heat.

The storm broke just after midnight on the fourth day. I was on watch. Everitt was standing rigidly, the tiller lifeless in his hands, useless. Great banks of cloud were rolling towards us from the horizon. We could see sheets of lightning ripping through the sky.

'It's coming,' Everitt suddenly shouted, pointing to the east.

The sea rose in seconds and the sky turned black. There was a tremendous crash of thunder, tearing the sky apart, booming over our masts. Squalls of rain hit us like a thunderbolt.

'All hands,' Everitt yelled.

The first wind that hit us nearly knocked *Rechabite* to her port bulwarks. I saw Everitt lurch to the starboard bulwarks and then stagger back. He grabbed the tiller and hung on like he was afraid of seeing devils.

'Two reefs in the mainsail,' he started yelling.

Jack Walmsley and Nathan Chapman raced to the sheets. The wind lifted again and hit us like a hammer. *Rechabite* took water over the port bulwarks. The deck was awash. I hung on to the mainsail sheets with Jack Walmsley while Nathan tried to secure the reefs. As he worked, the sail boomed and cracked. A huge wave landed in the mainsail and I saw Nathan clinging on, his mouth wide open as he gasped for air.

'Reef the mizzen,' Everitt yelled.

We were making five knots on a starboard tack. We were in turbulent water, the sea rising all around us and *Rechabite* racing into the roughest ground at the edge of the Dogger.

Everitt clung to the tiller and Edwin Wallis stood beside him, ready to help if he was needed. The tiller was swinging wildly, lunging and heaving as the huge seas swelled and boiled underneath us and travelled in a storm of white water towards the coast. The howling wind seemed to be rising all the time.

'Another reef on mainsail and mizzen,' Everitt shouted. 'Fasten everything down below.'

I saw Francis Campbell going down the companion to help the new lad. Richard Buss followed him. The rest of us were on deck. At the tiller, Everitt was securing a rope round his waist. The wind dropped sickeningly and we plunged into a lull. The sky was fractured by lightning. The waves looked like walls of brown mud, threshing all around *Rechabite*. She rode the lull like a drunk, swinging from side to side.

Then the wind hit us again, shrieking out of the black skies.

A foaming, roaring waste of water fell out of the sky and knocked *Rechabite* to starboard. John Pinney was knocked off his feet and carried straight to the starboard bulwarks. I saw Jack Walmsley dive for his feet. He had hold of John before he reached the bulwarks. Together, they clung to the bulwarks, scrambling back to the mainmast as *Rechabite* righted.

'Take another reef in and reeve the fourth down,' Everitt was yelling. 'Settle the main a bit, Jack, and slack the gaff halyards. Sing out when you're ready and I'll shove her up into the wind.'

As Walmsley leapt to the gaff halyards, Edwin Wallis and Nathan ran to reef the mainsail. I grabbed the lifelines from the hatch at the top of the companion and started securing them down the length of the smack. We were going to need something to hang on to if this weather continued. Richard Buss saw what I was doing and started unravelling the other set of lifelines on the starboard side. At the tiller, Everitt waited for Walmsley's shout.

When the third hand yelled, Everitt put the tiller hard to lee and *Rechabite* lurched up into the wind, her canvas shaking and banging and the wind lashing and gusting in a hailstorm across the deck. Enormous waves thundered towards the tiny smack. There was water pouring down my face, and I hung on to the rope, staring into the black sea, tasting the salt in my mouth. I knew this was going to be the end of us.

'Set the storm jib and reef the staysail,' Everitt was shouting. 'Lee the bowsprit in about four feet before you pull the storm jib out, Edwin.'

Edwin lurched to the bows with two of the lads.

I was thrown violently against the mainmast and felt the blood running down my face, mingling with the salt in my mouth.

'Strike the topmast,' Everitt yelled as another huge wave crashed across our decks. 'It's still coming, Edwin. Batten the hatches and secure the companion.'

'Right you are, skipper.'

Everybody was working at the sails, trying to reef the smack down without taking her to bare masts. We had to have something to keep control, unless the direction of the wind settled and we could ride the seas until the storm blew itself out. With the gales pounding us into the roughest water, Everitt had to keep some canvas on the masts to right the vessel when she was buffeted.

At last, he seemed to get the balance right. *Rechabite* settled into the weather. The wind howled in our ears. The smack was reefed down.

Everitt was struggling to keep his feet. In a brief lull, he shouted for a relieving tackle to be rigged between the weather bulwarks and the tiller. It was the first time I had seen him do so. He already had a rope secured round his waist to the mizzen. With Edwin's help, he got the tackle fixed and then went on with his relentless fight with the immense tiller. In the storm, the carved tiller was like a thing come alive.

I clung to the main lifeline and waited for the weather to change.

There were lulls when it was steadier and we thought the worst might be over, but then enormous, thundering seas lifted the sky out of our eyes, and we were plunging back down into drenching darkness. When the squalls came, sea after sea filled the decks to the rails, and we were hanging on to the lifeline for dear life. Then another lull would becalm us, and *Rechabite* would seem to become still, floating lifeless on the dead water, drifting in terrifying silence. The sky would brighten for a few seconds. We all prayed the storm was over.

In the middle of one of these lulls, 'Tea up,' Matthew Whalley shouted. I thought I was going to choke, I was laughing so much. He clambered up through the companion and slammed the hatch behind him with his foot. As he carried the steaming mugs, he lurched drunkenly into the mizzen and cursed the weather.

'Can't you keep her steady, skipper,' he shouted at Everitt.

Several of the men burst out laughing, but Everitt glared at him as if he was insane. We took what was left of the tea, and tried to drink it. It tasted of salt and sugar. In a sudden swell of water, I spilled most of mine down my waterproof. Another squall was shivering out of the sky towards us and Matthew disappeared down the companion.

When the last huge wave hit us the sky had gone pitch black, and Nathan Chapman was trying to get the storm lanterns into position on the masts. The lifelines were all safely secured between the masts now, and men lurched backwards and forwards on the tilting deck, trying to do their jobs, yelling at each other and laughing. There was always a kind of excitement in a storm. The wind hit us out of nowhere. The rain poured down like water out of a bucket. At the tiller, Everitt raised a fist and glared into the pouring darkness, his teeth gritted, his black waterproofs running with seawater as if he was already drowned. The savage wind howled and shrieked in the rigging as if it was alive and determined to wreck *Rechabite*. Wave after enormous wave thundered out of the horizon towards us. Then another hammer of wind knocked us to starboard and the waves came out of nowhere, crashing into *Rechabite*'s stern and flooding the stern deck round the mizzen. As *Rechabite* tried to right herself, we heard a loud crack, and the gaff on the mizzen splintered. The mizzen sail was shredded to rags.

'Hang on to your lifelines,' Everitt shrieked in the booming gale.

In the darkness I thought we were done for. *Rechabite* rolled like a demented animal. Three huge waves hit us one after another, torrents of water, mountains of spray and green sea. We were in the heart of a boiling cauldron. She could have gone over with another wave. There was nothing Everitt could do. With the shredding of the mizzen, and the mainsail reefed down to the fourth reef, we might as well have been riding our masts. There was a great tearing noise, and another crack as the mizzen gaff came apart, and then suddenly complete silence.

Nobody moved.

Francis Campbell was crying.

Edwin was muttering his prayers.

We might have hit another lull. The seas were still racing past us. *Rechabite* was as good as becalmed. She went on rolling, but the rolling was steadily coming under control. The skies overhead lightened.

'She's past,' I muttered, struggling to catch my breath.

'Thank the Lord,' Edwin said at my side.

We clung on to the lifelines for minutes. They seemed like hours. All around us the sea was racing. White water thundered past. But there were no swells, no mountainous green waves. The sky seemed to flatten above us. The sea went from black to brown: muddy sand churned up by the turmoil. We were stranded over the roughest grounds.

Then the storm was over.

For half an hour, we lay stunned in the calm. The tempest had lasted three hours. Already, the sky was turning pink at the horizon. Towards land, we could see nothing but blackness. We rested, and then Everitt started giving his orders. His voice was hoarse. We could hardly hear him. The men worked from instinct. We got the mainsail rigged and ran out the bowsprit. The mizzen was gone and we couldn't rig the spare because of the broken mizzen gaff. Three of the storm lamps were shattered. The wooden rails of the starboard bulwarks were badly splintered. When *Rechabite* was back under mainsail, Everitt changed course for the coast.

I was standing by the tiller. I had a patch over my cut forehead.

Everitt said nothing for an hour.

When he spoke, his voice was still hoarse with all the shouting, and with something else. It sounded like fear.

'We're making for Whitby, Samuel.'

I nodded numbly.

'Yes, skipper.'

'As you requested.'

'Skipper?'

'Have you powers, Samuel?'

I glanced at him, alarmed. His eyes were black with fatigue.

'I don't understand?'

'Have you powers?' he insisted, his teeth clenched together.

'No,' I said angrily.

'Have you!'

'No,' I shouted back. 'Don't be mad, man.'

The rudeness of my reply seemed to shake him. He pressed a finger against the side of his forehead and then frowned.

'You wished to go to Whitby?'

'That was all.'

'I see.'

I was feeling frightened. Edwin Wallis was watching us from the companion, listening to the raised voices. Several of the men turned to look. Jack Walmsley came across and asked the skipper if he was all right.

'I can take us into Whitby, skipper?' he suggested quietly.

'No thank you, Mr Walmsley.'

'Right you are, skipper. You got work to do, Samuel?'

'Right,' I answered quickly.

I went down below and helped Francis and Matthew sort out the mess. *Rechabite* was moving steadily through the calmer waters. I could hear seagulls, squabbling above our masts. They would have flown inland, away from the storm. I hardly listened while the two lads talked. By the time we had things sorted and I returned to the deck, we could see the Yorkshire coast.

Twenty-four

A shipwright in Whitby said he could replace the gaff in twenty-four hours. He knew Everitt was on his way to Iceland. The ruined mizzen and storm lamps could be replaced on the quays while *Rechabite* was waiting.

'You can see to your business after all, Mr Vempley,' Everitt said with wary sarcasm.

'Thank you, skipper.'

'Don't thank me, Mr Vempley, if you wouldn't mind.'

'This won't take long,' I said.

'Make sure it doesn't.'

He could have kept me on board *Rechabite* if he wanted. I had signed for the voyage. I had no right of free coming and going.

'I am grateful.'

I slipped into the narrow streets of the steeply cobbled town and asked around for the address on the letter. It was a tall, thin house not far from the bridge across the water. I knocked on the door and stood back, staring up apprehensively at the latticed windows. When the door opened, I stepped forward again.

The woman holding the door was young and pretty: fair-haired and with pale green eyes. She looked at me warily.

'Are you Jane Apted?' I asked her, showing her Ann's letter.

'Where did you get that?' she asked quickly, her eyes

searching my face, her grip tightening on the door. She had gone pale at the sight of the letter.

'It's all right,' I said. 'It was given to me by Ann Babb.'

'Is that so?'

'I'm Samuel Vempley,' I explained.

She touched her mouth quickly, a rapid, nervous movement. Her cheeks were white with shock. She held the door open and waited for me to step inside. In the hall, she turned and went through to a small front room. I could hear children playing upstairs, a woman singing in the kitchen.

'I didn't think you would come yourself,' the woman said.

'I loved her,' I said in a rush. 'I had to find out.'

'I know you loved her.'

'Do you?'

'She said so.'

'I had to learn what happened.'

'It doesn't do any good,' the woman said kindly. She still looked nervous, clenching her hands together, watching me with a soft smile. 'It won't bring Miriam back.'

The words made me feel faint. I sat down in one of the chairs and then stood up quickly. 'I beg your pardon.'

'You can sit down, Mr Vempley.'

'I didn't mean to fret you. I came to see the wise woman. I came to find out how she died.'

The woman tensed, became watchful.

'She's a decent woman,' she said quickly. 'She helps girls out.'

'I don't mean to hurt her.'

'You don't know the plight of some of these girls.'

'I know.'

'And women. Women with too many children already. She helps when others that could refuse. You must not come here bringing her trouble.'

'That isn't why I've come.'

'Then why have you?'

'Because she was the last person to talk to Miriam. The last one to see her, probably.'

'No. Miriam came here at the end. When she was sick.'

I was confused, didn't know what to say.

'Did she tell you she loved me?'

'I told you.'

I stood up again, going to the window and staring out into the narrow cobbled lane to hide my feelings.

'Why did she run away?' I asked desperately. 'Why did she not say, tell me what she was doing?'

'She felt she couldn't,' the woman said quietly.

'I don't understand.'

'She knew her own heart, Mr Vempley. She was only here a few days, but she did what she thought was for the best.'

'And ended up dying.'

'She caught an infection. That was nothing to do with the wise woman. She caught the infection here, in my house.'

I stared at the woman. There were tears in her eyes. She stood in front of me, wringing her hands together and crying. I turned from the window and offered to leave, going to the door. She rushed after me, and held my arm.

'You mustn't go.'

'I didn't come to upset you.'

'She caught the infection in my house,' the woman said hurriedly, 'being with the children. I told her she ought not, but she said they cheered her up, she found them company. My little boy had dysentery. There has been dysentery in the town. She was feverish, and we couldn't fetch a doctor. A doctor would have known immediately, or he might have guessed. The wise woman came and gave her some herbs, but it was too late. She died on the third night, after she returned from Boggle Hole.'

I listened in a kind of trance. It was hard to believe I was hearing these things: about my Miriam, the girl who had danced on the ice, worked on the farlins on the quays. I couldn't see this Miriam I was hearing about in the busy lanes around Yarmouth. I couldn't imagine her lying in my arms. If she hadn't, she would not have died.

'I must go,' I said, finding it difficult to speak. 'I'm grateful to you for your words.'

She smiled. 'Be kind to the wise woman. She lives in Boggle Hole.'

'Yes.'

'Let her tell you.'

'Yes.'

I left the room and went to the door into the street. The woman followed me. I turned suddenly and held out my hand.

'You mustn't blame yourself.'

'I can't help it. It was my child.'

'But you mustn't.'

'No,' she said sadly. 'Nor you.'

I shrugged and laughed bitterly. 'That's different.'

I left the house before she could answer.

It took me several hours to reach Robin Hood's Bay, following the road along the coast. I stopped for a lunch of beer and bread and cheese along the way, and paused frequently on the cliffs, thinking about Miriam, remembering our time together. She was slowly coming into my mind, smiling at me out of the terrible emptiness. I could see her now in Whitby. I understood why Ann Babb was her friend. I drifted along the pathway, with hardly a thought for *Rechabite*.

In Robin Hood's Bay, I explored the narrow streets and lanes, the tiny squares and miserable chapels. Miriam had spent hours here. I wanted to walk where she had been. I had heard strange stories about Robin Hood's Bay. The whole village was supposed to be undermined by caves and tunnels where the sea flooded darkly underground, washing the walls. Smugglers moved easily in the tunnels and passageways, the ginnels and alleys leading down to the cobbled slipway where small boats struggled to reach the shore. A beck ran down through the village, making the cobbled streets slippery and dangerous. As I walked around, I began to feel as if I were in a trap.

The streets were all linked with short flights of steps or cobbled slopes, and heavy seas vibrated through the buildings at the bottom of the hill. The main square was very old and the houses stood with their backs to the sea, so that you could hear the surf and the huge white rollers pounding into the bay. I walked all the way down to the bay, and felt the spray flying in my face, watching a fishing boat unloading its catch.

When I was ready, I walked to Boggle Hole.

Boggle Hole was about a mile from the village. A stream splashed on to the beach from a narrow valley. There was a watermill standing upstream. I walked down a narrow, overgrown lane. The whole placed seemed to be running with water. The air was filled with the sound of the stream. The lane was heady with the scent of wild garlic. I soon found the wise woman's house.

She opened the door to my knock. She was quite young. Her hair was completely white but her skin was fresh and pink. She had very blue eyes, and wore a blue cotton dress. A string of blue stones hung round her neck: coloured pebbles from the beach.

'I thought it might be you,' she said after a moment.

'How did you know?' I asked, surprised, then guessing that Miriam must have told her about me.

'You had to come. Miriam said you would.'

I showed her the letter.

'I don't need that.'

'Can I come inside?'

'That's what you came for.'

She showed me into a clean, tidy kitchen. A turf fire was burning in the grate, and there was a stack of dry wood beside it. She threw some of the wood on to the fire and it crackled and exploded into flames, bright tongues dancing up the back of the chimney. There was a bed in the corner of the kitchen, hidden behind a thick curtain, and herbs strung in packets over the fireplace. The room smelled of earth and flowers, a stew cooking on the stove, animals I couldn't see.

'I need to know,' I said, sitting down at the kitchen table.

The woman smiled: a sharp, kindly smile. 'I know that.'

'I saw Jane Apted.'

'I know that as well. I heard about you asking questions.'

I was startled. She couldn't possibly have found that out before I arrived. I had passed nobody on the cliff walk. I felt uneasy, not liking her sharp eyes, her brisk manner. I wondered if Miriam had found her kind.

'I don't do it unless it's needed,' the wise woman said firmly.

I blushed. I looked away from her. She let out a harsh laugh.

'I don't do it for sovereigns,' she said gaily.

I couldn't understand her. She was watching me intently. She seemed to be listening even when I wasn't speaking.

She got up suddenly and started making two cups of tea. The tea tasted of peppermint. I glanced at her warily but she drank her own cup empty and waited for me to drink mine. The taste was bitter. I heard the sea drumming in my head, felt the warmth from the fire making me drowsy. The woman kept throwing turf on to the fire.

'I need to ask,' I said desperately, feeling the tears in my eyes.

'I know you do.'

'She had to do it alone.'

'You let her.'

'I didn't know.'

'Is that right?'

It was an accusation.

I glared furiously into her sharp eyes, but she didn't flinch or turn away. She wasn't frightened by me.

'She didn't tell me,' I tried to protest.

The woman nodded seriously, her eyes wide with mockery.

'Maybe you didn't listen,' she said without changing her expression.

I couldn't understand what she was saying. I glanced

nervously at the bed in the corner. The sheets were clean. The cover was decorated with patterns of wild flowers, blue and delicate green, pink. I looked back at the woman.

'Please?' I said. 'Tell me.'

She nodded thoughtfully for a moment, and then smiled briskly.

When she spoke, the words were like a song.

'There is water,' she said. 'A dark-coloured liquid. The sea makes a great deal of noise: the tide coming in, the water rushing through the tunnels. You suck the life from a reed between the woman's legs. She feels no pain. The child is too young for pain. There is blood. There is darkness. Then you rub ointment into the soreness. The pain floods her mind: you take it away and heal it. The ointment makes her feel cool and sleepy. There is laudanum in the cordial. I don't mind what's natural. I mend the fire and sit beside the bed, holding her hand. She sleeps, and wakes in the morning.'

When she finished speaking, I got up and walked down to the beach. The wise woman followed me. The beach was limestone and blue shale, water washing down from the moors, ammonites and coloured pebbles scattered between the rocks. The wise woman told me that the moors had been infested with snakes when St Hilda was made abbess of Whitby, and she prayed that they would be drowned, cutting off their heads with a whip before throwing them into the sea. The ammonites were said to be the ghosts of the drowned snakes. We found sea urchins and limpets among the rocks, tiny green crabs and oysters and dogwhelks. There were hermit crabs in the deep pools, and curlews digging for lugworms along the shore. There were fulmars and cormorants on the cliffs, guillemots and a kittiwake. There were badgers and foxes on the moors, the wise woman told me, as black-headed gulls screamed at the slumbering seals.

'Did I know?' I asked her when it was time for me to leave.

'In your heart.'

'Then why didn't she tell me?'

'You must learn that for yourself.'

'You know?'

'It isn't something you can tell another person. It isn't something you learn with your mind. Go away, and she will come to you. She did love you, she told me that, but she did what she felt was right. The dying was misfortune. The dying was nothing to do with your child.'

I walked away, and wept on the moors. I spent the night raving and mad. I had no words. I was swept wildly with passion like *Rechabite* tossed in the storm. If the darkness had not lost me, I would have thrown myself over the edge of the towering cliffs.

I returned to Whitby as *Rechabite* was preparing to leave. Everitt had found another boy.

'This is Daniel Waghorn,' he told me proudly. 'He's from Grimsby, visiting an aunt here in Whitby. He's signed on for our Iceland voyage. He's sixteen, and willing to work. His mother wants him to learn to be a fisherman.'

I stared unhappily at the new boy. He was beaming and dangling in front of me, a long-limbed, jerking, dancing and slightly crazed innocent, his blond hair too long and curly, his cheeks pink and delicate with down. He grinned at me and moved about as if he was incapable of standing still. My heart went cold. He was the perfect victim for *Rechabite*.

Iceland

Twenty-five

I was feverish. There were hot shadows in the corners of the cabin, wraithlike, lambent, flickering on the dark panelling, stretching across the cobwebby beams. Grotesque figures whined as the wind blew the lamp, guttered the yellow flame. A mouse scampered across the floor, darting from beneath the bunks and then sniffing at the cold air, lifting its nose for danger. It disappeared so abruptly I wondered whether I was dreaming. I heard scrabblings in the night, the soft, insidious scufflings of rats. I was drenched with sweat, my head full of strange sounds.

A woman screeched in the cold. She was wearing a starched apron and black silk dress. The dress scratched the filthy floor. Rats ran around her leather boots. She was binding a young woman to a treadmill. There were muffled cries. A sullen, red-faced girl was helping her. They stuffed a gag into the woman's mouth, and then ripped her gown, loosening her stays and blindfolding her. There was no sound. I could hear the night shuffling round the treadmill, ghosts leering out of the blackness. With a bunch of osiers, the woman in the starched apron started flogging the woman on the treadmill. She lifted her arm and brought the osiers down in a frenzy until the ends split into pieces and the blood trickled down the victim's back. When the osiers were no longer any use, she repeated the flogging with a wooden cane until the tender flesh was black with diffused blood. On the treadmill, the bound woman finally lay still, her breathing harsh in the darkness like wind sighing through a broken window.

My grandmother cackled in a corner. She lifted her hands before her face and stared sightlessly at the ceiling. Then she was weeping.

'They won't let me speak,' she cried out. She collapsed back against her pillows. I was trying to tell her the woman in charge of the workhouse had been sent to prison. She wouldn't believe me. She had heard the stories about the flogging. I sat beside her bed, weeping, sweating, water running down my face. 'It wasn't you, Grandmother,' I kept telling her, but she wouldn't listen. 'They won't let me speak,' she whispered, 'they won't let me speak.' I cried because I hadn't seen her for months. I hadn't heard her rambling, grumbling voice, her endless stories. I had known her all my life, and sat listening to her stories for hours ever since she went blind. They had kept us apart since the day we arrived at the workhouse. Talking was her great pleasure, I kept telling them, but they wouldn't listen. Talking was her way of seeing the world, and in my loneliness and distress, I wondered who she was talking to, whether she was missing me. I thought she might be going mad.

'Samuel,' a voice hissed at me.

I struggled to turn away. I didn't want to hear.

'You all right now, Samuel?'

I tossed and heaved on my pillow. I recognised Jack Walmsley, his face peering close to my own, his eyes wide with alarm. He was holding a cloth on my forehead, dipping it into a bucket of cold water. The water ran down my neck. I was crying again. I felt my head burning, my throat full of pebbles. I swallowed the water he lifted to my lips, and stared at him in horror, waiting for him to knife me as I tried to drink. He lowered me back down to the pillow and went on soaking the cloth in cold water and bathing my head. I tried to talk to him, to keep him from hurting me.

'Then they fetched me to sit with her,' I whispered to Jack Walmsley frantically. 'They fetched me because she was dying. I'm not sure she even recognised me. Two years is a long time. She was a bit deranged. I sat with her, and listened to her talking, but she was talking to ghosts from the moon, sitting up in bed and pointing to people she said were standing in the corners of the room, having a conversation with her own past. I couldn't make sense of what she was saying. It was a kind of monologue, only talking to the past. I sat and listened. I hardly recognised her.'

She talked about Ringmer.

I could actually hear her talking: sitting in the darkness of the cabin, warming herself at the stove; I could hear the voice of her stories, like a child frightened of the night.

'We had bread and cheese for supper,' she said, 'and a glass of porter, then your grandfather always had his pipe of tobacco. He liked his pipe of tobacco. We didn't go hungry. There were loads of wheat for the poor. Potatoes on our own land. We didn't get them from the religious. There were all the religious in Ringmer: nasty lot, nasty narrow minds: Quakers and Baptists, Calvinists and Unitarians, Presbyterians and ranting Independents. You want to avoid the religious, Samuel. They didn't read their Bunyan. They didn't know Tom Paine and William Cobbett. Your grandfather knew all about them, with their devious, pious ways: do you ill to make a penny: tailors and leather-sellers, soap-boilers, weavers and brewers, tinkers selling their souls. He knew them all.'

'You got to calm down, Samuel.'

I shivered uncontrollably. I held on to Walmsley's hand, my hands wet with sweat, my body frozen.

Then my grandmother was talking again in her hypnotic dead voice.

'You keep clear from London, boy, you listen to what I'm saying: the great snare they call it, the mere, the foulness. City of Temptation and the Man in Black. He preached the dealer in old clothes to me, boy, and a sheep's-head seller, a coach-painter and mangle-maker, a footman all liveried out, a tooth-drawer and breeches-maker, a drunken coal-heaver. He preached the last night. You know *Pilgrim's Progress*, boy?'

'Grandmother!'

'Mr Money-Love and Great-heart, Mr Save-All and Mr Hold-the-World. Old Man Pope and Beelzebub, Bloody-man, Maul and Slay-good the giants, the Hill Difficulty and Doubting Castle, Vanity Fair, the Enchanted Ground. You fear the Enchanted Ground, boy. Lord Carnal Delight, Lord Luxurious, Lord Lechery, Sir Having Greedy. The Valley of Humiliation is where I lived my life, boy. You fear them all for me.'

She struggled to finish the words, choking on her phlegm. She was cold, clammy. I could hear death rattling in her throat.

In a frenzy, she threshed on the pillows, a trickle of blood running down the side of her neck. By the time the nurses arrived, she was dead.

I felt the stove exploding in my head, and Jack Walmsley leaping up to leave the cabin. 'Help here,' I think he was crying. 'Help here, down below.' I tried to get out of the bunk before the stove set fire to the cabin. He had done for me in the end, leaving me in the blind inferno. I sank back on the wet pillows, and passed out.

When I woke, I was in the workhouse. The room had high windows, letting in very little light. It was like a coffin. Three men sat at a long table. I was standing before them, trying to see their faces in the dismal light. It was raining outside, and the rain thundered on the roof.

'Your grandmother has been saying strange things,' one of the men said in a harsh, impatient voice. 'Vile things. You hear me, boy?'

I wasn't listening. I noticed he was wearing a cravat, white ruffled silk at his throat. He drummed his fingers on the table all the time he was speaking as if he couldn't wait to get out of the cold room.

'You hear me, boy?'

'Sir?'

'Your grandmother has been talking sedition.'

'I don't know, sir.'

'He doesn't know,' a second man said with a barking laugh.

'Tom Paine, boy: *The Rights of Man.*'

'She read that.' I nodded.

'She *talked* it,' the man with the cravat shouted.

'I don't know, sir.'

He scoffed angrily.

'You don't *know!*'

'I don't know what sedition is, sir.'

'He doesn't know what sedition is,' the second man said with another barking laugh.

The third man groaned and raised his eyes to the ceiling.

'She could be *hanged*,' the man with the cravat boomed at me from behind the table. '*Hanged!*'

I heard the rain pounding on the roof, pouring in torrents down the gutters. A waterfall cascaded past one of the tall, grimy windows.

'I don't know, sir,' I said again.

The man with the cravat thumped the table furiously. He got up and walked round the table. He poked a finger in my chest.

'You awake, boy?'

'Yes, sir.'

'You deaf, boy?'

'No, sir.'

'Got all your senses, boy?'

'I think so, sir.'

'Hah,' the man roared at me.

He turned abruptly and went back to his place behind the table.

'A person may be hanged for sedition, boy,' the second man said wearily. 'It is a crime.'

I nodded. I didn't know what to say. I had no idea what

they were talking about. I wanted my dinner and I wanted to get out of the dreary coffin room before they buried me under the cold earth.

'My grandfather was hanged for rioting,' I said, trying to be helpful.

In the silence, nobody moved. The rain continued. I watched the three men, surprised at their silence: they glanced at each other, fidgeted with papers on the table. The man with the cravat stared at me as if I was insane, or a dangerous fever-sufferer. I waited for them to speak, but they said nothing. After a few minutes, a warder came to fetch me, and I left the tall, hollow room. I walked back to the empty ward, and sat down on my bed. I waited for something to happen.

That was six months before my grandmother died.

The coke hissed on the stove. Shadows flickered round the cabin.

'Take it steady, Samuel, it's hot.'

I was sitting up in the bunk, leaning against a pile of pillows. John Pinney was spooning broth from a wooden bowl. I felt a dull grief aching in my mind. My chest was hurting: tight, sore, as if the ribs were bruised from coughing. I took a spoon of broth and closed my eyes. The broth made me feel sick. When John tried to give me some more I shook my head weakly, refusing.

'You got to take something, Samuel.'

'Not yet.'

'That's three days.'

'Tomorrow.'

I don't know why, but I started telling John Pinney about my grandmother. I wanted to talk. I wanted to talk about her. He listened, frowning and concerned. He tried the broth again, but I was too upset to take food. I had to tell somebody about my grandmother.

'I suppose she talked an awful lot about her life,' I said. 'She was a scratchy, irritable old woman, and blind towards the end, so she talked even more, trying to fight the dark.

She told me things might have been stories, might have been true. I never asked her. By the time I could have asked, she was dead. She hadn't many listeners but me.

'She worked as a kitchen maid until she married my grandfather. He was a quiet, easy-going sort of man, decent and good-natured, a bit sentimental. He worked for a miller. He never moved outside of West Sussex. He died in 1831, before he was twenty-two. I find that hard to grasp, my grandfather dying younger than I am now, but he didn't die natural, he was hanged. He was hanged for his part in the agricultural riots.

'I don't know much about that time. There was a lot of trouble, my father told me: men demanding higher wages, a fairer deal from the workhouses. They also wanted all the threshing machines smashed: it was the threshing machines putting them out of work. Hundreds of men paraded the streets demanding food and higher wages, saying they were fed up with potatoes and starvation. Gangs of men roamed the countryside, burning stacks and destroying threshing machines. There was a lot of violence.

'The daft thing about it is that my grandfather took no part in the riots. He was a shy, nervous man according to my grandmother. He was at home on the night of the riots, celebrating the birth of his son, my father. Several neighbours called round to join in the celebrations, and afterwards, as they walked up the street, they were embroiled in the riot. My grandfather was arrested and charged with conspiracy because the men had been meeting in his house.

'He hardly knew what was happening to him at the trial. He shouted out my grandmother's name. He was crying when they sentenced him. My grandmother was left a widow with a child to look after. She had no time for mourning. She must have been a much stronger character than my grandfather and not just because she had to find her own way. She always struck me as being hard, and she resented what happened. She never forgave them.

'She couldn't stay in Ringmer. Her parents were living in

a village not far from Stamford so she decided to go back home. The miller my grandfather worked for had a cousin who travelled regularly up to London, and she decided to make the journey with him. It must have been a strange journey, with the ricks burning in the fields, broken threshing machines lying out in the morning daylight. A disturbed world, and I wonder if it disturbed her more than I ever realised. She talked about it, but in a mad kind of way.

'In London, she spent the night at an inn. There was a preacher staying there. I think he must have been terrified out of his mind, and kept talking to stop himself shaking. Only he troubled my grandmother for his own comfort. She sat up all night with her baby son, listening to his nonsense. She daren't lie down and go to sleep. The preacher told her about the dangers all around her, the mudlarks and scuffle-hunters, bludgeon men and morocco men, flash coachmen and grubbers, bear-baiters, strolling minstrels and pedlars. He must have heard gossip about all the criminals in London: thieves and drunkards, coiners and gamblers, murderers and receivers, gypsies and whores. She never mentioned the whores.

'In the last stages of her journey, she went through the southern part of Lincolnshire with a gang of migrant field workers, mainly women with their children. There was a lot of drinking and cruelty: tiny children working from five in the morning until darkness; women selling theirselves for bread. She had no other way of getting through Lincolnshire but travel with them. It took her seven months to reach her parents. I don't know why my father didn't die on the journey: a babe in arms.'

I lay back against the pillows, exhausted. My eyes were full of tears. I brushed them aside. John Pinney sat silently beside the bunk. I could hear the creak of *Rechabite*'s timbers, the boom of her sails. We were sailing under a full rig of sail.

'What is it, Samuel?' John asked.

'I betrayed her,' I said desperately, choking back the sobs.

'Don't, Samuel.'

'I betrayed her.'

'You mustn't fret.'

'I told them my grandfather was hanged.'

'You were a child.'

'I was fourteen.'

'That's a child, Samuel. You couldn't know what they were asking.'

'They wanted to know about her talking,' I said. 'She must have been rambling on. She must have mentioned Tom Paine and William Cobbett. That's what they asked me about anyway. But I told them they hanged my grandfather for rioting. I must have wanted to hurt her. She was alive and my parents were dead. They moved her to a room on her own for the rest of the time. She died a few months after that.'

I couldn't stop crying, and then I slumped into a restless sleep. When I woke, John Pinney had gone. A pitcher of fresh water stood on the floor beside the bunk. I was too weak to reach it.

I lay still and listened to the sea. I knew what was buried in my mind. I did blame my grandmother for living after my parents died. I did blame her for being blind. What did I understand: I was a child. Did I betray her about her poor hanged husband, speaking his death when the words were not mine? I closed my eyes, and sank into a bleak sleep.

Twenty-six

I dreamed that night about Miriam: snakes and tunnels twined in my dreams, ammonites and dark-coloured liquid, an awful sucking noise thundering like a whirlpool in the black sea. Limestone and blue shale slithered beneath my feet. A weird woman in a long grey veil stood on the top of the cliffs, berating the keening wind. As she wailed, she held snakes up to the light, cutting off their heads and hurling them out to the sea. I felt my feet being gnawed by tiny green crabs and oysters and dogwhelks. Lugworms moved in my hair. Curlews stabbed their long beaks into my eyes.

Then I was walking with Miriam along the foreshore at Yarmouth.

It was a morning towards the end of February. The sea froze that winter. The shores were deserted. The shallow tidal run rippled over the shores and then froze to a solid sheet. Ice formed on the groynes and the wooden struts of the piers. The bait-diggers had to break through two inches of ice to dig for the buried lugworms. It was the coldest winter for decades, and the men on the pontoons had to work night and day to prevent the cod freezing in the cod-chests.

Joseph Proctor had been dead seven weeks.

The hymns from the funeral were still in my mind. *Wings of Morning* had moved to Aberdeen, and all the men I had known for seven years had found berths on other smacks. I did not know what I felt: resentment at Joseph for dying; grief at being alone. I was too desperate to know my own mind, lonely despite Miriam. When I wasn't working, I slumped into bleak depression. I would not let Miriam get near to me. We walked the deserted shores together, and I hardly heard a word she was saying.

Miriam seemed depressed, worried: she knelt down and drew a curlew in the firm sand, using the end of her finger. As she drew, she glanced up at a curlew digging for lugworms at the tideline.

I watched her for several minutes, and then knelt down beside her.

'That's not how a curlew digs,' I said, for some reason feeling irritation. She ought to get the bird right.

She didn't look at me. 'I know that.'

'It's a much more rapid movement. You have to show the beak going right into the sand.'

'I know!'

She glared at me, and stood up, kicking sand over her drawing.

'I'm not an artist. In case you hadn't noticed.'

Her voice echoed down the deserted foreshore. The curlew at the tideline lifted from the sands and went wheeling away into the grey distance. Miriam pushed her hands into her pockets and walked away.

I was hurt, surprised.

'I'm sorry,' I shouted, but she ignored me.

I followed her, trying to grab her arm.

'Leave me alone,' she said, turning round and speaking very quietly, threatening, warning.

'Miriam!'

'I said, leave me alone.'

'I'm sorry, I didn't mean anything.'

We stood and glared at each other: I was aroused, flushed with anger; Miriam was shaking with temper and then suddenly laughing harshly, seeing how ridiculous we must look.

She bit her bottom lip and stared down at her boots. Her
face was white and tired. I hadn't noticed.

'I am worried,' she said abruptly.

'Worried?' I stared at her vacantly.

'Yes, worried!' she snapped, losing her temper again then
biting her lip. She shrugged and there were tears in her eyes.
She reached out and touched my arm. 'I'm sorry.'

'Miriam.'

'I know,' she said, turning away. She was crying now, her
pale face drawn and ashen with tiredness. She turned back
suddenly and held my hand, keeping us apart. I put my
arms round her shoulders and held her for a long time.

'It isn't us,' I said.

'What?'

'I can't help it. You know . . .'

She sighed and shook her head.

'I know you loved him,' she said briskly.

'Yes.'

'I understand.'

She blew her nose and looked away, watching a schooner
making for the roadsteads under full sail. She walked a few
yards down to the tideline and stood with her back to me.

'I do understand,' she said with a brief nod of her head.

'Do you?'

'He was a lovely man. He was kind to you. You are bound
to miss him.'

'Yes.'

'So much a part of your life.'

I felt vaguely ashamed. I searched in my pockets and
walked down to the tideline where she was standing. I
offered her my hand.

'What is it?'

'Take it.'

It was a perfect scallop shell, white and delicate pink,
flecked with strands of brilliant blue.

'It's lovely,' she said, taking the shell from my hand.

'It must have been in the oyster beds,' I said.

'Oh?'

'To turn blue. I don't know what the blue is.'

'No.'

She handed the shell back to me but I shook my head.

'No, it's for you. A present. I brought it for you.'

She looked at the shell again and smiled.

'I am sorry,' I said.

'I know. It doesn't matter.'

'You said you were worried about something.'

'It doesn't matter.'

We walked back along the foreshore. Men were burning fires on the pontoons to keep from freezing. They roasted chestnuts on the open fires and children came down to eat the chestnuts and watch the frozen sea.

I pointed to the tideline. 'Turnstones,' I said.

Miriam looked where I was pointing. The tiny birds were darting among the shells and wrack, pecking at the frozen sands. A flash of sunlight shone on the ice. Further down the shore, sanderling ran in swarms along the tideline, an enormous oystercatcher darted backwards and forwards.

'Do you know all the birds?' Miriam asked me.

'Yes.'

She frowned swiftly, hiding her smile. She pretended to be interested.

'I think you *should* know the names,' I told her. Seabirds wheeled and circled above us. There was a smack making for the pontoons, a three-masted schooner far out in the main channel, heading down the coast. 'It's a way of acknowledging things.'

'Is that what Joseph believed?'

'Yes.' I nodded briefly, my eyes watering.

She stopped and smiled at me.

'You're a kind man,' she said.

'Am I?'

'Don't you know?'

'I suppose.'

I started telling her about the birds: curlew and godwit,

oystercatcher and grey plover, the red-legged redshank and the swarming knot, dunlin, turnstone and sanderling.

'You get three kinds of tern along this coast,' I told her. 'The sandwich tern, the little, and the arctic. They all have different calls.'

I stopped and stood very still. I cupped my hands to my mouth and made the strange, keerreeing sound Proctor had taught me, my voice carrying along the miles of sand.

'That's the arctic tern,' I told her with an embarrassed smile as she clapped, delighted with the imitation.

I lifted my hands again, and made the tirricking call of the sandwich tern and then the kik-kik of the little tern which visits mainly in the summer. The cries drifted out to sea, and Miriam listened fascinated, watching me as I enjoyed showing off, laughing at my obvious pride. As we walked back towards the pontoons, she pulled her arm through mine.

Was that the last time we were happy together?

I was away on the whelkers, working to ease my mind, stop myself thinking. Miriam was busy on the farlins. When we met, it was for a drink or walks. We didn't make love. It seemed the wrong thing. I was always tired. Miriam was restless and exhausted. She had been on edge for weeks. I thought she was probably worried about my going back to sea.

At the end of April, we went for a drink on the quays. Pale sunlight flickered over the horizon. A soft breeze blew through the open door of the beerhouse. We sat with the drinks outside and watched a late smack tying up at the bollards.

'Will you stay on the whelkers?' she asked me when we had been quiet for several minutes.

I shook my head. 'I don't know.'

'It seems easier. You get home more.'

'That's true.'

'I think the wives of fishermen must envy the men who work on whelkers. So much time at home with their families.'

'But it isn't the sea. It isn't fishing.'

'You feel that now?'

I shrugged. 'I'm not sure. It isn't, but I don't know whether I feel it.'

'Wouldn't it be nice to be home winter evenings?'

I shrugged.

'I only know the sea. The fishing. But I don't know how I'd be on any other smack than *Wings of Morning*.'

She smiled, watching me while I talked.

'It will come,' she said with a sigh. 'You'll make your mind up.'

We finished our drinks, and then walked back to Miriam's lodgings in the Rows. She held my hand and rested her head against my shoulder. We could hear singing from one of the houses: a woman singing to a child. Miriam stopped and listened for a moment, and then we walked on slowly, swinging our hands together.

'It's going to be a lovely summer,' she said softly.

At the house, she wouldn't let me come inside. She held me briefly against her shoulder, and kissed me on the mouth, and then she was gone. I walked back to my own lodgings. I didn't even regret the lost night. I was too distracted, too miserable to be any company. I stopped outside my own lodgings, and then walked on to the nearest beerhouse. I needed another drink before trying to sleep.

Twenty-seven

I woke up with a start. *Rechabite* was rocking backwards and forwards, and I could hear Everitt calling for a full rig. We must have been hove-to, fishing from the stern. The sound of laughter on deck made me struggle out of the bunk too quickly, banging my head. I hung on to the side, waiting for the cabin to stop spinning, the dizzying sickness to pass. Three days without food and I was light-headed and weak. When the cabin righted, I sat for a moment, trying to think what I was doing. The laughter was noisy and boisterous: men fooling at the lines, dealing with the catch, other men shouting at the halyards. Coming out of my sleep, my first thought had been Benjamin Bulpit. But Benjamin was all right: nobody could harm him any further. He was lost in his own restless sleep.

I groaned and the pain swept through my mind.

I could hear Benjamin talking as clearly as if he was in the cabin.

'He means it.' He began to blubber.

'No he doesn't.'

'He treats us real cruel,' he went on. 'He says he's going to kill us.'

I touched his arm and smiled at him. It was that or listening to what he said.

'Benjamin,' I said very firmly, laying down the law.

'Yes.'

'You listening to me?'

'Yes.'

'Good. He can't treat you cruel when I'm around,' I told him. 'I'm the new hand, let him try and make a meal of my eyes. Right?'

'Yes.' He nodded unhappily. I laughed at him, punching him on the arm.

I didn't ask him if he believed me. I hadn't the imagination to listen. I hadn't the heart to hear what he was saying. If I had listened, he might not have died. I let him die, because I knew there was something wrong on *Rechabite*, I knew there was going to be violence. If I had kept watch, he might have lived. Even when he died, I hadn't the courage to face Everitt: tell him there was some terrible mistake, Benjamin's death had been no accident. I let out a groan and clutched the sides of the bunk until the wood splintered in my hand. I had betrayed Benjamin simply because I *knew*. Any fisherman alive would have known.

In the fumey cabin, I thought suddenly about Robert Allison.

His frightened eyes stared into mine.

His teeth were chattering with the cold.

'What did you see, Robert?' I asked him.

'Nothing.'

'There must be something.'

'No.'

'Were you in here when you heard Benjamin cry?'

'No.'

'When you heard him screaming?'

'No!'

I heard the sails creaking in the silence.

Ice moaned in the frosted air.

'I see nothing,' Robert said abruptly.

'All right.'

'I ent going to tell.'

'It's all right, Robert.'

'I ent going to speak.'

'You don't have to,' I tried to say, but he wasn't listening.

'I gone blind,' he said in a sudden rush, and then opened the fishroom door and was gone, slamming the door behind him. 'I gone blind,' I heard him say in the darkness.

If he had stayed on *Rechabite*, would Robert have died as well?

I climbed down from the bunk and took a deep breath. I had to struggle into my fearnoughts and gansey jersey, clumsy with weakness. The seaboots were so heavy I could hardly lift them. My arms seemed to wave in front of my eyes. I could hear the loud laughter on deck again, and Everitt giving orders for the gutting of the fish. They would be gutting everything this time, not wasting time with live fish for the well. I stumbled as *Rechabite* took a large swell to starboard.

The dark thoughts pressed into my fumbling mind as I tried to get dressed. Did Miriam die because I was too pre-occupied with my own grief over Joseph Proctor to listen to what she had to say? Or was I full of resentment at Proctor's dying, too driven by hatred to turn to Miriam's love? Did I know Miriam was having a child, seeing the way she was: the sickness, the depressed moods; the way she stood outside the house in the Rows and listened to the mother singing to her child on the last night I ever saw her alive? Was she listening to the ghost of her own singing, a lullaby she would never be able to sing? Was I judging her because I knew the kind of girls who ended up pregnant?

'No,' I cried out, slamming my fist into the locker door and reeling from the pain. 'No,' I muttered as I sank to the deck, clutching my bruised hand. That wasn't true: that couldn't be true. I loved Miriam. I felt the tears running down my cheeks: I *loved* her, I almost shouted to the empty cabin. I loved her.

Then I saw my grandmother's sad, blind eyes. She was listening to the men in the workhouse asking me questions in the tall, dank room, sitting arrogantly behind their long table.

'My grandfather was hanged for rioting,' I shouted, 'my grandfather was hanged for rioting . . . my grandfather was hanged for rioting . . .' as the rain poured down the windows.

I stood up.

'This is not me,' I said quietly, taking a deep breath.

I had my fishing gear back on.

My heart steadied.

'This is not me.'

It was time I went back on deck.

There was a cheer when I climbed up from the companion. John Pinney rushed across and shook my hand. Jack Walmsley raised a fist and called for three cheers. The skipper watched me with a cynical, cold smile.

'You had a good rest then, Mr Vempley?' he said as the men cheered.

'Thank you, skipper.'

'Ready for some work now, are you?'

But I was not paying attention to the skipper.

On the deck below the mainmast, Daniel Waghorn was doing a weird dance. Henry Purvis was playing his accordion, and Richard Buss and Nathan Chapman were clapping. Walmsley was by the bulwarks, keeping time with a wooden club he kept beating against the deck. Daniel was like some apparition from the madhouse: he was wearing an enormous pair of fearnoughts and a gansey jersey that came down to his knees. As he danced, the jersey flapped and billowed, floating round him like a smock. His hair was wild and flaming around his head. I hadn't noticed when I first saw him how red it was, and loosely curled. The curls swivelled and bobbed like straw blowing across a field in the wind.

'What's happening to the lad?' I asked Everitt.

He glanced at me, surprised, disconcerted.

'He offered to do a dance,' he said, too taken aback to resent my tone. 'We caught some fine cod, and he said he would dance to celebrate.'

I paused, wondering whether he was being sarcastic. I still felt light-headed and suddenly my stomach gave a loud, rumbling, gurgling protest at the days of hunger. I touched the side of my head and stared at Daniel's bizarre dance. I knew there was something I had to say.

'I don't think he should be disciplined,' I said bleakly.

Now Everitt turned from the tiller and stared at me as if I had truly gone mad. He was still amused, in a good humour, but I could see the dangerous shine in his eyes. He smiled icily.

'For what?' he asked very quietly.

'For anything,' I said firmly.

He watched me for a moment, and then smiled: understanding.

'Do you not?' he said mildly, calm, indifferent.

'No, skipper. He's a boy, he's never been on a smack.'

'They're all boys when they first sign, Mr Vempley. I should have thought that was obvious, even to you.'

'He's a child.'

'He's sixteen, not that I wish to argue.'

'He is still a child. Benjamin Bulpit . . .'

I saw Everitt tense. The smile disappeared and his fingers tightened on the tiller.

'You haven't eaten for three days, Mr Vempley.'

'That's beside the point.'

'The *point*,' he said with vicious emphasis, 'is that you are fifth hand on my smack. You take orders like everybody else. I thought we had already had this conversation.'

'I heard you.'

'The need for something more than *kindness*.'

'I heard you,' I said with absolute calm, the harshness brittle in my voice.

Everitt stared at me for a moment, and then glanced up at the mainsail. We were ploughing through the water, tacking at five or six knots. He seemed to consider for a moment, and then shook his head, smiling to himself. He took a deep breath and pretended to yawn.

'I will leave the lad to you, Mr Vempley.'

'Skipper?'

'He needs to learn the fishing. We need another man on the lines. You can teach him how to catch fish. If you teach him to be a good smacksman at the same time and to understand the need for orders, we shall get along fine. The boy is your responsibility.'

I was shaken, wary of the man's deceit, his craftiness.

'Is that good enough for you, Mr Vempley?'

'It is, skipper.'

'I am pleased.'

I tried to smile at his sarcasm, but the dizziness was back in my head, and I felt my hands trembling.

'I was only concerned . . .'

'I know you were only concerned, Mr Vempley. You are that sort of man. Go and get yourself some food from the galley. The main meal is finished. Tell the galley boy I said he was to cook fresh food for you.'

I turned to leave.

'One last thing, Mr Vempley.'

I turned back and waited for Everitt to continue.

He smiled at me, still watching the mainsail.

'I will discipline the members of this crew as I see fit,' he said after a pause. 'I hope that is understood.'

'Yes, skipper.'

'It includes you.'

'Yes, skipper.'

'Then I would suggest you look after Daniel. Make sure Mr Walmsley doesn't take a liking to him. Mr Walmsley has to be watched. He has a temper. These things can be taken too far. By these things, I do not mean discipline: that is my responsibility. But the fooling about, the horseplay. You understand. You should make sure Walmsley doesn't go too far. You can have a care for your charge by keeping watch.'

He dismissed me then and I went down to the galley for some food.

Daniel was still dancing weirdly by himself.

Henry Purvis had stopped playing his accordion.

I was more confused than I had been since the day I signed on for *Rechabite*'s Iceland voyage.

When I had eaten my fill, I went back on deck to find Daniel.

Twenty-eight

Daniel was standing by the mizzen, watching the skipper at the tiller with wide-eyed amazement. Now that he was no longer dancing, the loosely fitting clothes hung about him like a shroud.

'He steers without a chart,' he told me, not taking his eyes off Everitt when I clapped him cheerfully on the shoulder.

'Ready, Daniel?'

'How does he do that?'

I pulled at his arm, seeing Everitt's look of irritation. 'Come on. Let's get you fitted out with something you can wear.'

Daniel followed me clumsily down the companion and we went for'ard through the starboard fishroom to the store-room next to the boys' cabin. The storeroom was used for the spare sails and ropes, but there were also shelves of old fishing gear and seaboots.

'Try this,' I said, offering Daniel one of the gansey jerseys. 'That looks more your size.'

He pulled the gansey over his head and came out with his hair standing on end. He turned round, trying to see the decorations on the back.

'What do the patterns mean?' he asked.

'The moon and star shapes on the waistband tell you how

many children and grandchildren a man has. Anchors are a sign of hope.'

'I have hope,' Daniel said proudly. 'Hope is a virtue.'

'Is that right? The zigzag patterns are lightning and they warn us of the turmoils of married life. You need hope for that.'

He burst out laughing.

'My mother had turmoil. She had turmoil regular Saturday nights, and Fridays if he had any money. My father used to go drinking,' Daniel whispered, lowering his voice and blushing as if drink was the wildest sin of his imagination. 'He used to spend all the money my mother should have had by rights and then beat her for not keeping a table.'

Before I could respond, he pointed at the patterns on my own gansey.

'What are they for?' he asked.

'They're dreams,' I said quietly.

'Don't you prefer hopes?'

'No.' I laughed.

'Hope sounds more reasonable than dreams,' he mused.

I handed him a fresh pair of heavy woollen fearnoughts and some seaboots. As he struggled to get into them, falling back against the door of the fishroom and sprawling out on the floor, he went on admiring my gansey.

'Did you knit that yourself?'

'No.'

'A lot of fishermen do.'

'Yes, or their girlfriends, wives.'

'Didn't your girlfriend knit yours?'

'Hurry up, Daniel.'

He stood up and banged the seaboots on the deck. They fitted well, and he looked almost normal in his tighter gansey and boots.

'You know what my father used to say?' he asked me.

'We should get on.'

'We're used to being drowned. Don't you think that's funny?'

It was an old fishing saying. A lot of fishermen wore the patterned jerseys as a means of identification so that their families might have some chance of finding them if they were drowned. Few fishermen could swim. There wasn't much reason to learn if you were working deep waters: the cold would often freeze you to death.

'Don't talk about that,' I told him seriously.

'I'm sorry.'

'It's bad luck.'

'Right.' He nodded solemnly, full of understanding.

'Let's get back on deck.'

Edwin Wallis and John Pinney were baiting lines at the coaming. *Rechabite* had her first set of lines down and was hove-to, waiting for Everitt to give the command to make the haul.

'We need another good catch,' Edwin said cheerfully, 'and we'll have enough in the fishrooms for Wick.'

Daniel knelt down and watched fascinated as John cracked a whelk and plunged the hook on the snood through the soft flesh.

'Doesn't that hurt?'

'He don't feel a thing,' Edwin said, and burst out laughing.

'But the whelk,' Daniel said seriously. 'I meant the whelk.'

We all stared at him for a second, and then I told him to take a hammer and have a go himself. He shuddered and shook his head.

'I couldn't do that.'

'You'd better,' John told him. 'The skipper might put one through you if we don't get these lines baited ready for putting down.'

'We'll be hauling any minute, Daniel,' I told him.

'Hauling?'

'Get on with it.'

I almost shouted. He never stopped asking questions. I knelt down beside him and showed him how to crack the shell and get the whelk on to the hook. There were dozens of snoods yet to be baited. He watched me intently and then tried himself, cracking his thumb with the hammer and then smashing another whelk to a pulp.

'You pay for those, lad,' Everitt shouted from the tiller, watching Daniel's performance. 'Just watch what you're doing.'

The next whelk was got clumsily on to the hook with a great deal of groaning and shuddering, and then Daniel picked another out of the net. I saw Edwin bait twenty snoods in the minutes it took Daniel to make his selection. He held the whelk up and admired its delicate colours.

'Get on, Daniel,' I hissed at him, elbowing him sharply in the ribs.

He gasped. 'Don't do that.'

'Then *get on*, for Christ's sake.'

Edwin blinked woefully at the blasphemy and showed the boy how he was working.

'You got to learn the trade, boy,' he said, 'otherwise you will hold us back. You want to be a fisherman, don't you?'

'Yes.' Daniel nodded quickly, beaming at him.

'Come on then, let me show you. Samuel is a bit on the impatient side.'

He showed Daniel more slowly what we were doing, and soon we were all working steadily, lulled by the rocking of the smack, the rhythm of the work. The rest of the crew were lounging about the deck, talking and smoking, drinking mugs of tea. Walmsley was chatting to the skipper.

'This is easy,' Daniel told us.

'You've a lot to learn yet, Daniel,' Edwin said with his friendly drawl.

'I know the fish,' Daniel told us.

'The fish?'

'The fish we catch.'

'Do you now?'

'Brill and cod,' Daniel said proudly. 'Torks, scad and dory.'

'All right, lad.'

'Bream, cuckoo wrasse, dab and flounder. Cornish sucker and butterfly blenny. Haddock, corkwing, hake, halibut.'

'He said all right, Daniel,' I hissed at him.

Several of the men had turned to listen. Daniel went on happily, showing off his fishing knowledge, enjoying himself and cracking whelks with a cheerful relish now that he knew how.

'Goldsinny, wolf-fish and herring, rock gob, butterfish, ling, mackerel, pilchard, saury, greenland cod, saithe, father-lasher, plaice, frigate mackerel, golden mullet and witch.'

He stopped, out of breath, his wide eyes shining with excitement, sweat running down his face, his hair damp and flattened to his high forehead. The men on deck were standing up, laughing and waiting for him to go on, encouraging him with their shouts.

'How about garfish?' Nathan Chapman called sarcastically.

'And don't forget pollack,' Henry Purvis joined in gleefully.

Daniel was impervious. He thought they were applauding him. He ignored the skipper's dark frown.

'Three-bearded rockling,' he said with great relish, 'ray, skate, redfish and gurnard. Lumpsucker, sole, sprats, scaldfish, tunny, lemon sole, shanny, turbot, solenette, whiting.'

'Haul the lines,' Everitt suddenly shouted.

I jumped up and grabbed hold of Daniel's arm.

'Lines baited, skipper,' I managed to call before Everitt could make his own enquiries. John Pinney was desperately cracking the last of the shells. He had the whelk on the hook before Everitt could lose his temper.

In the chaos of hauling the lines, I didn't have time to see how Daniel fared. This was one job he couldn't help with yet. Once the lines were on board, we had to begin gutting the catch. Everitt wanted none of it for the well. Daniel had to watch us for the first half-hour, and then Edwin began to show him how to use the knife. Henry Purvis, Richard Buss and Nathan Chapman were busy getting the new set of lines down while Jack Walmsley worked with Francis Campbell on the gear: Everitt laid the lines under mainsail, jib and staysail; there was enough breeze for that. It took us a good hour to gut the catch, and then I went down to the fishroom to show Daniel how Henry Purvis stored the dead fish in ice.

'That's a lot of fish, Mr Purvis,' Daniel said with admiration. 'Did I help catch that?'

'You helped bait the lines for the next haul, Daniel,' I told him.

'I shall write and tell my mother.'

'You can write?'

'I can read too. I had schooling in Grimsby. When my father wasn't drinking. When he was drinking, there was no money for schools. And I was needed on the barrows. I worked the barrows on the market.'

'That's where you learnt the names of all the fish?'

'I knew them better than anybody.' He beamed.

'I bet you did,' Henry Purvis said, without a hint of sarcasm.

Back on deck things were more relaxed. The lines were down and *Rechabite* was hove-to. Matthew Whalley brought plates of hot food up the companion and shouted us to come and get it. He took Everitt's plate to him: meat duff and treacle pudding. Daniel ate as if he had never seen food. We sat by the well coaming, leaning back against the hatches. The sun was high in the sky and enormous herring gulls wheeled across the calm water, taking bread out of Henry Purvis's fingers.

'That's wasting good food, Henry,' Jack Walmsley told him.

'They're all God's creatures,' Purvis laughed, holding out another lump of bread.

'You tell that to young Matthew Whalley.'

The galley-boy had to bake the bread in the oven. He wouldn't be too pleased to see it thrown away to the gulls.

With hot tea to finish the meal, we lounged about the deck and waited for hauling. Edwin Wallis closed his eyes and smoked his clay pipe. Henry went to fetch his accordion.

'How long will it take us to reach Iceland?' Daniel asked Edwin.

'It's about fourteen days from King's Lynn to Iceland,' he told him. 'That's doing seventy miles a day. But we're stopping off at Wick, and then Orkney and Shetland.'

'Why?'

'They're good markets. Sell the fish as we go. We might do the Faroes. Depends what we catch, how keen the skipper is to get to Iceland.'

'I bet you're a good fisherman, Mr Wallis.'

'Oh yes,' Edwin said, laughing with pleasure. 'They trust me, you see, they know my ways.'

'The fish?'

'That's right.'

'I bet they do, Mr Wallis.'

'But I ent got Samuel's touch,' Edwin went on. 'He can call the fish from the floor of the sea.'

Daniel stared at him open-mouthed. 'I don't believe you,' he said in a whisper.

'I ent being jocular,' Edwin told him seriously. 'If you spend your life at sea, you don't mock the wonders of nature.'

'Give over, Edwin,' I told him. 'You'll fill the lad's head with daft ideas.'

'No, I want to hear,' Daniel said, getting excited. 'I want to know things.'

I could see Henry Purvis and Nathan Chapman laughing. Even the skipper was listening now. Edwin puffed at his pipe and beamed solemnly at Daniel.

'Samuel talks to the fish, you see, Daniel. He talks them on to the lines. Persuades them, if you like. I seen him singing their names and the fish rise to the surface like they was long-lost relatives. I seen him dip his hand in the water, and the cod suddenly disappear, like magic. I heard him tell us one night to drop our lines, and they come up, shining with fish from the Lord. Wonders, that's the only word. Wonders that make you tremble.'

Several of the men applauded, and I saw a smile on Everitt's hard face. Edwin was enjoying himself.

Daniel was mesmerised.

'What does it mean?' he asked, turning to me.

I shrugged. 'It's all tricks,' I said. 'Edwin never saw me do any of them, but they're tricks any fisherman knows.'

'Tell me.'

'You can sometimes tell when cod are about because they like herring spawn,' I explained. 'The herring spawn shows on the lines.'

'Yes.' Daniel nodded seriously, frowning as he listened.

'Just tricks, you see.'

'Like magic?'

'No, tricks.'

'Tell me. Go on. I want to learn.'

'Cod move in huge shoals, feeding on other fish. They're very fond of herring spawn. If you want to know when cod are around, you drop a greased line and if it comes up with herring spawn you've probably got cod feeding.'

'So you didn't sing them from the bottom of the sea?' Daniel said with a disappointed frown.

Edwin tapped his pipe out on the deck and smiled at the lad. 'I once saw a shoal of herring swimming close to the surface,' he said. 'Nobody else was on deck but me. We had the lines down. I knew the cod would be rising to feed, so I went and had a joke with the lads down below, and when we hauled the lines we came up with some giant specimens. They never realised how I guessed. They weren't real fisher-men.'

'What about the fish disappearing?' Daniel asked.

'Cod don't like cold water,' I said. 'If there's a sudden cold current they can vanish in seconds. You put your hand in the water, and feel the change. You can't do it unless you're working from the smack's longboat. Any fisherman could make a guess like that. Cold water, and the cod disappear. Nothing magic.'

In the silence, I closed my eyes and thought about *Wings*

of Morning, the hours I had spent yarning with the men when we were hauling, the stories Joseph Proctor told with such deep pleasure. There was nothing Joseph liked better than a good yarn, unless it was a good catch. But he enjoyed telling stories best of all. I couldn't imagine Everitt ever sharing a yarn with his men.

Then it was time for the last haul before *Rechabite* made for Wick, and I was busy showing Daniel how to work the lines, sweating at the final gutting of the catch. Through all the work, Daniel went on smiling and asking questions. He never stopped talking. You would have thought he had never had such pleasure in his life.

Twenty-nine

'Do you know Wick, Samuel?' Daniel asked me as we stood in the bows and watched the dismal town approaching.

'It's carved in my flesh,' I said with a brief laugh.

A fine spray flew from the bows, and Nathan and Richard were preparing to get the bowsprit run in and stowed. Everitt was giving orders for the sails to be reefed down and the drogue unloosened in the stern.

Daniel's hair was soaked with the spray, but he seemed not to mind.

'I don't understand?' he said with one of his lopsided smiles, as if he knew he ought to follow but really thought I was mad: he treated half the things we told him as if we had made them up.

'I fished off here one summer,' I told him. 'On another smack.'

'*Wings of Morning*.' Daniel nodded with quick satisfaction. I had told him all about Joseph Proctor. The things I had learned when I was first apprenticed.

'That's right. We worked out of Wick and spent the season fishing the grounds west of Orkney. It was a good year for fishing, but the town was a helltown.'

'You said that about Grimsby.'

'There's more hells than one, Daniel.'

'Give a hand here,' Nathan Chapman grunted as the

skipper shouted for the bowsprit. 'Make yourself useful, Samuel.'

I showed Daniel how to work the bowsprit loose, and as *Rechabite* slowed into the crowded harbour, we hauled the bowsprit back into her locks and made her secure. Everitt was still shouting orders for the drogue, and I could see John Pinney and Francis Campbell heaving it over the stern. Jack Walmsley was on the sails as usual, arguing with Henry Purvis.

'It's a disease-ridden town,' I told Daniel. 'Typhoid and dysentery. They had smallpox the summer I was here. You heard endless rumours about cholera. There are forty drinking houses right down on the quays, and they don't keep regular hours.'

'Sounds like paradise to me,' Nathan said with a broad grin, wiping the sweat off his forehead.

Richard Buss glanced at the skipper and got the starboard ropes ready for the bollards. We were tacking rapidly towards the granite quays.

'I knew a woman in this town,' Nathan said with a leer.

'Did she love you?' Richard asked promptly.

'She wasna mithered,' Nathan said. 'So I left her with a nice plum in her duff pudding.' They both burst out laughing.

Once *Rechabite* was safely moored, Everitt climbed over the bulwarks and went to see the merchants on the market. Jack Walmsley went with him. Henry Purvis took the younger lads down into the fishrooms and started unpacking the ice round the catch.

As we watched the bustle and chaos of the quays, Edwin Wallis strolled over to the bows and stood beside us.

'I heard you talking,' he said with a nod towards the quays.

'Miserable place,' I said.

'It's a helltown right enough,' he said. 'It's a damnation.'

'Damnation for what, Edwin?' Nathan asked with his crude laugh.

'Sin,' Edwin said solemnly.

'What do you know about sin, Edwin?'

'I was here when the curers went on strike,' Edwin said quietly. 'There was no work to be had on the quays. There were families living in sail lofts and barns, old people left to die in cellars and sheds behind the curing houses. The destitute lived in upturned boats on the sands. There were young children starved. In times like that you find sin.'

'I know about sin,' Daniel said very seriously, frowning and creasing his pale forehead. 'My mother told me about lying and stealing. People steal when they're hungry but it is still a sin. They do all sorts of wrong things when they are driven to it. My father was driven to sin.'

'With your mother?' Nathan joked, winking at Richard and Matthew Whalley who had come up from the galley.

I remembered the crowds I had seen on the quays. There was disease and starvation that year because the herring shoaled late. The streets were wild and lawless: thousands of strangers in the town, sleeping in the sprawling slums, looking for work on the herring. They were soon going hungry. The streets were filthy with steaming offal, sewage ran in the open gutters. The heat was terrible.

'You just watch yourself,' Joseph warned me. 'Be careful.'

I walked the streets and heard the cries for help, saw the beggars in the overflowing gutters: a middle-aged woman with bleeding varicose veins; a man's neck crusted with angry boils; children blistered with weeping sores. There were riots and fights every night in the crowded, stinking alleyways. The dead sometimes lay in the streets for hours.

Then when the herring shoals arrived and the drifters started catching fish, everybody forgot about the dead. There were dances and concerts at the weekends, plays, ceilidhs and drinking parties. Travelling shows arrived overnight. The churches were packed, fifteen hundred people attending the Gaelic services and prayer meetings of a Sunday. People sang hymns while they worked.

'Superstition,' Joseph Proctor growled bad-temperedly. 'They should remember the dead. They should remember the children they buried.'

'Are we going ashore, Samuel?' Daniel suddenly asked, breaking into my memories.

'If you want a look round.'

'Don't we have to help unload the catch?'

'Mr Purvis does that.'

'Why?'

'He's second hand.'

I saw Everitt coming back down the quays with Jack Walmsley and one of the merchants off the market. The bobbers were already swarming aboard, ready to unload the catch. Henry Purvis was shouting up through the hatch for the baskets to be lowered into the hold. I waited until the skipper was back on board, and then climbed over the bulwarks with Daniel. We walked down the long quay, and round to the miles of farlins. The sea was a cold, dazzling blue. There were still a thousand herring drifters working from the port, although the herring would soon be shoaling southwards down the coast. As we walked, I pointed out the drifters to Daniel, and asked him how he was getting on with *Rechabite*.

'It's all right,' he said after a moment's thought. 'I didn't think the work would be so hard. I like the fishing, but I don't like it when we have to cut the fish. I think that hurts them.'

'They're dead mostly.'

'Not all of them. They go on breathing. I've seen them moving.'

'They're our living, Daniel.'

'I know.'

He seemed sad for a moment, charging along beside me, his hair blowing in the slight breeze, shining in the afternoon sunlight.

Then he cheered up.

'There are hundreds of drifters, aren't there?' he said happily.

'Like butterflies skimming over the spring tides,' I said, remembering something Miriam had said about the years she worked on the herring fleets, travelling with the drifters. Countless drifters joined in the annual journey from Lerwick to Lowestoft, thousands of girls following them to gut the herring in the farlins. 'We were like the tribes of Israel,' Miriam told me with her delighted laugh, 'swarming across the seas, searching for the promised land.'

'That was pretty,' Daniel said. 'Did you make it up?'

'A girl I knew used to say it.'

'Did you love her?' he asked straight off, innocent, direct.

'Yes,' I said quietly. 'I loved her.'

'But you didn't marry her?'

'She died.'

'I'm sorry,' he said, turning and staring at me with fierce alarm. He was like an ancient child, bobbing and weaving in front of me, blushing with his watery concern. 'I didn't mean to hurt you. I shouldn't ask so many questions. My mother always says I ask too many questions.'

'It's all right, Daniel. It doesn't matter.'

'Was she a herring girl?' Daniel asked me, but I wasn't listening. I was remembering the things Miriam had told me about the life on the herring. 'Samuel?' Daniel said again, but I hardly heard him.

The voice I heard was Miriam's.

In Wick, the women lived in long huts with no ceilings, only the exposed rafter beams above their heads.

'You could see what was happening in the rooms below by climbing up and looking over the beams,' Miriam told me with a giggle.

'That's not nice behaviour, Miriam.'

'Who said I was nice?'

There were melodions playing all night, dancing and singing, lovemaking and corn brandy. One night, Miriam and a friend climbed up on to the rafters and watched a couple making love. It looked uncomfortable and violent, scrabbling about on the mattress, the woman crying out, the man banging up and down into her. Miriam was frightened but she couldn't stop giggling.

'How old were you then?' I asked her.

'Fifteen or sixteen.'

'I knew nothing then.'

'I didn't know a lot,' Miriam said with a crude laugh.

For the journeys south the girls had to travel in the over-crowded boats, lying for long hours on the deck, or crowded together down below. Miriam always preferred sleeping on deck where she could watch the stars and hear the sounds of the sea, the gulls skimming the darkened water, the lulling wash of the tide against the bows. She loved the sea almost as much as I did.

In each port, the women swarmed ashore and laboured at the farlins. Accommodation was provided by the curers. In Grimsby, they often slept three to a bed, six to a room. In Yarmouth there were the wooden huts built along the quays where she had introduced me to some of her friends. Each hut had a coke stove, glowing and warm in the darkness. The girls could boil water on the stove and keep their clothes clean and fresh, cook simple meals on the fires. On Saturday nights, they made merry with hymns and vigorous dancing, the kind of dancing I had seen Miriam doing on the quays. On Sundays they rested or went to church before another week's hard work.

'It was like dipping your spoon in honey going for the herring,' Miriam said in one of her sentimental moods. 'It was like bringing the sweetness up into the light and getting money for the pleasure, it was that easy. Easier than working the farlins.'

I was upset.

We had reached the end of the quays where the farlins were set out. Hundreds of herring girls were working on the latest catch. Daniel was fascinated by everything. He kept rushing about, watching what the women were doing, laughing at their broad accents. He was excited by all the bustle and the shouts and laughter of the women.

I could hardly see: imagining Miriam on these quays, seeing her working at the farlins.

She was sixteen when she first took the voyage to Lerwick.

I tried to hold back my tears.

'How do they do it?' Daniel asked me, too interested in what was going on to notice that I was upset.

I gritted my teeth and told him.

The women always worked in crews of three: two gutting and sorting, and a third packing the fish into barrels, sprinkling each layer with salt. Miriam did the salting until she was old enough to handle the razor-sharp gutting knives. 'My hands tasted of salt for years afterwards,' she told me. 'A barrel could hold about seven hundred fish, and in a day we gutted and packed thirty barrels. Imagine that: that's a fish every five seconds or the curers would want to know why.' She sighed mournfully, remembering the vicious pace of the work, the tempers of the masters. The girls never worked less than ten hours a day. When a barrel was full, the lid was fitted and left for a week, then the pickle was run out through the bung hole and the barrel was opened so that it could be topped up. After the lid was refitted, enough pickle was poured back through the bunghole to fill any empty spaces.

'I don't know how you stood it,' I told her. 'Gutting on deck's hard enough, but we don't do it for hours on end.'

'I had to earn a living,' she told me wryly.

'Are you all right?' I suddenly heard Daniel asking.

'What?'

'You look upset?'

I stared at him, trying to think where I was.

'This was where my girl worked,' I said bleakly, blurting the words out. I didn't need to talk to a boy. I shouldn't be upsetting him. But I had to talk to somebody. I had to say the words. I stared blindly at the herring girls and every one of them was Miriam. Daniel stood at my side, waiting for me to go on.

'It looks hard,' he said quietly.

'It is.' I nodded. 'Long hours. They start at six, work until they're finished. You couldn't stand it aboard a smack. She was out in all weathers. The only protection they have is their working clothes: high leather boots, hessian aprons and woollen shawls. She used to wrap cotton rags round her fingers.'

'Why?'

I stopped, gulping back the tears. Miriam had dozens of tiny white scars on her fingers: her long, white fingers, which were so delicate in our warm hours. I took a breath and smiled bleakly at Daniel.

'She was always getting cuts and ulcers from the brine. Too tired to see what she was doing. They were expected to go on working, as long as there was a catch. Didn't matter about the weather, or the dark. She spent hours at the far-lins, ankle-deep in quagmires of mud, wet sand and fish refuse. She spent hours of her life at the farlins.'

I couldn't go on. I led Daniel to a beerhouse down one of the alleys off the quays and we sat for several minutes, drinking beer and saying nothing. I felt better in a dark corner of the beerhouse: nobody could see my shame; nobody bothered us. I drank two glasses of beer and told Daniel to stop looking so worried.

'I asked you to show me round.'

'I needed to come back,' I told him. 'I needed to see.'

'I don't understand.'

'Then be grateful,' I said bluntly.

I stood up and collected my loose coins. It was time we were getting back to *Rechabite*. I stood outside in the sun, and when Daniel finished his drink and joined me, we set off back down the quays towards our berth.

We could hear the shouting a hundred yards away from *Rechabite*.

Jack Walmsley was chasing round the deck, yelling after

Matthew Whalley, threatening him with a length of knotted rope. The lad scrambled behind the mainmast and dodged round the hatches to the holds. When Walmsley got near, he leapt for the mainmast boom and jumped from the gaff, swinging out of Walmsley's reach. Walmsley lashed at him with the rope and then paused to take a gulp of water. He was carrying a jug of water in his left hand, and kept tipping the jug back and taking huge swallows. I clambered aboard and guessed the skipper had gone to finish business on the market: he wouldn't have allowed this racket if he was down below in his cabin. Several men were standing round, laughing, and fishermen on the quays watched us and gossiped, making bets on whether Walmsley would catch up with the lad.

'What the hell's going on, Walmsley?' I shouted, grabbing his arm.

He glared at me and pulled free violently. 'That bastard put curry in my stew. He could have poisoned me.'

I knew the skipper kept a special box of curry powder in the galley: he liked it once in a while for a change. None of the crew were supposed to touch it.

I could see Whalley laughing at us from the mainmast. He had climbed well out of reach. Walmsley was draining the jug of water.

'You near burned my tongue out, you little sod,' he yelled at the boy.

'It was a mistake, Mr Vempley,' the lad said with a brazen grin.

'Liar,' Walmsley yelled.

'You'd better not let Everitt hear you using language like that,' I told Walmsley. 'Why not let him come down? He says it was a mistake.'

'He can come down.' Walmsley grinned viciously.

'Let him alone, Jack.'

'You let him alone. You got your own pet, Vempley. You leave me to mine.'

I could smell the curry on his breath.

Suddenly, as the lad was trying to climb down the mainmast without us seeing, Walmsley lunged round and went for him. He had his left foot before the lad could scramble to safety. Letting out a roar, he hauled on the foot as if he was hauling the halyards in a stiff gale. Matthew cried out in pain.

'You'll break my ankle.'

'I'll break your fucking neck.'

Whalley screamed again.

The next second I saw Edwin Wallis disappearing down the companion, and Nathan Chapman suddenly very busy with the lines at the stern. John Pinney was scrambling down the hatch into the fishroom. At my side, Daniel watched with growing concern as Walmsley yelled and dragged at Matthew's leg, making grabs for the boy's waist as they fought and clung their way along the boom. Glancing round, I saw Everitt walking rapidly down the quay.

It was too late to warn Walmsley.

'Mr Walmsley,' Everitt shouted, clambering over the bulwarks and going straight up to the third hand.

Walmsley turned on him and for a moment I thought he was going to hit the skipper. 'Who the hell . . .'

'Who the hell indeed,' the skipper roared. 'Get below, Whalley. Wait outside my cabin.'

Matthew leapt from the boom and fled for the companion.

'Are you an animal?' Everitt shouted into Walmsley's face.

'There's no call for that,' Walmsley said with a startled look, stepping back out of the skipper's way.

'Are you a wild animal?'

'Sir, the boy . . .'

'I will not have foul language aboard my *Rechabite*.'

'I was provoked, sir.'

'I will provoke you, Mr Walmsley. I will flog you until the blood washes your mouth clean of foulness.'

'Sir, I was doing my duty . . .'

'Shut your mouth, Mr Walmsley, shut your mouth.'

The skipper turned and stood with his back to Walmsley. I started moving away from the mainmast, gripping Daniel's arm and forcing him to go with me. He was trembling. He kept stuttering as if he was going to say something. Everitt must have heard him and turned suddenly in a fury.

'What is that boy saying?' he roared at me.

Before I could speak, Daniel answered for himself.

'Curry,' he said helplessly, his teeth chattering together.

'What!' Everitt screamed, blind with rage.

'Curry,' Daniel repeated as if he couldn't help himself.

'What about it, you fool?'

'I don't know what it is,' Daniel said. 'I never heard of curry.'

I thought Everitt was going to kill him. He stared at the boy with eyes wild with contempt, and then with an abrupt jerk of his neck, looked away and seemed to count the seconds. A vein at the side of his forehead was pumping violently: I thought he might have a seizure if he went on yelling. I kept trying to push Daniel backwards towards the companion. I could hear Matthew Whalley down below, standing at the bottom of the iron ladders: the fool was laughing. I pushed Daniel after him.

After a moment, Everitt stiffened and appeared to collect himself.

He turned very slowly, and faced Jack Walmsley.

'You're a fool,' I heard him hiss with frightening contempt.

Walmsley stared him out. He had recovered himself. He was still holding the empty water jug in his hand. 'Yes, sir,' he said, his voice quieter than I had ever heard it. 'If you say so, sir.'

It was then Everitt hit him, a single blow straight across the face, as hard as he could. There was a harsh crack. Neither man moved. They faced each other in silence. There was not a sound on *Rechabite*.

'You may go,' Everitt said quietly.

I saw Walmsley smile. He turned, and went below. With his back to me, he winked as he went past.

I was left alone with the skipper.

'Curry?' he said after a pause.

I didn't answer.

When he turned and walked to the tiller, I went below.

Thirty

Down below, I found Jack Walmsley alone in the cabin. He was standing by the stove, his broad shoulders hunched forward. He was shaking. His hand was held flat on the top of the stove, and when he flung round at me, his face was contorted with pain. The iron lid of the stove was red hot. He clenched his burned hand into a fist and held it under his arm, glaring at me with wild hatred. His eyes were red from tears of fury.

'What the hell are you doing?' I asked him, bewildered by the pain in his face. 'You want that in cold water.'

'Says you, Samuel Vempley.'

I went through to the galley and got a pan of cold water from the tub. I made Walmsley plunge his hand into it. There was a hiss as he writhed in agony. His eyes never left my face.

'That was a stupid thing to do.'

'You talking again?'

I shrugged. 'You'll enjoy hauling the halyards,' I told him.

I got some ointment from the galley and he smeared it on the wounded hand. The angry redness was gone. He flexed his fingers and then stood morosely by the stove, his hands hanging at his sides. He looked sick with pain, his eyes clouding over as he stared into the red glow of the fire.

'Can't play a practical joke these days, hev a bit of fun.'

'You'd have killed that lad.'

He flashed a malevolent grin at me. 'Might still do it.'

'Not with me around.'

'That's right, with you around. You brought this piety to *Rechabite*, Samuel Vempley. You turned us all soft.'

'Have you finished with that ointment?'

'But you ent got me.'

'You frighten boys, Walmsley.'

'You ent got the skipper neither, though you thinks you hev. That's your mistake. You'll learn. You'll see the way the weather goes once we hit a bit of rough. Bad fishing, few icebergs. You'll get the smell of the *Rechabite* then.'

There was a shout from the deck for all hands.

'Go to hell, Walmsley,' I told him.

I didn't wait for the rest. I went straight on deck and told the skipper Walmsley had burned his hand, stumbling against the stove. He glanced at me quickly, instantly suspicious.

'Is he drinking?'

'No, skipper.'

Everitt frowned and then looked back at the sails.

'You'd better take over with the halyards.'

'Right you are, skipper.'

'We'll put out for the grounds east of Orkney. See what we catch and maybe call at Westray. Get the mainsail hoisted, Mr Vempley. Mr Purvis, you give a hand.'

We all leapt to the sails. *Rechabite* tacked out of Wick and away to deep waters. She ghosted the waves with a fine easterly wind. She was like a bird eager to be away. We were soon lost in the work.

Everitt never left the tiller.

He hardly spoke.

He was tense with some strange anger, and his unpredictable mood made everybody nervous. Jack Walmsley being useless for two or three days didn't help. When the skipper changed the dressing and bandaged his hand, Walmsley winced with pain. The skipper made a point of doing the dressing every few hours. 'Make you think twice,' he said, tying the bandages with a vicious twist. The two men hardly spoke, avoiding each other's eyes.

In his fury, Everitt wouldn't let the men rest. Everything aboard *Rechabite* had to be scrubbed and polished. I could see the sense in that: keeping things clean saved a lot of trouble when you started gutting and icing the fish; you only needed a speck of dirt on the gills and you could lose the whole catch. But Everitt kept us at it until the dark hours: he even made us scrub the grid to the well, though he had no intention of stocking live fish. He just had to keep us at work.

Slowly, the routines made him easier.

He began to relax.

Not having Walmsley around seemed to help. He let me take the tiller when he drank his tea, and chatted amicably with Edwin Wallis. I loved being on the tiller. There's nothing like it: the spray flying in your face, cormorants and seagulls following in your white wake. I felt exhilarated, sensing *Rechabite* respond to my hand.

'How do you like her, Mr Vempley?' Everitt asked me one afternoon.

'She's a fine smack, skipper,' I told him.

He seemed pleased. 'Compared to *Wings of Morning*?' he asked.

I shrugged. '*Wings of Morning* was always easy to handle. She could turn on a splash of white spray and lift out of the waves as if she was made to fly. But I don't know that she had *Rechabite*'s speed. I've never known a smack like *Rechabite* for speed.'

I thought Everitt was going to slap me on the back. He drank his tea without looking at me, and then beamed up into the brilliant sunlight, his hands firmly clenched behind his back.

'You're a fine judge of a vessel, Mr Vempley,' he said quietly.

It was the nearest he ever came to paying me a compliment.

On the night watch, I heard him singing hymns at the tiller.

Once we had the lines over the side and were earning a living, he forgot about his fury with Jack Walmsley.

We caught fine fish working off Orkney.

I kept Daniel always at my side.

'This will do us,' Edwin said happily as we were baiting the lines one afternoon. 'Nothing like fishing when you're getting full lines.'

'I agree,' Daniel said solemnly. He spent hours talking to Edwin, chattering about the sea and his life in Grimsby, telling us about his mother's struggles to keep her home. 'I think I will become a fisherman,' he told us as he grabbed another whelk, still squirming every time he put the hook through the fat flesh, but doing the work with a will. 'I think I will have my own boat,' he added, with an innocent smile at Edwin.

We all burst out laughing.

'Good for you, Daniel,' John Pinney told him. 'Can I come and be second hand? We'd make a fine business of catching the fish.'

'Cast the same side as the Lord,' Edwin said seriously.

'Oh yes,' Daniel agreed with an emphatic nod. 'But I can't imagine a better life, can you, Mr Wallis?'

Edwin cracked another whelk and sat back for a moment, thinking. He took a puff at his pipe and rubbed his nose with the back of his hand.

'Can you?' Daniel asked with some surprise.

'I was thinking about the crofting.'

'What's that?'

'Farming on Shetland,' I told him.

'With some fishing,' Edwin added. 'They do that to help out when the farming's hard. I might have enjoyed crofting. I allus liked the land. But I weren't never given the chance. You take what you're given. But I had a grandmother knew about crofting. She spent her childhood on a croft at South Voe, on Shetland. She was always telling us yarns about that.'

'Tell us, Mr Wallis,' Daniel said eagerly. 'I never heard of crofting.'

'She was my father's mother,' Edwin said slowly. 'Lived with us in Yarmouth towards the end. I don't recall much about her, but the night she died, she talked about the crofting for hours: I do remember that. I was sitting by the bed with my old mother. My father was away fishing, working Tea Kettle Hole. He didn't get back before she died. But she did her talking: I suppose that was what she wanted, as long as somebody heard.'

'What did she say?' Daniel asked impatiently.

Edwin cracked another whelk and stared pensively over the stern.

'She told us about the croft. She said the walls were blackened by smoke, and they had a pot-shelf and open peat fires. Men lit their pipes from tinder boxes. They had oatmeal and bread if they were lucky, and always fish. She had a right taste for smoked herring, the old lady. The smokesheds were near the house. In good weather, the women used to sit outside, shelling the mussels for baiting the lines, getting the hooks through the soft flesh.'

'Ugghh.' Daniel shuddered and Edwin smiled at him.

'It's a hard life, Daniel, no matter where you get your living. But she never minded overmuch, growing up with it like. They had just the one crowded room to live in, with a table, stools, box-bed and truckle. There was salt-fish and onions hanging from the beams, oars and fishing lines. Her father suffered with rheumatism and used warmed skatebree for the pain. Outside, there were mounds of blue-grey mussel shells glinting along the green turf. The women waded waist-deep in the rock pools looking for mussels, feeling along the crevices, sitting in the sun afterwards and splitting the shells with a sharp knife to get the fish. Bare legs in the sunlight. Fingers slashed and scarred while they gossiped and concentrated on the shelling.'

He stopped for a moment, gazing across the blue sea. We were hove-to with the lines down and *Rechabite* rode the tide gently. A blue mistiness filled Edwin's pale old eyes.

'There was always broth cooking over the open fire, stirred with a heavy iron ladle. That was her first job, from being a wee girl. Light from a crusie lamp. Comfort from the peat fires. Then mornings listening to the plingies, crying over the ocean, the souls of the dead come back as seagulls, so you mustna harm a plingie.'

We nodded our agreement over that.

The souls of the drowned come back as mollies. That's what we believe. You can tell your friends from the way the birds strut and scavenge for food. You don't kill the mollies if you want to hear your friends yarning on the wind.

'The men took oatbread and cheese to sea with them,' Edwin went on in his dreamy voice. 'They sometimes rowed fifty miles out into the sea. They wore tight woollen jerseys when they were fishing, canvas trousers tied at the knees, and leather sea-boots up to the thighs. The women took haddock to the market at Lerwick in a creel. She said her mother had a cauldron over the peat fire and used to swing it out for ladling or filling. The men all played mouth-organs and fiddles. She danced to the fiddles, my grandmother. They touched iron for good luck and put a hare's foot out-side somebody's croft if they wished them harm. She had a lover's gift: a pearly conch shell, gleaming pink and blue and turquoise. She said there were mermaids and fairies on Shetland, and witches who lived in the sea. The men were away three days at a time, the boats undecked, nowhere to cook or shelter. At sea the men baited the lines themselves, and the women cut peat for winter while they were away. They used sandeels for bait if they couldn't find mussels.'

Edwin lapsed into a deep silence, preoccupied with his own memories, dark with a sudden sadness. We didn't like to speak. Even Daniel managed to keep quiet.

It was the following day that the skipper decided to head for Lerwick. 'We have a fine catch,' he said. 'No need to delay. I want to get to Iceland. Take the tiller, Mr Vempley, and show me you can get us there. I might begin to think you're a fisherman if you keep working the way you have.'

I took the tiller and checked the lie of the wind.

The last of the lines were up and Henry Purvis and some of the crew were sorting the catch. Jack Walmsley was back on deck now, helping coil the lines. We would be hand-lining after Lerwick. I gave the orders for full sail and set a course north-west for Shetland. At my side, Daniel beamed with admiration: you would have thought he was com-manding *Rechabite* himself.

We berthed *Rechabite* in Lerwick and Everitt sent Edwin and Henry Purvis to the market. The rest of us got the catch out of the fishrooms and into baskets on deck. When the merchants arrived, Everitt told Walmsley to go and buy mit-tens and guernseys and some spare oil for the lamps. Most of the skippers bound for Iceland bought tobacco and corn brandy when they were in Lerwick, but Everitt wouldn't stand for that. As the merchants' men began to unload the catch, I went off to have a look round. Daniel said he wanted to stay and watch the unloading.

I hadn't visited Lerwick for two years. There were crofters in town for the fish market, and crowds working on the quays. The houses built around the harbour jutted crazily into the sea, wooden piers leading directly from their back doors. Many of the doors were open in the warm weather. There were women on the piers, mending nets and prep-aring crabs and shellfish for hawking round the farms. Children tumbled and splashed joyfully in the shallow water, cartwheeling through the hot sun. I walked round the piers and sat on one of the stone bollards.

A dark-haired girl walked past me two or three times, swinging her skirts and giving me the eye. Relaxing in the sun, I felt easy in my mind for the first time since we'd left Yarmouth. I smiled at the girl absent-mindedly, and she came and sat on the next bollard along the quay.

'Are you with that liner?' she asked.

'*Rechabite*.'

'She's a fine vessel.'

'We're going to Iceland,' I told her.

'You might call in on your way back?'

'We might.'

I lit my pipe and grinned at her. She was outrageous in her flirting. 'You're very friendly,' I told her. 'I'm not going to find myself in a fight with your husband, am I?'

'No,' the girl said. She had the same dark laugh as Miriam, the same grey watchful eyes and dark hair coiled and fastened behind her neck. Her face and hands were tanned deep brown from the weather. I guessed she worked on the quays. 'Do you have a girl?' she asked me brazenly.

'No.'

'I don't believe you.'

'It's true.'

I felt the aching in my heart, but it was numb, lifeless: I smiled at the girl without emotion, observing her with my dead heart.

The girl laughed delightedly. 'I don't believe you,' she said, shaking her head, mocking. 'A tall man like you.'

'I *am* going to find myself in a fight,' I sighed wearily.

'Over me! You wouldn't fight over me!'

I got up and emptied my pipe. She looked up at me, swinging her bare legs from the bollards. She had lovely direct eyes. There was no mistaking her meaning. She had gold earrings in her ears and a wedding ring on her finger. I felt suddenly tired and wanted to get back to *Rechabite*. A group of men were watching us from the piers.

As I reached *Rechabite*, the merchants were leaving the deck. They looked disgruntled. Everitt was standing motionless by the tiller. I climbed aboard and glanced at Edwin Wallis.

'Anything wrong?'

'The market wasn't much good,' Edwin said quietly.

Everitt heard us. He glared after the merchants, disappearing down the quays, and then glanced furiously at his watch.

'We leave when Jack Walmsley gets back,' he said brusquely.

I nodded.

'Bad news about the market, skipper.'

Everitt registered my words, his eyes focusing on mine. He sniffed and straightened his back.

'We seem to be having our share of misfortune, Mr Vempley,' he said angrily.

I said nothing. I would have to keep out of his way.

I could see Jack Walmsley passing the merchants, greeting them cheerfully and hefting a huge package of mittens and guernseys across his shoulders, a can of spare oil for the lamps in his free hand. The merchants ignored his greeting.

A crowd of women and children had gathered on the quays to watch our departure, the children playing noisily round the bollards, the women chattering and knitting, their shawls hanging loose around their shoulders. The girl with the dark hair was nowhere to be seen.

I went down below and found Daniel in the galley. He was seated on a stool, drinking a mug of strong tea. There was a cut down his left cheek.

He did not look up when I entered the galley.

'Who did that?' I asked as he finished his tea.

'What?' he asked numbly.

'You know, Daniel. Who did that to your face?'

'Nobody.'

'Nobody!'

'I fell.'

He refused to tell me. I made another pot of tea, and when I filled his cup, his hand was shaking. He wouldn't speak, but there were tears in his eyes.

Thirty-one

We started fishing off Seydhjisfjordhur as soon as the skipper found his favourite grounds. Daniel was stunned by the coastline, the spectacular mountains right behind the shore, the sheer cliffs and plunging waterfalls, snow gleaming in the distance. In the intense blue water, fragments of ice drifted into the sea from the inland lakes, black from the lava sand in the mountains, white and pure in the brilliant sun. He stared in wonder at the floating ice, the clouds of seabirds spuming above the waves like screeching whirlwinds. It took me all my time to make him concentrate on the work. The hand-lines were down in deep water within minutes of making our destination. It was a thousand miles from Harwich to Seydhjisfjordhur, and once *Rechabite* reached Langanes just up the coast we would be within hours of the Arctic Circle. There was no time to waste staring at the landscape.

I made sure Daniel did the night watch with me, and whenever he was sleeping in the boys' quarters for'ard John Pinney looked out for him. John Pinney had no idea who had cut Daniel's face: he had been busy with the merchants when the accident happened: he did not see Daniel fall. Daniel still refused to tell me. As we worked the lines, he brightened and chattered as before, and seemed to forget the wound: the healing sunlight tightened the skin, and the cut was not a bad one.

The hand-lines were worked over the weather rail. The lines were played out through wooden tomboys fixed to the rail roughly four feet apart to give everybody room to work. Each line was thirty or forty fathoms in length and carried a lead weight of five to seven pounds. The hooks were fitted to a sprawl wire threaded through the top of the weight. In hand-lining, the snoods were not tanned and the lines not tarred. It was a very different kind of fishing from the long-lining we'd done so far.

'You have to adjust the snoods to the height of the rail,' I explained to Daniel, showing him how to get started. 'Then you can haul the line up to the side and use a net to get the fish aboard.'

'If I catch any,' Daniel giggled nervously.

'You'll catch something,' Edwin told him confidently.

'With big fish about,' I told him, 'maddened by hunger, you'll feel the sinkers striking their backs as the line sinks to the bottom. There'll be so many cod darting about you won't be able to miss them.'

Hove-to, *Rechabite* rocked gaily with the tide, held steady by the backed staysail. Everitt had two reefs in the mainsail. If there were fish about, we would be working the lines night and day. The gutting and icing would continue as long as we were catching fish.

'This is fun,' Daniel shouted excitedly, feeling the bite of the fish on his line, his face shining with pleasure as he hauled a massive cod aboard and landed it with his net. Edwin left his own line to help him.

'You should leave your line down,' I explained to Daniel.

'I felt the bite.'

'Wait until you've got fish on both snoods. They can't get off the hooks.'

'But I felt it bite!'

'Just keep your lines *down*,' I whispered harshly.

He nodded firmly, showing he understood, and then shrieked with pleasure as he felt another tug on his line. I nearly had to go across and stop him hauling. At his side, Edwin started talking to keep his mind off the abrupt jerks that shook the line.

'You got thirty fathom of line there, Daniel.'

'Is that right?' Daniel said excitedly, still thrilled by having his own place at the fishing.

'I prefer thirty fathom,' Edwin said ponderously.

'Why's that?'

'Easier fishing.'

'I'm a hundred-fathom man myself,' Henry Purvis shouted from his own tomboy.

'A hundred fathom!' Daniel gasped.

We all laughed at that.

'You don't want to listen to him, boy,' Edwin scoffed. 'Forty fathom of line is more than enough. You can work in water as deep as you like but forty fathom is the longest line I ever heard of being used.'

'And a thirty-pound weight,' Henry said gleefully, trying to rile Edwin.

'Seven pound on shoal ground,' Edwin went on stolidly. 'Scraggy Bank and them such places. Eleven-pounder off Faroes. I did hear of that.'

'But Mr Purvis just said . . .'

'He's mad, boy.'

'And fishing through midnight,' Henry went on imperviously.

'I prefer dawn or dusk myself, for hand-lining,' Edwin mused. 'What about you, Samuel?'

'Dawn for me,' I agreed.

'You get the biggest fish at dawn,' John Pinney said.

'Fair enough.' Henry Purvis laughed ruefully from further down the weather rail, giving up the argument. 'But it's always daylight in Iceland, remember. You don't get much of a dawn or a dusk.'

'Daylight,' Daniel said with wonder.

'That's the Arctic summer,' Edwin explained. 'It's always daylight when the smacks are fishing. When the daylight goes, it's time to be thinking about getting home. Otherwise, you get froze in.'

At the tiller, Everitt suddenly spoke.

'Let's get some fishing done, you men,' he said curtly. 'In the sweat of your brows you shall eat. And find me some fish. There'll be time for thinking about home when I've got my catch.'

'Yes, skipper,' Edwin agreed without a blink.

Nathan Chapman had already hauled his line heavy with two huge struggling cod and John and Richard Buss were busy with the gutting. As each man caught his fish, he measured it by the six-inch deck planks. On the Iceland fishing, all twenty-four-inch cod were entered in the skipper's notebook to count for a bonus of twopence a score. The skipper watched everything from the tiller, keeping his eye on the backed staysail and the run of the tide, listening to our casual conversation. Soon, we were all hauling our lines, unhooking the huge cod and throwing them to the gutters for heading, splitting and cleaning, getting the lines back overboard. Everitt wanted nothing for the well this trip. John Pinney and Richard Buss worked at the gutting until the sweat shone on their faces and their hands were red and swollen with fish slime and offal.

'The Lord is with us today,' Nathan Chapman chanted as he hauled yet another line heavy with threshing cod, the sunlight shining on their green backs, a spray of water dazzling like a cloud as they were lifted in the laddenette out of the water.

'Don't be blasphemous, boy,' Everitt told him briskly.

'Blasphemous, skipper? The Lord's name ent blasphemous.'

'It is in your mouth, boy.'

He scowled humourlessly, but the fish kept coming, and we were all too pleased to be bothered with the skipper.

'I don't care whether it's the Lord or the bait,' I managed to whisper to Daniel without anybody else hearing. 'The money we get will be just as easy to spend.'

But Daniel was fascinated by what Edwin Wallis was showing him.

'That's a candle,' he said, watching as Edwin cleared his line of fish and then crouched down to bait the hooks on the snoods. He used lengths of candle, ramming them through the hook. Daniel was still using the whelks we had in a bucket between us.

'Some of the lads used to carve bait out of potatoes,' Henry Purvis told him. 'Doesn't matter as long as they attract the fish.'

Edwin nodded, finishing his line and letting it go through the tomboy. 'I had a wooden bait one trip,' he said. 'Painted it silver. Cod like silver. Worked a wonder, but I lost it over Glettinganes way.'

Daniel snorted, showing doubt for the first time since we left the Humber. 'Cod don't like silver,' he said in a deeper voice, mocking us.

'Must do, they're that fond of herring,' Edwin said solemnly.

Down the weather rail, Henry Purvis and Nathan Chapman were already switching to candles for bait. Daniel watched them with wonder.

Edwin laughed when he saw his face, and decided to put him out of his misery.

'The thing is, Daniel,' he explained, 'the fish are sometimes so abundant you can catch them with unbaited lines, they're that greedy they'll gobble anything they can get their mouths on to.'

Daniel remained sceptical, until I showed him how to use candles on some of his own hooks and they came up with huge cod just as lively as the ones that had taken the whelks off the line.

'I told you fishing was all wonders.' I smiled at him.

He nodded, his eyes shining with the excitement of the catch.

As the fishing went on, we had even more wonderful stories. Edwin Wallis was full of yarns, and even Henry

Purvis relaxed, pleased with himself for the fish he was hauling, enjoying the warm sunlight and the relaxed routine at
the lines. The men doing the gutting did most of the hard
work when you were hand-lining.

'It's a rum place, this Iceland,' Henry said as we fished
our third afternoon.

'Is that right?' Edwin replied promptly, urging him on.

'You know they only get two hours' daylight come winter?'

'Two hours!' Daniel exclaimed.

'It's the truth,' Henry said with his quick nod. 'Two
hours. They sleep the other twenty-two. Not much else they
can do. Feed the cattle once a day, spend the rest of the time
sleeping. They're so poor the women use old sacks for skirts.
They take them off in the summer for keeping potatoes.
The men wear sheepskins turned inside out and tarred to
stop the water getting in. On my word as a fisherman.'

We all laughed at that.

'They always say the biggest catches come from the
biggest liars,' Jack Walmsley said dryly from the tiller where
he was checking the fishroom figures with the skipper.

Even Everitt seemed to be relaxing, pleased with the catch
and the easy weather, enjoying listening to the men talking.
When Matthew Whalley climbed out of the companion with
plates of fried fish and roast potatoes, every man on deck
cheered. We were ravenous after hours of fishing.

And still I kept up the night watches with Daniel.

The lad hardly seemed to need any sleep, and he was a
pleasure to work with, he was so interested in everything that
you told him. The night watch was the shortest, because of
the Arctic sunlight, but Daniel didn't want to miss any of it.
He stared at the endless seas, and was startled by the haunting cry of a herring gull. He leaned over the starboard
bulwarks and felt his hand freeze in the rapidly moving
waters. There wasn't a light to be seen on the calm ocean,
except the stars in the sky, the fire burning in the stern of
Rechabite.

'Why aren't there any other smacks fishing?' he asked me one night.

'We're late, for this season,' I told him. 'Most of them will be working further south. There are never any drifters this late in the season. They'll all be down Lowestoft way by now.'

'Why?' he asked.

'The herring shoals start moving in the spring. They're off Lerwick by the beginning of May, and Scarborough and Grimsby come late August. We didn't pass a single drifter on our way up here. Must be a fast season.'

'Or else they were fishing a long way out, or closer to the shore,' Daniel said, sounding very knowledgeable.

'Who told you that?'

'Edwin.'

'Right. And they do most of their fishing at night. They could have been there. We just didn't see them. You can sail for days in these waters and not see a vessel, and then suddenly find yourself in the middle of an enormous fleet: a hundred smacks trawling together, four or five hundred herring drifters.'

'Is drifting hard work?' Daniel asked.

'It can take an hour to haul the herring nets, but I've seen a drifter catch a thousand herring in twenty minutes.'

We were silent for several minutes. I leaned against the tiller, watching the movement of the stars, the moonlight radiant and pure. Everything was strangely quiet. A gull cried over the waves. In the silence, we held our breath and waited. The sky was changing to a rich orange colour, and then suddenly the horizon exploded, a luminous meteoric rainbow fragmenting in all directions, a vast electric storm illuminating the still seas to the horizon. Stars began to shoot through the night.

'The Lord's about,' Daniel whispered.

I stared at him. His face shone in the light. I saw Edwin climbing out of the companion. There was a shower of stars and lights, sudden flowering explosions. It was like fireworks, shimmering in brilliant moonlight. Daniel stood in a sort of awe, mesmerised by the bewildering colours. He was crying, but never took his eyes off the immense skies.

Edwin was standing at our side.

'It always affects you,' he said quietly, watching Daniel.

'Yes.' I nodded.

'Makes you realise.'

Daniel suddenly gasped.

A shooting star fell out of the sky and floated down to the horizon.

'Time for home,' Edwin said in a whisper.

In the midst of the dancing midnight, dawn was creeping up the skies.

Thirty-two

After about a week's fishing, *Rechabite* had run out of fresh water. We used the fresh water for cooking and drinking. If you wanted a wash it was a mitten thrown over the side and pulled up full of seawater. My skin tasted of salt after years of washing in green water.

'You'd better take the longboat, Mr Vempley,' Everitt said. 'Daniel can go with you, being as you're so friendly.'

There were sniggers from Purvis and Nathan Chapman, and Walmsley stood grinning by the water tub.

'I'll see to the longboat, skipper,' he said with alacrity, getting in before Everitt could give his orders.

'And get the smack hove-to, Mr Purvis.' The skipper nodded.

With Walmsley and the two young lads helping, we soon got the longboat tilted up and secured by ropes between the mainmast and mizzen, and Daniel helped me scrub the well out and mop it dry before plugging the holes with short wooden pegs. We put canvas round the pegs to make certain there was no leakage. Henry Purvis got *Rechabite* nicely hove-to while the skipper went below to check the figures for the catch.

'This is a good berth, Daniel,' Walmsley said as we lowered the longboat over the side. 'Have a look round. We don't often get the chance to set foot on hard ground on these Iceland trips.'

'I will,' Daniel told him seriously.

By the time we got the longboat lowered into the water, Everitt was back on deck.

'Take all the buckets we've got,' he shouted over the side.

Several buckets were thrown down into the bottom of the longboat.

With the men cheering from the bulwarks and the skipper ordering them back to their lines, we put our backs into rowing the longboat ashore. *Rechabite* had tacked a couple of miles north to Lodmundarfjord, a tiny fjord just to the north of Seydhjisfjordhur. We were working the lines in less than eight fathoms, but the fish were still taking the bait.

'Just head for that stretch of shore,' I told Daniel.

'Have you been here before, Samuel?' Daniel gasped as he looked over his shoulder and pulled with a will at the oars. He did everything as if it might be his last chance. He was one of the hardest workers I had ever known aboard a smack, and even Everitt acknowledged that.

'I nearly got frozen in one season,' I told him.

'Frozen in!'

'We'd gone ashore for water, just like *Rechabite*. There's a stream just behind those rocks, near the shore. You see them?'

'Yes,' he nodded.

'A couple of apprentices were hauling the longboat up for mooring and we were having a look round. There used to be an old feller lived there, in a hut. Lonely life. He smoked like a curing house, black shag tobacco. You never smelt anything like it. We'd just got back to the longboat when the second hand yelled out about ice.'

'Ice!' Daniel exclaimed with horror.

'I could see it creeping round the point. I thought the skipper was going to up and leave us.'

'He wouldn't do that,' Daniel said with wide eyes, jerking forward as the longboat plunged into the shingle beach and lurched violently to one side. I laughed at his terrified expression.

'Well he wouldn't want to be caught off Lodmundarfjord for weeks on end,' I said. 'I could see him talking to the second hand at the tiller. We got back in that longboat faster than it could freeze, I can tell you. I wasn't going to spend a winter with that crazy old bugger staring at the snow. Ice was closing behind us just as we went into Seydhjisfjordhur. We spent six weeks there that season, froze in. But at least we had comfort and good food.'

Daniel stared at me with admiration, and then frowned doubtfully.

'I never know whether to believe you half the time, Samuel,' he said seriously. 'I sometimes think your stories are too wonderful to be true.'

'I'm telling you the truth.' I laughed at him.

'Have you ever hit an iceberg then?' he asked. 'Jack Walmsley says he once hit an iceberg.'

'Don't talk us into bad luck, Daniel,' I told him.

'I only asked. Have you?'

'No, but I've seen them.'

'Seen them!' His eyes shone.

'Hundreds.'

'What are they like? Tell us?'

'Blue ice,' I said wistfully. 'Blue ice sailing in the water. They're beautiful things to look at. Freeze you in faster than you can haul the lines.'

'That sounds wonderful.'

'Maybe,' I grunted. 'But they're not something you'd ever *want* to see. Always get away before the sun kisses the water, my old skipper used to say. He never stayed this far north once the nights began to darken. That's when your Arctic winter is coming. It's too dangerous, being trapped by icebergs. Men die, Daniel, frozen black in the ice. They go mad, without food and water, raving as the sun sinks below the horizon. *Wings of Morning* always left long before there was any danger of being caught by bad weather.'

Daniel shivered, staring out to where *Rechabite* was riding the tide beyond the headland. In the sunlight, we could see the men working their lines. From the shore, *Rechabite* seemed a long way away.

'Let's get this water,' I said briskly.

I wanted to get back to *Rechabite* before the tide started running against us.

We took the buckets and found the stream behind the rocks. It was still running deep and clear. The hut where the old man had lived had long gone, but there were charred bits of wood buried in the sand. We filled the buckets and went back to the longboat, emptying them into the well. The water was ice cold on our hands, and Daniel took a long drink, closing his eyes as the water trickled down his neck. The sun was brilliant and high in the cloudless sky, but further down the coast I could see a bank of white mist floating from the sea. Seabirds wheeled and mourned all along the shore.

When the well was full and we had the buckets safely lodged in the bottom of the longboat, Daniel wanted to take a walk. 'Not for long,' I warned him, glancing down the coast towards the fog, 'we don't want to get trapped,' but he seemed entranced by the shingle beach, the rocks climbing to the green cliffs of the mountains, the glittering snow and ice in the distance.

'I heard about Iceland,' he said as we walked along the narrow shore. 'My father came here. A realm of midnight sun and perpetual darkness, he called it. Storms and fog, and wild sunsets and torrents of erupting water. He said there were volcanoes and lakes full of icebergs. I didn't know if that was true.'

'The icebergs drift down from the lakes into the sea,' I told him.

'It is true then?'

'Yes.'

'And the volcanoes?'

'Yes.'

He was reflective for a moment, kicking at the shingle, then went on searching among the pebbles, kneeling down and finding shells.

'I love shells, don't you, Samuel?'

'I suppose.'

'I know their names,' he said proudly. 'I was good at learning. Ottershell and striped venus. Blue-rayed limpet. There's a beautiful violet sea-snail you don't get often. Slipper limpet and tortoiseshell, common periwinkle, sting drill, tiger scallop. My mother had a tray in the kitchen where she kept her collection. She used to ask my father to bring them back but he never did. He said there wasn't time when you were fishing. I think he was right, now I know. Faroe sunset-shell was one of her favourites. She loved the names.'

He stood up and skimmed a handful of shells out to sea. He seemed to be moody and abstracted, reluctant to go back to the longboat. I had not seen him like this.

'Why don't you tell me what happened?' I asked him quietly.

He glanced at me nervously, taking another handful of shells to throw into the sea.

'Tell you?'

'Come on, Daniel.'

'There's nothing to tell.'

'Your mother wouldn't want to think you were being hurt,' I said unkindly. 'She wouldn't want that.'

He looked surprised, considering my words.

'I told you I fell.'

'But it isn't the truth.'

'No,' he said vaguely, feeling the faint white scar on his cheek. It soon wouldn't show, with the salt wind and sun. He was already tanned and his hair shone golden in the late-afternoon sunlight. He shrugged and sighed, dropping the shells he held in his hand and kicking at them with his long seaboots.

'My mother says you must be kind to people,' he said quietly.

'If they're kind to you.'

'No,' he said firmly. 'That wouldn't work. There wouldn't be any point then, if they were kind to you first. You must be kind to people always, because you never know their difficulties. We don't know what goes on in people's minds, what they've had happen in their lives.'

I scoffed angrily.

'That's nonsense, Daniel. A man like Jack Walmsley would just stab you in the back, and then what happens to your kindness?'

Daniel smiled radiantly.

'I like Jack Walmsley,' he said. 'He says funny things.'

'Oh yes!' I said angrily, staring at him in amazement.

'Yes.' Daniel nodded. 'Like the other morning, when he said water's wet. I thought that was funny.'

It was an old fisherman's saying. I took a breath and tried to control my temper. I wasn't going to persuade him with shouting.

'You might think that, until you felt the knife going in,' I said quietly, trying to shock him out of his stupidity.

He just smiled.

'At least you wouldn't be the one doing the stabbing,' he said.

I thought he must be a fool. I turned away and stared out to *Rechabite*. We ought to be getting back. But my heart was suddenly aching, and my eyes were blinded with tears. I could hear my grandmother talking, spinning her endless yarns beside the fire. She had a soft, lilting voice when she wasn't angry. She told me stories I would never forget.

I walked away a few yards and tried to stop the choking at the back of my throat. I couldn't grasp what was happening to me. I heard Daniel kicking his way along the tideline, whistling some tuneless song. I heard Miriam's dark voice calling to me from the tide, the surf tumbling and thundering up the beach, the great breakers pounding towards the shore. I could hear her singing in the twilight, walking towards me out of the foaming waves.

'God help me,' I gasped, staring up into the blue sky, letting the tears run down my face. 'God help me.' There was no reply. The sun burned my face, my mouth was full of salt. I cried into the empty desolation, and heard voices keening in the sunlight: Benjamin Bulpit screaming in pain; a young woman weeping over her child; an old woman endlessly repeating my name. I cried into the dark sunlight, and choked on my own phlegm.

'We must go back, Mr Vempley,' Daniel was calling.

Helpless, I stood and watched the light dazzling from the horizon, fluffy white cloud drifting across the intense blue sky. The cloud was pink with flashes of sunlight but full of dark shadows, travelling fast over the restless water. There was mist hovering over the surface of the sea. I felt the immense silence: intense, hard silence, gathering round us like the weather.

Daniel seized my arm and shouted and started dragging me back towards the longboat.

Thirty-three

We rowed through the choppy seas to *Rechabite*. Banks of black cloud were suddenly racing across the horizon. How had I failed to notice them? A cormorant flew low over the water like a black ghost skimming the waves. White surf tumbled and spumed over the bows of the longboat and the oars lifted into air as the swells took us by surprise. As we got nearer to *Rechabite*, we heard yells coming from the deck, saw the men on the lines turning and watching.

'What's happening?' Daniel asked, gasping for breath and half turning to look over his shoulder.

At the helm, I had no time to answer. I plunged my own oars and steadied the longboat as she rocked. I could hear the cries quite clearly now. It sounded like one of the boys. I could see nothing through the bulwarks once we were close enough to reach for the rope. We had to make for the stern of the smack because the lines were still down, stretched taut against the pull of the tide. As the longboat hit the stern of the smack, we were almost tipped over, and then I had the rope and was clambering up the side of the smack. Daniel followed me, and we tied the rope to the bulwarks. The longboat drifted clear with the tide.

Edwin Wallis was standing nearest to the transom stern. I caught my breath and watched what was happening. The skipper had Matthew Whalley tied to the mainmast, his shirt ripped open to the waist, his hands tied in front of him round the thick trunk of the mast. The skipper was flogging him with a length of frayed rope. Strips of flesh hung down between the boy's shoulders and there was blood pumping out of the wounds, running down his back and soaking his trousers. Each time the rope hit him, he writhed and screamed against the wood, clawing his hands into the oak. Every man in the crew was watching. Even the men on the lines had turned from their work.

I could feel Daniel trembling at my side. I reached out and gripped his arm. 'Take it easy.'

'Why's he doing that?' the boy stammered.

Matthew let out another cry and I saw John Pinney look away. Richard Buss went back to his lines. Edwin moved closer.

'He put cod livers in Walmsley's bunk,' he said quietly.

'Cod livers!'

'Stupid thing to do.'

'Stupid to get caught,' I muttered.

The skipper paused for breath, leaning against the boom, his chest heaving with his exertions. There was a line of sweat running down his brutal face: his skin looked like mahogany, with the features carved out with a knife. Nobody moved as he rested. Walmsley was standing by the mizzen, shaking his head miserably, staring at Whalley's bloodied back.

Then Daniel suddenly broke free of my hand.

He was blubbering, shouting incoherently. I couldn't make out what he was saying. Before I could move, he lurched across the deck and stood in front of Everitt. He was stammering and waving his arms in the air.

'You don't do that,' he seemed to be shouting at Everitt. 'You don't have the right to do that.'

Several of the men stepped forward but then hesitated.

'You can't hurt him,' Daniel went on stuttering and stammering, waving his arms about. 'You can't make him bleed.'

Everitt swung out with the rope and lashed Daniel across the chest. He stumbled and fell backwards into Henry Purvis's arms and then broke free and lurched towards the skipper. Everitt flinched and stared at him as if he had gone mad.

'You're hurting him,' Daniel shrieked at the top of his voice.

Everitt's face went black. His cheeks sucked in air and his eyes seemed to bulge out of their sockets.

'Is this my ship!' he roared with a violence that stopped Daniel in his tracks. Several of the men cowered back. Two or three of them turned and pretended to be busy with their lines so that the skipper wouldn't see them watching. 'Is this my ship!' Everitt roared again, and took a step towards Daniel, who danced and twisted in front of him as though he were treading barefoot on hot fires. 'Speak, you degenerate creature!'

Daniel seemed to stiffen at that. He stopped moving. With a single blow, the skipper brought the rope crashing across his shoulders and I leapt forward to try and get between them. I was yards away when Daniel went flailing across the deck. He seemed to spin and crouch for the floor, and then run as the rope hit him again. The thwack hissed in the air and Daniel let out a yell of pain. Stumbling, he fell straight against the tiller. There was a tremendous thud as his head hit the massive tiller beam. Then the smack was lurching out of control.

'Get the tiller,' Everitt screamed as Walmsley darted forward.

But it was too late. The tiller swung violently to starboard and suddenly *Rechabite* veered round into the wind. The wind flung her out of control. I heard the crash of the longboat against the stern, and then a yell as the men at the bulwarks started struggling with their lines.

'She's going,' Edwin yelled from the stern as he tried to reach the painter for the longboat.

'Hold her,' I heard Everitt screaming.

But *Rechabite* was like a drunk on slippery cobbles. She

swung rapidly against the lines, and then lurched back as Walmsley tried to regain control of her. Everitt was already at the tiller and shoving Jack Walmsley out of the way. With a tremendous screeching, tearing noise like fingernails going down a blackboard, the staysail parted from its ropes and flapped loosely in the breeze. Then the lines twanged, tightened to breaking point by the violent movements of the smack and then snapping apart as the longboat was dragged backwards right through them. In thirty seconds, we lost a complete set of lines.

I had Daniel's head in my arms by the time Everitt got *Rechabite* righted. The crew worked without a sound to fit the new staysail and bait a fresh set of lines. Everitt hardly seemed to notice. He stood at the tiller, staring at the darkening skies. He seemed rigid with shock. Edwin Wallis and Francis Campbell had taken Matthew down to the for'ard cabin to bathe his wounds. The skipper gave them the keys for the medicine box in his cabin. He was acting like a machine: jerking and stiff at the tiller; wild-eyed when anybody spoke to him.

I could see Daniel's eyes fluttering. He opened them and looked straight at me. He smiled, and then the smile passed: his face went white and he reached out to feel the back of his head. There was no blood. He had been stunned and no worse. He struggled to sit up and rubbed the back of his head, staring at the heap of broken and tangled lines on the deck. When he saw the skipper, he flinched, and then tried to stand up.

Everitt heard the sound. 'Has that man recovered?' he asked without looking at me.

'I'll take him below, skipper.'

'No you won't.'

'He needs that head seeing to.'

Everitt suddenly looked straight into my eyes. He smiled. It was the worst smile I had ever seen: remorseless; evil. He lifted his hand, and suddenly Nathan Chapman and Jack Walmsley were behind me.

'Stand aside please, Mr Vempley,' the skipper said icily.

'I won't let you touch the lad.'

With a curt nod the skipper told the two men to hold me. They had my arms before he had finished speaking. Walmsley twisted my left arm hard behind my back and Nathan Chapman yanked at the other. I struggled while Everitt watched, fighting to break free, but I couldn't move my arms.

'Samuel!'

I glanced up. It was Daniel speaking. He was standing clear, watching me try to get free. He shook his head.

'Don't get into trouble,' he said calmly.

'You leave him alone,' I shouted at Everitt, sweat running down my face at the pain in my shoulders. I think Walmsley was trying to break my arm.

'You be still, like a good feller,' he whispered sneeringly against my ear. His breath stank of whisky. I stared at Everitt: how could he not smell the alcohol? He was laughing at me. He was enjoying himself. With a quiet smile, he turned back to face Daniel.

'I think I am the skipper of *Rechabite*,' he said with a sneer.

'Yes, sir,' Daniel said promptly.

'Is that right?'

'Yes, sir.'

'I was beginning to imagine otherwise.'

I saw some of the men watching. Edwin Wallis and John Pinney kept their backs to the scene, concentrating on the fishing. There was a line of sweat on Everitt's thin top lip, and his mouth was twitching.

'I didn't mean to offend . . .' Daniel tried to say, but Everitt lifted a finger and waved it arrogantly in his face.

'Be quiet, boy.'

'Yes, sir.'

'I understood you to say that I had no right to punish members of my crew?'

Daniel stared at him silently: blushing, confused.

'You don't speak now.'

'I don't know what he did, but I can't bear the sight of blood.'

'Really?'

'Sir?'

'Even your own?'

'No, sir,' Daniel answered, his voice trembling.

I couldn't stand much more of this. I threshed against Nathan's grip and then tried to swing him round into Walmsley. Walmsley laughed and brought his knee crashing into my groin. I went over in agony, the sweat pouring down my face. I couldn't hear a sound for several seconds, a black buzzing drowning my brain.

Everitt was pointing towards the bows.

'This is a forlorn vessel, Daniel. Forlorn and unlucky. We have been unlucky ever since we left Yarmouth, but I can't put that down to your presence. Your presence has been joyful and willing. You have impressed me. You have done your work well. But I think you have been keeping bad company. Unlucky company. A man of many misfortunes. I think he has led you astray. Is that right?'

'I don't know what you mean, but I like Samuel, he's my friend.'

'So I hear,' Everitt said coldly.

'He is my friend,' Daniel protested. 'He's taught me a lot.'

Henry Purvis grinned behind the skipper's back. So that was the story they were putting round. Hanging on brutally to my arm, I could feel Walmsley nodding vigorously, Nathan trying not to laugh.

Daniel stared at the skipper blankly. He had no idea what they were talking about. His face shone as he called me his friend. He glanced at me, and I saw the pity in his eyes, the look of terror.

'Go to the bows, Daniel,' the skipper suddenly ordered.

'Sir?'

'Go to the bows. You know where the bows are, don't

you? Hasn't your friend Samuel taught you that? Go to the bows and be our figurehead. We need a forlorn figurehead for our forlorn vessel, and you are a forlorn creature, a deranged creature sent from God to be a warning to all men. Go to the bows, Daniel, and be our figurehead.'

I saw Daniel stare round him in bewilderment and then stumble towards the bows. Everitt followed him. He carried the length of rope and shouted at Daniel to hurry up. When Daniel reached the bows, Everitt made him climb up on to the bowsprit and stand facing the sea. The smack lifted and rolled and I saw Daniel reach out for the jib sheets. He clung on desperately. Everitt stood right behind him, swinging the rope and shouting his insane orders.

'Be our figurehead, Daniel, be our forlorn figurehead.'

Then Daniel stumbled and nearly fell over the starboard bows. He let out a cry. Everitt leapt forward and grabbed his arms. He was still shouting about figureheads. He pulled Daniel back on to the for'ard deck and yelled at Henry Purvis to bring a rope. I saw Purvis running with a length of tarred rope.

'Get undressed, boy,' Everitt was shouting.

In his panic, Daniel started to undress.

I tensed and watched what was going on. I had to wait for my moment. I was going to hurt Walmsley, and then get the skipper. Great banks of black cloud raced above our heads. Gulls screamed and mourned over the sails. The seas were white with surf and tumbling waves. Daniel flung his shirt to the deck in his hurry and pulled uselessly at his seaboots. Henry Purvis had to help him. When he had removed his trousers, Everitt told him to get rid of his pants. He stood naked before the skipper: a thin, white child, shaking in the evening cold. A low wind was moaning in the rigging.

Everitt seemed delighted. He stroked his rope down Daniel's chest, and then let out a cold laugh.

'Now be our figurehead,' he told Daniel quietly, in a hiss that carried the length of the boat.

Without a word, Daniel climbed back on to the bowsprit,

and Henry Purvis climbed after him to tie his hands to the jib ropes. At least he would not fall overboard and drown.

I could sense Walmsley and Chapman watching, tense with the angry drama. I had to move now. I held my breath and then kicked out with all my strength. I gave a yell as my feet left the deck and I flung both men backwards. Nathan went crashing into the mizzen and then I was on my feet struggling to get round for Walmsley. But this time Walmsley was ready. He must have guessed I would try for something. Before I could focus, he was moving behind me, and as I began to turn, he hit me with all his strength with a wooden codbanger. The club came down on the back of my neck, and I was gone into blackness before my head hit the deck.

Thirty-four

A faint green luminous glow filled the cabin from the stove fire. My throat and mouth were dry. I could hear a voice chanting in the darkness, far away across the water, muddled with the cries of seabirds. I opened my eyes and winced at the chronic pain. As I tried to sit up, I started choking, the fumes from the fire acrid and strong. The chanting voice floated nearer: it was coming from *Rechabite*'s deck.

I rolled out of the bunk and went to the door. It was locked. I hammered on the door but nobody came. There was no sound from the galley. Getting my gutting knife from the locker I forced it into the lock and twisted the blade. The lock gave slightly. I rammed the blade in and worked at it furiously. The lock was rusty. There was a snap, and the lock flew open, breaking my blade in half. I glanced at the jagged edge, and then listened to the chanting voice. It was Everitt, coming from the for'ard part of the deck: it was much louder now, and frantic.

I forced the door open and ran to the bottom of the companion. There were shadows moving at the top of the iron ladder. I pulled my seaboots off and scrambled quickly up. Halfway up I stopped to listen. Everitt's voice raked at the cold air, blunt and relentless in the dark. The madman was singing.

'Come, O my guilty brethren, come,
Groaning beneath your load of sin!
His bleeding heart shall make you room,
His open side shall take you in;
He calls you now, invites you home:
Come, O my guilty brethren, come.'

I climbed the rest of the ladder and peered over the hatch.
Walmsley was standing with his back to the companion. A
fire burned in the brazier in the stern and there were flares
guttering and blazing along the bulwarks of the smack. The
crew were standing about in desultory groups, watching,
sullen. It was cold and dark: the brief Arctic darkness.
Edwin Wallis was for'ard, standing slightly in front of the
men, stiff, rigid: in a moment's insanity I wondered if Edwin
was taking part in what was happening. I was still stunned
and confused from the blow to the back of my head.

Daniel was parading up and down the for'ard deck. He
was naked. Swirling mist danced through the garish light of
the flares. Cold shivered in the shrouds. As Daniel stalked
up and down, dragging wearily along the deck, Nathan
Chapman kept throwing buckets of cold water over him. I
heard the water hit Daniel's flesh. I saw him shiver and
stumble at each drenching.

'Throw! Throw!' Everitt screamed, and then suddenly he
was chanting again, following Daniel up and down the
ghastly shimmering deck, yelling into his face in a voice that
sounded like iron chains rattling.

'Oh hear me, you children of Israel. My soul is filled with
such a sense of God's love, as makes me weep before Him.
Weep, weep, you children of Israel. For one night I dreamed
that I was in Yorkshire, in my working clothes going home –
I heard a mighty cry, as of a multitude of people in
distress – ALL on a sudden they began to scream and tumble
over one another; I asked, what was the matter; and they
told me, Satan was let loose among them – Then I thought I
saw him in the shape of a red bull, running through the

people as a beast runs through the standing corn, yet not offering to gore any of them, but making directly at me, as if he would run his horns into my heart. Then I cried out, "Lord, help me!" and immediately caught him by the horns and twisted him on his back, setting my right foot on his neck, in the presence of a thousand people. Oh weep, weep, for the coming of the Lord.'

As the skipper came to the end of his ranting, Daniel stumbled and fell and began crawling along the deck. Everitt seized another bucket and hurled it over his writhing body. I saw the cod livers cascade over Daniel's back. The stench of cod livers and urine polluted the damp midnight air. Daniel groaned helplessly and Everitt started kicking him, yelling, 'Up! Up!' in a terrifying scream, flailing and kicking frantically as the men began to murmur.

I knew there was no point tackling Walmsley.

I climbed rapidly back down the companion and dragged my seaboots on. In the cabin, I furiously broke locker doors until I found a gutting knife: it was Edwin Wallis's, shining razored steel with a bone handle. I pushed the knife down the inside of my right seaboot and left the cabin.

In a sweating panic, I ran through the starboard fishroom and opened the door into the for'ard quarters. There were groans coming from the for'ard cabin. In one of the bunks, Matthew Whalley lay flat on his stomach, crying and feverish. His back was inflamed and tight with hard red skin. He kept muttering, 'Please, please,' in a racking whisper. I could hear the shouts going on above me, Everitt's wild fury.

'Hang on, Matthew,' I said close to his face. He was burning, sweat pouring off his face and soaking his hair and pillow. He grabbed my hand and went on begging, 'Please, please,' and his hand was wet with fever and blood. The blood was still oozing from his torn back. I had to leave him.

I broke free and climbed the for'ard hatch.

Everitt's voice was getting louder and more hysterical.

He was still kicking Daniel, who lay motionless on the watery deck.

'The Whore of Babylon and all the Clergy of the Land are abominated by the Lord,' Everitt yelled into the darkness. 'False Shepherds and Liars adulterate my Bible as an adulterous man commits fornication with an adulterous woman – Oh Lovers of Jezebel, children of SIN and adultery!'

Incredibly, he burst into song.

> *'Still the fountain of Thy blood*
> *Stands for sinners open'd wide;*
> *Now, even now, my Lord and God,*
> *I wash me in Thy side.'*

He finished, and went on flailing at the helpless body before him. I had to move before he killed Daniel. I leapt out behind Nathan Chapman and snarled his name. As Nathan swivelled round, I bunched my fist and hit him as hard as I could in the throat. A choking, gargling sound came out of his mouth as he crashed to his knees. His eyes were wide with surprise, and then he opened his mouth to speak and collapsed. His head hit the deck with a sickening thud.

I turned on Everitt.

Daniel was lying lifeless on the deck.

With the iron-nailed heels of his boots Everitt was hacking away at the flesh of the boy's hands and arms. The flesh was coming off in lumps. There was blood and skin on Everitt's boots. In the light of the flares, I could see that there was no skin on Daniel's hands, and his back was smeared with foul excrement, daubed all over his shoulders and thighs. There was a sudden murmur among the men.

In less than seconds, I saw Jack Walmsley start for'ard and then several men hurl themselves in his way. John Pinney went straight for his legs, and Richard Buss and Francis Campbell tried to grab his arms. Walmsley let out a yell of pain and began knocking them aside. He floored Campbell with a single blow, and turned savagely on Buss, trying to kick John Pinney at the same time. In the frantic struggle, I heard a cry, and then Henry Purvis darted right in front of

Walmsley and hit him in the face with a wooden club. Walmsley stared at him in amazement, and then stumbled forward on to his knees. His eyes were wide open as he went down. I saw Edwin in the same seconds: too stunned to act, the shock racking his old face; he watched everything as if he was living a nightmare. The men in the stern finally over-powered Walmsley. It took all four of them to hold him, until suddenly he seemed to give up. He went slack in their arms, and shuddered. His hands hung limp at his sides.

Then Everitt came out of his trance and turned to face me.

He seemed to recognise me for the first time.

He smiled.

Thirty-five

Arctic dawn was lifting around us, frozen silence. The sluggish green seas drifted out of the dark: a pale white sunlight shimmered through the veil of mist; a low wind soughed through the rigging. There was a knocking, bumping sound against the sides of *Rechabite*. I could hear strange grinding noises, abrupt cracks in the air. The sunlight was weak and watery, a desolate sun shrouded like a white moon.

Then I saw the icebergs: the sea was bobbing with icebergs, blue shards of ice swirling beneath the surface, Arctic winter floating down from the frozen north to surround our stranded vessel. Like rainbows, the icebergs were surrounding us: blue and pink, white and garish green, black with seams of lava. *Rechabite* turned and knocked drunkenly against the ice. She moaned like the wind in her rigging.

Everitt was watching me with cold condescension.

He began chanting again, this time very quietly, his voice hoarse with the night's work, his eyes inflamed and lifeless. As he chanted, his voice became gradually firmer. His mouth was flecked with spittle. All the time he was speaking, he moved steadily closer towards me.

I knew he had gone mad.

He whispered his words like a maniac in an asylum.

'Come out! Come out! Let Sodom feel its doom. Where now is Lot? At Zoar safe! Where is his wife? Is she not salt all? The writing is on the wall – Thou lewdly revellest with the bowls of God . . . Let Bel asunder burst! . . . The saints now judge the earth. The omnipotent is here, in power, and spirit in the word – The sword, white horse, and King of kings has drawn the flaming sword! Rejoice, ye saints, rejoice!'

At the final rejoice, he made a lunge and grabbed my arm. For a moment I couldn't move, mesmerised by his ranting voice. I was hypnotised by the blank, cruel eyes.

'Rejoice!' he spat into my face.

I had my knife ready. I brought the handle down on his wrist and he reeled back in pain, gasping with surprise.

'Rejoice!' he said with a bewildered stare, as if he had been trying to do me a kindness.

I backed away, keeping myself between Daniel and the skipper.

I saw Edwin kneel down and lay a coat over Daniel's naked body.

Everitt went on speaking, hissing the words into my face.

He had recovered his venom, massaging his aching hand.

'Great Og and Agag where are ye!' he sneered. 'The walls of Jericho are thou, fall flat! Joshua's ram's horns, the seven and twelve, pass Jordan's stream . . . The Lord's anointed reigns – The rods or laws of Ephraim, ten unite in one, and hold by Judah's skirt – The Son of Man o'er Israel reigns – The dry bones now arise . . . The bride is come – The Bridegroom now receives the marriage seal. The law and gospel now unite – The moon and sun appear – Caleb and Joshua pass the stream in triumph to restore – Where now thou Canaanite art thou? Where all thy maddened crew?'

With his relentless chanting, he had backed me craftily to the bows, and suddenly lunged forward yet again. He had a gutting knife in his left hand and the length of frayed rope in his right. As I stumbled against the bowsprit he lashed out with the rope and the frayed end cut straight across my mouth. The knife slipped from my hand. I leapt frantically for the bowsprit and hauled myself upright, clinging on to the shrouds. As he came forward, I leaned back and kicked him with all my force. The nailed seaboot crashed into his shoulder and he reeled into the bulwarks, dropping his own knife. Before he had time to recover, I leapt from the bowsprit and ran to the coaming over the well: we kept spare gutting knives there. I grabbed one from the locker and was spinning round as Everitt came for me. His slashing blow caught me on the arm. I let out a grunt of pain. The knife sliced through the flesh and my blood was suddenly spurting out on to the deck. He lifted his arm to strike again but I ducked out of the way and dodged behind the mainmast.

I had time to catch my breath. Edwin was kneeling with Daniel, wrapping his body in a blanket Francis Campbell had brought for'ard, holding the boy in his arms. At the companion, Walmsley had given up struggling. He was sitting on the hatch, his head miserably slumped on his chest, his arms tied behind him. Nathan Chapman and Henry Purvis were standing beside him.

Everitt was chanting again, following me round the mainmast, hissing the words in the weird blue dawnlight. The blood was still pumping out of my left arm. I had to keep my eyes on him. I had to listen for the break in his voice when he would attack. His eyes never left my face. He was smiling all the time he spoke.

'The Earth shall be filled with My Goodness,' he hissed in a savage whisper, 'and hell shall be filled with My Terrors . . . My fury shall go forth – and My Lovingkindness shall save to the utmost all them that now come unto ME.'

'Amen,' I heard Edwin whisper in a low voice.

Everitt didn't hear him.

'Awake, awake, O Zion,' he sighed, 'put on thy beautiful garments, O Jerusalem: for the day of the LORD is at hand . . . I will break down the pride of the Lofty, and I will exalt the Spirit of the Meek . . .'

We were round by the starboard bulwarks when he came for me.

'SATAN!' he screamed in a wild, hysterical cry, and the next minute I was pinned against the bulwarks and he was forcing my back over the side. I brought my right hand up and slammed the handle of the knife into his neck but the blow incensed him. 'SATAN!' he screamed again, and brought his knee up into my groin. I felt the blackness sweeping across my mind. I was going to pass out. I tried to change my grip on the knife to plunge the blade into his back but he wrenched my arm down and then brought his elbow up into my neck, forcing it into my windpipe. As I choked for air, I heard the knife clattering on the deck, and the wooden bulwarks behind me splintering. There was a savage cry from Everitt, and then I was slipping backwards through the broken bulwarks. Everitt was standing over me with his gutting knife. He let out a shout of joy, and plunged the knife down towards my stomach.

It was Edwin who grabbed his arm.

For a moment, the two men faced each other, Everitt lurching round with surprise, Edwin staring at him with blank amazement. Then the knife fell from Everitt's fingers, and with a terrified cry, he was flailing backwards over the bulwarks, stumbling in wild panic and plunging down into the sea. With a heft of his shoulder, Edwin had forced him over the side.

'SATAN!' we heard the skipper screaming.

Then there was a splintering crash as he hit the water.

'SATAN!' he screamed again.

I managed to heave myself up against the bulwarks. The men rushed across the deck. Edwin stood motionless at my side.

Rechabite was surrounded by broken ice floes. We could see the blue lumps of ice bobbing and floating with the tide, grey blobs sticking out of the water, slithers of darkness lurching with the fast-running tide. Seabirds wheeled and dazzled in the watery sunlight. Grey mist hung over the horizon. There were blue icebergs floating all around us.

Everitt was scrabbling about on his hands and knees,

trying to stand on a lurching watery shard of ice. The ice was underneath the surface of the water, a dark, slippery shadow, bouncing and bumping against the side of *Rechabite*. Each time he managed to stand, the ice lurched away from the vessel, and he stumbled down to his knees. He was shouting and waving his fists at *Rechabite*. He was screaming in terror in the bleak dawn silence.

Then the sheet of ice bounced violently against *Rechabite*, and began to drift away from the vessel. The tide carried her out. We could see ripples of water running across the dark shadow.

Everitt let out a cry of fear.

'Edwin!' he shouted. 'Edwin!'

At my side, Edwin stared back at him. There were tears shining in the old man's eyes. He was trembling, but when I tried to stand, he put his hand on my shoulder.

'My Loving-kindness shall save to the utmost all them that now come unto ME,' he said very softly. His voice was weary with grief. He wouldn't let me stand.

'Jack Walmsley!' the skipper was screaming. 'You do your duty. You know what I done for you! Jack Walmsley! You do your duty, man!'

At the companion, Jack Walmsley never moved.

Everitt was drifting further away. He had managed to stand and was rigid on the island of ice. We could see his body tense with fury and fear. He could only keep his balance by standing perfectly still. He couldn't move his arms. He started chanting, glaring at *Rechabite*. His voice was rough in the chill air. His eyes blazed with a fierce agony.

'The axe is laid to the tree, and it must and will be cut down; ye know not the days of your visitation . . . The midnight-hour is coming for you all, and will burst upon you. I warn you of dangers that now stand before you, for the time is at hand for the fulfilment of all things. Who is he that cometh from Edom, with dyed garments from Bozrah; that speaketh in righteousness, mighty to save all that trust in him; but of my enemies I will tread them in mine anger, and trample them in my fury; for the day of vengeance is in my heart, and the year of my redeemed is come.'

Then we could no longer hear him. He was drifting out to sea with the ice floes. His voice grew fainter and fainter, his desperate cries lost on the low wind, and then he was a black shadow, like a scarecrow standing on a field of ice, spinning into the Arctic winter, floating towards the distant hills of blue.

Thirty-six

Edwin had *Rechabite* turned for Shetland as soon as Everitt disappeared. He was the senior hand now: Walmsley was locked below, and Henry Purvis had simply given up: dejected and keeping his head down; depressed when there was no work to be done. Purvis and Nathan Chapman were both told they would be reported once we reached Lerwick. They helped with the sailing of the smack, desultory, lifeless, but hardly spoke during quiet hours. We had to get away from Iceland before the ice began to freeze and we were trapped for the winter. It was because we had come so late that we had almost been caught by the first of the drifting icebergs.

Walmsley was secured in the skipper's cabin. He gave no trouble. He seemed to have lost his will: when we took him food he watched us with a bewildered expression, and scarcely bothered to eat; if we spoke to him, he avoided our eyes, refusing to reply. At night, he talked to himself in the cabin. Half the time he didn't seem to know where he was.

'You didn't touch Bulpit, did you?' I asked him one night.

He glanced up, his eyes dull with hunger and weariness. He sat crouched in a corner of the cabin, his head hunched forward on his knees. He didn't move: would sit like this for hours. I could see the blank incomprehension in his blood-shot eyes.

'You didn't push his hand into the boiling fat?'

He didn't speak, but I already knew the answer.

I had seen Everitt outside his cabin, moving towards the galley, pretending to be shocked by Benjamin's scream of pain. I had seen him hacking the skin off Daniel's defence-less hands.

'You must eat,' I told Walmsley gently.

He seemed like an animal, trapped in a weird cage. He had no understanding of what had happened. Everitt must have driven his life for years. Without Everitt, he didn't know what to say.

'He was a domineering man,' Edwin told me one night as we took the watch together. I was on the tiller. Edwin was watching for the lights that would show us we were near Shetland. 'He ran our lives.'

'You admired him.'

'I thought he was truly religious.'

'All that violence and discipline? Break the will of the child?'

'I read that in Wesley.'

Edwin stared unhappily through the darkness. Winter was moving in fast now, the northern autumn bleak with cold and ice, the skies brilliant with stars. The night was bit-ter. No more bitter than Edwin's regrets.

'You couldn't have protected the boys,' I said.

'I could have tried.'

'He would have got rid of you. He wouldn't have had you on *Rechabite*.'

'I know that,' Edwin said quietly. 'But it is on my con-science. I can't disown that. I could have done better.'

'We could all have done better,' I said quietly.

In the silence, I saw a shooting star falling to the horizon. I felt the immense loneliness of the sea: the life I had lived since leaving the workhouse. I heard Joseph Proctor's kind old voice in my mind. I heard the icebergs floating in the blue darkness, creaking and freezing in the misty cold. I wondered if I would ever return to Iceland.

'Everitt once said that being a good man is not enough,' I said.

Edwin shrugged wearily.

'I wouldn't know,' he said.

'I think you do, Edwin. He said when the moment came I would need something else. Something other than kindness.'

'Did you?' he asked after a long silence.

I felt *Rechabite* move steadily beneath me, gliding over the rough waves, pitching and rolling towards the lights of the far islands.

'No,' I said quietly.

In the for'ard cabin, Daniel spent his time sleeping. We bathed his arms and changed the dressings every few hours. He was fretful and hot, and feverish for the first two days. When his temperature went down, we managed to make him drink some water. The water wet his lips, and he opened his eyes: when he saw me, he started crying gently: I held him in my arms for hours: I held him, and sang lullabies I remembered from my childhood, hearing Miriam's sweet voice in my mind, hearing my mother singing by the fireside. I held him even when he slept, and changed his dressings myself, bringing him weak broth to drink, using cold water on his forehead.

'It is over?' he whispered to me as Lerwick finally came into sight.

'Yes, it's over,' I reassured him.

'It wasn't nice.' He began to cry, his voice weak and piping, his eyes such a deep blue I almost cried myself with wonder. 'It was cruel,' he told me with his trembling firmness, determined to control his voice.

'It was cruel.' I nodded, gritting my teeth to stop the tears.

I nursed him like a woman with a child.

On the last afternoon, as Edwin was berthing *Rechabite* in Lerwick, Daniel leant against my shoulder and talked about the fishing.

'I will always remember Iceland,' he said proudly.

'So will I.'

'I will remember the blue icebergs. Nobody will believe I have seen them, but you and I know what was true. We did see the icebergs.'

'We did.' I nodded with a laugh. 'They nearly did for us.'

'But you will stay with the fishing?' Daniel said after a moment's silence. 'You know you love that.'

I shrugged.

'I don't know anything,' I told him.

'Yes you do. The fishing was nothing to do with *Rechabite*.'

'Maybe.'

'No.'

'There's plenty more men like the skipper, Daniel.'

'No,' he said again firmly.

We carried him ashore, and stayed in Lerwick until he was well enough to move. I visited the cottage hospital every afternoon. The doctor said the skin on his arms and hands would soon grow again. There had been no broken bones despite the brutal kicking. Daniel grinned when the doctor said he would quickly be well: he was most concerned that his mother should not be shocked by his return.

In the afternoons, I walked the quays at Lerwick or talked with Edwin. I had to go back to Grimsby with Daniel and tell his mother what had happened. She had to know the truth, even if Daniel insisted on going on with the fishing. If she agreed, I would help him find a decent smack. I would find one of the skippers who knew what the fishing was about.

After that I had to return to Yarmouth. Benjamin Bulpit's mother had no idea how her son had died. I had to tell her the truth, or find a truth that would help her survive her grieving. I could not leave the death of her son such a harsh, unbearable blankness. I could not be silent, unless she needed me to be silent. But I had to go back and find out.

Then I must visit the graveyard in Whitby, say goodbye to my Miriam.

And go back and thank the wise woman.

I have a lot to do with my life. I have to make a fresh beginning. And there will always be the fishing, until the sun kisses the horizon.

THE LAST MUTINY

Bill Collett

Dogged by mutinies and accusations of tyranny throughout his distinguished career, Vice Admiral William Bligh had looked forward to a relatively peaceful retirement.

But it seems there is to be no rest for the wicked. Insolent neighbours, marauding geese, rebellious daughters and his own failing health all conspire to disrupt the tranquillity of rural Kent, encouraging the beleaguered Bligh to seek a kind of solace in looking back over his eventful life. Cook's last voyage, the Governorship of New South Wales, tussles with Napoleon and of course the mutiny of Fletcher Christian are all re-lived with candour and insight, as Bligh reflects on his current problems and morbidly inspects his 'nightsoil' for clues to his maladies.

Frank, exuberant, and witty, *The Last Mutiny* is an inspired testament of a man convinced he is more sinned against than sinning.

'[It] has an authenticity that is compelling, but it is the fiction that lifts the novel far beyond the predictability of history'
Australian Book Review

ABACUS FICTION
0 349 10643 6

THEORY OF WAR

Joan Brady

Elegant and passionate, *Theory of War* is the haunting story of Jonathan Carrick, sold into white slavery as a child, in post-Civil War America.

Jonathan is cruelly treated by his master, Alvah Stokes, and it is Alvah's son George who becomes the object of a hatred that endures half a century. Forced to submit, but never submissive, Jonathan's escape to a new life as a railroadman, then as an itinerant preacher, opens up a new world for him. But within him lies the need for revenge – a war against George, in fact – that must be satisfied.

A chronicle of human triumph over adversity, *Theory of War* also provides as breathtaking and visionary an account of life in the primitive West as any to be found in the novels of Jack London or John Steinbeck.

'It resonates beyond the particular experience of one family, [becoming] an allegory of American society, and a commentary on notions of freedom everywhere'
Independent on Sunday

'Absolutely brilliant' Mary Wesley

Whitbread Book of the Year 1993

ABACUS FICTION
0 349 10457 3

SUMMER IN FEBRUARY

Jonathan Smith

Sir Alfred Munnings, retiring President of the Royal
Academy, chooses the 1949 Annual Banquet to launch a
savage attack on Modern Art. The effect of his diatribe is
doubly shocking, leaving not only his distinguished audience
gasping but also the many people tuning in to the BBC's
live radio broadcast. But as he approaches the end of his
assault, the speech suddenly dissolves into incoherence when
he stumbles over a name – a name he normally takes pains
to avoid – that takes him back forty years to a special time
and a special place.

Summer in February is a disturbing and moving re-creation of
a celebrated Edwardian artistic community enjoying the
last days of a golden age soon to be shattered by war. As
resonant and understated as *The Go-Between*, it is a love
story of beauty, deprivation and tragedy that could never
be forgotten by those marked by its passing.

'Jonathan Smith's style is in keeping with the breezy
naturalism with which Munnings and Laura Knight
painted' – *Times Literary Supplement*

'An excellent and subtle novelist' – A. S. Byatt

'Subtle, accomplished and absorbing . . . A real and
serious talent' – Margaret Drabble

'A first-rate writer' – *The Times*

ABACUS FICTION
0 349 10746 7

Abacus Books now offers an exciting range of quality titles by both established and new authors. All of the books in this series are available from:

Little, Brown and Company (UK),
P.O. Box 11,
Falmouth,
Cornwall TR10 9EN.

Alternatively you may fax your order to the above address. Fax No. 01326 317444.

Payments can be made as follows: cheque, postal order (payable to Little, Brown and Company) or by credit cards, Visa/Access. Do not send cash or currency. UK customers and B.F.P.O.: please send a cheque or postal order (no currency) and allow £1.00 for postage and packing for the first book, plus 50p for the second book, plus 30p for each additional book up to a maximum charge of £3.00 (7 books plus).

Overseas customers including Ireland please allow £2.00 for postage and packing for the first book, plus £1.00 for the second book, plus 50p for each additional book.

NAME (Block Letters) ....

....

ADDRESS ....

....

....

☐ I enclose my remittance for ....

☐ I wish to pay by Access/Visa Card

Number ⬚⬚⬚⬚⬚⬚⬚⬚⬚⬚⬚⬚⬚⬚⬚⬚⬚⬚

Card Expiry Date ⬚⬚⬚⬚